CYBELE'S
SECRET

1874

CYBELE'S SECRET

Juliet Marillier

Alfred A. Knopf

New York

THIS IS A BORZOI BOOK PUBLISHED BY ALFRED A. KNOPF

Published in the United States by Alfred A. Knopf, an imprint of Random House Children's Books, a division of Random House, Inc., New York.

Knopf, Borzoi Books, and the colophon are registered trademarks of Random House, Inc.

Visit us on the Web! www.randomhouse.com/teens

Educators and librarians, for a variety of teaching tools, visit us at www.randomhouse.com/teachers

Library of Congress Cataloging-in-Publication Data
Marillier, Juliet.
Cybele's secret / Juliet Marillier. — 1st ed.
    p. cm.
Summary: Scholarly eighteen-year-old Paula and her merchant father journey from Transylvania to Istanbul to buy an ancient pagan artifact rumored to be charmed, but others, including a handsome Portuguese pirate and an envoy from the magical Wildwood, want to acquire the item as well.
ISBN 978-0-375-83365-6 (trade) — ISBN 978-0-375-93365-3 (lib. bdg.)
[1. Antiquities—Fiction. 2. Fathers and daughters—Fiction. 3. Merchants—Fiction. 4. Pirates—Fiction. 5. Supernatural—Fiction. 6. Magic—Fiction. 7. Cults—Fiction. 8. Sisters—Fiction. 9. Istanbul (Turkey)—History—Fiction. 10. Turkey—History—Fiction.] I. Title.
PZ7.M33856Cyb 2008
[Fic]—dc22
2008004758

The text of this book is set in 11-point Book Antiqua Turkish.

Printed in the United States of America

September 2008

10 9 8 7 6 5 4 3 2 1

First Edition

To my granddaughter Katy

Acknowledgments

A number of people helped me with this book. Erudite tour guide Jane Taylor and translator Canan Barim Alioglu provided insights into Ottoman culture during my trip to Turkey. Mr. Ali Tüysüz of the Galeri Kayseri Bookshop in Istanbul found me a wealth of reference material. I've had supportive and professional guidance from my editors—Michelle Frey at Knopf, Brianne Tunnicliffe and Anna McFarlane at Pan Macmillan Australia, and Stefanie Bierwerth at Macmillan UK. My agent, Russell Galen, has played a valuable role in all stages of the book's journey to publication, and Danny Baror has done excellent work on foreign rights. My family has continued to provide moral support and to participate in brainstorming sessions as required.

For proper pronunciation of and details about selected non-English terms, please turn to the back of the book.

CYBELE'S
SECRET

Chapter One

The deck tilted to port, and I tilted with it, grabbing at a rope to keep my balance. One day out from Constanța, the wind had turned contrary and the waters of the Black Sea rose and fell under the *Stea de Mare*'s belly like a testy horse trying to unseat its rider.

"You have excellent sea legs, Paula," my father commented. He stood perfectly balanced, a veteran of more merchant voyages than he could count. This was my first.

The sail crackled in the wind. The crewmen, grim-jawed and narrow-eyed, were struggling to keep the one-master under control. When they glanced my way, their expressions were hostile.

"It unsettles them to have a woman on board," my father said. "Ignore it. It's superstitious nonsense. They know me, and you're my daughter. If the captain doesn't like it, he shouldn't have accepted my silver."

"It doesn't bother me, Father," I said through gritted teeth. Having good sea legs didn't mean I relished the bobbing motion of the boat or the constant drenching in salt spray. Nor did I much care for the sense that if the *Stea de Mare* sank, these sailors would put the blame on me. "Is this going to delay us, Father?"

"It may, but Salem bin Afazi will wait for us in Istanbul. He understands what this means for me, Paula—the opportunity of a lifetime."

"I know, Father." There was a treasure waiting for us in the great city of the Turks, the kind of piece merchants dream of laying their hands on just once in their lives. Father wouldn't be the only prospective buyer. Fortunately, he was a skillful negotiator, patient and subtle.

When he had first agreed to take me with him, it had been to allow me to broaden my horizons now that I was in my eighteenth year, to let me see the world beyond the isolated valley where we lived and the merchant towns of Transylvania that we sometimes visited.

But things had changed on the journey. Just before we were due to embark, Father's secretary, Gabriel, had tripped coming down a flight of steps in the Black Sea port of Constanţa. The resultant broken ankle was now being tended to in the physician's house there while the *Stea de Mare* bore Father and me on to Istanbul. It was most fortunate that I spoke perfect Greek and several other languages and that I had Father's full trust. While I could not take Gabriel's place as his official assistant, I could, at the very least, be his second set of ears. It would be a challenge. I could hardly wait.

The wind had brought rain, the same drenching spring rain that fell on our mountains back home, flooding streams and soaking fields. It scoured the planks of the deck and wrapped the ship in a curtain of white. From where I stood, I could barely see the sail, let alone the bow cutting its way through choppy seas. The crew must be steering our course blind.

Father was shouting something above the rising voice of the wind, perhaps suggesting we should go below until things calmed down. I pretended not to hear. The tiny cabins we had been allocated were stuffy and claustrophobic. Being enclosed there only emphasized the ship's movement, and one could not lie on the narrow bunk without dwelling on how exactly one would get out should the *Stea de Mare* decide to sink.

"Get down, Paula!" Father yelled. A moment later a huge, dark form loomed up behind us. A scream died in my throat before I could release it. Another ship—a tall three-master, so close I screwed my eyes shut, waiting for the sickening crunch of a collision. It towered above us. The moment it hit us, we would begin to go down.

Running steps, shouts, the clank of metal. I opened my eyes to see our crew diving across the deck, snatching implements to fend off the approaching wall of timber. Everyone was yelling. The helmsman and his assistant heaved on the wheel. I clutched on to Father, and the two of us ducked down behind the flimsy protection of a cargo crate, but I couldn't bear not knowing what was happening. I peered over the crate, my heart racing. Aboard the three-master, a motley collection of sailors was busy hauling on ropes and scrambling up rigging while an equally mixed group had assembled by the rail, long poles extended across and downward in our direction. There were about two arm's lengths between us.

"Poxy pirate!" I heard our captain snarl as he strode past.

A shudder went through the bigger ship, as if it were drawing a difficult breath, and then the two vessels slid by one another, a pair of dancers performing a graceful aquatic pavane.

The wind gusted, snatching my red headscarf and tossing it high. As the scrap of scarlet crossed the divide between the boats, I saw a man set a booted foot on the rail of the three-master and swing up with graceful ease to stand balanced on the narrow rim. He took hold of a rope with one casual hand, then leaned out over the churning waters to pluck the scarf from midair while the ship moved on under full sail. The sailor was tall, his skin darker than was usual in my homeland, his features striking in their sculpted strength. As I stared, the fellow tilted himself back with the ship's natural movement and leaped down to the deck, tucking the red scarf into his belt. He did not glance in my direction. The big ship moved away, and I saw its name in gold paint on the side: *Esperança.*

"Close," muttered Father. "Altogether too close."

Despite my pounding heart, I felt more intrigued than frightened. "Did the captain say *pirate*?" I asked, unrealistic images of weathered seafarers with exotic birds or monkeys on their shoulders flashing through my mind.

"If he did," Father said, "we must be glad the fellow didn't seize the opportunity to board us. I want to get my goods to Istanbul in one piece. Perhaps he knew all I had was hides and wheat. We'll be more of a prize on the way back."

I looked at him.

"Don't worry," Father said. "This crew has transported me dozens of times, and we've never yet lost a cargo. Come, we'd best go below. It's obvious we're in the way, and you should cover up your hair again."

I raised no objections. In my tiny cabin, I wielded a hairbrush as best I could, then tied on another scarf from my collection. There were rules for this trip, rules designed not only for my safety but for the success of our business venture. To win the trust of those we traded with, we must abide by certain codes of behavior, including standards of dress. I would be wearing a headscarf, along with my most decorous clothing, whenever I went out in public.

In fact, the greater part of our business would be conducted with other Christian traders, men from Genoa or Venice or farther west, in whose company these rules could be relaxed. Father would need me to record transactions and check figures, at the very least. When he consulted with Muslim merchants, I would be banned, for Father had told me women of that faith did not mix with men other than those who were their close kin, and then only within the safe walls of the family home. Fortunately, Father and his colleague Salem bin Afazi, who would be meeting us in Istanbul, had a very good understanding. I hoped Salem might arrange for me to be admitted to libraries or to gatherings of female scholars. I had dreamed of that for a long time.

"Father," I said a little later when the two of us were squeezed into his cabin space as the *Stea de Mare* pitched and rolled, "if you meant what you said about our being a bigger prize once we have the artifact, perhaps we'll need to take further precautions on the way back. I didn't think it was the kind of thing pirates would want, but I suppose if they knew its value, they could try to seize it."

Father looked unperturbed. In the dim light that filtered down the steep ladder from the deck, he was writing notes in the little leather-bound book he carried with him everywhere. "When we reach Istanbul, I'll hire a guard for you," he said. "Salem should be able to recommend a trustworthy man. You may receive some invitations from the wives of my fellow merchants, and I won't always be able to accompany you. A guard can ensure your safety. Without one, you'll find yourself confined indoors most of the time. Women don't go about on their own in such places. I do plan to look at other goods while we're in Istanbul, if only to distract attention from our principal business there, and I'll take you with me when I can. Nobody's going to offer me the item I want openly. I'll need to pursue it through Salem's contacts." Father's voice was held low. The transaction we sought to carry out was delicate in the extreme, and we could not be too cautious.

"Is there any chance I might visit a library, Father? I've heard there are many rare books and manuscripts in Istanbul."

"The best of those are in the libraries of the religious schools or the personal collections of high-ranking officials," Father said. "As a woman and as a non-Muslim, you could not have access to those. There are some female scholars in the city, of course. Irene of Volos, for example."

"Who is she, Father?"

"I haven't met the lady, but she's a long-term resident of Istanbul and has an excellent reputation as a patron of worthy causes. She's wealthy; her husband is a personal adviser to the Sultan. I understand Irene's hospitality extends to women of various backgrounds, including the wives of foreign merchants. I think you'll find her invitations are much prized. Perhaps we could make an approach to her."

"That would be wonderful, Father. Of course, I know a lot of the material in any Turkish library would be in Arabic script, but there must be works in Greek and Latin as well, the kind of thing that one day I may be wealthy enough to buy for myself."

"Is that what you'd do if you made your fortune, Paula? Establish a grand personal library?" Father laid down his quill, which promptly rolled off the fold-down table. I caught it, splashing ink on my skirt.

"Not exactly," I said, feeling a little defensive. "I was thinking more of a book-trading enterprise. Braşov would be an excellent base for that kind of business. I could provide a service for scholars, teachers, and priests. Once the business became well established, I'd have a partner in Istanbul, another in Venice or Genoa, a third in London. I could expand it in time to include my own printing press."

Father gazed at me, his dark eyes thoughtful in his narrow, gray-bearded face. "An ambitious plan," he said. "You realize, Paula, that this voyage may well make our fortunes—mine, yours, those of all your sisters and Costi as well?" Costi was Father's business partner and was married to my sister Jena. He was also our second cousin. Our family had expanded quite a bit over the last few years. Two of my four sisters were married with children, and only Stela and I were still at home with Father. As for my eldest sister, Tati, it was very possible we would never see her again. The forest that surrounded our home housed a portal to another world. Six years ago, true love had carried her through that doorway, never to return.

"If we acquire this artifact and get it safely back to Transylvania for the buyer," Father went on, "there's a substantial profit to be made. And it could lead to more commissions." There seemed to be something he wasn't saying.

"But the risks almost outweigh the opportunities?" I ventured.

"That is unfortunately true, Paula. With the *Esperança* plying Black Sea waters, we'll need to be especially watchful."

"So you did recognize the ship," I said.

"I recognized the name. I thought the fellow was confining his activities to southern regions these days."

"Fellow?"

"The ship's out of Lisbon. Her master's called Duarte da Costa Aguiar."

"That's a grand sort of name for a villain. He's a long way from home."

"Indeed. For a man who's prepared to engage in theft and violence, there must be rich pickings nearer the English coast. But Aguiar's not the kind of man folk mean when they say *pirate*. He's a trader, a dealer, and he has an eye for antiquities. It's not very hard to guess what's brought him to these parts."

"Aguiar," I mused. "Like the Latin *aquila*—eagle." I recalled the proud features of the man who had caught my scarf and the nonchalant way he'd tucked it into his belt. I'd bet a silver piece to a lump of coal that he was this Duarte. "Theft, you said. How does a person like that dispose of the things he steals?"

Father smiled. "There's always a black market for these

items, purchasers who are not scrupulous about the goods' provenance. Almost anything can be disposed of covertly, though the profit may not be quite as high. This Portuguese is astute. He knows what he's after and chooses his targets accordingly. Some of it's quite legitimate buying and selling. When it isn't, he's expert at avoiding being caught. Nobody's ever been able to pin anything on him."

"He must be doing well," I commented, recalling the size of the vessel that had almost rammed us.

"Indeed. A man doesn't maintain a ship like that without resources and good planning. Of course, there are actual pirate operations hereabouts, but they're mostly small, spur-of-the-moment ventures."

I glanced at him. "If you're trying to reassure me, Father," I said, clutching the table as the *Stea de Mare* rolled again, "you're not succeeding. What would have happened if they'd boarded us?" At the time, it had not occurred to me that the poles and hooks with which the crew of the *Esperança* had reached out to fend us off might just as well have been for the purpose of grappling us fast to her side, the better to leap aboard and—and what? Set about slaughtering crew and passengers alike? Sink the ship with all of us still on it? Or go through our cargo with the appreciation of merchants, help themselves to the best bits, say thank you, and sail away into the sunset? "And don't tell me not to worry," I added severely.

Father sighed. "There's always a possibility of violence," he said. "The fact that you are a girl puts you at particular risk. It makes me question why I agreed to bring you."

"Because I'm useful, Father. And because I've been asking

for years and years. With Gabriel not here, you'll need me in Istanbul. Father, do you think Duarte Aguiar is after the same thing we are?"

"There's little doubt that at some point in our negotiations we will find ourselves face to face with this pirate. We'll need to be watchful. It would be exceptionally ill luck for us to be waylaid with the artifact in our possession—that's supposing we do succeed in acquiring it. I expect Aguiar can be bought off, if necessary, with a payment in gold or jewels, or maybe a fine Damascene blade or two. Such a man cares principally for profit."

In official documents, the great city was still called by its old name, Constantinople. Poets described it as a city of porphyry and marble, a jewel among jewels, its mosques and palaces rising above the water as if reaching toward the heavens. It was a place rich in history, a seat of imperial power, the conjunction of great trade ways, and a melting pot of cultures.

To a girl who had never traveled beyond the borders of Transylvania, the sea path toward that pale forest of minarets and towers, with the sun breaking through heavy clouds above us and the water surging past the *Stea de Mare*'s sides, was nothing short of magical. There had once been a great deal of magic in my life, but not recently. I had given up the hope of ever returning to the Other Kingdom, the enchanted realm I and my sisters had been privileged to visit at each full moon all through the years of our growing up. The way in had been closed to us six years ago, when we lost Tati. Today, sailing along the Bosphorus as my father pointed out the fortress of Rumeli Hisari, the landing from which the Spice

Market might be accessed, and the high walls and green gardens of a grand private residence, I felt brimful with excitement, as if I were on the verge of a great discovery. Maybe the magic was back. At the very least, an adventure lay ahead.

We had come here to buy Cybele's Gift, the fabled treasure of a lost faith. Somewhere amongst those steep ways clustered with shops and houses, mosques and basilicas, it was waiting for us. If we succeeded in our bid, my work as Father's assistant would earn me a small share of the profit. I had plans for my earnings. They would enable me to take the first steps toward establishing my book business.

Neither Father nor I knew what the artifact looked like, although I had done some rapid research into the subject before we left home. I had found no physical description of the piece in the writings of scholars, but word of mouth suggested it was extremely old and of great beauty. I envisaged a marble tablet incised with rows of neat writing. It was said to contain a message of wisdom from an ancient goddess, her last words before she withdrew from the mortal world. Every merchant worth his salt had heard of this artifact, and when they spoke of it, they did so in hushed voices. Sometimes there is an item everyone wants, an object with some special quality that places it almost beyond valuation. Cybele's Gift was one of those pieces.

My reading had told me Cybele was an Anatolian earth goddess associated with caves and mountaintops and bees. She was a wild kind of deity, her rituals involving all-night drumming and ecstatic dancing. I had not passed on to Father the most shocking detail I had uncovered, which was that her male followers mutilated themselves to become more like women, then dressed in female clothing. The cult of Cybele had long since died out, but the legend of Cybele's Gift survived. If the artifact fell into deserving hands, the owner and his descendants would be blessed with riches and good fortune all the days of their lives. As is the manner of such promises, the thing worked both ways. In the wrong hands, the artifact would bring death and chaos. This had not been put to the test in living memory, for nobody had known the whereabouts of Cybele's Gift for many years. Until now.

If I had been a collector, I would have steered well clear of such an acquisition, for my experience with the folk of the Other Kingdom had taught me the danger of such charms. However, when Father received word that an Armenian dealer would be offering Cybele's Gift for sale when a certain caravan came into Istanbul, he quickly secured a potential buyer, a scholarly collector who helped finance our journey. And so we had come to Istanbul, the city glowing in the sunset above its scarf of water, to purchase this prize of prizes and bear it safely home.

The *Stea de Mare* made its way across the wide channel of the Bosphorus and into the narrower waterway, the Golden Horn, that opened from it, dividing the city. A rich aroma wafted in the air, made up of spices and sandalwood, hides and salt, and a hundred other cargoes—the smell of a great trading center.

Officials in small boats came out to halt us while our captain gave an inventory of the goods on board and the passengers he was ferrying. An impressive personage in a snowy turban and a robe of purple silk was asking all the questions. When the formalities were complete, he gave Father a little bow and the hint of a smile, and they exchanged courteous greetings in Turkish. Then the chain-link barrier across the Golden Horn was lowered for us, and we sailed into the docks. We had arrived.

I had expected carts by the waterfront to carry our cargo to Salem bin Afazi's warehouse, but the bales and sacks were unloaded onto the dock, then borne away on the backs of workers whose every move was watched by a hawkeyed overseer with a coiled whip at his belt. I had known there would be slaves here, but the sight gave me a cold, uncomfortable feeling in my stomach.

Father was in intense conversation with a man who had come on board. The newcomer was wearing an expertly tailored short robe over wool hose and felt boots, and a velvet cap on his head. He had the well-kempt, well-fed look of a successful trader. They were speaking in Greek. I let the talk drift past me as I scanned the craft moored around us, my gaze moving from tiny, weather-beaten fishing boats to grand three-masted carracks, from merchant vessels swarming with activity to swift, elegant caïques that served as ferryboats. I looked back along the nearby docks and my gaze stilled. The *Esperança* was moored at some distance from us, her sails furled now, the only sign of life a solitary crewman making a slow patrol of the deck. I could not see if he was armed. Perhaps Duarte da Costa Aguiar was already out there in the city somewhere, making a generous offer for Cybele's Gift.

I narrowed my eyes. What was that patch of black, a tattered length of cloth next to the *Esperança*'s mast? It was flapping as if stirred by a capricious breeze, yet nothing around it moved. Wasn't that . . . No, it couldn't be. And yet that was what I saw: Halfway up the mainmast was the figure of a woman clad in a black robe whose folds billowed out on that uncanny wind. Her head was turned in my direction, but I could not see her face, for she wore the style of veil that conceals all but the eyes. She seemed to be beckoning. And I heard a command, not aloud but clear in my mind: *It's time, Paula. It's time to begin your quest.* Goose bumps broke out all over my body. Without a shred of doubt, it was a voice from the Other Kingdom. A familiar voice. I could have sworn the speaker was my sister Tati.

"Paula!"

I dragged my eyes away from the unearthly figure on the pirate vessel; then, seeing my father's expression, I went quickly to his side. "What is it, Father? Are you unwell?" It had been a long time since that terrible winter when he had been too ill to stay at home in the mountains. Father had been much better of late. Still, I worried. Right now he looked old. "Father, you should sit down," I said, motioning to a bench. I glanced back toward the *Esperança*; the apparition had vanished.

"I'm fine, Paula. This is Master Giacomo of Genoa, another colleague of Salem bin Afazi." Out of courtesy, he continued to use Greek, which he had told me was a shared tongue of traders in these parts. There would be few who spoke our own language here. "Giacomo, let me present my daughter Paula, who is here as my assistant."

The Genoese sketched a bow, his shrewd eyes evaluating what he could see of me behind my modest scarf and demure gown.

"There's been a change of plan," Father said. He was twisting his hat between his hands; it would need steaming to regain its shape. He had not sat down. "Master Giacomo has procured lodgings for us in the Galata district. It's in a *han,* a trading center, where there will be storage for our goods as well. He says it will be quite proper for you to stay there; many of the Genoese merchants live nearby with their families, and Giacomo and his wife will be in residence on the upper floor. The establishment is well guarded. Our cargo will be taken there, not to Salem's warehouse."

I observed the lines on my father's face, the grayish tinge around eyes and nose. I waited for him to speak again.

"Salem's dead, Paula," Father said flatly. "It happened not long ago. In keeping with Muslim practice, he was buried within a day."

"Oh, no!" It was a shock even to me. Father and Salem had had a close trading partnership for years, exchanging sensitive information, helping each other to achieve audacious deals, supporting each other in negotiations. They had built a delicate bridge between cultures. They had been friends. "I'm so sorry, Father. What happened?"

The Genoese trader cleared his throat, glancing at Father, and Father gave a weary nod.

"He was murdered," said Master Giacomo. "Done to death in an alleyway not far from his home, the perpetrators unknown. We must all be watchful."

We walked from the docks up a steep, winding street. Despite the bad news, I could not help feeling excited by the color and life and sheer difference of the place. I realized that no matter how much I had read about Istanbul and its history, nothing could have prepared me for the real thing. There were so many people here, more people than I had ever seen at one time before, even in the very center of Braşov on market day. My head went from side to side as I tried to take in everything at once—little shops by the roadside piled high with strange-looking fruit, a man in a tall hat balancing a stack of round, flat loaves, another with a donkey bearing a pair of bulging skin bags.

"Water," Father said, seeing me staring. "He's making a delivery to one of the houses; most folk have a cistern near their gate. Fresh supplies come in daily."

The noise was overpowering—folk calling out to advertise their wares, donkeys braying, cart wheels rumbling on the stones of the street—as if the place could barely contain its bustling human traffic. I had heard that more than three hundred thousand people lived in Istanbul, most of them Turkish. Here in the trading district of Galata, the faces I saw around me were more of a mixture. Turbans mingled with the looser headdresses of southern regions, merchants' velvet hats went side by side with the skullcaps of Jews. The crowd was almost exclusively male.

"The Galata Tower," Father said, pointing up the hill. "Built by the Genoese before the Ottoman conquest. This district was once an independent city-state. Those times are long past, but a good many of the fortifications remain. Business continued to flourish under the sultanate. Very sensibly, the Ottomans saw the advantages of a tolerant approach to successful foreign traders in the city and made an arrangement with the Genoese. Our han is along this way."

The trading center where we were to stay was an imposing building shaped in an open rectangle of two stories, set around a courtyard with trees and fountains. The ground floor was bordered by a broad cloister with arches to the court. From here, doors opened to a series of chambers in which cargoes could be safely stored. Under the covered area's shade, traders had goods set out for inspection: carpets and fine pottery and silks. Small clusters of buyers were conducting intense conversations. On the upper level, reached by steep stone steps, were living quarters and private rooms for business meetings, along with privies and washing facilities. By the time we reached our allocated apartment, my feet were hurting and my head was reeling as I tried to absorb everything.

It was a relief to see another woman; there had been so few out in the street that I had begun to feel uncomfortably conspicuous. Giacomo's wife, Maria, came bustling along the upstairs gallery, introduced herself, and promised to bring us coffee. She showed us the amenities of our quarters, which were not luxurious. Most of the rooms, she explained, were designed for merchants traveling alone and consisted of a small bedchamber and a slightly larger meeting room. Ours had the added feature of a closet-sized extra space with its own tiny window set with red and blue glass. This little chamber was where I would be sleeping. I eyed it dubiously but thanked her in my best Greek. I would be getting a lot of practice in this language, which we would be using for most of our business negotiations in Istanbul.

"Well, Paula," Father said when Giacomo and Maria were gone, "here we are. A loss, a challenge, but I suppose we can do it. I've asked Giacomo to put the word about that we're looking for a guard. We'll interview the applicants first thing tomorrow."

"First thing" apparently meant before breakfast. I had been awake since dawn anyway, roused abruptly by the ringing voice of a muezzin chanting the morning call to prayer from a nearby minaret. A motley collection of men was waiting in the courtyard below our quarters. Father called them up to the gallery one by one, and I observed from just inside the doorway of our apartment, my veil over my head. Some of them spoke only Turkish. Some could not provide names of past employers. Some balked when it was explained that they would be protecting me rather than my father. One or two looked as if they wouldn't have the strength to fight off a stray terrier.

Father and I had a good understanding. It needed no words for us to agree on a short list of three men, whom Father asked to wait in the courtyard. We sat out on the gallery, where a small mosaic-topped table and two chairs had been placed for us. In this Genoese quarter, it was recognized that not all visitors were used to the Turkish habit of sitting cross-legged on cushions.

From our vantage point, we could look down on the would-be bodyguards standing awkwardly around a small fountain.

"You choose, Paula," Father said. "I'm happy with any of those three. They all speak adequate Greek as well as Turkish, and they've got plenty of brawn."

"Are you sure you want me to make the decision, Father?"

"The fellow's going to be spending more time in your company than mine." His attention was caught by movement farther along the gallery. "Excuse me, I won't be a moment. I must catch Giacomo before he goes out." He got to his feet and headed off in the direction of the Genoese merchant's living quarters, leaving me to mull over the bodyguard question on my own.

In fact, I had not liked any of the applicants much, although I could see they were suitable. The first had looked pugnacious. The second, spotting me, had used a moment when Father's attention was elsewhere to give me a look I did not care for. There had been something in the third's tone of voice that suggested he was confused as to my reasons for being in Istanbul at all, let alone needing a personal guard. I glanced down to give them another look over. Now there were four men waiting on the grass by the fountain: A newcomer had joined our short-listed three. I watched him question the others and be given what was clearly a negative. A brief, intense dispute ensued, then the new arrival headed up to our floor, taking the steep external steps in three easy bounds.

I looked along the gallery, but there was no sign of Father. The man was advancing toward me in big strides. He came to a halt four paces away from where I sat. I took a deep breath and looked up at him. A long way up. He stood head and shoulders over the others Father had interviewed and was, quite frankly, the most intimidating-looking young man I had seen in my life. His eyes were of an unusual yellowish green shade and had an intensity that suggested he was poised to attack. His face was broad, with well-defined cheekbones and a strong jaw, and his complexion was winter-pale. A jagged scar ran from the outer corner of his right eye down to his chin. His dark hair was thick and wayward; an attempt to discipline it into a plait had not been entirely successful. He was of athletic build, the shoulders broad, the arms bulging with muscle. He wore loose trousers under a long white shirt with an embroidered waistcoat over it. A broad sashlike belt held an assortment of knives, and there was a curved sword in a scabbard on his back. I waited for him to ask where my father was. I wished he would get on with it; I was developing a crick in the neck.

Abruptly, the large young man dropped to one knee, taking me by surprise. Now his eyes were closer to my level. "You are the merchant seeking a personal guard?" he asked in fluent Greek.

I grinned. I couldn't help myself. If it had been up to me to interview further applicants, I would have hired this giant on the strength of that question alone.

"You laugh?" the large young man said.

"Not at you. My father is the merchant. I am his assistant." I glanced over my shoulder. There was still no sign of Father, and the men down in the courtyard were starting to look restless. It was against the rules of social etiquette for me to conduct an interview alone with a young man, even if, as his behavior suggested, this one was not a Muslim. Should I ask him to go back down and wait, or make a start and save Father time and effort? I was here to help, after all, to prove my worth. I gathered my composure and arranged my features into a severely capable expression. "Your name?"

"I am called Stoyan, *kyria.*" He used the polite form of address for a lady. "A Bulgar."

"My name is Paula. My father is Master Teodor of Braşov." This was the name my father used in his official dealings; the merchant town of Braşov was his birthplace and mine. "We come from Transylvania. Is it too much to hope you speak Turkish as well?"

"My previous employer was the merchant Salem bin Afazi, kyria. My Turkish is not that of an educated man, but I speak and understand the language adequately. I am twenty years of age and in good health. I am very familiar with the city and well trained in the skills required for a bodyguard."

Salem bin Afazi; that was an odd coincidence. I could hardly say what sprang first to my mind: that Stoyan did not seem to have done a very good job of guarding his last employer. I hesitated. Only twenty. He looked older. Stoyan remained kneeling in front of me, his eyes fixed on the floor of the gallery. He offered nothing further. I willed Father to return, but he remained invisible along the gallery. In the end, I decided to come right out with it. "Salem bin Afazi was a friend of my father's," I said. "We were shocked to hear of his death. What happened?"

Stoyan addressed himself to my feet. His voice had shrunk to a murmur. "He gave me three days' leave. I traveled away from the city. When I returned, he was dead."

This was uncomfortable. "Look at me," I said.

Stoyan looked up. His eyes were desolate. "If I could have that time back, Kyria Paula, believe me, I would not move a finger's breadth from my master's side. I would defend him with the last breath in my body. But I cannot. I was not there. He died."

"Why have you come?" I asked him, fighting back an urge to give him a comforting pat on the shoulder, then offer him the job immediately. I was supposed to be Father's assistant; I must behave in keeping with that. "You must realize that what you've told me hardly inspires confidence in your abilities as a bodyguard. And we have other suitable applicants."

Stoyan rose to his full, towering height. "Of course," he said quietly. "Forgive me." Before I had time to start framing a reply, he was at the bottom of the steps.

"Curse it," I muttered as at last Father came along the gallery to join me in gazing down to the courtyard. At the rate this young man was able to travel, there would be no calling him back. "Why did I say that?"

As I spoke, the Bulgar paused for the briefest moment to glance back over his shoulder, straight up toward where I was leaning on the rail. The piercing yellow eyes met mine. Shouting would be unseemly. I framed one word with my lips, making it quite clear: *Wait.*

I had thought Stoyan might march right on out the gate, but he moved to stand by the fountain, brawny arms folded. One look at him would be enough to scare off a small army of assailants; surely I'd be safe with him. I looked at Father, and he looked back with a question in his eyes.

"That one," I said.

Father smiled. "He's certainly the best-looking," he said. "Perhaps I shouldn't have left the choice to you, Paula."

"Don't be silly, Father." There was no doubt it was true; Stoyan was a very fine specimen of manhood. Not that I had any interest at all in that as long as he was fit to guard me. "Such a thing never entered my head."

Chapter Two

Stoyan was a man of few words. On hearing that he had been hired for the duration of our stay in Istanbul, subject to satisfactory performance, he went off briefly and returned with a small bundle of possessions, announcing that he would sleep across the doorway of our quarters, on a blanket. Neither Father nor I raised any objection. There was, in fact, nowhere else for him to go. The apartment was sparsely furnished, with a bed and a chest in Father's chamber, a pallet and a smaller storage box in mine, and a low table and cushions in the central chamber, which also had a narrow hearth capped with a chimneypiece like a pointed hood. There was no spare bed, and, as Stoyan explained concisely, it was best that he stay close at night. I had not considered there might be any risk here in the han, which had a pair of regular guards on the gate and was used only for trading, but he looked so grim and serious that I said nothing at all.

We were both a little in awe of the way the young Bulgar immediately took efficient control of our personal arrangements. I was soon convinced that Stoyan's passionate words about his previous employer had been true, for he carried out every aspect of his duties with dedicated efficiency. I wondered what his own story was. It did not seem likely he would ever tell it. He spoke only when he had to as part of his duties. His idea of what those duties entailed proved to be far wider than ours had been.

There were vendors of food and drink close by the han, and Stoyan made arrangements to collect our meals regularly. Within our courtyard, an enterprising man had set up a tea and coffee business, evidently realizing a constant supply of these beverages was essential to the smooth conduct of trade negotiations. We purchased a hanging brass tray and a set of glasses. We had not intended using our bodyguard to fetch and carry, but we learned quickly that there were many things Stoyan did without being asked.

I was an early riser but not as early as he was. Every morning when I emerged from my closet, he had already fetched warm water for washing and hung a curtain across the main doorway. He stood watch outside while I performed my ablutions. By the time I was clean and dressed, my hair neatly plaited and the veil loosely around my neck, ready to be slipped on as required, Father would be stirring. Stoyan would take away the buckets and bring me back a little pot of coffee. I would sit out on the gallery to drink it while Stoyan escorted Father to the nearby *hamam,* the public bathhouse. He had made an arrangement with the gate guard to keep an eye on me in their absence. This was unnecessary, for I was perfectly capable of looking after myself for an hour or so. My life in Transylvania had not been that of a sheltered young girl, even though our home was isolated and quiet. But I found that I was quite enjoying being looked after. This reaction shamed me. It seemed unworthy of an independent woman.

The accommodation was full to bursting—I wondered what influence Giacomo had brought to bear to secure our apartment for us at such short notice—and the day's trading saw many visitors come and go. At one end of the building was a place for horses and camels, which added another rich set of smells to the mix. The courtyard was accessed from the street outside through an arched way with double gates. The gate guards, one for day and one for night, were each armed with a serious-looking curved sword. Nobody was admitted without appropriate credentials of one kind or another.

Introducing a young female as his official assistant must have been awkward for Father, despite the fact that I was his daughter, but he took a pragmatic approach. When folk came upstairs to speak with him, they would find me seated cross-legged on the floor in a corner, my skirt modestly arranged, my veil in place, a quill, ink, and a bound notebook on the low table before me. Father would explain my role briefly. I would offer a nod and a smile, then apply myself to taking notes.

"Even in the more liberal Genoese or Venetian circles, it's unusual for a young woman to take such responsibility," he told me. "On the other hand, they like novelty, and they do want to do business with me. If any of them decides to take issue with the situation, I expect his opinion will come back to us via the tea shops or the hamam. If that occurs, we may need to revise our strategy."

Several days passed. I recorded business conversations and kept a ledger of sales. I did not mention that I was itching to get out of the trading center and see something of the city. The weather was perfect for walking, the spring far warmer than ours at home. The sudden, drenching showers that came from time to time were soon over, leaving the air fresh and damp. Each day I grew more weary of figures and more desperate to be let out. Stoyan knew his way around; I was sure he could take me to look at the riverside parks and the great church of Aya Sofia, which was now a mosque surrounded by tall minarets, and the Sultan's walled palace down by the Bosphorus. . . . Perhaps not. To reach those places would require crossing the Golden Horn by boat. But at least he could walk up with me to the Galata Tower. From there, I could get a good view of the city. Or we could go to the docks, or the fish market, or just about anywhere as long as it was not within these walls. Despite my fondness for books and scholarship, I was used to regular exercise. I wondered if I should remind Father about Irene of Volos and her library. He had been too busy since our arrival to do anything but attend to commercial matters. Perhaps if I could get outside the trading center, I might see the woman in black once again. I might hear that voice, the one that sounded like my lost sister's.

While the men were at the bathhouse or otherwise occupied, I got into the habit of walking around the han with my ears open for useful information. Gossip around the tea stall one morning told me the Portuguese, Duarte da Costa Aguiar, had been making inquiries about antiquities and had visited a certain Armenian twice since the *Esperança* had docked in the Golden Horn. Thus far, Father's covert inquiries about the rare item we were seeking had proven fruitless. The death of Salem bin Afazi had set the trading community on edge, and folk were reluctant to talk.

We sat over a tray of tea, indoors this time, Father and I on the cushions, Stoyan standing by the door with a tiny ruby-red glass in his big hands. I was feeling quite awkward, for I wanted to pass on this information quickly, but with Stoyan present, I hesitated.

"Father?"

"Yes, Paula?"

I glanced at Stoyan, trying not to be too obvious about it. "I heard something just now that could be useful," I said. "It relates to our business here. Our principal business, I mean."

"Stoyan, could you leave us for a little?" Father's tone was courteous.

Stoyan hesitated, then added, "I will wait on the gallery, if you wish. I should tell you, however, that I know already what business has brought you here. I worked for Salem for some time. I was fully in his confidence—necessary, in view of the risks he took in his line of work. He spoke of you and of how he had sent you word that this item was coming to the city. I must tell you also that I believe Salem lost his life because of his involvement with the trading of this particular artifact. If I am to keep Kyria Paula safe, it may be better if you allow me to be present when you speak of your plans."

We stared at him. I felt a trickle of unease go down my spine. This was the longest speech I'd ever heard Stoyan make, and he sounded as if he knew what he was talking about.

"Why didn't you tell us all this right at the start?" I asked him. "When you first spoke to me? Didn't you realize this would have been very useful information for us?"

Stoyan looked down at his hands, still holding the little glass. He was avoiding my eye. "This matter is not only confidential, it is fraught with risk," he said. "To pursue this artifact is to step amongst dangerous men, powerful men who will stop at nothing to achieve their ends. It seemed too soon to tell you what I knew."

"You veil your true meaning, Stoyan," Father said. "But I understand you. You waited until you were convinced we were trustworthy."

"I intended no insult, Master Teodor. Salem bin Afazi had a high regard for you. He spoke of your integrity. But experience has made me cautious. It is a matter of profound regret to me that I let that caution slip at the time of Salem's death. I made a grievous error."

"I find it hard to believe that my old friend was killed over this artifact," said Father. "Salem made it clear in his note to me that he did not intend to bid for the piece himself."

"It is complicated, Master Teodor. Even if I had proof, there are reasons why I could not make my suspicions public. And there is no proof, only my instincts."

"I hope you will tell us more in time, Stoyan. Meanwhile, please stay and let us hear what Paula has heard."

I passed on my information as accurately as I could: the Armenian merchant, whose name had been mentioned in the message Salem bin Afazi had sent Father; the fact that the Portuguese had visited him twice, asking about antiquities. "I heard the man say something about a blue house," I said. "The Armenian was staying there. Near the Arab Mosque, I think that was what he said. It's up a lot of steps and apparently very hard to find."

"Interesting." Father set his glass down on the tray. "Your sharp ears have served us well, Paula. This is the first indication we've had that the item we seek is already here in Istanbul, and the seller with it. However, we cannot march over to this blue house and knock on the front door. We'd best send a discreet message. If we can locate the place." He glanced at Stoyan.

"It sounds as if the pirate was prepared to knock on the door, Father," I pointed out. "As a result, he has the advantage right now."

"And has therefore put himself in the path of danger, where we, thus far, have avoided it. Stoyan, is it possible someone believed my old friend Salem was actually in possession of the item we are discussing? That he was done to death in a bungled attempt at robbery?"

"I cannot say," Stoyan said. I could see on his face that the subject was raw and painful for him, even though he had raised it himself earlier. "The house of Salem bin Afazi is in the same quarter of the city as the mosque Kyria Paula mentioned, and he was close to home when . . . when it happened." His voice fell to a murmur. "This artifact . . . a myriad of tales surrounds it, tales certain parties find deeply unsettling. For some time there have been rumors. . . ." He fell silent, clearly uncomfortable under two sets of shrewdly assessing eyes.

"Go on," Father said.

"I accompanied Salem on many missions and into many houses and places of trade. I am not a man of learning, but I have learned how to listen. This piece, Cybele's Gift, has a long history. For some time now, since before we heard it had been found and would be offered for sale, there have been stories circulating in the city. Stories that have made the imams uneasy."

"I have wondered why Salem did not want to deal with Cybele's Gift himself," Father said. Now that Stoyan had said its name, there seemed no reason to hold it back, but he, too, spoke quietly. In a trading center such as this, there were ears everywhere. "It was exceptionally generous of him to allow me the opportunity to bid for it. There must be many collectors in Istanbul and the regions nearby who would pay handsomely for such an artifact. Salem could have made a big profit."

Stoyan seemed about to speak, then thought better of it.

"What is it, Stoyan?" I asked him.

The strange eyes lifted to meet mine. "He would not have done so, kyria. Salem was a Muslim. He made his devotions daily; he lived his life in accordance with the principles of his faith. As a trader, he took risks. One such risk was to alert your father to the probable arrival of this rare piece in the city. To handle it himself would have been . . . ill advised."

I was missing something. "I don't understand," I said.

"You mentioned the imams." Father was several steps ahead of me. "Are you saying the Islamic religious leaders didn't approve of the sale? Why should it trouble them? Cybele's Gift may be a pagan artifact, but it's extremely old. The cult it related to died out hundreds of years ago. Of course, there is a great deal of superstition attached to it, but . . ."

"There was a story." Stoyan seemed reluctant to say more, but in the face of our expectant silence, he went on. "A rumor. That somehow the cult of Cybele had been revived, here in Istanbul. An ancient ritual, idolatrous, shocking, and violent. The idea sparked outrage amongst those in positions of influence at the mosques. Salem never found out if it was true."

"But if it was," I said, thinking out loud, "that would give other people reasons for wanting the piece, apart from pursuing it for profit or because it's supposed to confer good fortune."

"If there were such a cult, possession of Cybele's Gift would strengthen it," said Father. "A pagan revival of that kind must be seen as a threat by Islamic leaders. That's if the story is true."

"What do you know about Cybele's Gift, Stoyan?" I asked him. "What did Salem tell you about it?"

"That it holds the last words of an ancient goddess. This Cybele, it is said her feet were like the roots of the deepest tree and her hair a nesting place for birds and insects of a thousand kinds. To touch this piece would be to touch the power of the earth itself."

His words sent a shiver through me. This seemed a far more profound interpretation of the lore than the one we had heard, that the artifact bestowed good fortune on its owner and his descendants. "You sound as if you believe it," I said, then regretted it, for Stoyan's face closed up as if he were offended.

"Of course," he said, "I am not an educated man."

This seemed to be a sore point for him. I wondered what he would think if I told him my own story, in which eldritch forces of nature had played a significant part. "If someone really has revived the cult," I said, "then I suppose it could be argued that the piece belongs with that person, not with a buyer like ours. On the other hand, the man who financed our trip is a genuine collector, scholarly and responsible. He would value the piece and look after it."

"We could debate that issue at length and get nowhere," Father said. "The fact is, as merchants, we are only ever middlemen, buying and selling on behalf of others, and while we spend time pondering motivations, our competitors are likely to seize the advantage in the deal. I'm not going to let that happen with Cybele's Gift; there's too much riding on our securing the piece. Stoyan, I will give you a message to take to this blue house. I won't put anything in writing. Ask if there is an Armenian merchant in residence, and if the answer is yes, please let him know the trader Teodor of Braşov wishes to speak with him on a sensitive commercial matter. I can attend him at his convenience."

Stoyan nodded, then glanced at me as if expecting that I would add my own contribution to the message.

"Go safely," I said.

We were expecting a party of Venetian merchants before midday, to discuss arrangements for a future supply of hides and furs. Father was anxious to secure the deal on favorable terms, without too many conditions. In particular, he was keen to gain access to fine glassware. If the Venetians would ship our supplies as far as Istanbul, we would use the *Stea de Mare* or another vessel of similar size to get them to Constanţa, where the landward part of the journey would commence. Father and Costi had reliable carters and excellent guards. In addition, they understood the importance of making certain payments on the way, not just the taxes imposed by our Turkish overlords but unofficial sums that would ensure a shipment was not held up for months in a warehouse somewhere. It was all part of doing well in the competitive world of trading, and since I had unexpectedly found myself in the role of Father's assistant, I was trying to learn it as fast as I could.

I had been luckier than most girls. My father had seen the value of educating me, and after several years under the tuition of our local priest, I had spent the last few winters staying with a friend of my aunt's in Braşov, sharing the tutor she had employed for her sons. It was a highly unorthodox arrangement, but then, we were an unusual family. My sister Jena had already traveled south to Venice and Naples and north to Vienna with her husband on trading trips. My next sister, Iulia, had married a man whose family bred fine riding horses. While busy producing her children, Iulia had developed that sixth sense that allows a person to see which foal will develop into a top-quality mare or stallion. When we were younger, I had thought Iulia flighty. I'd believed she would grow up interested only in parties and finery. I knew now that she had something of Father's business acumen. Her husband's family seemed quite in awe of her.

My little sister, Stela, was only eleven. It was too early to say what she would turn her hand to as a grown-up woman, but she was certainly clever. She could be a scholar like me, or a merchant like Jena, or a wife, mother, and influential family adviser like Iulia. Or she might be the one out of us all who managed to find a way back to the Other Kingdom. Unlike me, Stela had never given up hope that she would one day do just that.

As for my eldest sister, Tatiana, whom we called Tati, we did not expect to see her again. She had fallen in love with a strange young man in a black coat and had gone where we could not reach her. Six years; it was a long time. Jena's son, Nicolae, was three now, Iulia's son a toddler and her daughter a bonny infant. Tati had missed so much. I wondered if they had children of their own, she and Sorrow, and what they were like.

Father and I sat out on the gallery drinking tea and preparing for the meeting with the Venetians. There was a constant stream of folk across the courtyard below us, like a smaller version of Istanbul's colorful tide of humanity. Most of the occupants of this han were Genoese, but their customers came from everywhere. A party of Turkish officials in elaborately embroidered robes came in to speak with Giacomo and his partner. They were escorted by armed men wearing tall hats. Janissaries, Father told me—the Sultan's military force, formidable in battle and faultlessly loyal. The han guard did not give his usual ringing challenge but let them pass without a word. They did not stay long.

The Sultan would not buy here, of course. Those who purchased goods on his behalf dealt almost exclusively with business enterprises that were within his own personal control. If there was a need to go beyond those, perhaps for a particularly specialized dyestuff or a rare manuscript, an emissary would be sent out to summon the merchant to the palace. Even the most respected traders would be admitted only to the outer court of that establishment. The Sultan and his household were surrounded by layer on layer of security and protected by rigid codes of protocol. That did not always keep them safe. In a hierarchy where any male of direct lineage could ascend the throne, covert killings were a fact of life. I had heard some terrible stories.

"Concentrate, Paula," said Father. "I need you to be observant during this meeting. Watch their eyes and their expressions. This fellow Alonso di Parma is known to be manipulative. We need to be clear on the taxes; who pays the fee on entry of the goods to the harbor here and whether there's an additional impost on transfer to our own ship for the journey north. If they pay that, we could offer to set it against the tax on the furs."

"Yes, Father." I had been distracted by the appearance of a female visitor to the han. A shapely, stylish woman of about thirty was going up the far steps now, probably to visit Maria or her friend Claudia, who was married to another Genoese trader. Her hair was covered by a very fine veil in dark green stuff with a row of tiny gold medallions sewn around the edge, framing her face. Under it she wore a long overdress in the Greek style, green and gold, with a flowing skirt beneath. The ensemble was complemented by gold slippers.

I glanced down at my own garb, finding it suddenly a little lacking. I had selected my outfit for decorum, not for style. I had on a dove-gray gown with some unobtrusive braiding at neck and wrists, and a blue headscarf. In short, I had dressed not as a single woman of seventeen but as my father's assistant. For a moment or two, I allowed myself to want gold slippers and a gown that would make me beautiful.

The elegant lady had vanished into Maria's quarters. Her guard, a big man in a caftan and turban, was standing out on the gallery waiting. I caught his eye without intending to, and he gave a slight nod. There was something odd about him—a fleshiness of the features, a certain manner. I could not quite place it.

"A eunuch," said Father, noticing my curiosity. "You'll

see them from time to time in Istanbul, generally escorting dignitaries from the palace. Among the Sultan's most trusted slaves are both black and white eunuchs. The former guard the harem, the latter see to the business of the household in general, including the education of the Sultan's sons and those of his nobles. They are employees of high status. But slaves nonetheless."

"Oh," I said. "But he came with a lady who looked like a buyer. Greek, maybe."

"I didn't notice her. It would be unusual. Infidels—that is, foreigners, non-Muslims—rarely have the opportunity to employ such a person in their households. Don't stare, Paula."

Embarrassed, I brought my attention back to the matter at hand. We went through our figures once again. The Venetians were late. We discussed how we would handle things if they did not come. When we heard the guard at the han gate challenge someone, Father and I both rose to our feet, sure our visitors had arrived at last. But it was Stoyan who came into the courtyard; he strode to the steps and ascended them with his usual athletic speed. He hurried along the gallery to us. I observed that he was slightly out of breath; that was a first.

"Is something wrong?" Father asked him.

"No, Master Teodor. I have been to this blue house. The merchant invites you to come now, immediately. I made my way back as quickly as I could, knowing you viewed the matter as urgent."

Father was not a man given to cursing, but he muttered something under his breath that sounded suspiciously like an oath. "I can't go now," he said. "I have traders coming to see me at any moment. If I put them off, I may lose an important deal."

Stoyan was getting his breathing under better control. I suspected he had run all the way. "I am sorry, Master Teodor. At first, the steward of that household did not wish to hear my message. I thought it prudent to mention Salem bin Afazi. I was then admitted. I told the merchant you were Salem's friend, all the way from Transylvania."

"I wonder if he would see me in the afternoon."

"He did say"—Stoyan's tone was apologetic—"that he must keep your appointment brief, as others were coming to visit him later."

"This is infuriating," muttered Father. "To have the opportunity laid before me on a plate and not be able to take it . . . I can't be in two places at once."

"I could go," I said.

"I don't think that's wise." Stoyan's response was instant and emphatic.

I stared at him, outraged. "It's not up to you to decide!" It was all very well for him; he wasn't shut up in the han all day. "I'm perfectly capable."

"I'm in complete agreement with Stoyan," Father said. "This Armenian will not be prepared to receive a young woman on such sensitive business. Besides, it's too risky." He sighed. "It does seem we must let this opportunity pass."

"If I may suggest?" Stoyan spoke up, surprising me. "Kyria Paula could deal with these traders, could she not? I can request that the han guard remains within sight. Provided the negotiations take place out on the gallery, I believe it will be quite safe for her. You will need me to show you the way to the blue house, Master Teodor. It is not so easy to find."

Father opened his mouth to say no—I could see the doubt in his eyes—and shut it again as I lifted my chin and fixed him with my most capable look.

"I can do it," I said. "I know everything about the deal, including how to stop Alonso di Parma from trying to double-cross me. I'll explain that we can reach provisional terms subject to your signature. Go on, Father. You must see this Armenian. It may be our big chance."

"I don't know—"

"I can do this, Father," I repeated.

"It's a lot for you to take on. . . ." He was already fetching his short cloak, his hat, his best gloves.

"I like a challenge, Father. You know that."

As they left, I met Stoyan's eye and he gave me a little nod. I did not respond. I wasn't quite sure how I felt: cross or grateful. I only knew he had surprised me yet again.

By the time the Venetian merchants were making their farewells, I was holding on to my temper by the merest thread and my whole body was clammy with nervous sweat. Alonso di Parma had not only tried to double-cross me, he had patronized me, attempted to trap me into giving away trade secrets, then, once he realized I knew what I was doing, flirted with me outrageously. The man was old enough to be my father.

Alonso had brought his two trading partners with him. One had wanted to leave immediately on discovering they would be dealing with me. The other was tired from the walk to the han and preferred to stay long enough for a glass of tea and a rest. I seized the opportunity, procuring the tea from downstairs and handing around the glasses like any demure young lady while making certain introductory statements— just enough to get them interested. A very considerable time later, after many more glasses of tea and a great deal of maneuvering, we had agreed on terms.

I curbed both my jubilation and my annoyance, bidding my visitors a courteous farewell. I stood on the gallery watching until they were out of sight. Then I slipped my veil off my head, ran my fingers through my hair, and whirled around in a little private dance of triumph. As I came to a halt, I realized there were two people watching me. One was the eunuch, still stationed by Maria's doorway. The other stood down in the courtyard, looking up at me with a blank expression on his hawkish features. He was wearing riding gear, serviceable and plain, in muted grays and browns. His only touch of color was twisted around his neck: a red scarf.

Suddenly I was aware of how tired and sweaty I was. My hair had been neatly plaited this morning, but now it was everywhere, curling over my brow and spilling onto my shoulders. I pulled my veil back up and retreated swiftly into our apartment. What was Duarte da Costa Aguiar doing in the Genoese trading center? Not looking for me, that much was certain. His eyes had passed over me as if I were of no more interest than the brickwork of the han walls. I would go down there on the pretext of returning the tea jug to the vendor, and I would ask the pirate to give back my scarf. But not looking like this.

Some time later, I emerged from our apartment wearing a clean gown, with my hair brushed and pinned up high. The

woman in the gold-decorated veil was down in the courtyard chatting to Maria beneath a bay tree. Her attendant
stood behind. Three or four Genoese merchants were gathered close, like a swarm of bees around an exotic bloom. That
was unsurprising, for the woman was lovely. Her face was a
perfect oval, her skin smooth olive, her features flawless.

Someone stepped out from the shadows a little way
along the gallery, making me jump.

"That looks nice," said the pirate in accented Greek, his
eyes running over my neatly ordered curls and fresh gown.
"Blue suits you. But I think I prefer your hair down."

As I tried to find words, Duarte Aguiar hitched himself
up to sit on the gallery railing, from which elevated and precarious position he would be fully visible to anyone in the
courtyard. He was breaking so many rules of acceptable behavior I could not think what to say to him. Foremost in my
mind was the thought that he had been waiting for me out
here while I changed my clothes with not much more than a
curtain between us. I tried to look past him for the han guard,
but the Portuguese was effectively blocking my view. I was
not quite prepared to run away; that would suggest an inability to cope with the situation.

"I don't believe I know you," I said in my frostiest tone.

The pirate smiled. He was a startlingly attractive man,
lean and tall, his dark hair caught back with a ribbon, his
eyes sparkling with mischief in a face like that of a fine Greek
statue, only with considerably more character. His close
proximity troubled me for reasons that were not all to do
with the impropriety of the situation. "You're blushing," he
said. "Most fetching. I think I have the advantage over you.
Paula of Braşov, isn't it? I am Duarte da Costa Aguiar, master

of the *Esperança,* out of Lisbon. There, now we are introduced, and it is perfectly proper for you to talk to me. How
are you enjoying Istanbul? Has your father taken you to see
Aya Sofia yet? Or to the covered markets? You'd like the
booksellers, I'm sure."

It sounded as if he'd been gathering information about
me, for what purpose I could not imagine. Anxiety was making my palms clammy. Eyes would be on us from all over the
han. I did not want Father to return to the news that his
daughter had been entertaining male visitors alone. Alonso
di Parma's visit had been a scheduled trading meeting, during which the han guard had kept me in sight continuously
as instructed by Stoyan. Once Alonso had departed, the
guard had gone back to his normal duties. I needed to extri-
cate myself swiftly and, if possible, politely.

"Why would you assume that?" I inquired as Duarte
folded his arms, apparently settling in for a lengthy chat.

"Gossip travels fast in the Galata quarter," the
Portuguese said lightly. "You must know how people talk in
the hamam. All that steam loosens their tongues." When I
did not reply, he narrowed his snapping dark eyes and gave
me a droll look of scrutiny. "Don't tell me your father hasn't
let you visit a bathhouse," he said. "It's an essential part of
being in Istanbul to submit to the steaming and scrubbing
and pummeling. You won't know yourself, Mistress Paula. It
would give me immense pleasure to introduce you to the delights of the hamam personally, but unfortunately I am too
much of a man for that."

I felt my blush flame still brighter. "This is most unseemly," I spluttered. "*Senhor* Aguiar, I cannot conduct a private conversation with you, and I suspect you know it. If you

want something, tell me what it is and then leave. Please. My father is out on business. If you need to speak to him, you should return later."

"Master Teodor? I am not ready to speak to him yet. I came here to offer you an apology."

I gaped at him. "For what?"

His hand went up, long-fingered, elegant, to touch the red scarf. "For this," he murmured.

"It wasn't a gift," I said. "If you feel sorry for taking it, all you need to do is give it back."

"I suppose I could do that. I find myself disinclined to part with it. It has become something of a good-luck charm, Mistress Paula. I think I will retain this little part of you for myself, to hold close."

That sent a shiver through me, mostly unease but, I was forced to recognize, partly pleasure as well. I could not help feeling just a little flattered. "I want you to leave," I made myself say. "Please."

"Am I embarrassing you?"

"Of course not," I lied. "But you must know how wrong it is for me to receive you up here on my own. It's not as if we're talking business."

"Ah!" He came down off the railing in a graceful movement and stood before me, perfectly relaxed in his good, plain clothes and his highly polished leather boots. The red scarf did set off his manly beauty rather well. "So business is allowed? Then let us speak of that. Your father has brought a cargo of hides, furs, grain, yes? I'm not dealing in those. I want to know what he's come to buy."

My heart gave a lurch. "You have goods for sale?" I

asked, squashing the response that sprang to my lips—*That's none of your business*—and keeping my tone cool.

"None at all," Duarte said, spreading his hands with a shrug. "But I think Master Teodor and I may be in competition for a certain item. I understand he is making a series of visits. As his assistant—that is what I have heard you are— you might perhaps be able to provide me with further details. If I ask nicely." He smiled again, a look I suspected had been practiced on young women for years and years with devastating results. I wished I had listened all those times when my sister Iulia had tried to give me tips on dealing with men; her advice would have come in handy right now.

"There's a way these things are done, Senhor Aguiar," I told him, surreptitiously wiping my clammy hands on my skirt. "And this is not the way. Have you never heard of confidentiality? I thought you were a trader—that is, when you are not pursuing your other activities."

His gaze altered; it became suddenly dangerous. "And what activities might those be?" The tone was like silk wrapped around a blade.

Piracy. Stealing. Murder. "I've heard certain things. Enough to know I cannot do business with you, senhor. I'll wish you good day. I will tell my father you called." I made to walk away along the gallery, but suddenly he was there, not blocking my path exactly, for if this man was anything, he was subtle, but somehow making it too awkward for me to get past.

"Not so fast," the pirate said. "I can't have wild rumors spread about, especially not if they reach the ears of lovely young women such as yourself. What exactly did you hear about me, and—"

"Senhor Aguiar!" The confident female voice cut Duarte's speech short. We turned to see the woman from the courtyard walking along the gallery toward us, her pace unhurried, her eyes fixed on my companion. There was an expression in them that could only be described as withering. "At your age, have you not grown weary of playing silly games with vulnerable young women? We'll bid you good day. Mistress Paula has an appointment with me."

The pirate surprised me by sketching a mocking half bow, then obeying without a word. At the top of the steps, he turned his head and gave me a wave and a crooked smile. A moment later he was gone.

"Thank you," I said uncertainly. "Do we have an appointment?" I tried to recall whether Father had expected any more visitors today.

"Officially, no, though I did obtain Maria's opinion that you would be prepared to receive me. It appeared to me that Senhor Aguiar might be embarrassing you; I know the man well enough to read his moves. I hope you didn't mind being rescued."

"No, I welcomed it. Are you a friend of Maria's?"

"How remiss of me. I am so sorry! My name is Irene of Volos. Maria told me you were here in Istanbul with your father, of whom I have heard many good things. She tells me you are something of a scholar."

Irene of Volos. That explained a lot. No wonder Duarte had obeyed her without question, though he had ignored my requests for him to leave. "I'm honored to meet you," I murmured. "May I offer you some tea?"

At closer quarters, her Greek descent was more evident.

It was in the patrician nose with its slight downturn and the confident carriage. Her sloe-dark eyes were rimmed in artful black. Her brows had been expertly shaped. Behind her, the eunuch had come silently up to the gallery and stationed himself near the steps.

"Tea?" She gave a rueful smile. "To tell you the truth, I am awash with it after a morning's visiting. Let us sit down here and talk a little, Paula. Maria says you have been very busy helping your father with his business. I like that. Most men would not be prepared to allow a young woman to take such responsibility, however much aptitude she showed. You speak excellent Greek."

"Thank you." I was assessing her earrings, which hung to striking effect down her long, graceful neck. Those were not pieces of faceted glass but real emeralds. The pearls were the size of quail's eggs. "I do love reading and study. I'm more of a scholar than a merchant."

Irene smiled. "Don't underrate yourself, Paula. Wasn't that Alonso di Parma I saw leaving not long ago with a self-satisfied look on his face?"

"First him and then Duarte Aguiar," I said with a grimace. "It's been quite a day." A moment later I realized I had spoken to her as if she were someone I knew and trusted. I had addressed her as I would one of my sisters.

She chuckled. "I can see Maria is right; your father expects a great deal of you," she said. "She tells me you have seen nothing of the city as yet. You are too young to spend a visit to Istanbul entirely in trade negotiations. Do you think your father could spare you for a morning? My home is not far away, in the Greek quarter. You could come early, before it is too hot for the walk, and stay to take some refreshments with me. It can be very difficult for an outsider to access the company of educated women here in Istanbul. Indeed, it is even a challenge for us to meet amongst ourselves. My home is a gathering place for women who love books, music, high culture, and meaningful discussion. You must feel free to make use of my library."

My attempt to be coolly professional crumbled. A library, scholars, an outing . . . "Oh, thank you!" I could not control the grin of delight that was spreading across my face. "I'd love that!"

"Good, Paula. My collection includes many interesting texts: philosophy, poetry, the classics. There are books in Latin and Greek as well as a selection of manuscripts in Persian and Arabic. I know you will handle them with respect."

"Of course."

"My home is very comfortable, cool even on the fiercest days of summer," Irene went on. "And I have my own private hamam, which you are welcome to use."

That was almost more of a lure than the library. I longed for a proper bath. Duarte's comments about the public hamam had been painfully accurate. Father had refused to let me attend the one he and Stoyan visited most days, although I knew it had a separate section for women. He did not think I would be safe there.

"That would be wonderful. Of course, my father will need to approve such a visit. And I'll have to bring my body-guard."

For the first time, Irene looked doubtful.

"I'm sorry," I said, knowing how angry it was going to

make me if Stoyan's caution lost me this opportunity. "Father won't let me go anywhere without Stoyan. On this particular issue, there will be no changing his mind."

"Men!" Irene rolled her eyes heavenward. "I have to tell you, Paula, that men are seldom admitted to my home. I understand that you have certain rules to follow. So do I. My steward, Murat"—she glanced toward the eunuch, who responded with an inclination of the head—"is the only man who enters my gate when my husband is away, which is frequently the case. I do have guards stationed outside, of course. That is only common sense. I have chosen to create a place of privacy for women in my home, a place where they can pursue their personal interests with complete freedom. The rule safeguards that privacy."

I was deeply impressed and bitterly disappointed. "I do understand," I said. "But I think it means I can't visit. We hired Stoyan as my personal guard. I am quite sure Father would not think it adequate for him to wait in the street."

There must have been a wretched look on my face, for she smiled and said, "Well, perhaps in your case the rule can be bent a little. You hired the man who used to attend Salem bin Afazi, yes?"

"That's right." Information did indeed spread widely within the Galata quarter.

"And you believe him trustworthy?"

"I wouldn't have hired him if I didn't," I said.

"Oh, *you* hired him? Not your father?" Her attention was caught by this; she scented something intriguing.

"Father was called away; I ended up conducting the interview, and I chose Stoyan. He's reliable and polite, he speaks Greek and Turkish, and he's . . . well, he's of impressive physique. And he makes rules for me, unfortunately, rules Father respects. I could not visit unless he came with me and stayed with me."

"Even in the hamam?" Irene's brows rose; a dimple appeared at the corner of her mouth.

"Hardly," I said, recalling Duarte's stated desire to introduce me to the delights of the bathhouse. "If I bathe, he can wait outside. But if men aren't allowed into your house at all . . ." It seemed a little extreme, even in the light of her admirable wish to provide a haven for women.

"I will make an exception for you, Paula. Ask your father if you can come tomorrow, and bring this man of impressive physique with you. Murat can find a corner for him, I expect."

I thought of Father's errand to the blue house. Our primary business must always take first priority. "Thank you so much, kyria. If I can come, I'll send a message later today to let you know."

Irene waved her hand dismissively. "No need for a message," she said. "I will be at home—I go out very seldom. I'll look forward to seeing you, Paula." She rose to her feet. "I'm happy I was able to help you with the Portuguese. That man has no sense of propriety. Now I must be off. I do hope we will be friends."

"I hope so, too," I said. "Farewell, kyria."

"Farewell until tomorrow, Paula. And do call me Irene."

She made her way down the steps and across the courtyard. I watched from the gallery. The gates stood open, and in the street outside, waiting for her, I glimpsed a kind of sedan chair carried by two brawny men in loose shirts and voluminous green trousers. As Irene of Volos stepped gracefully in and was borne away, her eunuch walking in front to clear the path, I realized I had forgotten to ask her where she lived.

Chapter Three

After my success with the Venetians, I think Father felt he could not refuse me a morning off to visit Irene of Volos. His delight with the deal I had negotiated was dampened by frustration over his own mission. He had met the Armenian merchant, who went by the intriguing name of Barsam the Elusive, and had established that Cybele's Gift was indeed in Istanbul and available for purchase. However, the artifact would not be presented for viewing until all interested buyers had submitted preliminary bids. Father had done so and had been told to wait for further word. Secrecy surrounded the whole proceedings, with Barsam advising Father to avoid discussing any aspects of the sale with other merchants.

"I do not see how I can avoid speaking of it," Father said in the morning as Stoyan and I prepared to leave for Irene's house. "It's the way these things are done—finding out how much each player is prepared to risk and who may be prepared to withdraw a bid if offered sufficient incentive, perhaps forming partnerships. . . . But there's certainly a danger attached to this particular piece. The fact that the blue house was almost impossible to find, and heavily guarded, underlines that. Paula, you must stay close to Stoyan in the street. A Turkish girl doesn't go to the hamam or on a visit without a bevy of older female relations to accompany her, and she isn't seen walking in the open."

"What if they need to go to the markets?" I asked. "Or to the mosque?"

"The men of the family would escort them to the mosque for Friday prayers or for religious instruction. But it's more common for Muslim women to make their devotions at home. As for shopping, generally it's the men who go out to buy food. Sometimes female servants or slaves may do it."

It occurred to me that once a woman was draped in cloth from the top of her head to her ankles, with only her eyes showing, nobody would know whether she was a servant or a princess. "Did you ever meet Salem bin Afazi's wife and children, Father?" I asked him.

His smile was sad. "His sons, yes. When I was received in his house, the women remained secluded. This custom is strictly observed in Muslim households."

"I think I would find that difficult."

"It's part of the code for daily living observed by all devout folk of that faith, Paula. So is the wearing of a certain style of dress, including the veil. There are rules of dress for men as well. You should speak to some Turkish women about it while we are in Istanbul."

"Perhaps there will be someone I can ask at Irene's house."

"I'm not sure it's wise for you to go out at all." He frowned; he was looking pale and tired.

"I've got Stoyan, Father. I'll be fine." I kissed him on either cheek, feeling a little worried myself. He'd been working hard, perhaps too hard for a man of his age and uncertain health. "I do so much want to get out for a bit." I did not add that visiting Irene would allow me to find out more about Duarte Aguiar, who had been much on my mind.

"Go." He shooed me away with a smile. "Books, manuscripts, scholarly female company—how can I hope to compete with that?"

"You forgot to mention the bath," I said.

Istanbul had many *mahalles*, or districts. Stoyan seemed to know all of them, from the Sultan's walled compound on the water's edge to the leafy northern hills, where, he had said, the tomb of a heroic Muslim warrior was set among cypresses; from the grand residences of pashas to the modest quarter inhabited by Gypsies.

He had had no difficulty in obtaining instructions for finding the residence of Irene of Volos. It was in the Greek quarter, set amongst tall houses near a fountain. We were to look out for olive trees growing in a walled garden.

We walked along paved streets lined with a curious assortment of buildings. The valley where I lived was remote and quiet; it was the opposite of this place of myriad smells and sounds and exotic colors and shapes. A thousand villages like mine could be fitted into this city and there would still be room left over.

The streets were alive with activity. Vendors of foodstuffs, with trays on their heads, threaded expert ways through the crowd, and riders on horses and camels came past with scant regard for those on foot. Stoyan did his best to maintain a safe margin between me and anyone who sought to come closer than he thought was quite proper. It was noisy and chaotic. I smelled horse dung and spices and something frying; I smelled flowers and herbs and fish that had been thrown out into an alleyway. Glancing down the shadowy gap between the houses, I saw a tribe of skinny cats hunched over this unexpected bounty. I tried to look every way at once and felt dizzy and overwhelmed.

The more imposing buildings and open spaces of the Galata district were surrounded by a maze of steep, narrow ways lined with modest, low-doored dwellings. After making our way through several of these little streets, we emerged into a square. A patch of grass in the center held a shady tree laden with purple flowers. Under the tree a man in dark robes sat cross-legged, talking, and around him squatted an entranced audience, mostly of small children, though men, too, were listening, some seated on the rush-topped stools provided by a coffee vendor who had set up his brass-decorated cart in the shade.

"A storyteller," Stoyan murmured. "Before the sun is high, others will bring their wares here: fruit sellers, purveyors of sherbet, all those who see an opportunity. And beggars. We should move on, kyria. Already we attract stares."

It was true. The coffee drinkers were looking in our direction and exchanging remarks. An extremely large guard and a pale-skinned woman of seventeen, modestly clad as I was—perhaps their interest was not so surprising, even in a mahalle that housed more than its share of outsiders. I drew a fold of the veil up over my mouth and nose and turned my eyes down.

"*Destur!*" came a shout in my ear, and a moment later my arm was caught in a powerful grip, my whole body pulled sharply sideways. A porter bent double under a huge, laden basket came striding past, unable to see anyone who might be in his way. In a moment he was gone. I was standing against a house wall, with Stoyan between me and the street, his big hands holding both my arms, not tightly now but more gently as he looked down at me, his stern features softened by concern.

"Did I hurt you, Kyria Paula?"

I felt a flush rise to my cheeks. "I'm fine," I muttered, disengaging myself as my breathing slowed to normal. I looked over toward the tree. The glances had sharpened.

"We must move on," I said. "I don't like the way those men are looking at us."

My bodyguard eyed the men in question. He seemed unperturbed. "You are safe with me, kyria," he said. "I think it cannot be far from here to the house we seek. The tall dwellings over there match the description I was given."

They were tall indeed: three floors high, with each level jutting forward a little farther than the one below. Rows of windows were set with colored glass: red, green, several shades of blue. Some of these were screened, perhaps denoting women's quarters. I had grown up in a castle, and a most eccentric one at that. All the same, I was impressed.

We passed between two rows of the tall houses. Their shade made the street dark. A man with a monkey on his shoulder walked by; the monkey turned its head to peer at us, bright-eyed. A veiled woman all in black scuttled off down an alleyway, averting her face.

"I think that is the house of this Greek lady, Kyria Paula." Stoyan pointed ahead to a long screening wall above which the gray-green foliage of olive trees could be seen. The dwelling house beyond the wall was low and white-painted; among the imposing three-story buildings it looked graceful, cool, and pleasing.

We identified ourselves to a gate guard. Within moments, Murat came out of the house to greet us courteously. I got a better look at him this time and noticed what I had not before—his eyes were light blue, the eyes of a man who most certainly had his ancestry outside the borders of Anatolia. I wondered if, under the turban, his hair was fair.

The eunuch ushered us through to a shady tile-floored colonnade with arched openings to the garden. The arches were decorated with filigree work in wood and plaster. Across the garden, fountains made a soft, whispering music and small birds dipped in and out of the sun-touched curtains of water. What was it Father had told me about fountains in Istanbul—that their sound not only soothed the heart but also made an excellent cover for the exchange of confidential information? Perhaps that was why every garden seemed to have one or two. Peach trees spread branches thick with new season's foliage, with olives providing a darker frieze beyond. Closer to the house were clipped cypresses and beds of white and blue flowers. The sward beneath was like emerald velvet.

"Ah, Paula! I'm so happy you could come!" My hostess emerged from within the house, her glossy dark hair dressed high. Today she wore a tunic and skirt of rose-colored silk damask embroidered in gold thread. Her earrings matched the outfit: rose quartz and gold. They were not as valuable as those she had worn yesterday, but their design, in which each stone formed the carapace of a fanciful beetle, gave them charm. My little sister, Stela, would have liked them.

Irene's eyes were on my companion, assessing him in much the same way as I had just valued her jewelry.

"This is Stoyan, my guard," I said.

"You may wait in the servants' quarters, young man. Murat will show you where to go."

Stoyan shot me a look. We had discussed the possibilities before we left the han, and I knew that if he was not permitted to stay close to me, we would be going straight home.

"Could Stoyan remain near enough to keep me in view, Irene?" I asked, hoping this would not offend my hostess. I was deeply impressed that she had opened her home as a meeting place for women, and I felt awkward asking for a further bending of her rules.

Murat looked pained. I could understand that. I had just implied that the house where he was steward was not a safe place to visit.

"Father insisted," I added. "I'm sorry."

"Very well," Irene said. "Murat, please arrange some light refreshments for us. We'll take them here on the colonnade." Murat melted away like spring snow. It seemed to me he had begun to move before she made her request, as if he knew his mistress well enough to read her mind. "And then the library; it's almost empty today, so you will have plenty of peace and quiet for reading. Your guard may wait over there." She gestured toward a shady area by the wall, and Stoyan, features impassive, walked over to station himself there.

A young woman brought icy cold drinks of a kind I had not tasted before, a sweet fruit nectar. There was a pottery bowl of nuts and dried fruits and a platter of little honeyed wafers. Stoyan stayed where he was as we partook of this delicate feast. I did not think I could ask him to join us, but I felt uncomfortable. Back at the han, it had never occurred to Father and me to treat him as less than an equal.

"Could my guard be provided with water to drink, Irene?" I asked.

"Of course." She clapped her hands, and another servant came soundlessly along the colonnade to do her bidding.

"Had your large young man been prepared to let you out of his sight long enough to visit my kitchen," Irene said in an undertone, smiling slyly, "he would, of course, have been offered a little more by way of sustenance. He's very serious about his duties, isn't he?"

"He's good at what he does," I said, knowing how much I would hate to overhear such a conversation about myself.

"Really?" Behind the light tone, the little smile, was the undeniable fact that Salem bin Afazi had been done to death in the streets of the city not long ago.

I changed the subject. "Thank you so much for inviting me here," I said, sipping my drink. "To tell you the truth, I've been quite desperate to get out for a little. And I am looking forward to seeing your books."

"Not at all, Paula. As soon as I heard you were a scholar, I felt I should extend the invitation. Here I have reversed the policy of the great libraries of the medreses, which are open only to men. My collection is exclusively for the female sex— I make it available to any woman who wishes to visit. I know how frustrating it is to be close to that wealth of knowledge and be unable to tap into it. To be female and a scholar in Istanbul is almost a contradiction in terms. But possible; you'd be surprised."

"I owe you thanks for another reason, too," I said. "I did

appreciate your intervention yesterday. I was finding the conversation awkward."

"With Duarte Aguiar? Yes, I thought so."

"Do you know him well?"

"Everyone knows Duarte. He's one of Istanbul's more colorful characters." Irene's expression was thoughtful, the lovely eyes suddenly distant, as if she were searching in her memory. "You're aware that he's not only a trader but a pirate as well?"

"So my father said."

"He planned to visit your father, I take it."

"I suppose so," I said cautiously.

"You should beware of Duarte Aguiar, Paula. He has great superficial charm, as no doubt you've noticed. Women follow him about in droves. But there's a dark resolve hidden below the surface. And you're young. You should not tangle with such a man."

"I'm duly warned," I said with a smile, my tone expressing a confidence I did not feel. Although the little I knew about the Portuguese was all bad, in a way I had enjoyed our awkward encounter and his easy banter. It had certainly added excitement to my day.

Our refreshments finished, we walked along the colonnade to a tall, arched doorway with panels of colored tiles on either side, red on blue. Irene made it clear Stoyan could not come into the library. Without comment, he placed himself just outside the door.

Irene's collection was housed in a vast, airy chamber on two levels. The upper was furnished with crimson-cushioned divans and cunning brass stands to hold items at a convenient height for reading, while around the lower level, a step down, were shelves on which numerous bound books were stored flat. There were low tables holding writing materials and cedar chests suitable for scrolls and other documents.

Two Turkish women in robes and veils were seated cross-legged in a corner, poring over a faded manuscript laid out on a table before them. Their faces were uncovered, and they looked up and nodded to us as we entered.

"We have started a catalog," Irene said, indicating a bound notebook lying open on a stand. "You're welcome to look at that, or perhaps I can find something of particular interest?"

I hesitated. It had occurred to me last night that I might use this visit as an opportunity to seek out information about Cybele, something that might give Father and me the edge in our trading negotiations. Knowledge, I believed, was the strongest weapon in any battle, and a fierce bidding contest was quite like a war. If I could find material about Cybele's legend here, or about the mysterious inscription on the artifact, we might use that to convince Barsam the Elusive that we were the right buyers for the piece, even in the face of some other merchant making an equal offer. But I wasn't going to reveal trade secrets to Irene, friendly as she was. "I like myths and legends," I said. "Is there anything about the local folklore? The only thing is, although I can read Greek, Latin, and French, I would have problems with Arabic script. I learned a little Turkish when I was in Braşov, but only speaking, not reading."

Irene's lovely eyes widened. "Your education must have been remarkable. We may have something of that kind. There have been several recent donations to the collection, and we still need to go through them. You realize, I suppose, that the high language of the Ottomans, used for scholarly documents, is a peculiar mixture of Arabic, Turkish, and Persian? If you wish to pursue your studies here in Istanbul, you'll need help with translation."

"I know," I said, wondering how long it would take to learn Arabic.

"I will ask Ariadne to see what she can find for you," Irene said, beckoning to a young woman in a green gown who had been working at another table. "Meanwhile, perhaps you'd like to leaf through the catalog, as far as it goes."

I settled myself in a spot where Stoyan could keep me in view while Irene went over to talk to the Turkish women. After a while, Ariadne returned, her pretty face bearing an expression of apology.

"Kyria, I cannot locate anything of the precise nature you require," she said. "That is not to say it does not exist somewhere in the collection. A great deal of our material is yet unsorted. Our storeroom holds many loose papers, individual leaves of manuscripts and so on."

"Perhaps I could look through some of those papers?" I asked her. "I could make a note of what they are as I go—that might be useful for your catalog. I have experience at that kind of work." I looked around for Irene, not sure if it was appropriate for me to make such a suggestion, but it seemed she had gone out. I caught sight of Stoyan in the doorway, his eyes steady on me.

Ariadne did not invite me to investigate the storeroom, but she brought out a large box filled with single leaves of paper and parchment, none of which appeared to have come from the same original manuscript. "There are numerous boxes of this kind," the girl said. "Kyria Irene receives many such gifts. In time they will be itemized and recorded. I hope you will find something of interest." She placed the box beside my table.

For a scholar like me, this was akin to being handed a treasure chest. I explored the box's contents, handling each sheet with delicacy. Most were in Arabic script. Some were illustrated, perhaps poetry or histories. Some I could read; there was a single sheet from a play in Greek, perhaps torn from a bound book, and a page of figures with Latin annotations. I set out each item neatly on the table as I worked my way deeper into the box.

A fragment caught my eye. I lifted it out with extreme care, for it was ancient and fragile. The script was ornate and regular. I guessed the language was Persian, for one or two such pieces had passed through Father's hands over the years, and I recognized the style of decoration: tiny, vivid illustrations and elaborate hand-drawn borders full of scrolls and curlicues.

The pictures were indeed strange. It was not clear whether the figures in them were of men, women, or animals. They reminded me vividly of the Other Kingdom, the fairy realm my sisters and I had visited every full moon through the years of my childhood. While my sisters were dancing, I had spent the better part of those nights in company with a group of most unusual scholars, and they had taught me to look beyond the obvious. Either these were images of just such a magical place, or they were heavy in symbolism. I could see a warrior with the head of a dog, a cat

in a hooded cloak, a blindfolded woman with a wolf, someone swinging on a rope . . .

The little paintings were so finely detailed I needed my
spectacles, which I kept on a chain around my neck and generally used only for very close work. After I had been staring
at the page for a while, I started to see a pattern there beyond
the regular design of the decorative border. Almost hidden in
the dancing confusion of images was a sequence of tiny
squares, each different, each showing a sprinkling of lines,
twists, and blobs. They were executed in a contrasting style,
almost as if they were an afterthought. They seemed familiar,
teasing at my memory.

I glanced up. Ariadne was seated at a table on the lower
level and was busy writing. Irene had not returned. In a
shadowy corner of the library, there now sat another woman,
black-robed, with a needle and thread in one hand and a tattered old cloth in the other. She was fully veiled, save for her
eyes, and in the semidark where she sat, even they could not
be clearly seen, but I sensed she was watching me. I shivered,
remembering the strange figure I had seen, or thought I'd
seen, on the *Esperança* at the dock.

I turned my attention back to the manuscript. What was
it about those little squares that was so familiar? They looked
quite out of place, as if designed to catch the reader's attention. A code? A secret message? Frowning, I turned the page
over and saw something I had missed before, words in minuscule writing inserted between border and main text. It
was not Persian. It was not Greek, Latin, or any other language I knew. And yet I understood. *Find the heart,* someone
had written, *for there lies wisdom. The crown is the destination.* A
cold sensation passed through me, like a warning of danger.

I was gripped by the disturbing feeling that this message, scrawled here by someone I didn't know, was meant for me. It was an instruction, an order.

I glanced up, shaking my head to clear it of such ridiculous notions. Across the library, the black-clad woman unfolded her rag of embroidery, and I saw on it, executed in rich color and with what looked like immaculate stitchery, an image of a girl dancing: a girl with rippling black hair and violet-blue eyes, just like my sister Tati. The woman gave a nod and folded her work away.

This was crazy. I was letting my imagination get out of control. If someone was trying to send me cryptic messages about a quest or mission, they would hardly do so in Irene's library. I drew a deep breath and turned my attention back to the manuscript. Before I went home today, I would work out what those squares in the border meant.

I did not realize how much time had passed until I heard my hostess's voice. She was standing by the next table, gazing at me quizzically. "Your powers of concentration are extraordinary, Paula," she observed.

"I'm so sorry," I said, rising ungracefully, for my legs were badly cramped. I glanced over toward the door. Stoyan did not appear to have moved at all. His gaze was intent, watchful. "I do have a habit of getting caught up in my reading." I was tempted to show Irene the manuscript and ask her if she could see the pattern I had been poring over without success. I hesitated. There was something strange going on here, and I could not explain it without revealing that I was familiar with matters magical and otherworldly. This was something my sisters and I did not talk about, save amongst ourselves. I picked up the leaf of paper to put it back in the box, then hesitated, looking at the fragment again. Where a few moments ago there had been small, clear writing squeezed into the narrow space between the text and the border, now there was nothing at all.

"Is something wrong?" my hostess inquired with a little frown.

I put the paper back in the box, slipping it partway down the pile of documents. "Nothing," I said. "I didn't get quite as far as I hoped this morning, that's all. It's a frustration common to scholars."

"You're tired," Irene said with a smile. "You've been working too hard."

I glanced around the library. A number of folk were now seated there reading or writing, unobtrusively dressed women who might perhaps have donned these plain robes or cloaks or gowns to pass through the streets to Irene's haven without attracting too much attention. I had been too absorbed to see them come in. The black-clad person with the embroidery was gone.

"Do tell me if you'd like any translation done," my hostess went on. "We'll help all we can. But now you most certainly need a rest from study. Ariadne, please tell Murat we'll take coffee in the *camekan* after our bath."

The green-clad girl bowed and left us. I could not be sure if she was a superior kind of servant or a scholar in training. I did like her name, which I knew from the legend of Theseus.

"I imagine you would like to make use of the hamam, Paula," Irene said. "I have a woman who does a wonderful massage; just the thing after sitting still over a book for so long."

"Thank you." I was still puzzling over the woman in black and the disappearing writing, wondering if I could actually have imagined both. I didn't think I was as tired as that.

The bathhouse was in a separate building at the end of the long colonnade that sheltered Irene's house from the noonday sun. I could see from the tight look on Stoyan's face that he wanted me to give Irene a polite refusal and head for home, but I made it clear to him that I was not prepared to sacrifice this opportunity, and he settled to wait once again, this time in the garden by the hamam entry. My hostess and I walked into an airy outer chamber, marble-floored and furnished with shelves and benches. It was both light and private; openings in the domed roof let in the sun, while the windows were shielded by screens pierced with small apertures in a flower pattern. On the wall were pegs from which clothing might be hung. A robed woman with skin darker than any I had seen before offered us folded cloths. I took one, hoping I could guess their purpose without needing to ask.

"I imagine your upbringing was quite restrictive. You will not be accustomed to disrobing before others," murmured my hostess as another attendant closed the door behind us. "I am so used to this, I hardly think about it anymore."

"I have four sisters. We all shared a bedchamber." I followed Irene's lead, slipping off my gown, shift, and smallclothes and wrapping the cloth around my body. I could not help noticing that while my wrap covered me from armpits to thighs with its edges overlapping by two handspans or more, my hostess's generous curves were barely contained in a cloth of the same dimensions. Irene's skin had an olive sheen against the white of the linen. Beside her, I felt like a winter creature, a pale thing that seldom saw the sun.

"Give your things to Nashwa; she will look after them. This little wrap is called a *peştamal*. Another word of Turkish for your vocabulary. Did you bring fresh clothing?"

"Oh. No, I didn't think—"

"I'm sure we can find something for you. It is so refreshing to put on clean linen after the bath." She spoke to the bath attendant in Turkish.

"There's no need . . ." Now I did feel embarrassed. Istanbul was full of public bathhouses, wells, fountains, and cisterns. Islamic prayers were always preceded by ritual ablutions, so it was unsurprising that facilities for washing were so common in the city. I wondered if Irene thought me grubby and uncouth.

"Come, Paula, let us go through. Take a pair of these slippers; they'll keep you from coming to grief on the wet floor of the hamam."

I selected a pair from a shelf by the inner door. They were set on little wooden stilts that lifted my feet a handspan from the ground and carried their own kind of peril. I staggered after my hostess into a chamber whose heat hit me like a blow. Sweat broke out instantly all over my body. Basins were set at intervals around the walls, with copper piping running along above them and spouts extending over each receptacle. This roof, too, was domed but was far higher than that of the entrance chamber. Holes pierced in the stone admitted sunlight; in the chamber's corners burned lamps in intricately wrought brass holders. In the center stood a big marble slab, damp with condensation. On various benches a number of women sat chatting. All were completely naked and apparently quite at ease. At one of the basins, a girl had been washing her hair; it hung down her slim form to her knees, ebony-dark. On the far side of the slab, a small, capable-looking female clad in a shiftlike garment and sandals was administering a massage to a lady who lay on her stomach, eyes closed.

"Here we sit awhile and sweat," Irene said, seating herself on a bench and slipping out of her peştamal in one movement to expose her ripely mature body, all lush curves and smooth bronze skin. Her dark eyes met mine. I saw it as a challenge and took off my own wrapping before sitting down beside her.

"You have not been in a hamam before?" she asked me.

"Never."

"It is quite significant in the lives of Turkish women, Paula. A visit to the hamam is not simply an opportunity to bathe. It is a social event, a highlight of the week. At the bathhouse, women can exchange their news, look over prospective daughters-in-law, enjoy the company of a wide circle of friends and acquaintances. Some stay all day."

"Really?" Clearly I had been missing quite a bit as a result of Father's extreme caution over my personal safety.

"After the sweat, we wash here in the hot room, and if you wish, Olena will provide the massage," Irene said. "She has magic hands; I recommend it. There is a small, deep pool in the next chamber, not so hot. I like to immerse myself there before drying off. You will not find that in the public hamams; it is a refinement I chose to add. As a child, I swam in the ocean. I miss such freedoms. When we are dry, we take refreshments and chat. If you enjoy the experience, you must come back and repeat it whenever you wish."

"You're very generous."

"Not at all. I am a strong supporter of opportunities for women, which places me severely out of step with the culture in which I live. It delights me to encounter a girl with such a thirst for knowledge. You deserve every bit of encouragement that comes your way, Paula. You remind me of myself as I once was." She sighed, putting her hands behind her head and stretching out her long legs, feet crossed. It showed off her figure to startling advantage. I kept my eyes on the marble slab, where the masseuse had finished her work and was rearranging her supply of oils, soaps, and sponges. "I imagine young women have few opportunities in Transylvania," Irene added.

"In such a place, the opportunities must be found or made," I said a little stiffly. "Fortunately for me and my sisters, our father saw the value in educating us."

"Your level of knowledge and your breadth of interest seem somewhat beyond what might be expected even for a young man of your background," Irene observed. "Are all your sisters scholars?"

"Not exactly. Jena studied mathematics. She works in the business, with her husband. When I'm at home, I teach Stela, who is only eleven. She's quite clever. We're making a start on Greek."

"A little sister, how sweet. Does she stay at home with your mother while you accompany your father?"

"My mother is dead."

"Oh, I'm so sorry."

"I can't really remember her; she died so long ago. While we are away, Stela is staying with Jena and Costi. They live next door. Though 'next door' is actually quite a long walk through the forest."

"And the other sisters? You said four."

"Iulia's married with two children. And Tati . . ." This was always difficult, even though my sisters and I had practiced the half-truth over and over. "She lives a long way away. We hardly ever see her now."

"She wed a man from another land? A merchant, a traveler?"

"Something like that." I drew a deep breath. It was indeed hot in here. "May I ask you about your family?"

"Of course."

"You seem very . . . independent. You mentioned your husband. Do you have children?"

Irene threw back her head and laughed. "That is rather direct, Paula. No, no, I'm not offended. My husband is considerably my senior. He was a widower, a man with grown-up sons, when his eye fell on me. A good match, so my friends told me, and I have come to agree with them, for my own reasons. My husband's duties take him away a great deal of the time, and that gives me space for my projects. One might say those are my children. You will have observed the women who study in my library—Jew, Christian, and Muslim together."

"Don't the authorities frown on your allowing Muslim women to come here for such a purpose?"

"Ah," she said, "that is one reason for my ban on male visitors." She glanced in the general direction of the garden with a rueful smile. "Apart from the troublesome few who will not take no for an answer, that is," she added. "I wish women to feel quite safe in my house. Because this is known to be a female preserve, the husbands of my guests view it as a suitable place for their wives to go for an outing. They know there's a hamam here, and I suspect they believe we spend the day bathing and gossiping, only in more salubrious surroundings than those of the public bathhouse. And, of course, some of the husbands don't object to their wives' scholarship; they sanction it provided the women do their study in private, in an all-female setting. My library is ideal for that. I do request discretion. I ask all my guests not to speak of whom they have met here."

"I won't, of course." I thought of the strange woman in black and decided not to ask who she was. "I do admire you for doing this, Irene. If more women of learning were prepared to follow your example—"

She raised a hand to silence me, clearly embarrassed. "I do it because I enjoy it, Paula. Women have so much to offer. It is regrettable that social custom and religious stricture limit those possibilities. And it can be dangerous to offend the wrong people here. Istanbul is a place of high culture and refinement. It can also deliver sudden and deadly violence. Shall we wash now? Do allow Olena to assist you. She will do wonders with your hair. Tell me, are all your sisters formed like you, slim as willow wands and pale as snow?"

I felt myself blushing. "Jena's like me," I said as we went to the basins, where Olena began to sluice my sweating body with warm water that ran from the pipes at the turn of a little spigot. "The others are far more beautiful."

"You speak without rancor."

"I don't care much about such things," I said. "Good health and intellect are more important to me than beauty." Olena had applied soap and was scrubbing my body with a rough sponge; it felt as if she was scraping away my skin.

"Oh, but you are lovely in your own way," Irene said, lifting a scoop to trickle water over her shoulders. "Hasn't anyone ever told you that? A young man at home, perhaps?"

I grimaced. "Hardly," I said. "Young men like curves and smiles, blushes and modest speech. I have yet to discover one who meets up to my expectations."

"I'm certain you will change your mind in time, kyria," said one of the other women seated close by. "Wait until you meet the right young man. Or are you too much of a scholar?" Her Greek was good. I could not tell what her origins were; since nobody was wearing a stitch of clothing, all I had to go by was general appearance, and these women were quite a mixture.

Irene took the opportunity to introduce me. The names were Turkish, Greek, Venetian, all sorts. I nodded and smiled, still not quite used to conversation without clothing. Several of those present did not speak any Greek, and I stumbled through some basic phrases in Turkish, trying hard to follow their questions while Olena scoured every inch of my skin, rinsed me off with a deluge of fresh water, washed and combed my hair, then laid me on the slab. She proceeded to pummel and knead me until my body felt boneless. During this process, I found myself unable to conduct a conversation at all, and I drifted into a daze while the women chatted amongst themselves. I only came back to full awareness when I heard the name Cybele.

They were speaking Turkish. Something about a fascinating

story, or a rumor. Something about danger. I struggled to pick up enough of it to understand. "What are they talking about?" I asked Irene in Greek.

"Gül here has heard some scandalous gossip, Paula," said Irene in the same language as Olena rolled me onto my back and started in anew. "Talk of a secret religion right here in Istanbul. It's very shocking; the imams would be outraged."

"A secret religion?" I murmured against the fists working on my rib cage. "What kind of religion?"

"A pagan cult," said one of the Greek women. "Based on the worship of an ancient earth goddess. Gül's husband heard that the Sheikh-ul-Islam himself is investigating it."

"The Sheikh is the Mufti of Istanbul, Paula," Irene explained. "The Sultan's chief adviser on religious law. A highly influential man. He is certainly not the kind of individual one would want as an enemy. But perhaps this is not true about the cult."

There was a silence, almost as if these women were waiting for me to make a comment.

"I did hear something along the same lines," I said. It seemed safe to offer that much, since they knew about it already, and perhaps I might glean useful information for Father. "What would this Sheikh do if he discovered who was running the cult?"

"The consequences would be dire," Irene said. "It's not like one of the mystic dervish cults associated with Islam, such as the Bektaşi, whose devotees combine adherence to Muslim beliefs with certain freedoms—for instance, in that group men and women worship as equals, and there is a certain degree of celebration involved, music and dancing and so on. But the Bektaşi are recognized by the religious authorities, even if frowned on by the more conservative leaders. This—Cybele cult, I suppose one might call it—would not be acceptable to Muslim, Christian, or Jew, since it would be based on ancient pagan ways, idolatry and sacrifice and so on. Its practices sound somewhat wild."

Olena was finished with me. I got up very slowly, dizzy from the massage and the heat, and another woman took my place on the slab.

"You look almost ready for sleep, Paula," Irene said. "Come, let's use the deep pool and then have our rest. We will leave these ladies to their thrilling gossip. I daresay the whole thing is a false rumor, perhaps put about for some political reason that will become plain in due course."

A little later I found myself in the camekan, or resting chamber, being served with coffee by Murat while Irene offered me honeyed fruits from a platter of beaten brass. She had given me a length of green silk in which to wrap myself. I considered this to be completely inadequate garb in the steward's presence, but my hostess seemed at ease in her own meager covering, so I made sure my misgivings did not show, even if some other parts of me did. None of the other women had come through with us. Perhaps they were still engrossed in conversation.

Murat was gone before I remembered my guard. "Stoyan," I said, my cup halfway to my lips. "He's been waiting a long time. Perhaps . . ." I could hardly run out there with a cup for him, half naked as I was.

"Murat was displeased earlier when his household

arrangements were criticized." Irene said this with a smile. "That will not prevent him from offering your man refreshments."

"I'm sorry if he was offended. Stoyan was just trying to do his job."

"Murat is a little sensitive on such issues," Irene said, reaching to top up her coffee from the elaborately decorated pot, whose holder was of silver filigree wrought in a pattern of vine leaves. "We acquired him from Topkapi Palace. You may not realize how unusual it is for a court-trained eunuch to move to a position outside the control of the Sultan and his powerful advisers. The acquisition of such a rare jewel requires money, influence, and connections. Fortunately, my husband possesses all three and put them to good use on this occasion. In his previous position, Murat had attracted a powerful enemy. He was anxious to move on, and we were in a position to help him."

"That must have been difficult. Dangerous, even." I knew the palace was the scene of hair-raising political intrigues.

"Money changed hands," Irene said casually. "A sum that would shock even a merchant's daughter. The exchange was done expertly, and in secret."

"And Murat was content to become a household steward?"

"Oh, that's only his official title," Irene said. "Murat is a great deal more than a domestic manager. His talents are many, his inside knowledge invaluable. I have never considered him a slave, although I do keep slaves in my household: Nashwa and Olena, whom you met in the hamam, for instance." Irene's tone was matter-of-fact. "I can see that shocks you, Paula. But you do not know this country. If I had not secured responsibility for these women, it is entirely likely they would have been sold into an existence of utter hardship and degradation. Here, they are trusted members of the household, with all their needs taken care of. Ariadne, the young woman who helps in the library, is not a slave. She's more of a protégée, someone I thought worth educating."

"I'm sorry I seemed critical," I said. "What you're doing here is admirable. It makes my own life's ambition fade into insignificance."

Irene's eyes sparked with interest. She leaned toward me. "Oh, do tell me!"

Feeling a little awkward, I explained to her about the bookselling business that would eventually expand to include a printing press on which I would publish scholarly texts.

"It's a fine ambition, Paula." She did not sound in the least patronizing, and I took heart from that. "As a dream, it has practicality. At least you did not tell me you hoped to wed a prince and live in a castle."

"Actually, I do live in a castle." I felt obliged to mention this. "But there's no prince, and the place has leaky roofs and collapsing floors. Like Murat, it's a jewel in its own way. One of a kind."

Irene gave a lazy smile. "He is certainly that. Now"—she rose gracefully to her feet—"we'd best get you into some proper clothing and send you home before that ferocious young man bursts in and demands to know what I've done with you. And look—what perfect timing! Here is Ariadne with some garments for you. I want to dress you in the Greek style. I think the look will suit you, Paula. The line of the skirt and coat is ideal for a slim figure."

My protests fell on deaf ears. The clothes, she assured me, were surplus to needs. They had belonged to a member of the household who had moved on. If I liked them, I could keep them. On went fresh smallclothes and shift, then a narrow skirt with little pleats at the side and a blouse with embroidered borders and over it a long waistcoat in a fabric that seemed either cobalt blue or rich bronze, depending on how the light caught it. It fastened with cunning silver clasps shaped like tulips. On top of this, I had a knee-length coat in a lighter blue, with sleeves to the wrists and a pattern worked in many colors of silk thread around the hem. This was worn open in the front. Ariadne rolled my curly hair into a neat bundle at the back and put a little blue hat like a round box on top of my head. Over that went a gauzy scarf anchored with hairpins.

I was shown my reflection in a bronze mirror and found it startling. The outfit covered me up quite well. Yet it seemed designed to catch the eye, to make men look at me. I was not at all sure it was appropriate wear for a walk through the streets of Istanbul.

"Thank you," I said, feeling a sudden longing to be back at the han with my father. "If I can repay your kindness in any way, please tell me."

"I will, Paula. Do come back soon. Would tomorrow suit you?"

"I will come if Father doesn't need me." I hoped he wouldn't. Irene's house seemed a very special place.

Surrounded by women who shared the same sort of interests as mine, I had realized how much I was missing my sisters. It was not just being in Istanbul, so far from home. It was having three of them move away, Tati to the Other Kingdom, Jena and Iulia not so far but separated from me by the profound difference marriage and children create. Stela was a child still. I loved my little sister, but I could not confide in her as I might do in Jena.

Besides, Irene's library was full of secrets: the symbols I had recognized without knowing why, the writing that had appeared and disappeared, the woman and her embroidery that seemed to have an image of Tati on it. There was a puzzle here to be worked out, and I was good at those. Given a little more time, I would find the answer. I remembered the words I had heard at the docks when I'd seen the black-robed woman the first time: *It's time to begin your quest.* Maybe someone was setting clues for me—leading me on a journey. Once, back home, the folk of the Other Kingdom had set a quest for Tati's sweetheart. Jena and Costi had had their own mission that same winter. Maybe it was my turn. Could such a thing happen when I was so far from home?

"How is your father's business in Istanbul progressing?" Irene asked. "Well enough to allow him to spare you again?"

"I'll need to ask him," I said. I could see from her expression that she knew I was exercising a merchant's caution; she looked, if anything, amused.

"I mentioned Duarte Aguiar earlier." Her tone was delicate. "You might wish to pass on a warning to your father where the Portuguese is concerned. He's highly competitive and does not play by the accepted rules."

"I don't think it's very likely Duarte Aguiar will be doing

business with us," I told her. "I don't think he trades in the kind of goods we have brought."

"He was at your han and went out of his way to talk to you," Irene said. "If I was a merchant, that would be sufficient to make me ask a few questions. I speak only as a friend. I know of this man. He is not trustworthy, Paula."

"I'll pass it on to Father. I think he probably knows that already. He's been trading here for many years, on and off."

We stepped outside. Stoyan was still standing just beyond the hamam doorway.

"I'm ready to go home now," I said, not meeting his eye. In the lovely new clothes, with my skin still tingling from Olena's scrubbing and my limbs heavy after the massage, I felt curiously raw and exposed before his gaze.

"Yes, Kyria Paula."

On the way back, we saw a band of red-clad musicians with drums and cymbals and horns, and a juggler tossing up plates. The midday call to prayer rang out over the city when we were only halfway back to the han. We paused under a shady tree, not wishing to draw particular attention to ourselves while the streets were half empty.

"We will wait here awhile, then walk on," Stoyan said.

I sat on a bench and he stood nearby, looking particularly grave. After a little I ventured, "Have I done something to make you angry, Stoyan?"

"No, kyria. I was becoming concerned. You were out of my sight too long."

"That's unreasonable," I said. "It's all right for you and Father to go to the hamam, but as soon as I get the opportunity, and in a private bathhouse at that, you raise objections."

"You hired me as a guard, Kyria Paula. As a guard, my

judgment is that I cannot keep you safe in such places if I am required to be out of sight." His tone of calm reason did nothing to improve my mood.

"If I followed your rules, I'd never go anywhere," I said, folding my arms belligerently. "You can't know how desperate I've been for a walk, an outing, just to see some of the city. And books; I miss those most of all. This was perfectly safe. There were only women there, and all we were doing was bathing and reading."

"You should be with me, or with your father, at all times when you leave the han. You are not accustomed to a place such as this—a place where death is only an eyeblink away."

This speech chilled me. I understood why he believed this; it had been true for Salem bin Afazi. But my situation was quite different. "I think you've misjudged Irene," I said. "She does some wonderful things, Stoyan, providing opportunities for people who have none."

He was silent awhile, then said, "Yes, kyria. What opportunity does she offer you that you do not already have?"

"Access to a library," I said. "The chance to expand my knowledge. I'm hoping to discover something more about Cybele's Gift."

"Shh!" It was a fierce hiss of warning, and I heeded it, mortified that my bodyguard had needed to remind me this particular topic was not for discussion in public places.

"I'm sorry." It came out despite me. "As I said, it seemed perfectly safe."

"You believe you are in no danger because you are in a private house or garden? That shows how ignorant you are of this city and of the perils that lie in wait for the unwary."

"Don't call me ignorant!" I snapped. How dare he? My

scholarship was my one great strength, and to dismiss it thus was, in effect, to call me worthless. How would Stoyan know anyway? A man like him was incapable of understanding how far learning could take one. "A man who earns a living with his fists should not be so ready to dismiss the opinions of an educated woman," I added. It came out sounding terribly pompous, and I was instantly ashamed of myself, but it was too late to take it back. The silence between us was almost vibrating with tension. After a while, when the time of devotions drew to a close and the street began to fill up with folk again, we walked back to the han an arm's length apart, and neither of us spoke a word.

Chapter Four

Run! My chest heaved. A cold sweat of utter terror chilled my skin. Which way? Openings yawned to the left and right of the dark passage. I stood frozen a moment, then chose a path at random and pushed myself on. Ancient webs draggled down to cling in my hair; small things skittered around my ankles and crunched under my feet in the gloom. Run! Run! A strong hand gripped mine, tugging me forward. Behind me pounded the heavy feet of the pursuers. They were gaining on us. Run! But I could go no farther. I bent double, gasping, and my guardian's hand slipped out of my hold. The darkness descended. All was shadow. Which way was onward and which way back? I thought I could feel the enemy's breath hot on my neck. His steps had slowed. Now his tread was the prowl of a creature about to pounce. . . .

"Father!" I cried out. "Stoyan!" I sat up abruptly, my heart going like a hammer. Beyond the door of my tiny sleeping chamber, nothing was stirring. Perhaps I had shouted only in my dream. One thing was certain—I wasn't staying in here by myself one instant longer.

I threw on a cloak over my nightrobe and stumbled out to the gallery, almost walking into Stoyan, who was standing by the railing, fully dressed.

"Kyria," he murmured, stretching out his hands to halt my wild progress. "You walk in your sleep. Come, sit here."

I obeyed. Seated on one of the little chairs overlooking the darkened and empty courtyard, I couldn't stop shaking. It had all been so real—the shadows, the flight, the menacing presence. . . .

Stoyan crouched in front of me as he had the first time I met him and put his big hands around mine to steady me. Gradually the shivering subsided and my breathing slowed.

"Kyria," he said, "the night guard has a little brazier down below and a kettle. I will fetch tea for you. You wish me to wake Master Teodor?"

"No, please, don't worry him. I'm fine. I had a nightmare, that's all. I just don't want to be by myself in there right now. Did I scream?"

"No, kyria, or more than I would have woken. Sit quietly. I will not be far away. You can see the man from here, and his fire."

"Thank you. Tea would be good."

What he fetched tasted more like sugar syrup than anything, but I drank it gratefully. The glass shook in my hands. Stoyan refilled it without comment. At last he said, "This happens often? Night terrors, sleepwalking?"

"Night terrors, no. My sisters used to tell me I walked in my sleep. They kept our bedchamber door bolted so I would be safe. There are lots of steps at Piscul Dracului, and some of them are very uneven."

"Piscul Dracului. That is a strange name for a house."

"It's an old castle in the forest. The name could be translated as *Dragon's Peak* or *Devil's Peak*. It's isolated. Full of strange surprises."

Stoyan nodded, not pressing for further explanations.

"That dream was horrible," I said. "Someone was chasing me. Underground, a dark, deep place with many ways and no map to say which was right. I knew the moment they caught me they would kill me."

He took my hand again. Here in the darkness, with the city sleeping all around us, the rules of custom that would have made this improper didn't seem to apply. His touch warmed me.

"You spoke my name," Stoyan said. "Your father's, and then mine. In your dream."

"I was awake by then. I've never been so glad to wake up."

"I could swear you were still asleep when you walked out here. I thought you would go over the railing."

"It felt so real. Someone was holding my hand, pulling me forward. And someone was coming after us. . . ."

Stoyan got up, fetched his blanket, and put it around my shoulders over my cloak. "Better?" he asked.

"Much better, Stoyan. Thank you. I'm sorry to be such a nuisance and disturb your sleep. I don't usually go to pieces like this. I'm generally quite a capable person." His opinion of me must have plummeted today. First my unpleasant remark on the walk home, and now this.

"I know you are capable, kyria."

"Stoyan?" It was time to swallow my pride.

"Yes, kyria?"

"I'm sorry I was so unpleasant to you before, when we

were walking home. What I said was inappropriate and offensive."

"You are forgiven. Besides, I am your hired guard. You may say whatever you wish to me."

"It doesn't give me an excuse for bad manners. I'm not used to servants, Stoyan. I felt quite awkward at Irene's house when she told me some of her folk are slaves. At home, the old couple who look after things for us are viewed as part of the family. Occasionally, if they're feeling put out about something, they address me as Mistress Paula, but mostly they just use my name."

"It sounds a good place, this Dragon's Peak."

"It's an interesting place. Both the castle and the wild-wood around it are very old."

"You are fortunate to have so many sisters still living. And now some have husbands and children, Master Teodor tells me. Your father is blessed."

I wondered about that. There had been sorrows aplenty for Father: the death of our mother when Stela was born, the tragic accident that had claimed Uncle Nicolae, the loss of my sister Tati to a realm from which she could never return. But what Stoyan said was true all the same. Jena's and Iulia's children had brought a new richness to Father's life.

"The five of us were very close, growing up. We had exciting times. Adventures." I would not tell him of our visits to the Other Kingdom. We guarded that story with great care for fear of being misunderstood. "Do you have brothers or sisters, Stoyan?"

"Perhaps you should try to sleep, kyria. It is late."

"I don't want to sleep. I'm afraid the nightmare will come back. But there's no need for you to stay awake with me."

"I will stay."

He leaned against the wall by my chair, arms folded. After a little, he said quietly, "I had two brothers. One died at five years old in an accident. The other was taken in the *devshirme*, the collecting. You know of this?"

I shook my head. "Tell me," I said.

"The Sultan sends a Janissary, a senior officer of the army, as his representative to certain lands under his rule. This official travels with the purpose of taking a levy in boys who have not yet reached manhood. In this way, a supply of pure, healthy, and biddable slaves is maintained for the sultanate. Some go straight to the palace; some are sent to work for wealthy families until a position is found for them, generally as soldiers. Some endure surgery. A eunuch, unable to father children and limited in his capacity for physical desire, is regarded as a suitable person to guard the Sultan's women or educate their sons." He saw me wince and added, "My mother tried to hide us, me and my younger brother, but we were found. It is their policy not to deprive a widow of all her sons. I was allowed to remain at home. But Taidjut was taken."

I struggled for the right thing to say, imagining what it must have been like for young Stoyan. What a burden for a boy to carry, not just grief and family responsibility but probably misplaced guilt as well. "How terrible for you and your mother," I managed. "How long ago did this happen?"

"Taidjut was ten years old. He will be a man of eighteen now. I was too young to go after him then, only a boy myself. I have waited a long time to start a search for him. The farm is more prosperous now, and my mother does not need me all the time. Once I was sure she had sufficient help, I came here. When I was not in service to Salem bin Afazi or to others before him, I sought news of my brother. But there are places in Istanbul where an unbeliever, an infidel, cannot go, houses to which he cannot be admitted, secrets to which he can never be party. There are records, but they are beyond my reach. I do not think I will find Taidjut now. And if I find him, perhaps he will not want to know me."

"But you're his brother! Surely—"

"They have had eight years to educate him, Paula, eight years to impress on him that he is no longer a Bulgar farm boy running about with his dog and chopping wood for his mother. In all likelihood, he is serving somewhere in the Sultan's army, grateful to those who offered him this fine new opportunity."

The sorrow and resignation in his voice made me want to weep. "That's a sad story," I said. "When we lost Tati, my eldest sister, at least we knew she would be happy, even if we could never see her again. Do you plan to return home eventually, Stoyan? To go back to being a farmer?"

"I do not know. To do so is to give up hope of finding Taidjut. I made a promise to my mother that I would not return without some news at least. This journey has changed me, Paula. I cannot see the future with the clear eyes of my childhood."

"What does your mother grow on the farm?"

I saw him smile then.

"Many fruits: peaches, plums, apricots, and cherries. I would like you to taste our cherries. The winter chill makes the fruit as sweet as honey. Later in the season, there are pears and apples. And we breed dogs."

"Really? What kind of dogs?"

"The Bugarski Goran, the shepherd dog of my homeland. A hound of massive build and formidable strength, of great heart and exemplary loyalty. Such an animal is an honored member of any household, treated as if he were one of the family. Ours is a land of many wolves. With dogs like this, the flock is safe. My hope for the future is to breed a purer dog, true to the ancient bloodlines. If I go back."

Though it was dark, I could see how his eyes came alive with enthusiasm and the way he used his hands to illustrate with surprising grace. There were hidden depths beneath that impassive exterior. A sweet kernel shielded by a tough shell; dancing fire concealed in stone.

"I am boring you, kyria," he said suddenly.

"No, you're not. What you have to say is interesting."

"You, too, have an interesting story," he said, surprising me. "Where did this sister go—Tati, is it? Where is so far away that you speak of her as if she were dead?"

I swallowed. "I don't think I can tell you," I said.

There was an awkward silence. Stoyan stared into space. Beyond the complicated outlines of the roofs of Istanbul, the towers and domes and minarets, the moon now set a pale gleam over the city. It showed his strong features as a pattern of light and shade.

"You apologize," he said softly. "And yet you do not trust me."

"It's not that. It's a story we don't tell, that's all."

"There is no need to excuse yourself, kyria. I spoke too freely. I presumed too much."

I got up to lean on the railing, looking down at the small light made by the night guard's brazier. It had been placed in the center of the courtyard, well away from the chambers where precious cargoes were stored. "Some secrets are too dangerous to share," I said.

"I expect nothing from you, kyria," said Stoyan. "But I will tell you that before tonight I had not spoken of Taidjut save to my family and to those I thought might have knowledge of the boys taken that year. I have held this hidden, close to my heart. As for the farm and my hopes of the future, since I left there, I have never spoken of those things. Until now."

So he had trusted me and I had not returned that trust. I was afraid that if I spoke of the magical journeys of my childhood, folk would dismiss it as girlish fancy. Yet here in Istanbul, the Other Kingdom loomed close. The nightmare with its darkness and terror seemed part and parcel of the odd things that had been happening—the black-robed woman with her embroidery, the mysterious words, even the pattern I had seen on that manuscript today and half remembered. What I needed most of all was someone to talk to, someone who would neither laugh nor be upset if I spoke of such things.

I sat quietly, wondering if I could try it, wondering how Stoyan would respond. I remembered the way he had spoken about Cybele. As I held a debate with myself, he brought a second blanket to cover my knees. He went down to brew more tea and carried it up to me. The moon hung above us, pure and delicate in its meadow of stars. Stoyan's silence and his kindness helped me make up my mind. I would risk Tati's story. It would be a test.

"You asked about Tati, my eldest sister," I said. "She went through a portal to another place, a place that is not part of the human world. She fell in love with a man who had been taken there as a child and now cannot come back. She wanted to go, and we helped her, my other sisters and I. That's only a very small part of a long, long story, and we don't talk about it, not even with Father, because it still upsets him so much. Some people would hear it and think I was making it up. They'd assume I was a crazy girl with a wild imagination."

Stoyan nodded gravely. "I had guessed something of the kind," he said. "A difficult choice for you. They say the land of the Sultan swarms with giants, peris, and djinns. I would think this a place of many such portals, if one knew how to find them."

So, just like that, he accepted it. No questions, no reservations. It was remarkable. I realized, in a surge of delighted relief, that in this distant part of the world, I had found a friend.

We stayed there until the first hint of dawn lightened the sky and the early call to prayer rang out across the Galata mahalle. Gradually the han came awake, folk opening shutters, others carrying water, the tea vendor setting up shop to serve a stream of early customers. It was time to get ready for another day.

I didn't go back to Irene's library that morning or for several days after. We were busy buying and selling. I had plenty of opportunity to assist my father, and word soon went around the trading quarter that I was almost as tough to deal with as he was. It was good to feel genuinely useful. But the mystery I had stumbled into at the library was never far from my thoughts. A restless urge to find answers disturbed my sleep.

There was something I needed to do before I returned to

Irene's. I broached the subject one evening over supper. Stoyan had set out our meal on the little table: a platter of flat bread, a bowl of onion and cucumber chopped together, dark olives, and a paste of peas ground up with garlic. Father and I took the two chairs while Stoyan leaned against the wall nearby. He said he was more comfortable that way; the furniture had been made for folk of far smaller build.

"Father, I have a favor to ask."

"Mmm?"

"I'd like to go to Irene's library again soon. I may be able to find useful information there, something about Cybele that may help us with our purchase. I want to visit her hamam, too, but I need new clothes. The gowns I've brought from home aren't suitable for Istanbul. It was embarrassing that Irene needed to give me things to change into. Could we go to the public market so I can buy fabrics? Maria said she'd help me with the sewing."

Father glanced at Stoyan.

"Few women venture into the *çarşi*," Stoyan said. "You would attract much attention, kyria."

"Why don't you give Stoyan a list?" asked Father, scooping up ground peas with a chunk of bread.

I suppressed a sigh.

"I think Kyria Paula wishes to view the goods in person, Master Teodor." It seemed Stoyan had understood my thoughts perfectly.

"I'd be disappointed if I came all the way to Istanbul and didn't visit the covered markets, Father," I said. "And didn't you say you'd need Stoyan for a few days while you try to track down the other prospective purchasers for Cybele's Gift?" I had passed on the gossip about the Sheikh-ul-Islam and the secret cult, as well as giving him a much-edited version of my conversation with Duarte Aguiar. That had done nothing to deter him from pursuing his round of visits. "If I'm with Maria sewing, I'll be out of trouble while the two of you are away."

Father smiled. "Since you put the arguments so convincingly, I can only capitulate. We'll all go. The çarşi is a hive of activity. If we ask the right questions, there may be good information to be had."

The next morning we walked through the Galata mahalle down to the waterfront. Here the Golden Horn was fringed by little coffee shops and resting areas. We descended a flight of steps to a rickety wooden jetty crammed with people. Stoyan conducted a rapid, intense conversation in Turkish with an official in a green turban. Once the price was agreed, this man used his silver-tipped staff to indicate a small caïque tied up amongst an assortment of larger craft. Vessels were arriving and leaving all the time, accompanied by shouting and near collisions. Similar jetties projected into the water for some distance along the bank. At this early hour, all were bustling. Both men and women were being ferried. The bigger craft had separate sections at the rear for female passengers.

I was wearing a plain gown in a good light wool dyed blue, and over my head a white scarf. Father looked distinguished in his merchant's robe of deep red, with a flat velvet cap to match. Folk did glance at us; if our foreignness did not ensure that, Stoyan's height and broad shoulders surely did. But there were people of all kinds getting on and off the boats, and the looks did not linger on us. Stoyan helped me aboard the rocking caïque, and I sat in the stern. Father settled beside me, with Stoyan farther forward.

The boatman edged us out through the chaotic tangle of vessels, and we headed across the water. He used the single set of oars to propel the caïque on a swift, bobbing course amidst the heavy traffic of the Golden Horn. The water sparkled around us. Sails of red and brown and cream passed like exotic butterflies. Looking backward and upstream, I glimpsed the *Stea de Mare* moored at the merchant docks and, beyond her, the taller form of the *Esperança*. On either side of the waterway, the towers of Istanbul rose tall against a perfect blue sky.

Halfway across, a huge, high-powered caïque passed us at speed, manned by a crew of eighteen oarsmen in red and white uniforms. In the stern, under a tasseled canopy, sat a grand personage clad in gold-encrusted robes. The wake nearly swamped us. I clutched the seat, imagining what it would be like trying to swim in such a congested channel. I met Stoyan's eye and forced a smile.

"We are safe, kyria," he said quietly. "This man is expert."

"Mmm," I murmured. It seemed important not to show how troubled I was by the shallow draft and rocking movement of the caïque. After all, I was the one who had requested this outing.

"You do not swim?" Stoyan asked conversationally.

"I can keep afloat," I said. "But I'd rather not put my skills to the test clad in a woolen gown and boots."

Father made a comment, but I didn't catch it. In the back of a larger boat traveling near us sat several women robed in black. That in itself was nothing unusual; most of the female passengers I had seen from the dock were dressed the same way. But one of these travelers was staring straight back at me. A piece of ragged embroidery drooped limply from her hands like a small dead creature. I thought I could see a second girl on the cloth. Next to the black-haired dancer was a thin one with a cloud of curly brown hair and a frog balanced on her shoulder. My sister Jena. I shivered. What was this all about?

"Paula?"

My father sounded perplexed. I turned my attention to him.

"I'm sorry," I said. "I thought I saw someone I knew, but I must have been mistaken." And, indeed, when I looked back at the bigger ferry, I could no longer distinguish one woman from another. Anyway, how could I possibly have seen the details on her handiwork at such a distance? My imagination was playing tricks again. I applied my thoughts to what shade of fabric I would buy.

The çarşi was a warren of narrow alleys roofed with a series of domes supported by pillars. Here and there, openings in this roof admitted thin shafts of daylight.

"It's so dark," I muttered as we headed into a tiny street crowded with people. "Why aren't there more lamps?"

"Fire," said Father. "This place is full of hides and fabrics and papers. A single careless moment could send the whole mahalle up like a torch."

The streets were lined with small shops, each with its owner seated on a bench outside. There was a street for kerchiefs and embroidered goods, Father explained, and one for coppersmiths, and another for leatherworkers, and so on. I wondered where the booksellers were, the ones Duarte had mentioned. The place seemed to go on forever. I could smell spices and roasting lamb and freshly ground coffee. Now that I was out of the caïque, I was keen to start shopping.

"If we can find a street of fabric sellers," I said, "I'll make my purchases straightaway. And, if you don't mind, Father, I want to do the bargaining by myself."

"Would I interfere?" Father was smiling. "Just make sure you stay in sight. The place is a maze, and it's easy to lose one another in this gloom. Stoyan, will you go to the paper merchant's establishment for me? He should have my order already bundled up; the price has been agreed in advance. By the time you come back to us, my daughter may have brought her business to a conclusion."

For a little while, we could see Stoyan's dark head as he moved away through the crowd; then he was gone.

We worked our way down the cloth merchants' street. Father stood quietly observing the passing crowd, leaving me to exercise my halting Turkish. I was determined not to ask him for help. I drank a lot of tea and made a lot of polite inquiries as to the health of the merchants' families. Those steps were necessary before the vendors would allow me to inspect their wares: rolls of linen and wool, lengths of fine gauze, muslin for turbans. There was delicate tissue for veils and thick felt for winter cloaks and caps.

At the third shop, I saw some linen I liked, but the price was exorbitant and I could not seem to bargain it down. The man waved his hands, speaking too quickly for me to follow.

"Red linen—too expensive," I told him, hoping my Turkish was not as bad as his lack of understanding seemed to indicate. "I go elsewhere. Good day to you."

We moved on. As each merchant in turn inflated his

prices to ridiculous heights and refused to bargain the way he would with a male customer, it became plain to me that none of them considered me a serious purchaser. I suspected their best wares were not even being brought to the front of the shop. Father was busy talking to people in the street; everyone seemed to know him. I could hardly blame him for not helping me when I had insisted on doing this on my own.

I became more and more frustrated. I found myself wishing Stoyan would come back so I could ask him to stand beside me and look threatening. I was determined not to leave empty-handed; that was to admit defeat.

I was in a little shop with a narrow doorway to a shadowy inner room. I could see rolls of silk in there: a lovely plum red and a very good mossy green. To judge the quality, I'd need to run the cloth through my fingers and inspect the weave in adequate light.

"Those silks—bring here," I said, pointing. "If you please."

Farther down the street, Father had halted to greet two merchants whose style of dress suggested they were Neapolitan. Their wives were with them, in modest gowns and veils.

The vendor was saying I would not be interested in those silks. He waved his hands, telling me he would send his boy to fetch others from storage.

"No! No send boy." I adopted a more forceful approach, frowning and gesturing. "Those silks. Bring here, I look!"

The vendor shuffled his feet and mumbled at me, not meeting my eye. I was about to say something exceedingly impolite when a familiar voice spoke from behind me in Greek.

"May I assist?"

I turned. A tall, dashing figure stood there, clad in Turkish style in a red dolman and a wide sashlike belt over loose white shirt and trousers. A pair of dark eyes regarded me quizzically down an aristocratic, high-bridged nose. He was still wearing my scarf.

"You are too polite," said Duarte. "You must stamp your foot, shriek with fury, and threaten to put him out of business."

"I'm a grown woman, not a spoiled child," I retorted, my annoyance fueled by frustration. "I do not require your assistance."

The pirate grinned. His aquiline features took on a conspiratorial look. "We are friends, are we not, Mistress Paula? And I owe you a favor." His fingers went up to touch the scarf. "Let me help, please."

Without waiting for a reply, he addressed himself to the cloth vendor in fluent Turkish. I did not catch all of it, but he seemed to be saying that I was the daughter of an unbelievably powerful man and a personal friend of Duarte himself and that I needed to see everything in the shop right now or a terrible, unspecified pestilence would descend on the vendor and all his family. Then, less dramatically, that the trader could count himself fortunate that I had not yet spread word throughout the çarşi that he had insulted a lady.

The effect was stunning. The merchant produced a padded stool and invited me to sit. The tea glasses came out. I explained in Greek what I wanted to see, and, with a ferocious smile, Duarte relayed my wishes to the shopkeeper. The cloth was produced. I inspected it and assessed its quality. I mentioned shoes. The vendor said his boy would show us the best place to purchase fine-quality leather slippers. I spoke of braid and trimmings. The vendor told us how to find his cousin's establishment in the street of kerchief sellers. One mention of his own name would assure us of attentive service, he added, glancing at Duarte nervously.

I haggled over the price of the silks. By now, we had acquired an audience: my father, the Neapolitan merchants and their wives, and a gaggle of small boys. My Turkish was quite sufficient for this part, but Duarte kept interjecting, threatening the hapless trader with several alarming fates should he take it into his head to cheat me. I ended up with lengths of both the plum and the green at a price I knew to be very fair for middle-grade silk. All the same, I felt dissatisfied. I had so wanted to do this on my own.

We moved on to the shoe seller and then to the kerchief street, where I made additional purchases. Our entourage went with us. Father was watching Duarte closely but did not intervene. He was always alert to anything that might give him a trading advantage. I could see he had made a decision to be unobtrusive and keep his ears open, since I seemed to be coping. The others watched with undisguised interest. I did not like the idea that my visit to the markets would hereafter furnish an amusing tale to be told in the hamam or amongst gatherings of Neapolitan traders. However, the opportunity was too good to let pass.

I purchased a pair of soft leather slippers in dark red, with a flower pattern tooled around the upper edge, and a length of elaborate braid that would look well with the moss-colored silk. I acquired plain, light veils in several shades and a quantity of fine muslin for smallclothes.

Duarte remained close by, putting in a word whenever he

seemed to think it necessary. I was torn between irritation and curiosity. There was no need at all for him to do this. It went far beyond compensation for a cheap scarf, even if it had been my favorite.

As the vendor handed me the muslin wrapped up in protective cloth, Stoyan came into view with a package under his arm. The crowd parted as he strode toward us.

"Your watchdog is about to bark," murmured Duarte in my ear. Through the thin silk of my headscarf, I could feel the warmth of his breath.

A moment later, somehow our guard was between me and the Portuguese. "Kyria, I will escort you," he said, as if the other man were invisible.

Peering around Stoyan's bulk, I saw Duarte leaning on a pillar, looking not at all put out.

"Ah," the pirate drawled, "just in time. Mistress Paula has a great many packages for you to carry."

I saw Stoyan's right hand bunch itself into a fist, then relax as he checked himself. As a bodyguard, he knew what he was about.

"Finished, Paula?" Father spoke from the street, his tone calm. "My Neapolitan colleagues have suggested we repair to one of the coffee establishments near the waterfront to relax awhile before we cross back to Galata."

"Yes, Father, I'm quite finished. Stoyan, I'm afraid I do have rather a lot of parcels. I'll take some of them myself."

"I will carry them, kyria." He relieved me of the bundles.

I wondered if Duarte Aguiar was included in the coffee invitation, but when I looked up from dealing with the shopping, the pirate had vanished into the crowded maze of the çarşi, gone as suddenly as he had appeared.

I had not realized how exhausted I was until I sat down. The Neapolitans and their wives settled on the cushions of the coffee shop and introduced themselves to me while Stoyan put down the bundles and took himself off to procure drinks for us.

One of the wives, Fiorella, was asking me about Duarte Aguiar and how it was that I knew him so well.

"I don't," I told her. "He just stepped up and offered to help me."

"He is very handsome, in an aloof kind of way," put in the other woman, Gemma. "Those melting eyes and that strong profile . . ."

Father cleared his throat. "A man of his reputation does not volunteer to assist with domestic shopping on a whim. His behavior was odd."

There was a brief silence. Then one of the merchants, a man named Antonio, said, "It is possible all of us are in Istanbul for a single purpose, Teodor: you, I, and Duarte Aguiar. Have you been invited to call upon Barsam the Elusive in his blue house?" His voice had dropped to a murmur. Everyone was speaking in Greek, the traders' language. However, that in itself did not ensure confidentiality in this city of many tongues.

Father's bearded features took on the neutral expression he used during trade negotiations. He could have been thinking anything. It was a trick I practiced sometimes in front of a mirror and was much harder than it looked. "I have met the Armenian," he said noncommittally.

"I, too, have called on him," said Antonio. He held his voice quiet, although we had seated ourselves at some distance from others in the coffee establishment. The fact that there were three women in our party made such separation essential.

"You expect to be called back?" Father asked.

"I understand that, when the vendor is ready, there will be a formal invitation to a viewing. Perhaps then we will discover the extent of the competition."

Stoyan was threading his way back toward us, bearing a tray full of little coffee cups. As he placed it on the low table around which we sat, Duarte Aguiar came up the steps from the street and folded himself gracefully down onto his haunches beside me.

"Excuse me," he murmured in Greek. "You left this." He placed a small, cloth-wrapped package on the table by my hand. "My greetings to you, Master Teodor, Master Antonio, Master Enzo. I wonder if you have received an invitation to supper at the house of a certain Armenian merchant?"

There was a frozen silence. Father regained his self-possession first. "Would you care to join us, Senhor Aguiar?" he asked.

"Thank you, I will," said Duarte, promptly settling himself in Turkish style, one knee up, the other leg bent alongside the low table. He inclined his head to me, to Gemma, to Fiorella. The other women blushed and smiled; I tried hard not to do so. A round of awkward introductions followed.

"I suppose my daughter owes you some kind of thanks," my father said to Duarte, "though I'm not entirely sure she appreciated your assistance. Paula does not readily accept help. I know better than to offer it myself under such circumstances."

I scrambled for a little dignity. "If you wish to discuss me, please remember that I am present," I said, cheeks flaming.

"My apologies, Paula," said Father. "Senhor Duarte, you mentioned an invitation. Are we to take it that you have received such a summons yourself?"

"My message came only this morning," Duarte said, accepting a cup of coffee and looking at me out of the corner of his eye. "A supper to be held in five days' time, to discuss a certain item for purchase. Perhaps there will be a similar summons for you on your return to your lodgings."

"Who knows?" Antonio's tone was light.

"I hear you are a keen collector of antiquities, Senhor Aguiar," Father said. "Amongst other things."

The pirate's lips curved into an insouciant smile. "I share certain interests with you. I do not deny that," he said. "These old pieces have such interesting stories attached, don't you agree, Mistress Paula?"

"I have heard that you are a highly competitive trader, Senhor Aguiar," I said. His casually confident manner annoyed me. He behaved as if he were not just the equal of any respectable merchant but somehow superior. But he intrigued me, too. The man was like a fascinating puzzle, full of secrets. Right now, he deserved to have someone challenge him. "You've proved that by your performance in the market. I am obliged to admit that my shopping expedition went a great deal better after your intervention." I made myself look him in the eye. He had fine eyes, black, bold, and long-lashed. "However, my understanding is that you cannot be defined as a merchant in the way my father and his colleagues here might be."

There was a little silence. I knew I had been rude, but the man irked me. Still more troublesome was the fact that I half admired his style. And nobody deserved to be so handsome.

Gemma and Fiorella were staring at him, their faces shining with admiration.

Duarte's smile had faded. He regarded me gravely. "You hinted at this once before, Mistress Paula," he said. "My methods are a little unorthodox, true. Perhaps they are beyond the understanding of a young woman such as yourself. Your upbringing must have been sheltered. You have many years to learn that the world is not a place full of men like your father. If you stay in Istanbul awhile, that lesson will begin to make its mark on you. In a way I hope it does not. Best if Master Teodor spirits you back home before your freshness is destroyed by experience."

My father rose to his feet. "Your remarks are inappropriate, Senhor Aguiar," he said, and I saw an expression that seldom appeared on his face: that of deep-seated, well-governed anger. "I do not believe we have anything further to say to each other. Stoyan, the gentleman is leaving. Please escort him down into the street."

Stoyan approached, but the pirate remained seated. His pose was perfectly relaxed.

"No need for that," I said quickly. "It's all right, Father. The comments were addressed to me and I can deal with them. I prefer to counter cheap insults with reason." I turned back to Duarte, who was calmly sipping his coffee. "You are fast to judge me, senhor. You saw my apparent helplessness in the çarşi and leaped to the conclusion that I am a pampered child. It's foolish to make your assessments so quickly. A man of your mature years should know better."

Father cleared his throat. I could not tell if he was shocked or amused. Evidently deciding not to intervene further, he sat down again and murmured something to the Neapolitan merchants, who began a quiet conversation at the far end of the table. Stoyan's eyes remained on me and the Portuguese.

"Ah," Duarte said smoothly, "but did you not in your turn make a swift judgment of *my* character? Admit it, you have already dismissed me as a man of no principles, grasping and immoral. But with a certain dashing charm. Yes?"

"I did not base my assessment solely on appearances, senhor. You must know you have a certain reputation."

"You trust gossip and rumor?" His dark brows shot up in disdain.

"I'm an ignorant girl, aren't I?" I said. "How would I know the difference between rumor and fact?"

Duarte smiled, lifting the little coffee cup in elegant hands. His eyes were dancing with pleasure—it seemed he had appreciated my attempt at humor. "Shall we call a truce?" he murmured. "I never thought you ignorant, Mistress Paula. Your Greek is far too fluent. Has your father been training you as a merchant since infancy?"

"In fact, no. I study languages out of interest; I speak several others as well as Greek. When I'm at home, I spend most of the time reading."

"Of course, you are a scholar! How could I forget? Alas, while Istanbul is rich in culture, its libraries are not readily accessible to infidels. I have found this frustrating. Unless I experience a religious conversion, much of the city's wealth of knowledge remains beyond my grasp." He grimaced. "That was an unfortunate choice of words. You understand, I do not wish to liberate any of these works of scholarship, only to read them." He turned slightly, clicking his fingers in the direction of the brazier where the coffee vendor was working.

"You like books?" I studied his face, trying to decide if he was teasing me.

"Don't look so surprised, Mistress Paula. As you kindly reminded me, I am of mature years, at least by comparison with yourself, and I have had plenty of time to gain an education. Yes, I like books. I like anything with an interesting story attached. Myths, fables, folktales. Accounts of the strange and the heroic."

This remark hung between us, full of unspoken meaning. I was sure he was referring to Cybele's Gift, but I knew enough of merchant dealings not to mention that.

"Persephone's journey to the underworld," I said, an image of Tati dancing through my mind. "Atalanta, who could outrace all her suitors. I enjoy those, too, but I prefer the Greek dramas—Sophocles in particular. The plays may concern legendary figures, but they're really about human nature and human frailty. They are very strong stories."

"Some would say too strong for a young woman to be reading," Duarte said, smiling. "Oedipus, Antigone—their fates were terrible."

"Terrible things happen in real life," I said, warming to the discussion. I thought of Stoyan's brother and of the strange events that had overtaken my own family six years ago. "I think those plays were written to help people make sense of that."

"I am revising my opinion, Mistress Paula. I see that you are a woman of culture and learning."

"I hope you're not making fun of me. I don't care

for that." I felt a smile creeping onto my lips, despite my best intentions.

"I would not dare. Not with the eyes of your guard fixed on me in that intimidating fashion. Where did you get him? He's a tough-looking specimen."

I was not about to be drawn into a conversation about Stoyan and his former employer. "I want to ask you something," I said.

"Go on."

"You used the word *liberate* before. Can you possibly mean acquiring goods without making fair payment for them?"

It was unfortunate that I spoke these words during a lull in the other conversation, the one Father was conducting with the Neapolitans. Suddenly everyone was looking at me.

"You will hear me called a pirate," said Duarte. "Among other things. Some of what folk say is true, some not. I've plied these waters a long time, Mistress Paula. A man uses what methods he must to make a living."

"All the same," I said, delighted that he was prepared to engage me in a proper debate, "surely even the most admirable end should not be served by dishonest means."

"Paula." My father's tone was soft, a warning.

"Dishonest? I am more honest than a man who pretends to integrity while readying a noose for his rival's neck." Duarte's tone had changed; I could tell I had annoyed him this time. "I have never lied about what I am and what I do. I have been known to remain silent in the face of questioning. It has proven convenient once or twice, I admit."

The awkward moment was ended by the arrival of a fresh tray of coffee, carried by the vendor himself. A platter of sweetmeats followed. Duarte had procured these without needing to utter a word.

"Folk run to do your bidding," I observed. "Now why is that? From fear?"

"Do not discount my natural charm, Mistress Paula." He glanced at me, and I saw the flash of white teeth before I looked away. He was dangerous, all right—dangerous and irresistible.

"Thank you for the information about the supper, Senhor Aguiar," said my father politely. "We'll bid you good day."

"I deduce I have outstayed my welcome." Duarte glanced toward the steps to the street. A man I recognized was waiting there: the short, thickset fellow I had seen on board the *Esperança*. "We may meet in five days' time," the Portuguese said. "If so, we can resume this interesting conversation. Enjoy the sweetmeats." And, with the effortless grace of a wild creature, he was on his feet and away.

"Strange fellow," observed Antonio, helping himself to a dried apricot.

Father and I exchanged looks. We both knew that the conversation had yielded useful information and that we did not plan to discuss it in front of the Neapolitans.

"That was a little unsettling," Father said mildly. "More coffee, Paula?"

As we sailed back across the Golden Horn, I felt an unexpected sense of well-being. Maybe the caïque was bobbing about more than I cared for, and maybe I had not coped with the çarşi as well as I had expected to, but I did have two lengths of good silk and enough trimmings to make a pair of very becoming outfits, and all at an excellent price. Better still, I had just had a discussion of the kind I most enjoyed, one in which my opponent could match me for cut and thrust. I wasn't sure I liked Duarte Aguiar much. But I very much hoped I would talk to him again. Back in my tiny chamber at the han, I unpacked the purchases that Stoyan had carried for me. Plum silk, moss-green silk, braid and muslin, veils and shoes—I did like the elegant tooled finish on those. I might send Stoyan out another day to get a pair for Stela. Ah, there was the little package Duarte had so politely brought to the coffee shop, the item he'd said I left behind.

I unfastened the twine around the bundle—not easy, as the knot was a sailor's—and unfolded the wrapping. Inside was a length of cloth in deep red-purple, a darker version of the plum-colored silk I had purchased. As I lifted it, there was a faint tinkling sound. I shook it out, the fabric smooth in my hands, and saw that it was a generously sized headscarf of the kind I had so admired on Irene of Volos: smoothly draping and fringed at the front with a row of tiny medallions. Not gold; such headdresses were reserved for the storage and occasional display of the wealth of an entire family. These were disks of polished shell, each a small miracle of swirling light, in every shade from cloud to spindrift to stream-in-shadow. It was a garment for a fairy-tale princess, delicate, exotic, one of a kind. Not valuable, yet of a value beyond measuring in merchants' currency. As a gift, it was the kind of item that would appeal only to someone with a taste for the unusual. Instantly I loved it.

I decided I would not explain to Father that I had left nothing behind in the çarşi. Let him think I had bought this stunning garment for myself. Was it intended as compensation for my red scarf? What else could it be?

I arranged the scarf over my hair so the disks lay across my brow. There was no mirror here, but I let myself imagine it made me beautiful. *What are you playing at?* I thought. *What is it you want from me?*

"Paula?" Father called from the adjoining chamber. "After we've eaten, will you check our remaining stock against the inventory, or were you planning to throw yourself straight into a frenzy of sewing?"

"Of course I'll do it, Father." I took off the scarf with a sigh and put it away in the storage chest, where it settled like a soft red shadow: out of sight but definitely not out of mind.

Chapter Five

It was now urgent that Father call on the other merchants he suspected might be in the contest for Cybele's Gift, for not long after we'd got back from the markets, we'd received our own invitation to supper at the house of Barsam the Elusive. The invitation included me, provided I brought a chaperone. That improved my mood considerably, and in the morning I waved goodbye in good spirits as Father and Stoyan headed out on a round of visits. Then I went to Maria's quarters and settled to sewing.

I was good at dressmaking. It had been an essential skill for my sisters and me. When we were growing up, our monthly visits to the Other Kingdom had required dancing gowns of a style and quality we had no need for in our daily lives. We had become expert at creating dazzling confections out of limited materials. The new silks, feather-soft and glowing with subtle color, were an enticing invitation— almost enough to make me forget Irene's library, the manuscript, and the woman in black, but not quite.

Maria and her friend Claudia were also keen seamstresses. Perhaps it came with being married to merchants and constantly surrounded by lovely fabrics. One day, then another, passed in a whirlwind of creative activity, and on the third morning my new apparel was ready. I felt quite an urge to give it an outing.

Father and Stoyan had left early, planning to sail up the Bosphorus to see Antonio, one of the Neapolitan merchants we'd met in the çarşi. They would be gone until nearly suppertime. In the last two days, they had tracked down four other parties interested in Cybele's Gift, and Father had ascertained that none was prepared to enter into any kind of deal prior to the viewing. He had also made his own informed guesses as to how serious each trader was and how much each might be prepared to offer for the piece. When he returned in the evenings, there was a suppressed excitement about him, as if he were enjoying the challenges of this contest. Stoyan, by contrast, seemed on edge. I often saw him scanning the courtyard, the gallery, the dark corners of the han as if he expected danger to follow us right inside. Before they left in the mornings, he always had a long conversation with the han guard, which I suspected was to do with my safety. I could have told him there was nothing to worry about. What trouble was I going to get into while shut up inside sewing?

Now, with my project finished, I sat on the gallery in my moss-green outfit, frustrated that I could not go to Irene's without an escort. I knew the way and could walk there easily. I could request that same box of papers again and see if there were any other pages to match the one I had studied. I could copy those little pictures, the mysterious ones in the decorative border. I could look for information about Cybele. Besides, I wanted to see if the woman in black was there. If she was, I would ask to see her embroidery.

But I couldn't go. I'd promised not to take a single step outside the han walls unless Father or Stoyan was with me. It was infuriating. There were only a couple of days left until Barsam's supper, and my instincts told me there was a puzzle I was supposed to solve before then. The clues were in the library. I had to go there.

The morning wore on and my mood did not improve. I sent the tea vendor's boy out with a small purse and instructions to make some purchases for me and to keep his mouth shut about it. I wrote a letter to Stela, which I would dispatch when the *Stea de Mare* sailed. We would not be on it this time; buying Cybele's Gift was taking longer than Father had expected, and we would not sail for home until our ship came back on its next trip, about a month from now. I played chess with myself, using a board and pieces borrowed from Maria's quarters. The sun rose higher, and a light breeze tossed small clouds across the sky. It was a beautiful day for a walk. The boy came back. I thanked him and stowed away the items he had brought.

An hour or so before the midday call to prayer, Irene's steward, Murat, appeared in the han courtyard. He caught my eye and indicated by gestures that he had come to speak with me. I beckoned him up to the gallery, suppressing an urge to grovel in gratitude when he said he had come to fetch me, at Irene's request, so I could spend the rest of the day at her house. Only if it suited me, of course, he added politely.

I fetched what I needed for the hamam and left a message with the tea vendor that Stoyan should come and collect me before suppertime. Then, very glad that I had put on my new clothing, I set out for Irene's. Even Stoyan must agree, I reasoned, that I would be safe on the street in Murat's company. The eunuch was armed today, a knife in his sash, and made a fine figure in his green dolman and neatly wrapped turban, the latter fastened with a little clasp set with what appeared to be a real emerald.

Murat intrigued me. His manner was courteous in the extreme, but there was something about him that was the opposite of servile. The upright but relaxed stance, the piercing blue eyes, the impression he gave that he could perform the duties of a household steward more or less in his sleep— these intrigued me. There were many things I wanted to know about his past, all far too awkward to put into words. But there were other, related matters he might be prepared to talk about. As we negotiated a narrow street, I said, "May I ask you something, Murat?"

"Of course, kyria." His voice was high for a man's; Father had told me this was usual for eunuchs.

"I've heard of the devshirme, when they take boys for the Sultan's service. Do folk ever come here looking for their lost sons or brothers? And if they do, what is the chance of such a young man being found?"

Murat maintained his steady pace, walking to my right and one step behind. "It is possible," he said. "But unlikely. The families that lose sons to the devshirme are not wealthy. Few would have the resources to mount such a search. Besides, though no doubt the cause of much grief in the short term, to have a child taken in this way could be seen as beneficial. For a poor family, it is one less mouth to feed. For the boy, an opportunity to make something of himself."

"But—" I began, about to tell him that most boys would surely rather end up as simple farmers free to make their own choices than as highly trained, well-fed slaves. I stopped myself just in time. It seemed very likely Murat himself had been a child of the devshirme. "What about records?" I asked him, trying to make it sound like a casual question. "Which boys went where in which year, and so on?"

"I cannot say, kyria. Such records, if they exist, would be in the archives at Topkapi Palace and accessible only to the Sultan's librarians. Their availability would depend, I imagine, on who was asking to see them."

I could not pursue this any further. It was Stoyan's secret, not mine. If it had occurred to me that Murat might be able to help him, Stoyan must also have thought of it.

"Thank you, Murat," I said. "I apologize if I was too curious. This is a very different culture from the one I am used to at home."

"It has many secrets, kyria. Layer on layer. If you were to stay in Istanbul, in time they would begin to reveal themselves."

The library was almost empty today. After greeting me warmly and saying Ariadne would find whatever I needed, Irene went out. The black-robed woman was nowhere to be seen. I asked Ariadne to fetch the box of papers I had studied on my last visit and settled to look at them.

The first thing I noticed was that the sheet I had spent so long poring over before was on top of the pile. I knew I had placed it farther down, in a wish, perhaps misguided, to conceal the nature of my interest. "Ariadne?" I asked.

"Yes, kyria?"

"Is someone else currently working on these papers? I would hate to disrupt another scholar's research. . . ."

"They have not been touched since your last visit, kyria. Alas, I have been too busy to progress with the catalog, and nobody else has asked to see these. Why do you ask?"

"I couldn't remember where I'd put the piece I was looking at. Never mind, it should be easy enough to find. Thank you, Ariadne."

It was odd. There was no reason for her to lie about such a thing, but I could not escape the conclusion that someone had set the piece at the top in readiness for me. I felt uneasy. It didn't seem quite right to be in this house without Stoyan, even though all he had done the last time had been to stand by the door. I turned the sheet over, thinking I might make a copy of the symbols before I went home. The tiny, cryptic writing, the script that had appeared and disappeared before my eyes, was not visible today. There was no way to tell there had ever been anything written on that part of the sheet.

I was disappointed. Secretly, I had been hoping there might be a new message there, something that began to make sense of the clues that were coming my way. Never mind; perhaps that was too easy. I had not gone through the entire box last time. I would check the full contents today to see if there were other papers that matched this one. More pictures; perhaps more clues. If someone wanted me to solve a puzzle, I needed more information.

Because so many of the papers were old and fragile, it was a slow job. Time passed as I lifted them out onto the table, first the leaves I had looked at before, then those that were new to me. Just when I was deciding it was a wasted effort, I found it—another piece with matching borders and the same assured, ornate calligraphy, the letters curling and decorative, each a small masterpiece of control and flow. On this page there was only one picture. My heart gave a jolt; I knew immediately what I was looking at. It could not be coincidence. Whoever was setting me clues knew about Cybele's Gift. The woman and her embroidery, the mysterious words about a quest and finding the heart, the cryptic border symbols—they were all tied up with Father's business in Istanbul. I felt it in my bones.

The miniature was no taller than my thumb, but it captured her vividly. She was painted in ocher, a squat, round person, her face a mask with a flat nose, a wide mouth, and dark holes for eyes. Her hands were on her hips, her legs tucked under her. Gold earrings hung from her lobes, and her hair streamed out like a wild tangle of snakes. Around the exuberant locks, the artist had added a swarm of bees. I looked into the cavernous eyes and heard a deep voice say, *I am the beginning. Make me whole.* I started in shock. When I looked up, thinking others in the library must have heard the same strange words, the woman in black was seated opposite me at the table, her eyes fixed on my face through the narrow opening in her veil.

"Who are you?" I murmured, my gaze dropping to the embroidery that lay partly unrolled on the tabletop, far enough to show me that the two dancing girls had been joined by a third, curvaceous and graceful, with artfully dressed dark hair and bright blue eyes. My sister Iulia. After her, it would be me. Then Stela. Was that how long I had to work out the mystery, two more encounters with this woman? "Tell me! What do you want with me?" I looked at her veiled face once more. All I could see was her beautiful eyes, eyes of an unusual violet-blue shade, fringed by long dark lashes. They were just like my sister Tati's. My skin prickled with unease. "Tati?" I whispered, not quite daring to believe.

She did not speak. I heard it in my mind instead, my sister's voice saying, *The signs—you've got to look for the signs, Paula. And you haven't got much time left.* Then I was by myself at the table again, my lips still framing a question that would not be answered, for where Tati had been there was only empty space. Across the library, Ariadne worked on, oblivious to what had happened.

I was cold with shock. Tati—Tati, who had not once come back from the Other Kingdom in the six years since she went there to be with her sweetheart, Sorrow. What could this mean? That a quest had been set not just for me but for my sister as well? In our forest at home, the Other Kingdom paralleled the human world, the same hills and hollows, lakes and streams existing in both. They were linked by hidden portals, doorways guarded by magic. Did that apply everywhere? Was there an Other Kingdom in Istanbul, in Bulgaria, in Portugal? I remembered the mission on which Sorrow had been sent by Ileana, the forest queen, to win Tati's hand. That had involved an extraordinary journey, taking him to places within both our world and the other. So perhaps it was true. Perhaps concealed in the streets and gardens and palaces of Istanbul there existed secret entrances to another world, the same as the ones my sisters and I had discovered in the forest and castle of Piscul Dracului when we were growing up.

Think, Paula. My mind was awhirl. I prided myself on my scholarship, my ability to use my learning to work things out. There had to be a logical way of approaching this. I must set aside the thrill of seeing my lost sister and the bitter disappointment that she had disappeared before I could speak to her. Step by step, that was the way to handle things. I would proceed as I'd planned, starting by making a copy of the odd little patterns from the border of the first manuscript page. I could examine them at leisure back at the han.

I put them in my notebook, using the same order in case that was a clue to their meaning. There were thirty squares, each with its own decoration. As I worked steadily through the sequence, the tiny writing reappeared on the page. *Find the heart, for there lies wisdom. The crown is the destination.* I stared at it, looked away, looked back, half expecting it to vanish before my eyes. But it was still there. I drew more squares. Twenty-five, twenty-six . . . The more of them I set down, the more familiar they seemed. Perhaps they marked out some kind of mathematical sequence. I tried various possibilities for a while and got nowhere. Maybe they were a code that related to words in another manuscript or well-known book. If that was the case, it would probably be in Persian and I would have to trust someone to help me. I imagined the squares turned in various ways and tried to make them match the letters in the manuscript's text.

"Ready for some coffee, Paula? Or the hamam?" Irene was coming across the library, smiling. "You're looking quite pale. I can't have you fainting from overwork."

I slipped the manuscript pages back into their box and closed the lid. As I did so, I saw that the line of tiny writing had vanished.

Today even the hamam did not succeed in relaxing me. Ideas were racing around in my head, wild guesses as to what it was I was supposed to do and why Tati would be involved. Was I to ensure Father succeeded in buying Cybele's Gift? Stop Duarte Aguiar from "liberating" it? Or was the quest something entirely different, related to hearts and crowns? I was a scholar; I excelled at puzzles. I hated myself for being too stupid to work this one out.

"You seem tense today, Paula," Irene remarked as we sat together in the camekan after our bath. "Did you find what you were looking for?"

"I'm not looking for anything in particular," I lied. "I am rather frustrated at my inability to read Persian."

"I hear you've had another confrontation with the dashing Senhor Aguiar," Irene said.

The change of subject caught me off guard. I felt myself blush and lowered my eyes. Inwardly, I kicked myself. If I'd wanted to give Irene a perfect impression of a gauche country girl, I could hardly have done better. "I saw him briefly at the markets," I said, trying to look as if I was not the least interested in the dashing Senhor Aguiar.

Irene chuckled. "Paula, this may be a very big city, but in certain circles news travels fast, and gossip even faster. I heard he was showing a marked interest in you. I was told the good senhor and your large watchdog exchanged glances like sword strokes while you busied yourself intimidating the hapless merchants of the çarşi. I wish I'd been there to see it."

I was mortified. "A gross exaggeration," I said hastily. "It was just ordinary shopping. I've no idea why Duarte Aguiar decided to put himself out to help me. I hardly know him. He had stolen my scarf. That was how it started."

"Really?"

The story of the near collision at sea, the scarf, the appearance of Duarte at the markets, and his extravagant gift had her enthralled. After rewarding my narrative performance with laughter, Irene turned suddenly serious.

"It's an excellent story that can only improve with retelling," she said. "However, you should steer clear of Aguiar, as I advised you earlier. His past is shadowed by a hundred tales of dark deeds. This is a man who will stop at nothing to get what he wants."

"I know that," I said. "And I know his manner is sometimes inappropriate; I told him so. But he is interesting to talk to. We had a discussion about books. My father was present throughout," I added hastily.

"A man such as that does not offer a young woman gifts for no reason," Irene said with a crooked smile. "Duarte cuts a fine figure; women admire him. A man with a reputation has more glamour than an upright fellow with a spotless record. And, of course, girls love the notion that a bad man can be turned to good, as long as he has the right woman to help him."

"You sound very cynical."

"Your father allows you considerable freedom, Paula. I respect him for that. But you should heed my warning where Duarte is concerned. If he thinks he can use you to achieve a goal, he will do so without scruples. If he continues to pay you attention, you should question his motives at every turn."

I said nothing. Her speech had left me more than a little deflated. It was not possible, apparently, that a man like Duarte Aguiar could admire me for myself, as an intellectual foil. And as a woman.

"Do you think you will see him again?" Irene asked casually, rising to slip off her wrap, stretching like a cat, then stepping into her delicately embroidered undergarments.

"Maybe," I said. "My father has been invited to a supper; it's likely Duarte will also be there. I will be careful. The thing is, I did like talking to him. It made me feel . . . alive." It had made me feel as full of life as I had long ago in the Other Kingdom, debating all night with the scholars, wizards, and sages of that mysterious realm. There, nobody had worried about who liked whom or whether anyone had hidden motives. All had loved ideas; all had been excited by theories and argument. I thought of Tati, who had made that strange world her home. How could she have shown herself to me, then vanished before I could say any of the things I wanted to?

"You look sad." Irene's tone was soft. "What's troubling you, Paula?"

"It's nothing." I dropped my own wrap and dressed myself in the fresh set of clothing I had brought: my gray gown and a plain white scarf. I was saving the plum outfit for supper at Barsam's house.

"Come back in the morning," Irene said. "You need company, books, stimulation."

"Thank you. I will come if Stoyan is available to bring me. He may be busy again; Father has a lot to fit in."

"How long until this supper?"

"Two days."

"If you need Murat to fetch you again, just send a message," Irene said. "I do not want you to be alone at the han and unhappy, Paula. Besides, here you are safe from predators such as Duarte Aguiar."

I heard Murat's voice from outside and, answering, Stoyan's. I felt unaccountably relieved to hear him.

"Is it the supper that is worrying you?" Irene asked delicately. "A Muslim household, perhaps?"

"I don't think so, or I wouldn't have been invited," I told her. "All I was told was to bring a chaperone. Maria will probably come with us. I wish I understood a little better about the rules governing women's behavior here in Istanbul."

"If it is a Muslim household, Paula, you might perhaps accompany your father there, but you could be admitted only to the *haremlik*, the women's quarters. If the purpose of the supper is to conduct a business transaction—I am assuming this may be so in view of your father's occupation—any Islamic traders attending would not be prepared to continue if you were present. You might consider that grossly unfair, but it is the way things work in this part of the world. Those of us who live here discover our own forms of freedom, as no doubt you will if you stay among us long enough."

I did not answer. I could not do so without revealing the nature of our business and the purpose of Barsam's supper.

"You hesitate to say more." Irene was fastening a row of tiny clips down the front of her braided tunic. "I think it is time for complete honesty, Paula. There should be no secrets between friends."

I opened my mouth to say that the secret was Father's, not mine, but she spoke first.

"I will tell you what I know, and you can confirm it as truth or falsehood. I've recently been provided with some information. It concerns a rare artifact that is for sale in Istanbul. I've been told the vendor lives near the Mosque of Arabs and that competition for the item is fierce, with a number of merchants having traveled to the city for the purpose of bidding. I heard that the transaction is cloaked in the utmost secrecy."

"Secrecy?" I echoed, stunned. "It cannot be so secret if you've heard all this."

"I know more. Duarte Aguiar is one of the interested parties, and Teodor of Braşov another. I see you are shocked. You should not be. All I am demonstrating to you is that a woman can be more capable than a man of putting two and two together and making four. I have a wide circle of acquaintances in the city, Paula, and I'm a good listener. In this particular instance, it may set your father's mind at rest if I tell you I obtained my knowledge from a single source: a former acquaintance of Murat's at Topkapi Palace. The information will go no further, I promise you. The fact that I have not mentioned this to you earlier I offer as proof that I know when to keep my mouth shut. Your father's trade secrets are perfectly safe with me. My own collection consists solely of books and manuscripts, none of them particularly rare. I have no interest whatever in religious artifacts. Now tell me, is this supper to be held at the house of an Armenian?"

She had indeed shocked me. There seemed no point in holding back what she evidently knew perfectly well already. "Barsam the Elusive," I said, nodding.

"This is exciting for you, Paula. I see that. To be involved in the purchase of such an item must quicken the blood of any merchant. I have a warning for your father. You may pass on what I have told you, in confidence, of course, and add that Murat's source believed it will not be long before the Mufti's representatives carry out raids on the premises of all the potential buyers for this item. This relates to the matter the women were discussing on your first visit here—the revival of an ancient cult in Istanbul. It is Cybele's cult the rumors refer to. The Sheikh-ul-Islam, of course, is outraged at the possibility of pagan rites taking a grip in this devoutly Muslim city and will be keen to shut them down. On this issue, his Jewish and Christian counterparts in Istanbul are very likely to agree with him. His men will be looking for any evidence that will allow them to track the artifact and, through it, the leaders of this supposed cult, who, it is assumed, will be just as keen to acquire Cybele's Gift as everyone else seems to be. Let Master Teodor know it may be expedient to conceal any documentation related to this purchase. Such a visit will not be conducted gently."

"Thank you," I said, shocked that she knew so much and horrified at the thought that, without the warning, Father might have been caught unprepared by the Mufti's men. "I will certainly tell him. Now I must go; I hear Stoyan."

"Of course, Paula. I hope we will see you again tomorrow."

Stoyan was looking particularly impenetrable. It was late; long shadows stretched across the streets, and from the rooftops dark birds screeched to one another, offering their last territorial challenges before nightfall. We walked briskly.

"Thank you for coming to fetch me," I ventured.

A nod in response.

"Is everything all right? Was there a problem with the Neapolitan merchant?"

"It was complicated, kyria. Your father will explain."

"Complicated?"

"Master Teodor will tell you. The meeting did not proceed quite as he expected. Then, when we returned to the han, he was upset to find you gone."

"I left a message. You must have got it or you wouldn't be here."

Stoyan turned his gaze on me but did not slow his pace. "The house of Irene of Volos is the first place I would have looked for you, Kyria Paula. You think if you were missing, I would stay at the han and do nothing?" He sounded less than his calm self.

"I'm sorry if I upset anyone. It was a long morning, and Murat did come to fetch me. I'm not completely irresponsible." I did not tell him that I had sent the tea vendor's boy to buy me a set of robes like those the old women wore, black and all-concealing. I did not mention that I'd been on the verge of putting them on and going out by myself.

There was silence as we walked on. We crossed the square with the shady tree under which the storyteller was accustomed to sit. The man had shut up business and gone home; it was almost time for the evening call to prayer.

"I know that," Stoyan said quietly. "Your father received your message. But he was worried about you, kyria. Now we should make haste. Best if you are safely indoors before dark."

I lengthened my stride. We walked past a coffee shop where a lot of men were sitting or standing around a central brazier. Dusk was falling; the little fire glowed amber. Eyes turned toward us. Stoyan moved so that he was between me and the watchers.

"You keep up well for such a small thing," he observed when we were safely past.

"I was brought up in the mountains," I said.

"So," Stoyan said as we made our way along the narrow, shadowy street that led toward the han, "you can walk fast and climb. You can float in deep water, even with your boots on. A woman of many talents."

The smile in his voice surprised me. "You don't make jokes very often, Stoyan," I said.

"I have offended you?"

"Not at all. I liked your joke."

A group of men passed close by us, and Stoyan put his hand against my back, lightly, as if to reassure me that I had a protector. It felt nice—better than it should have to a woman like me, who had always believed she could look after herself. As soon as the men were out of sight, he took his hand away.

"May I ask you a question, Stoyan?"

"Of course," Stoyan replied.

"I heard some disturbing rumors about Senhor Duarte. You've been in Istanbul for some time. What do you know about him?"

"That man, Aguiar, he is not a suitable friend for you. I was troubled by his interest in you at the çarşi."

I could not think of an adequate response. "It wasn't exactly my choice," I said rather lamely. "He just came up and took over the shopping. I could hardly tell him to go away; that would have been rude."

"Such men, offered a pinch of salt, will take a bucketful, kyria. But you are a woman of independence; you will make your own path. See, we are almost home. Your father will tell you of his meeting. He is worried; you should hear him out."

I was worried, too, now and confused by the things he had said. "I will," I said. "Thank you for bringing me home."

At the han, Father was pacing up and down on the gallery, his face drawn and tired. This could not be solely from concern that I had gone out without prior permission. He'd already approved my excursions to Irene's. I deposited my bundle of clothing on my bed and returned to our central chamber while Stoyan went to buy supper.

"What happened?" I asked straight out. "Come, sit down, Father. You look exhausted. Stoyan wouldn't explain to me. Has something gone wrong?"

"Not exactly." Father sighed, then settled on the cushions opposite me. "I suppose it could even be interpreted as good news. Antonio of Naples is withdrawing his interest in Cybele's Gift. He no longer wishes to compete."

"You bought him off?"

"I never had the chance to try. Antonio received a warning. I was with him when it arrived. Whatever was in that message—it was in writing, and after he'd read it he consigned the paper to a brazier—was enough to turn him the color of goat cheese. He told me immediately that he was pulling out. This reduces our competition. Nonetheless, it troubles me."

He wasn't the only one. "You think the letter was a threat?" I asked.

"I don't know." A certain note in Father's voice told me he wasn't giving me the full story. He reached across and took both my hands in his. "It's not so very long since Salem bin Afazi was killed, Paula. I'm beginning to think I was foolishly naive when I decided it would be safe to bring you to Istanbul and to involve you in this particular business. When we returned here and you were gone, it alarmed me."

"I did leave a—"

"Yes, yes, I know. You did the right thing. But the situation has changed. I'm concerned about your welfare."

I could just see it. The next thing would be a decision not to let me come to the supper at Barsam's house. If someone outbid Father, I might never get to see Cybele's Gift. I bit back a childish protest: *It's not fair!* I must consider what was best—for Father, for Tati, for me. Just possibly, for the Other Kingdom as well. Before I could even think about Cybele's Gift, I needed to deal with the mystery of the manuscript and Tati's appearances. I had to solve that puzzle. As for Father, I must pass on the information I had been given without delay.

Stoyan came back up the steps, bearing a platter of steaming rice topped with chunks of roast lamb on skewers. It gave off a tantalizing odor combining lemon, mint, and spices.

"Thank you, Stoyan," said Father as this dish was set on the low table between us. "Paula, you know how badly I want this deal to be successful. You've worked hard to help me, and you've proven yourself an able assistant. But I don't like exposing you to this world of power plays and scheming. Nor, I find, am I as comfortable as I hoped to be about your situation as a woman in a man's world. You are vulnerable, like it or not. The Portuguese had a certain look in his eye. So, I am certain, did Alonso di Parma the day you struck your deal with him. I didn't much care for it."

"Maybe that's true," I said, "but surely there's an advantage to you in the very fact that I am a woman, and a young one at that. Men do tend to assume a girl is incapable of fully understanding a conversation about trading or related matters. I might hear all sorts of things you wouldn't. Father, I have some information for you. I think it's important." I told them what Irene had said—that raids on trading centers were imminent and that it might be appropriate to do a little rearranging of documents. That the Mufti was interested in Cybele's Gift and anyone who might be bidding for it. "Irene implied that their methods might be rather rough," I added. "It sounds as if this is not as secret as you've believed, Father. I've been careful not to talk about Cybele's Gift, even when the women at the hamam were discussing this underground cult. I didn't give away any secrets. But Irene does know a lot about what's going on, through her steward's contacts at Topkapi."

Father whistled under his breath. "It seems we are in your Greek friend's debt," he said. "It's very possible the agents of the Sheikh-ul-Islam will be here in the morning. As soon as we finish this meal, I will prepare for such a visit. I've been careful not to put certain information in writing. However, there are papers, including a promissory note from a bank in Venice, that must be concealed. And I have Salem's letters. Let us eat quickly; this has set me on edge."

Stoyan sat down beside us, and I passed around the small bowls we kept in our apartment.

"Paula—" Father began, and I sensed he was about to broach the topic of the supper and the risk to me of attending it.

"About the supper," I said, "I know you're probably concerned. Father, Duarte Aguiar seems to like me for some reason. Wouldn't it be useful if I talked to him some more? As for Alonso di Parma, he's such an outrageous flirt, he's likely to let slip all kinds of secrets without even thinking."

"A man doesn't use his daughter as a tool of that kind,

Paula." Father was sounding tired and grim. "I think I have to give you the full story about Antonio."

Something in his tone sent a chill down my spine. "What?" I asked. "Father, do you know who sent that letter to Antonio?" With a sinking heart, I recalled Irene's warnings about Duarte Aguiar.

"No, Paula," Father said heavily. "There are at least seven parties interested in Cybele's Gift, and I suppose the message could have come from any of the others. As for these searches by the Mufti, that kind of interference in the business of established merchants is highly unusual. Generally the Muslims are tolerant of 'People of the Book'—that is, Christians and Jews. We're not seen as ungodly, since we have our own holy scripture and live in accordance with its codes. Because of that, the Sultan allows us our places of worship in the city, even if the grandest have been converted into mosques. It's a different case with folk viewed as pagan, devotees of more primitive deities."

"Such as Cybele," I said.

"Indeed. This visit in the morning may be a little awkward. I'd prefer you to be absent from the han while the Mufti's representatives are here. It may be necessary not to lie but to withhold certain information. I've no intention of being the one who betrays the whereabouts of Cybele's Gift to someone who could only plan to destroy it."

"I've been invited back to Irene's. If you can spare Stoyan, he could take me there. Father, you were going to tell me about Antonio. About the threat."

"Antonio told me what was in the letter before he consigned it to the fire. The threat was not to himself but to his wife—you met her that day at the markets—and their children. It was precise, inventive, and ugly. Consider the fact that the man who sent that letter is likely to be present at this supper. I think it best that you do not come, Paula. You can spend the evening here with Maria instead."

I swallowed my first response. "I see. You think Maria can protect me better than Stoyan can?"

"I will leave Stoyan here with you. He was hired as your guard, not mine."

Stoyan half rose to his feet. "No, Master Teodor," he protested. "For you to attend this supper without my protection would be foolhardy—"

"You can't be in two places at once," Father said reasonably enough.

"I believe it is wiser for all of us to go, Master Teodor," said Stoyan. His tone was respectful. "Your daughter is a grown woman with a good head on her shoulders, resourceful and brave. If she accompanies you, I can protect you both. I do, in fact, believe that would be safer than leaving Kyria Paula here without us after dark. The han guards can do only so much."

"Besides," I put in, warmed by Stoyan's description of me, which was so unlike the empty compliments other young men had offered me in the past, "we shouldn't give in to bullying. That would be weak. If people threaten me, I don't cave in. I fight back. That's what we have to do."

Chapter Six

Something was stalking me. Its footsteps were soft as falling snow, its growl subterranean, menacing. It was gaining on me. I scrambled to get away, my feet skidding on the uneven floor of the tunnel, but something was clinging to my ankles, holding me back. I looked down and my skin crawled. A pair of long-nailed gray hands was clamped around my legs. I screamed and tried to wrench away. The creature clutched tighter, ripping my skirt and raking my flesh with scythe-sharp claws. Cackling laughter filled the dim passageway. *The signs*, someone whispered in my sister's voice. *Why didn't you work out the signs? You're the scholar, the clever one. How could you miss them?* From behind now came a sound of rustling and a susurration of wings, louder by the moment. An army of small scuttling things swarmed over my feet. I slipped and sprawled full length. Their shells crunched beneath me, splitting to spill their entrails over the stone. Then came a horde of insects, swarming around my head, landing to crawl into any crevice they could discover, buzzing into my ears, flying up my nose. I put my hands up to cover my eyes and felt my fingers instantly thick with their fuzzy creeping legs. I opened my mouth to scream and they crowded in. I couldn't breathe, I was going to die—

"Paula! Paula, wake up!"

I shuddered awake, sitting bolt upright in a tangle of blankets, my hands still clawing at my mouth. I could hear myself babbling in a mixture of terror and relief. My face was drenched in tears. I was in my little bedroom at the han, and Stoyan was crouched by the pallet with his arm around me. I was well beyond being shocked by that. The dream had been so real. I could still feel those things crawling on me. I could hear the sickening sound of their bodies breaking under me. I could feel them in my mouth, in my throat. . . .

"Put my cloak around you, Paula. Here."

Only half emerged from my nightmare, I still noticed that he had used my first name.

Now Stoyan was draping the cloak over my shoulders. "Breathe slowly. . . . That's better." I was dimly aware of his lifting a corner of his loose muslin undershirt to dry my eyes. I felt the brush of his fingers against my cheek, wiping away my tears, and then I was properly awake.

"Oh, God," I muttered. "That was horrible. I'm so sorry if I woke you." He was barefoot, clad only in the undershirt and light trousers, his mane of dark hair flowing unbound over his shoulders.

"You will not wish to be here alone in the dark. Keep the cloak on; we can sit on the gallery. It is not so cold tonight. I will stay with you until you are recovered."

"Thank you. If you're going to fetch tea, I'm coming with you." I didn't want to be by myself even for as long as it took him to walk down to the courtyard and come back again.

A little later, having obtained a supply of tea and a small shielded lantern, we were on the gallery once more. With Stoyan's big cloak over my nightrobe, I was both warm and decently covered. He had flung a sheepskin coat on top of his thin shirt and trousers and had thrust his bare feet into his boots.

I knew, as I had done that other night when Stoyan had sat up with me until dawn, that the situation might be judged by some as improper. But Stoyan made me feel safe. And I could not wake Father—he had enough to worry about. I did not think the night guard would gossip. All the han workers were in awe of Stoyan.

Our eyes met in the lamplight as he put a glass of tea in my hand. He was calm, as always, but there was something different in his expression, a wariness I had not seen before. I did not bother trying to interpret it. I was just intensely glad he was there to sit with me and help keep the dark things at bay.

"I don't want to talk about the dream," I said. "I want to forget it. I don't know what's wrong with me. I hate being out of control like this. I think someone's trying to warn me. To show me what might happen if I get it wrong, if I can't work it out."

"What is it you must work out, Paula?"

I made a snap decision. "I want to show you something, Stoyan. I need your advice. Hold this for a moment." Giving him back the glass, I went inside to fetch my notebook.

"I will not be able to help you," he said flatly when I returned. His gaze was on the book.

"You might." I was looking for the page on which I'd transcribed the little symbols. "Someone's given me a puzzle, something to do with Cybele's Gift. If you look—" I glanced up and was shocked by the expression on his face, which was suddenly as guarded as if we were total strangers. "What?" I asked.

"It shames me to tell you, kyria, but I cannot read. In your world, all men are scholars. I am not part of that world." He had to force this out, and my heart bled for him.

"I don't need you to read, Stoyan," I said, choosing my words carefully, "just to look at something. Most people can't read, you know. Most people aren't given the opportunity to learn."

"I have no wish to talk of this."

I had really upset him. "Stoyan," I said in a different tone, "we are friends, aren't we? Be honest. Forget that we hired you as a guard and speak from the heart."

His lips twisted into a self-mocking smile, but his tone was warm. "We are friends," he said.

"Good," I said. "It is not difficult to learn to read, provided you have a little time and a good teacher. I am a good teacher. I taught my younger sister, and she's becoming quite a scholar. This is something I could help you with, if you want to learn."

Stoyan hunched his shoulders and looked at his feet. "I cannot learn," he muttered.

"Cannot? I don't believe it."

"I am a man of the land, kyria. In my village, even the elders do not possess this skill. Only the priest has any knowledge of letters."

"What about a wager? I would lay odds on my ability to teach you successfully."

His lips curved in a sweet smile, taking me by surprise. "I have nothing to wager," he said. "Unless you are in need of a sharp knife or a pair of too-large boots."

I was silent for a moment. "You said you would breed dogs one day. I'll have a pup from the first litter, one that you don't want for breeding stock. A . . . a Bugarski Goran. Do I have it right?"

"That is an item of more value than perhaps you realize, Paula."

"If it's anything like our farm dogs at home, I have a fair idea of its worth."

"And what if you fail? What should be set against a creature of such price?"

"I won't fail."

"Nonetheless, you must wager something of equivalent value, Paula."

I thought about this. It seemed to me there was only one thing I could give him that he really needed. "I suppose, when Father and I leave for home, you will take up the search for your brother again," I said. "If you had funds, you could do so straightaway, without having to spend more time working as a guard. Once we've bought Cybele's Gift, I can reasonably ask Father for some money of my own—"

"No." Stoyan did not let me finish. His features had tightened and his eyes had lost their earlier warmth. "I will not take your charity, Paula. Finding Taidjut is my quest, my mission. I must earn the means to undertake it by my own labor. You insult me with this offer."

"Insult?" Clearly I had made an error of judgment, but I had not thought he would be so offended by my suggestion, which seemed to me perfectly practical. "Pride is all very well, Stoyan, but sometimes we have to be practical about these things—"

"I will not discuss this with you," Stoyan said. His voice was unsteady; I had really upset him. "You cannot understand."

Now I was the one who was insulted. "Cannot? I thought you said I was a . . . a grown woman with a good head on my shoulders."

"When I said so, I spoke the truth," he said, his tone once more calm and even. His ability to control his temper was much better than mine. "But this is a matter beyond your comprehension. Perhaps beyond any woman's."

After a moment I said, "I see." My heart was thumping; I realized I very much didn't want to have an argument with him. "I suppose it's immaterial anyway. I intend to win the wager."

"From what Master Teodor tells me," Stoyan said, "in one month you return to Transylvania and we part company. What can you teach me in a month?"

"Plenty," I told him. "All your letters—it will have to be in Greek, since I don't know your native tongue and you don't know mine—and how to write your name and a few other things, sufficient to get you started. Enough to write a very short letter to your mother, which the priest can read to her."

Stoyan said nothing. In his amber eyes I saw his image of his mother receiving such a missive, perhaps with news of the lost brother, Taidjut. The silence drew out.

"I'm sorry I upset you," I said eventually. "I hate arguing with you." It had made my stomach tie itself into a tight knot of distress.

"I too, Paula. Tell me, when might such study be undertaken? Your father pays me to guard his daughter, not to be the recipient of her wisdom."

"We'll make time. This is important."

"To prove you are right and win the wager? You like dogs so much?"

"This is not about the dog. I want to prove to you that this is something you can do. I can see you view reading and writing as an arcane mystery, and I know it isn't."

"I am not of a scholarly persuasion, Paula. What is easy for you will be difficult for me."

"Perhaps we should forget the wager, and you teach me something in return. Something that is easy for you and difficult for me."

A slow smile spread across Stoyan's face, lighting up his strange eyes. I wondered what I had started.

"I like this idea far better, Paula," he said. "Let us agree to it."

"Done," I said, thinking how much I liked it when he called me by my name. It was not something I could tell him.

"Now, if you wish, I will look at this book," Stoyan said, "though I cannot imagine I can be of much assistance. Tomorrow I will begin to teach you how to defend yourself against attackers. Unarmed combat. In that, I am expert."

I put my chin up and tried for a confident look. "All right," I said, as if lessons in self-defense were the kind of thing I did every day. "I suppose that might come in useful sometime."

I showed him the page in my notebook where I had copied the little border designs from the Persian manuscript. "I think it's a code or puzzle," I told him, "but I can't work out how to solve it. I thought of letters or numbers, a numeric sequence of some kind or perhaps a cryptic reference to another book. I cannot think what would be sufficiently well known."

"The Koran?" Stoyan suggested, surprising me. "No, perhaps not. A devout person would not use the holy book in such a way. Why do you believe this puzzle has been set for you? How could anyone know you would be in this library except the Greek lady herself?"

I hesitated. Did I trust him enough to speak of the strange words that had appeared and disappeared? Could I tell him I had seen Tati? I looked at him, and Stoyan looked back, his scarred face pale in the lantern light, his hair a shadowy cascade across his powerful shoulders. I saw trust in his eyes, and honesty, and something else, something that drew me to him, yet made me look away.

"There have been other things," I said in an undertone. "A woman dressed all in black. I've seen her several times now, at the docks, in a boat, in the library. She's been leading me on a quest, at least I think that's what it is. Back home, the folk of the Other Kingdom delighted in setting tests and trials. Usually they had reasons of their own, but it was also a way for human folk to learn lessons and become better people. When it happened to us before, it was all about keeping the forest safe, the place where they lived, and making sure our valley was looked after by someone fair and honest who respected the Other Kingdom. That turned out to be our second cousin Costi and my sister Jena. And at the same time, the quest was to help my eldest sister, Tati, and her sweetheart be together. The woman . . . When I heard her voice and saw her eyes, it was Tati, Stoyan. The sister who went away years ago and never came back."

"Remarkable," he breathed. "What is the nature of this quest?"

Somehow, I was not surprised that he had accepted my words without making the sort of remarks other folk would under such circumstances: *That's impossible* or *How could your sister be here in Istanbul?* Stoyan was different. I had known that from the first.

"I don't know, but I think it's to do with Cybele's Gift. That's why it's urgent to work out the clues. There was writing on the manuscript, writing that appeared and disappeared. 'Find the heart, for there lies wisdom. The crown is the destination.' Then, the next time I was in the library, I found another sheet of the same manuscript, and it had Cybele's picture on it."

Stoyan studied the little images awhile, brow furrowed. Then he said, "You spoke of a puzzle to solve. Perhaps it is less complex than you imagine. Put together in the right way, these fragments might make the image of a spreading tree with flowers and leaves, with small creatures at its feet and with birds and insects in its branches. A tree has both a heart, in the center of the old wood, and a crown, a canopy. Do you think?" His voice was hesitant.

"Why break the image up? Why make it so cryptic?" I wondered aloud.

"I cannot imagine," Stoyan said quietly, "unless it is somehow secret. If this quest is indeed for you, Paula, perhaps this message was concealed thus so it would only become apparent when you were ready to read it."

I was silent. Could Stoyan so quickly have solved a puzzle I had labored for hours to work out without success?

"We could put it to the test," Stoyan suggested. "A tray of sand in which we can re-create this tree, or some small scraps of paper . . . I know your Father's store of writing materials is not to be wasted, but . . ."

"We'll need a tray of sand to practice our Greek letters," I said.

"There is clean sand in the camel compound." A pause. "I do not wish to leave you here alone, Paula."

"I'll be all right if I can keep the lantern." It seemed wrong to let nightmares and apparitions get the better of me. I had always wanted to be my own woman, independent and brave. "But don't take too long. Stoyan?" I spoke as he was heading off along the gallery, and he turned his head. "I like it when you call me Paula," I said, against my better judgment. "And please don't answer that it's inappropriate."

"It is just for the nighttime," Stoyan said, his voice like a shadow. Then he was gone.

It was a strange thing to say, and I wondered if I had misheard him. I made myself concentrate on the images, putting them together in my mind to make a stylized picture, doing my best to work out what kind of tree it might be—something with broad, heart-shaped leaves, not needles; something with flowers; something much visited by small creatures of one kind or another. The more I imagined this tree, the more I saw the form of the bee goddess in it, the leaves her wild hair, the roots her strong feet, the bulbous trunk and generous limbs a mirror of Cybele's own body. *Make me whole,* her spectral voice whispered. I tried hard not to look along the gallery into the dark recesses at its far corners, where anything might be lurking.

Stoyan came back at a run, balancing a tray filled with damp sand. The lantern light was not ideal for fine work, but we set the tray on the small table, and while I held up the book with my notes, he marked the sand out as a grid with thirty squares, then began to copy the shapes with a twig, filling each square with one of the small patterns, trying to place them in the way he had envisaged would form the trunk, branches, and leaves of a tree. I tried to note which ones he had used so he didn't double up or leave any out. For a long time, we murmured instructions and suggestions to each other as he crouched by the table, making a line here, rubbing out a squiggle there, doing his best to make it work.

"If this theory proves correct," Stoyan said, erasing several images with a sigh and examining the notebook page again, "where does it take us?"

"I don't know. I stumbled on the manuscript at random when I was browsing through a box of bits and pieces that hadn't been sorted out. It's too much of a coincidence for me to find these, unless it's a trail I'm supposed to follow. I'm sure Irene didn't know what was in the box, nor did her assistant. Neither of them took much interest in exactly what I was studying. Stoyan, when I looked at the little picture of Cybele . . ." My words died away as he completed the last few pieces of the puzzle. He'd been right. The tiny shapes formed a spreading tree bearing flowers and fruit at the same time, with all sorts of creatures flying and roosting and foraging around the roots. A tree with a heart, for that was the way its sturdy trunk looked, and a crown of verdant foliage.

"How was it you saw that so quickly," I asked him, "and I spent days thinking about it and getting nowhere?"

"Perhaps you were looking for a more complex solution. A simple man sees a simple answer."

"Simple? You? I doubt that."

"You did not finish what you were saying." He regarded me gravely. "When you found this image of the old goddess, something happened."

"I heard a voice. Not Tati's; another voice, a deep one. It was like a command: 'I am the beginning. Make me whole.' There was another girl in the library, and she didn't seem to have heard it, nor did she see Tati when she appeared and disappeared. I wonder if you'd be able to see her?"

"I do not know. Paula, your past must make you a perfect choice to be entrusted with such a secret. I am unsurprised that clues have been laid for you to follow. A scholar by nature and training, and already a visitor to this kingdom of the shadows. . . . So someone has chosen you to be the holder of knowledge. This troubles me. I know you wish to visit Kyria Irene's library in the morning. I am not content to wait for you outside. Not this time."

"That won't work anyway," I said, impressed by his insight. "I want to show you the manuscript. Perhaps there's a way around Irene's rule. Let me think about it."

"Should you speak of these manifestations to Master Teodor? He fears attack by commercial rivals. He is unaware that other, more unusual forces are also at work."

"It's best that he doesn't know," I said. "We did tell him the truth about Tati, about why she was gone when he came home that winter, but not all of it. Not that she and Jena had met the Night People and . . . Well, it's a long story. I'll tell you someday. If Father knew that Tati had been here and that I might have a quest to fulfill, he'd probably send me straight home. He doesn't realize I can deal with these things."

"I believe you," said Stoyan. "It seems you have grown up with a knowledge of the uncanny and have less fear of it than most folk might. It is the more worldly dangers that give me pause."

"I thought you were going to teach me unarmed combat." I managed a smile.

"The same as the reading: enough to get you started," he said. "It cannot be sufficient to allay my fears for you. Not so quickly."

"You don't need to worry about me, Stoyan."

"You are a woman of spirited views, of independence and courage. I wish I could say you are right. But how can I do that when you wake suddenly and I hear terror in your voice? It cuts me to the quick that I cannot be there by your side in your dreams to lead you to safety."

I could think of absolutely nothing to say. His last remark had been deeply personal and seemed quite inappropriate from a hired guard. My cheeks were hot, and I was glad the dim light concealed this from my companion. Eventually I said, "They're only dreams." Perhaps I had misunderstood what he meant. After my earlier blunder, I was probably overreacting.

"My mother would say a dream is the key that unlocks the mysteries of the waking world."

"You seem remarkably ready to accept the eldritch and supernatural," I told him, steering the conversation away from the perilous track that seemed to be opening up with alarming frequency tonight. "You don't seem at all shocked by what I've told you. Unless you're just humoring me."

"I would not do that. I respect you."

"Does this openness come from your mother? At home, the mountain people distrust and fear the Other Kingdom. They hang talismans on the trees and erect crucifixes to keep out not just the devil's minions but fairies and dwarves and Night People as well. It's not that they don't believe. It's more that they hope those forces will set a wide berth around them and their loved ones."

"My mother's mother was a *znaharka*, a . . . What is the word? A wisewoman, one who dabbled in spells and cures. She taught us respect for what is beyond the commonplace; she imparted a love for the deep and wise truths of the earth. That is how I know of Cybele. There is not so much difference, I believe, between the kind of beings you spoke of, the denizens of your Other Kingdom, and a deity such as the bee goddess."

"I want to study that second page more closely tomorrow, the one with Cybele's picture on it. Maybe there are more clues there. I think it's important that we work them out before the supper." A yawn overtook me. I looked out over the rooftops and thought I could see a faint lightening of the sky. "That's if either of us can stay awake," I added.

"You have time to sleep a little before your father rises," said Stoyan. "What shall we do with this small work of art? Should we preserve it?"

I looked down at the little tray with its neat image in the sand, the squiggly lines that had resolved themselves into a pattern of trunk and branches, the parts I had thought only blobs and smears that were now, quite obviously, leaves, buds, birds, creatures. I wondered if too much learning had blinded me to what was right and true. "I don't think that's practical," I told him. "But we should try to remember it. There has to be a reason we were shown this."

"I will study it further before dawn, commit it to memory."

"You should sleep, Stoyan. I've kept you up half the night."

"Do not concern yourself. You must rest. You have a difficult task ahead of you."

"You mean trying to find clues that may not exist?" I got up, hugging the cloak around me and wondering if I dared try to sleep. The nightmare was not far away.

"I mean teaching a farm boy his letters. I think I will have more success as a tutor than you."

"Making a scholarly girl into a fearsome warrior? I doubt it. Stoyan, since you are staying up, would you mind not dousing the lantern for a while?"

"I will be here, just by the outer doorway. I will place the light where you can see it from your pallet. Sleep well, Paula. Your dreams will be good ones now. I know it."

I lay on my bed watching him through the half-closed door. The lantern light warmed his broad features and gave a glint to the long-lashed yellow eyes. His dark hair fell forward, tangling over his shoulders as he sat cross-legged with the sand tray on his lap. Once or twice he took his gaze off the little tree and glanced toward me, then turned his attention back to the task. His concentration was exemplary. I'd have him writing his name before he knew it. But that might be as far as it went, because in one month's time, when the

Stea de Mare was due for her next trip to Constanța, we would part ways and I'd never see Stoyan again.

As I fell asleep, it came to me that this would be like discovering a new book, a compelling one full of surprises, and then, just when I was becoming absorbed in the story, having it snatched away half read.

When I woke, I found I had slept right through the morning call to prayer, and I could not recall a single dream.

Maria had a stomach upset. It seemed unlikely she would be sufficiently recovered by evening to accompany us to Barsam's house. Anticipating the morning inspection, Father was edgy and distracted. I could not attend the supper without a chaperone. Claudia would be looking after Maria. Stoyan did not want me to stay at the han at night without him, nor did he want Father to go to the blue house without his guard to protect him. They were on the verge of a full-scale argument when I interrupted with what seemed the obvious solution.

"I think Irene would come as my chaperone," I said. "She's highly respected in the city, she's a friend, and she already knows about Cybele's Gift and the supper, so there's no problem with confidentiality. And if she brings Murat, we'll have two bodyguards. Shall I ask her?"

Father nodded agreement, his mind clearly elsewhere. He had not told me where he had hidden the papers concerning Cybele's Gift, but I knew him well enough to be quite sure they would not be found. All the same, the prospect of the Mufti's men performing a search of our private quarters was troubling.

They arrived while I was still eating breakfast. In addition to several men I took from their robes and hats to be imams, prayer leaders, there was a small force of Janissaries. I remembered Irene's comment on the nature of the visits the Sheikh-ul-Islam was carrying out and began to worry about Father. Giacomo was already down in the courtyard, welcoming the delegation.

"The Janissaries are only for show," Father muttered as he put on his hat in readiness to meet the visitors. "To intimidate us into providing whatever the Mufti's after. Don't look so worried, Paula. Leave me to deal with this. I'm used to providing just enough information to satisfy without revealing what I don't want known. They'll be talking to Giacomo first. Stoyan, slip out with Paula as soon as they've gone inside."

It had rained overnight. Stoyan and I walked to Irene's house between showers, and we talked very little on the way. There was a constraint between us this morning. Each of us had made certain remarks last night that fell outside the boundaries of convention. He was quiet and remote now, I reasoned, because he was regretting allowing that to happen.

"You must be tired, Stoyan," I observed as the wall of Irene's house came into view down the street.

"Not so weary that I cannot fulfill my duties, kyria."

I sighed. He was right back into mistress and servant mode. "That's not what I meant," I said, but probably he was wise. Mistress and servant was what we were, officially, and it would be a lot easier to keep things that way. Maybe, once tomorrow's supper was over, I would have no more nightmares. Maybe I wouldn't need a friend to hold my hand in the middle of the night and listen as if he understood everything.

Some time later, I sat with Irene overlooking her rain-soaked garden, sipping a cold drink. As soon as I had mentioned Maria's illness, my hostess had offered to chaperone me at the supper, which had saved me from having to ask her. She expressed the view that, at the very least, she could prevent Duarte Aguiar from spoiling my evening with his pestering. We made arrangements to get to the blue house—she and Murat would meet us at the han, from where we would all go on together. Now I was making a more awkward request.

"I would like to work here on the colonnade today, if you agree. It would mean bringing out the box of papers I have been studying. The light is better here. I will use a table, of course, and keep everything clean and dry."

Irene saw through it instantly. "And you can remain somewhat closer to your young man," she observed with lifted brows. Stoyan was standing not far from us.

"My guard," I corrected. "That is part of the reason for my request, yes. Father was expecting the Mufti's men this morning—he thanks you for the warning, by the way. He's sensitive about my safety."

"Paula." Irene lowered her voice. "You'd do well to avoid getting too close to this guard of yours."

I was so taken aback I could find nothing to say.

"You have not noticed the way he looks at you?" Irene murmured.

"It's Stoyan's job to look after me," I told her. "I have complete faith in him. Are you questioning my choice of guard?"

"Not at all, Paula, only what might arise from it. You are young. This is a fine specimen of manhood, an unpolished gem, one might say. But not for you. I see a certain affinity between you. I hear how quickly you spring to his defense. You know he used to work for Salem bin Afazi, don't you? The merchant who was done to death in the street not long ago?"

"Salem was a friend of my father's. We know all about it. The murder happened while Stoyan was away. He was devastated when he returned to find his employer dead."

"You discuss such personal matters with him?"

I was becoming acutely aware of Stoyan, standing a short distance along the colonnade. I judged he was not quite out of earshot. His face was turned away from us. "Why not?" I asked in an undertone.

"Again you spring to his defense. He is not your equal, Paula, and never can be. Ask yourself if such a man would ever be able to conduct a conversation with you about books or music or philosophy. Would he ever be able to share with you the pursuits you love, the ideas you are so passionate about? Besides, how much can you know about him on so brief an acquaintance? Has it occurred to you that his absence at the time of his employer's death might have been more than coincidence? If, let us say, a rival had wished to remove Salem bin Afazi from the scene, he would only have needed to offer a respectable sum to this large young man to ensure he would be far away from his master's side at the critical moment."

I was shocked. "I'm certain that's not how it was. I mean, maybe it's true about a rival being responsible for what happened to Salem. But Stoyan would never risk his employer's safety for money. We know him well enough by now to be quite sure of that."

"Really? I imagine his family back home, wherever that is, must be impoverished. There's another matter of concern,

HFM-SLS

Paula. I have heard of your guard's involvement in certain unsavory dealings prior to his time with Salem bin Afazi. Street fighting and other such activities."

"He has reasons for being here, and reasons for needing funds," I said a little defensively. Her comments bothered me. It was true that, in terms of our background, there was a yawning gulf between Stoyan and me. But there was no need for her to point it out, especially not within his hearing. Besides, there was nothing going on between us.

"And he has confided these reasons to you." Her voice was soft.

I wasn't going to let her probe any further. "Irene, I know you must be very busy. And I should get on with some work."

"I see my criticism of your watchdog hurts you," Irene said quietly. "I'm sorry. You are young, and young girls can be swayed by the longings of the heart, or by excess sympathy for those who seem in trouble, or by the all-too-powerful yearnings of the body. Before she knows it, a young woman can find herself swept into very deep waters."

Stoyan had moved slightly farther away and was busy adjusting the weapon he carried on his back. His mouth was set in a grim line.

"You don't need to warn me," I said. "I'm not one of those gullible types. Besides, I'm in Istanbul to assist my father. I've no plans to fall in love."

Irene smiled. "No, I suppose your first love will always be scholarship. How frustrating for you that we women are denied so many opportunities. If you had been a boy, perhaps you might have been a noted scholar, a teacher, a writer. As it is, I imagine that although your father allows you considerable freedom, he will eventually expect you to marry some worthy man and settle down to produce a batch of children. Such a waste of your gifts." She sounded unusually passionate, as if this genuinely angered her.

"It's not quite like that," I said, feeling I must defend my father. "Father has been delighted to see two of my sisters happily married, of course. But he knows I want to become a trader specializing in books. I suppose he would like me to marry as well. My sisters often tease me about that. They say that if I select a husband, it will be on the basis of how many languages he can read or his ability to sustain an argument on obscure points of philosophy. In fact, I am coming to the conclusion that a woman cannot succeed in both—I mean, conducting some kind of career of her own as well as being a wife and mother. My sister Jena is an exception, but then, she married an unusual man. There are no others like Costi."

Irene smiled. "It's my belief that a strong-minded and able young woman needs no husband, only the courage of her own convictions," she said. "There are hundreds of girls who can perform the role of wives and mothers. There are only a few with the capacity to rise above that and do the extraordinary. You could be one of those, Paula. Give it some thought. Now I will ask Ariadne to fetch your manuscripts. You may work here. Just be careful the wind does not carry the papers into the garden. Everything's wet today."

Chapter Seven

Stoyan wasn't happy. Whatever he had overheard had caused him to close in on himself completely. I gestured to him to come over and sit by me at the table, but he was slow to respond. Our hostess had moved away along the colonnade and was speaking to a group of women gathered there.

"Please, Stoyan," I murmured.

With visible reluctance, he squatted down beside me, peering at the fragment.

"This is the goddess with her bees." I showed him the tiny image. "I do think she looks a little like a tree, with her hair as foliage."

Stoyan spoke in a sharp whisper. "I am out of place here. I am a guard, not a scholar."

"Never mind that," I whispered back. "Tell me what you can see."

"Pictures, kyria. And words I cannot read. You do not require me here to tell you what you can see for yourself."

"I can't read this either. It's in Persian. Look closely. I want to know if you notice anything unusual." When he made no comment, I added, "I'm sorry if she upset you. I can't do this without you, Stoyan."

While he examined the ornately decorated pages, I got out my writing materials and made another copy of the hidden symbols, this time on a loose sheet of paper that I had divided up into thirty squares. I did not try to put them in the shape of the tree, only to copy each faithfully. Back at the han, I would cut the sheet up and assemble the pieces to form a more lasting version of our completed puzzle. I needed the sand tray for Stoyan's writing lessons. I was determined to make him realize he was capable of learning. He was bitter and angry about his lack of scholarship. There was enough sadness in his life. No point in adding to it when the solution was so easy.

Stoyan's attention had been taken by the miniatures on the other fragment, the one I had found first. "This looks like a game of combat," he whispered to me, indicating one of the images. "This being, who seems part man, part jackal, tosses the other, with his horselike head, over his shoulder and onto the ground. These others—men in women's clothing?— applaud the bout. I think this figure holds a circlet of leaves to crown the victor."

"Cybele's spring ritual," I murmured. "They enacted it every year when her lover was reborn. They used to . . . Well, never mind the details."

"If you look closely, you can see similar forms in the border—look here and here."

The border was intricate. Its scrolls and twists and spirals embellished not only the little squares and triangles that made up the tree puzzle, but also images of men and animals. The colors were vivid: rich strong blue, vibrant red, a touch of gold leaf here and there, a deep olive green. "In this picture," Stoyan said, "a woman converses with a cat. The creature has one blue and one yellow eye. In the next is a hawk-headed man swinging from a rope and a dog-faced one waiting to catch him."

"Maybe the spring ritual involves a series of tests." I peered at the tiny image. "You know, strength, agility, and wit or something like that."

"I wonder if—"

The words seemed to freeze on Stoyan's lips. When I glanced at him, he was staring at me with such horror that I looked over my shoulder to see if a monster had suddenly appeared. Irene and most of her group had gone inside the house, leaving only two women sitting farther along the colonnade quietly reading. Stoyan had turned ghostly white, his eyes like saucers.

"Wh—" I began, and a moment later had the sensation of floating out of my body, as if in a dream, so that I was looking down on my own seated figure and that of my companion from some point in the air above myself. But the person on the chair was not Paula in her demure gown and headscarf. It was a woman clad all in black, seated exactly where I had been a moment ago and fixing her lovely violet-blue eyes on Stoyan. Her embroidery trailed across her knees. On its surface, girls danced in a line. The fourth was slim and pale with wavy brown hair and spectacles on a chain around her neck: myself, executed in neat stitches. As for the real Paula, I was no longer part of the world of Irene's house but in some other realm, held separate until Tati had said or done whatever it was she needed to.

"Where's Paula?" Stoyan's voice was a strangled whisper.

"What have you done with her?" He was reaching for the knife at his belt. "Answer me!"

Frozen, suspended, I could not speak. I could not tell him to be calm and wait.

"Listen to me!" my sister said. As she spoke, Stoyan whipped the knife out of its sheath and stood up, blade ready to strike. It was one of the worst moments of my life. Every part of me was screaming to intervene, to stop him from doing something terrible, to warn Tati. . . . And yet I knew I could not. The powerful charm that held me immobile would not be released until this had unfolded in its own way. Along the colonnade, the two women now stood frozen, staring. One had her book clutched defensively to her chest.

"What is this?" Stoyan hissed. His voice shook, but he held the weapon perfectly steady. "What do you want with us?"

"You have to listen, Stoyan," said Tati, and she slipped the veil from her face so he could see that she was young and beautiful and as pale as frost on the hawthorn. "I can't stay long and I'm not allowed to talk to Paula, not properly; it's one of the rules. Each of us has a quest to fulfill, you and Paula and I. If you succeed, you will earn three rewards: one for courage, one for steadfastness, one for openness. Earn them well. Use them well. And please keep my sister safe."

"Your—" Stoyan began, lowering the knife slightly, and a moment later I felt myself descending, becoming flesh and blood again, and there I was sitting at the table, looking up into his face and trying to still my trembling hands.

"I . . . I saw her," I stammered. "I could hear her. But I was somewhere else. . . . Stoyan, sit down, you look as if you're about to faint."

"Paula!" He reached out a hand, touched my arm, my hair. He was as shocked as I was. "You are safe, unhurt? By all the saints . . . I do not know what to say." He sheathed the knife, glancing along the colonnade at the women, who were now conferring with apparent urgency. I imagined them running to Irene or to Murat and telling a tale of how my bodyguard had been waving weapons around on the premises. I didn't know exactly what they'd seen, but I'd need to reassure them or this could become very unpleasant.

"I'm sorry," I called, getting to my feet. My legs would scarcely hold me. "My guard thought he heard an intruder in the garden. Please don't be alarmed."

The women did not look convinced.

"Are you sure you are safe, kyria?" one of them asked in halting Greek. "It seemed . . ." She glanced at Stoyan. "I thought the young man meant to harm you. That was the way it looked. Should I call Kyria Irene?"

Stoyan gathered himself, bowed respectfully, and called something to them in Turkish, his tone placatory.

"Really, we're fine," I added. As the women seated themselves once more, I lowered my voice. "Stoyan, that was my sister," I told him. "Tatiana. I thought you were going to kill her." Something occurred to me; something odd. "What language was she speaking?" I asked. I had understood her and so, it seemed, had Stoyan. Since Tati had never learned Greek, that ruled out the only tongue Stoyan and I had in common. Had she spoken in the strange language of the Other Kingdom, universally understood yet so ephemeral we could never remember it in our own world? It shocked me to recognize how far my eldest sister had drifted away from her old life.

"That doesn't matter, Paula. We should leave right away. This is dangerous. What if you had not come back? If these forces draw you into another world, a realm beyond the earthly and human, I cannot follow you there."

"It sounded as if Tati expected you to do just that. She was giving you a mission to accomplish. You are involved whether you like it or not. The fact that you could see her and those women couldn't proves it. If they'd noticed me disappearing and being replaced by someone completely different, they certainly wouldn't still be sitting along there."

"I have a mission: protecting you while you are here in Istanbul. My instructions do not extend to dealing with manifestations like this. Against such a threat, I have no weapons."

"I think Tati was saying you do. Courage, steadfastness, and openness. Those are the weapons you need."

"For what? Why does this sister not tell us plainly what is required of us?"

I thought of Drăguţa, the witch of the wood. "She may not know," I said. "The folk of the Other Kingdom never play simple games. If she could meet us properly and explain it clearly, she would have no need to appear and disappear or to remove me while she spoke to you. Perhaps she's not very good at these manifestations yet. I mean, six years ago she was an ordinary human girl like me. But the longer she stays in that other world, the more like its inhabitants she becomes. That's why her sweetheart, Sorrow, can never come back—he was taken by the Night People when he was only about ten and now he's . . . different. The quest they set for him was extremely difficult. That's the way these things work: The greater the reward to be won at the end, the harder the mission. Quests can win people happiness, peace, knowledge. The stakes are high, because these missions affect many lives—they can alter the course of history. In the process, people can get badly hurt. They can die."

"You cannot be saying that our paths are set down for us by these beings?" Stoyan sounded deeply troubled. "They sound capricious. I cannot believe my destiny is in the hands of such wayward creatures. What of God? Or, indeed, of gods in general, Cybele included? Do these forces work together, or do they wage ceaseless wars, with human souls as the price?"

"I can't answer that. All I know is that we have our own quest, you and I. And Tati. I don't know how it all fits together. Maybe it won't make sense until the end."

"What if we will not play this game?"

I shivered. "When it happened to our family before, we would have lost everything if Jena hadn't played, and played well. I don't know where this is leading us, Stoyan. But I must go on. I can't ignore Tati. She's my big sister."

"Paula," said Stoyan, a new note in his voice. He was looking at the miniature of Cybele, his eyes narrowed.

"What?"

"See there," he murmured, pointing. "Your goddess bears some writing on her skin."

The squat figure stared out with her enigmatic smile and her blank eyes, hands on hips, legs crossed beneath her generous body. Stoyan was right. If I looked very closely through my spectacles, I could just make out that what had seemed to be a vine or cord flowing across her belly and around her hip was in fact a stream of minuscule writing.

"I wonder what it says," I murmured. "I don't recognize

the style of letters at all. It must be something very old. Or a code of some kind. This is so frustrating! Bits of clues, half signs, hints and suggestions, but nothing to tie it all together."

"She said—your sister—that she could not explain it to you. Why would that be, Paula?"

"It's typical of the Other Kingdom. A witch used a spell of silence on our second cousin Costi a few years ago. It was pretty cruel. It meant he couldn't explain to Jena who he really was. By the time he got his voice back, they were so angry with each other they weren't talking anyway. It did all get sorted out eventually—they're husband and wife now. There's always a reason for the use of these charms."

"What reason could there be for allowing your sister to speak to me but not to you, Paula?"

"I could think of a few. To show you that you are part of all this, that you can't hide behind your status as a hired guard. To make my quest harder for me and Tati's for her. The folk of the Other Kingdom make us suffer so we learn our lesson better. Whatever lesson it is. I hope I find that out soon, because I hate it when I can't make sense of things."

"How long do you wish to stay here? The Mufti's party may be finished at the han by now." Stoyan was looking seriously unsettled; I could see he was longing to leave.

"We need to stay a little longer at least. Irene would think it impolite if we rushed off, and if those women tell her you were waving knives around, we might face some awkward questions. Stoyan, I wonder if Irene could translate that tiny writing?"

"You do not believe this may be in some way secret?" Stoyan offered this with diffidence.

"The manuscript does belong to Irene," I pointed out. "Now that she's told me she knows about Cybele's Gift, there seems no risk in asking her. I won't mention the vanishing inscription—'Find the heart' and so on. I think that probably is something I'm not supposed to share with anyone."

"You shared it with me."

"That's different," I said.

I waited until Irene came out to suggest coffee before showing her the manuscript. As soon as Irene appeared, Stoyan moved down into the garden, where the rain had eased off again. He stationed himself just far enough away so he would not be able to overhear our conversation. My hostess bent over the table, dark eyes sharp with interest as she examined the manuscript. I heard her suck in her breath.

"Astonishing," she murmured, "that such a piece was in my collection and I did not know. . . . You found this quite by chance in one of the boxes?"

"That's right." It was clear from her expression that she had never seen this before. "I have a strong feeling that it's an image of Cybele. But of course I can't translate the words, neither this part on the figure nor the main text of the manuscript. I was hoping you might be able to help."

"I do not recognize this alphabet at all, Paula." Irene moved her graceful fingers over the miniature, not quite touching the band of tiny letters. "But I can translate the main text for you, of course. And the name of your earth goddess is certainly here. Let me see. . . ."

It was an account of the death of Cybele's lover, Attis, a tale full of high emotion. Irene's voice quivered as she rendered it, as if the scenes of blood and sorrow were unfolding right before her eyes: I'd been right about the other sheet, with the pictures of strange games. It concerned the goddess's spring ritual, held to celebrate the rebirth of this lost lover. Just before the writer described the actual details of the ceremony, Irene reached the end of the fragment.

"Fascinating!" my hostess exclaimed. "What a remarkable find, Paula! And how extraordinary that you were the one to stumble on this when your father is on the brink of acquiring this artifact. . . . I cannot believe it."

I could hardly point out that I was sure forces from the Other Kingdom were putting clues in my path. "Yes, it is quite surprising," I said. "To tell you the truth, I had been hoping there might be some information about Cybele here, something that could come in useful. I'm happy that I found this."

"Thank you for doing so—I must make cataloging the rest of these papers a priority, I can see. If you remain in Istanbul a little, maybe you would assist me."

"I'd be happy to do so." Flattering as this was, it was starting to look unlikely that I'd have the opportunity. Whatever quest the powers of the Other Kingdom wanted me to complete, I doubted very much that it would involve cataloging.

Over coffee, Irene questioned me on what I planned to wear to the supper and how I would dress my hair—she suggested putting it up so I would look older. I found it difficult to show interest in such matters. Stoyan was looking worried, and I was feeling confused. Tati's words to Stoyan had suggested urgency; the supper was tonight. And still I couldn't put the pieces together. I believed in the mission. I believed we had a task to accomplish. I just hoped it wouldn't be too much longer before I worked out what it was.

It was nearly time for the midday call to prayer when we got back to the han, and the Mufti's party was long gone. It seemed they had not discovered anything of interest, though their search had been extremely thorough. Father and Stoyan spent a good part of the afternoon restoring order in the chamber where our remaining cargo was stored, while I tidied up the living quarters, which had been turned upside down. It looked as if even my storage chest had been searched. I did not like the thought of those guards handling my clothing and my little personal things. Nothing seemed to be missing. Father did not say where he had hidden his papers, but they were safe. He had been a merchant for many years and knew how these things were done.

The invitation to the blue house had said we should be there as soon as convenient after the evening call to prayer. Timing was everything. To arrive early was impolite. To be late was to give the other merchants an advantage, for whoever reached Barsam's house first might gain a brief opportunity to speak with the Armenian in confidence. As it happened, all the merchants had the same idea, so we arrived en masse. The exception was Duarte da Costa Aguiar, who, with his usual flair, had managed to get there before anyone else. He was seated cross-legged on a cushion in the courtyard, chatting with our host to the accompaniment of murmuring fountains. Lanterns cast a warm light over the stone pillars and soft greenery of the enclosed space. Discreet servants, all male, moved about silently. There had been armed guards outside the gates. Before they had let us in, we had been required to answer a set of questions to prove our identity.

Barsam rose to greet us. He was wearing an embroidered caftan of pearly gray silk; his hair and beard matched the fabric. When my father introduced me in Greek, the Armenian murmured a greeting in the same tongue. I responded courteously, thanking him for his hospitality. The moment Barsam turned to speak to Irene, Duarte took my hand, bowed over it, then with a look in his eyes that was plain mischievous drew me away from the group of folk exchanging pleasantries.

"In this color," he said, keeping his voice down, "you resemble a rare butterfly, Mistress Paula. Or a tempting fruit, perhaps, rich red on the outside, palest cream within."

I struggled for a reply. If this was the man who had sent that horrible threatening letter to Antonio, I was not sure I wanted to speak to him at all. And yet his outrageous flattery made me want to smile. "I should thank you for this," I said coolly, adjusting the crimson veil. The fringe of delicate shell disks tinkled across my brow. Now I wondered if wearing it had been a mistake.

Duarte was clad in plain clothing of superior quality: trousers in a deep blue, a pale linen shirt that contrasted dramatically with his tanned skin and ink-dark hair, and a tunic of blue-gray linen with bone fastenings. His belt was the brightest note, a strip of fabric woven in exotic colors.

"It seemed a rather individual way to compensate me for the loss of my own scarf," I added. Out of the corner of my eye, I could see Stoyan watching us. He was standing guard at one side of the courtyard as the supper guests mingled.

The scar on his cheek was especially noticeable tonight; I thought he had his teeth clenched. On the other side stood Murat, impassive as always, his blue eyes watchful. I looked back at Duarte, who had reached into his belt to tweak up a corner of something red that was tucked beneath it.

"Isn't this fun?" the Portuguese murmured. "You're wearing mine and I'm wearing yours."

He certainly had a talent for the inappropriate. "Are you so superstitious, Senhor Aguiar, that you actually believe my scarf is lucky?" I asked him.

The devastating grin spread across his lean features. "Quite the opposite, Mistress Paula. I have no time for the fears and fantasies that beset so many seafaring men, the charms and amulets borne to ward off evil forces, the songs and tales of mermaids and monsters lurking in the deep. I carry this to remind me that I have something to prove."

"Oh? And what is that?" I noticed Father looking at me, his expression unreadable. He would not order me to stop speaking to Duarte. After all, I had offered to use my feminine charms to aid our mission if I could. But he was keeping an eye on me, ready to get me out of trouble if I needed him.

"That, with sufficient work on my part, you might begin to see that I am not the out-and-out rogue folk love to paint me," Duarte said. "Given time, I think you and I could become friends."

He must be joking. "Recent events suggest to me that such a development is not possible," I said. Across the courtyard, Irene, eye-catching even in her sedate dark blue, had most of the other merchants gathered around her. She lifted her brows at me, evidently displeased that I was not heeding her warnings about Duarte. Trapped as she was by her admirers, she could not fulfill her duty as a chaperone. "I could not befriend a man who gets what he wants by threats."

"Threats? Me?" His brows went up. "Mistress Paula, I think you've been listening to gossip again. My methods may not always be orthodox, but they are quite gentlemanly on the whole. Violence is a last resort. And it is generally not necessary to threaten. I am a more subtle man than that."

I scrutinized his features, trying to see past their charm and work out whether he was playing games again. "I'm not sure I believe you," I said. "It is hardly subtle to draw the wives and children of trading rivals into danger." Perhaps I should have kept my mouth shut, but I was angry on Antonio's behalf and on behalf of all honest merchants. And on my own. I felt a strong inclination to like this man, but if what my father suspected was true, I could not allow myself to give in to it.

"I cannot imagine what folk have been telling you, Mistress Paula. Ah—I believe we are being summoned indoors. I feel your watchdog's awful glare on me. I fear he does not trust me."

"Stoyan is doing his job. I had some difficulty persuading my father that I would be safe here." I made to turn away.

"Wait," Duarte said, his tone suddenly serious. "When you speak of threats, what do you mean? Threats to you personally?"

For the first time, I began to wonder if he did not know about the reason Antonio had pulled out of the bidding.

"Someone sent an unpleasant note to one of the other

bidders," I said. "That's as much as I'm prepared to say. If you were not responsible, I apologize. If you were, I don't want to talk to you. I can't be plainer about it than that."

"I see." Duarte was not smiling now. "This is a dangerous business, Mistress Paula. For all of us, I believe."

"I don't suppose anyone would threaten you, senhor. Folk appear to be in awe of you. Or in fear."

Duarte shrugged. "Let people believe what they will of me. What do I care for them? But you are an exception. I hope in time I may earn your good opinion. Shall we go in?" He was ushering me ahead of him toward an arched doorway into the house. As we moved forward, he whispered in my ear, "Please call me Duarte. The other thing makes me feel so elderly."

I attempted a quelling look, designed to freeze his inappropriate familiarity. His lips twitched and a dimple appeared at each corner of his mouth. I was unable to prevent myself from smiling. "I cannot do as you ask," I murmured. "It would shock everyone at this supper and embarrass my father."

In a generously spaced chamber inside the house, Barsam's guests were settling on the floor around a low table. The walls were tiled in blue and white, and a blue cloth with colored borders had been laid over the table. If our host was married, there was no sign of his wife—Irene and I were the only women present. My father had been waiting for me to come in and indicated a place beside him. Irene sat on my other side, and Duarte, with an eloquent shrug, settled himself a distance away, between Alonso di Parma and a man in a skullcap. Stoyan stood close behind Father and me. Murat had not come inside.

Servants brought bowls of scented water for us to wash our hands and immaculate embroidered towels for drying. Various dishes were then placed before us to share: goulash, fragrant rice, cucumbers with mint and yogurt. Stoyan did not eat.

"Alonso," my father said after a while, "I am a little surprised to see you here. I had thought your interest lay more in textiles and carpets." It seemed tonight's conversation would be in Greek, which suited me, as it meant I could follow the proceedings.

"I surprise myself." If deviousness could be given a voice, it would sound just like the Venetian merchant with whom I had struck my first Istanbul deal. "Of course, it is less the item to be displayed that has brought me here tonight and more the prospect of meeting you and your delightful daughter once more. You've been working hard, Teodor. You should not overstretch yourself; not at your age."

I opened my mouth to deliver a withering response. Irene gave me a subtle nudge, and I restrained myself.

"Overstretch?" Father did not sound in the least put out. "I've been in the business too long to make such a basic error of judgment. When you are a little older, you will begin to get an understanding of such matters, I suppose."

"Barsam, we thank you for your hospitality," said Enzo of Naples. "I know you must be aware of how eager we are to view the artifact at last. Can you tell us a little more about it? There has been much discussion of how it was acquired and from whom."

"We do understand," put in Duarte smoothly, "that such details may be commercially sensitive. It is up to our host how much he chooses to divulge."

There was a silence, which I interpreted as the merchants at the table refusing to acknowledge the Portuguese as an equal in the field of mercantile transactions.

"Of course," someone said delicately, "each of us will have performed his own investigations into the nature and history of Cybele's Gift." There was a collective release of breath, almost a sigh, as the item was named. "I am interested to discover if the information you possess, Master Barsam, supports or contradicts the scant knowledge we have of the piece."

"My guests, please enjoy your meal," said Barsam in softly courteous tones. "Time for this when all have eaten sufficiently. I welcome you to my modest dwelling." Out in the courtyard, someone began to play music, a plaintive tune on a reed instrument punctuated by the clash of small cymbals. The timing was impeccable; it was almost as if Barsam had planned it thus.

"We lack patience," my father observed. "My apologies, Master Barsam. Your hospitality is very fine. I do appreciate your extending the invitation to include my daughter, who, as you may know, is in Istanbul as my assistant."

"You have no sons, Master Teodor?" That was Duarte. "Nobody to carry on your trading business?"

"I was blessed with girls, senhor. The five of them possess sufficient funds of wit, beauty, and scholarship to make any father happy. I am fortunate enough to have three grandchildren as well, two of them boys. As it happens, I am in partnership with my son-in-law."

"You are blessed indeed, Master Teodor," said our host. "As fathers, we know it matters not if our children and our children's children become warriors or merchants, dervishes or administrators. We wish for them only good health and good fortune, love of family, respect for their ruler, and devotion to their God. Whatever our faith, whatever our origins, we are united in this."

There was a general murmur of acknowledgment.

"Irene," I whispered.

"Yes, Paula?"

"They will let us see Cybele's Gift, won't they?" I could barely eat; my stomach was churning with nerves. The presence of Duarte just along the table, glancing mischievously in my direction from time to time, did nothing to calm me.

"Don't worry so, Paula. You're giving yourself a permanent frown. Have a little more of the goulash; it is very good."

The men were talking about silk carpets now. My mind drifted from Tati to Stoyan to Duarte. . . . I was somewhat ashamed to realize the pirate's compliments had pleased me. The admiration of such an outrageously good-looking man was unsettling. I did have a strong instinct to like him despite all the bad things I had heard about him. Such a response could only make things complicated. I pondered this as I picked at my meal.

Some time later, I snapped back to the present when Barsam mentioned Cybele.

". . . an Anatolian scholar," the Armenian was saying. "He told me the piece was being conveyed toward Samarkand by a man who almost certainly did not appreciate its rarity. I then set out to pursue the caravan to which this traveler had attached himself, catching up with it halfway to Tabriz. I was able to secure Cybele's Gift with a payment in . . . Well, let us not go into details. I know the piece is genuine. It has been examined and valued in strictest confidence by an expert on religious antiquities. It is of the correct age and style, and the markings it bears are appropriate only to that particular region and period. I believe one glimpse of the artifact will convince you of its authenticity."

I hoped we would get more than a glimpse. I was intending to read the inscription—or at least remember it so I could have it translated in due course—and find out what it was Cybele had said before she left the world forever. Those words were the element that made Cybele's Gift so much desired; they created the belief that the piece would confer life-long good fortune on its holder.

"Valued," echoed my father. "I am intrigued to know how this expert went about setting a value on a unique piece of such antiquity."

"If this is the real Cybele's Gift," put in Duarte, "I would say it is beyond measuring in terms of silver or gold."

"Nonetheless," said Alonso di Parma, "it would be pointless to pretend we are here tonight for any other purpose than to bid for the piece, and I imagine each of us has offered a price that can indeed be measured in just those terms."

"I stand by my comment," Duarte said quietly. "Whatever value a merchant may place on this particular piece, it cannot be treated in the same way as a silk carpet or a piece of fine silverware. This is a symbol of genuine faith. And faith cannot be bought and sold."

It was an astonishing speech for such a man to make. I wanted to ask him what he meant but felt awkward in the company of the others, whose expressions, where not carefully masked, were cynical.

"That's pretentious claptrap," said one of the merchants. "This is a primitive artifact, Senhor Aguiar. It's not the same as trying to sell a scroll dictated by the Prophet or the thigh-bone of a Christian saint. Nobody still believes in this earth goddess—she's a figure of ancient mythology. Of course, there's the superstition attached to this piece; we all know about that. I'm in no doubt my buyer wants it not for its rarity but because he believes it will ensure generations of prosperity for him and his. We could probably all say the same."

"What exactly is your point, Senhor Aguiar?" Father sounded calm and assured. "I gather you are present as a bidder. And yet you say the item should not be traded. This makes no sense to me."

"Let us just say that should I be the successful bidder, my intentions for Cybele's Gift would not be the same as your own or those of our friends here." Duarte gestured to encompass everyone at the table. "Each of you has come here with a potential buyer in mind, I imagine. My own role is somewhat different. It might be said that I am present on behalf of the original custodian of the piece. It is for that party that I intend to acquire the artifact."

"Original custodian? What does that mean?" said Enzo of Naples. "The piece is offered for legitimate sale; nobody has a claim to prior ownership. Unless there's something Barsam hasn't told us." He glanced suspiciously at our host, who shook his head with a grave smile. "Besides," the Neapolitan merchant went on, "your high-minded comments don't change the fact that you've come with a pocketful of silver just like the rest of us."

"I am not so foolish as to carry my funds on my person,"

Duarte said. "The streets of Istanbul can be dangerous at night. But, yes, I am here to purchase, and when I have done so, I will return this piece to the place of its origins. Master Barsam, may we view the artifact now?"

The Armenian rose to his feet. Immediately the servants reappeared, bearing fresh bowls of water and towels so the guests could wash their hands once again.

"Let us repair to the courtyard," Barsam said. "I have fine musicians here this evening, including a very good player of the *tulum*. You are familiar with this? A kind of bagpipe; you will enjoy it. Then we will take coffee and you may see the artifact. It is closely guarded and carefully stored. I regret I could not offer this opportunity earlier and to each of you in turn. There were certain dangers attached. I'm sure you will understand."

Stoyan was waiting by the door and walked out beside me. Across the courtyard, I glimpsed the barrel-chested figure of Duarte's crewman, the one who had been with him at the market. Murat stood near the gate, talking to one of Barsam's guards. He looked alert but relaxed, as if he anticipated trouble but was confident he could deal with it.

The tulum player was an artist, wringing a desperately sad voice from his instrument. I could not listen to it without thinking about Tati and Sorrow. The music made me want to cry, but I did not. I sat on a bench between Father and Irene, drinking my coffee out of a tiny tulip-shaped cup in a silver holder. Duarte was perched on the stone rim of the fountain, watching me with his dimples showing. There was no chance at all of speaking to him. Everyone was edgy. Stoyan's face was in shadow. I could guess what images that bittersweet tune brought to his mind. To lose your only surviving brother at twelve years old was a terrible thing. To have to wait until you were grown up to go and look for him, knowing that every passing day was taking him farther away, if not in miles, then certainly in attitudes, must have been unbearable.

After what seemed an immensely long time, our host invited us to enter a different part of the house, farther down the courtyard. There were massive double doors with elaborate iron bolts. Outside stood an armed guard.

"These precautions are necessary," Barsam said. "Any buyer of such an item must be equipped to offer it suitable protection. Not all collectors possess such scruples as you do, my friends. And as you doubtless know by now, there is a certain official interest in the artifact. Taking it out of the city will require both ingenuity and excellent security."

At least one of those present, I thought, had no scruples at all. At least one of them had sent that horrible threat to Antonio of Naples and had perhaps killed Salem bin Afazi as well. I glanced at Stoyan as we went in, and his eyes told me he was thinking the same thing.

There was an antechamber floored with stone and another set of doors that led to an inner room lit by shielded lamps. The only furnishing was a marble-topped table in the center, on which stood a box fashioned of cedar wood and fastened with a heavy lock. We moved to make a circle around the table while Barsam took a key from his sash and turned it in the lock. By the inner door, Stoyan stood on one side and Duarte's man on the other. The air was almost fizzing with tension. We'd waited a long time for this.

The chest opened soundlessly, its hinges well oiled. Someone made a little sound of surprise as Cybele's Gift was exposed under the lamplight, nestled in a bed of fine straw packing. Eyes widened all around the circle. Here was no marble tablet with a neat record of ancient sayings, no slab of granite chiseled with antique script. Sitting neatly in the Armenian merchant's storage chest was a little statue fashioned in clay baked to a rich red-brown and shaped in the form of a generously proportioned woman. Her hair was wild, her nose broad and flat, her mouth stretched in a grin. Her eyes were blank dark holes. Her right ear was chipped, but her left still bore in its pierced lobe a tiny gold ring. It was Cybele herself.

Duarte recovered first. "This is unexpected," he said. "Master Barsam, may we handle the piece?"

Barsam passed him a pair of thin cotton gloves. At that point, no doubt all the others were wishing they had asked first. Alonso di Parma was frowning. Enzo of Naples wore an expression that I could only describe as avid. Even Irene had a glint of excitement in her eyes.

"Mistress Paula?"

It took me a moment to realize Duarte was holding out the gloves to me. A challenge; I had sensed the frisson of disapproval in the chamber as the Portuguese spoke. I felt my face flush as I slipped the gloves on. I was terrified that my hands would shake and I'd let go of Cybele and smash her to pieces.

"Is this wise—" someone began, then fell silent as I reached into the straw and lifted the statue, supporting it from underneath with one hand as I held the neck with the other. The piece was lighter than I expected, and as it left the box, I saw why. Where the Cybele of the miniature had possessed a round belly, crossed legs, and neat bare feet, this statue ended abruptly at around waist level. *Make me whole.* A deep shiver ran through me.

"Where is the inscription?" one of the merchants asked. "The lore is that Cybele wrote her last message on the piece. I see no markings of that kind here."

* "That's because this is only half of Cybele's Gift," I said, looking at Barsam. "The writing is on her belly and across her hip, or should be. This piece is broken."

A profound silence fell. As it drew out, I could almost hear the seven merchants thinking. I knew every one of them was mentally reducing his bid or withdrawing from the competition altogether. The deal had just been turned on its head.

Chapter Eight

I was asked to substantiate my bold statement and I did, describing the miniature I had seen in Irene's library and its stunning resemblance to the artifact. Irene confirmed that the picture had indeed shown the figure of a whole woman. I found a trace of ancient writing near the broken-off edge of the statue: all that was left of the inscription. I must have been convincing. The place began to clear quickly, each of the merchants in turn making his polite excuses to Barsam and departing forthwith. Our host appeared unperturbed. He murmured that he had not known Cybele's Gift was ever more than this half woman or that the inscription was so critical to its value.

Before we left the lamp-lit chamber, Father held the piece himself, subjecting it to close examination. "This is a remarkably neat break," he said quietly. "If the other part could be located, it would not be so difficult to mend. Wouldn't you agree, Paula?"

"Mmm," I murmured, my head buzzing. Had Tati intended me to make just this discovery? Surely the quest she was leading me on could not be to find the missing half of the statue. I had spoken out instinctively, shocked to find Cybele less than her full, exuberant self. It was clear my revelation had lost Barsam the opportunity to deal with most of those present; their buyers would not want the artifact without the goddess's last words and the luck they conveyed. Did that mean Father would also withdraw from the deal? I tried to read his expression, but I could not. He was wearing his merchant face.

When we got out to the courtyard, most of the guests had left. Duarte was over by the fountain, talking to Irene. He didn't seem put out in the least by what had happened, or by her glacial stare.

"You wish to leave, Master Teodor?" Stoyan had obtained our cloaks from Barsam's steward and now stood with them over his arm.

Father lowered his voice. "I wish to create that impression. But I want a word with Barsam after the others have departed. A few moments will do. Paula, the Portuguese seems to be settling for a long talk with your friend. I wonder if he can be persuaded to move farther out of earshot?" There was definitely something afoot; he sounded as if he was suppressing excitement.

"Of course, Father."

Farther down the garden, the musicians were still playing, not to entertain company now but for their own enjoyment. They were gathered beside an outdoor cooking oven, with a number of Barsam's household retainers as audience. The tulum had been joined by a drum and a stringed instrument; the rhythm set my feet tapping.

I gathered up Irene and Duarte with an announcement

that I was keen to move closer and listen to the music properly. Murat followed us at a discreet distance. Behind me, Father, shadowed by Stoyan, moved to engage our host in quiet conversation. Between the fountain and the tulum, I could not distinguish the words.

"You are fond of music?" inquired Duarte.

"When it's well played, yes."

"And dancing?"

"I don't have much opportunity for that kind of thing, senhor." I'd danced at Jena's wedding and at Iulia's. Apart from that, there had been scant occasion for it since our portal to the Other Kingdom was closed to us.

"Of course." He nodded sagely, but his dark eyes were dancing themselves. "You are a scholar, too serious for such frivolous pastimes. Since I am myself a lover of books, I salute you for that. On the other hand, it is a trifle early for you to be turning your back on the pleasures of youth. Are you not afraid of growing old before your time?"

"You are offensive, Senhor Aguiar." Irene's tone was unusually sharp. "Save your barbed comments for your own kind."

"Thank you, Irene, but I can defend myself," I said, squaring my shoulders. "Senhor Duarte, I am a grown woman, and I make my own choices as to how I will spend my time. Sometimes I read; sometimes I dance; sometimes I do neither. As far as I can see, you are a grown man and far too old for silly games."

"Once again you dismiss me," Duarte said, and I had no idea whether he was serious or not. "Like the rest of them, you believe I don't have an ethical bone in my body."

"Other folk's opinions are all I have to judge you by," I said. "Those and the brief impressions I've gained at our rather odd meetings. If your actions proved those opinions wrong, I would be quite prepared to revise my judgment."

"Paula, perhaps we should be moving on," Irene said. "Your father . . ." She glanced back toward the fountain, but the light was such that we could not see those who stood beyond it.

The music pounded and wailed its way toward a climax. The onlookers augmented the thumping of the drum with vigorous, rhythmic clapping. "I'd like to listen to the band just a little longer, until he calls me," I said.

"It might be better if—"

"You think your father has lost interest in buying, now he knows the statue is incomplete?" asked Duarte.

I scrambled to answer the unexpected question. "I would expect that," I said, even as it struck me that Duarte himself was showing no inclination to leave in a hurry. "It would be different if we had some information about where the other part is. If we found that in good condition and could repair the piece, it would still be worth buying. The value would be much lower, of course, even if the mending was expertly done. But Barsam didn't seem to know about the other half. It would be quite a mission to track it down."

"Agreed."

There was something arresting in Duarte's expression; I tried to interpret it. Was it possible he still planned to bid? How far would he lower his own offer, knowing only part of the artifact was on sale?

His lips twitched; his dark eyes twinkled. "You wish to read my mind?" he queried.

"I'm not so desperate for entertainment," I snapped, annoyed to be caught staring.

Irene came to my rescue. "Of all those present," she observed, "you, Senhor Aguiar, seemed the least surprised by Paula's revelation. And I note that you remain here in conversation with ladies when all others are gone."

"Ah." He gave an enigmatic smile, directed more at me than at my companion. It was as if he wanted to share a secret and, despite my better judgment, I felt a thrill inside me akin to that produced by the wild music of the tulum. "I am not here solely as a purchaser, Mistress Irene. I came also to renew my acquaintance with the charming Paula. As unrelated men and women do not mingle in public places here in Istanbul, I must seize what opportunities come my way to speak with her." He glanced at me. "You're blushing again," he murmured. "How sweet. When you look like that, it becomes obvious why you need a chaperone."

"This conversation is finished!" snapped Irene, moving forward to take my arm. "Senhor Aguiar, you are old enough to know better."

"Senhor Duarte has yet to prove that," I put in. "Thus far I remain unconvinced."

"Of my age or of my wisdom, Paula?"

"I don't know how old you are, nor am I especially interested," I said. "But I do have a question for you. What did you mean before, when you said you'd take Cybele's Gift back to the place of its origins if you bought it? What place? I thought all that was known was the general region it came from, not an actual location."

The tulum played on; the fountain added a soft accompaniment. It seemed to me that both Duarte and Irene had become suddenly very still, as if my speech had possessed some meaning far beyond what I had intended. I had strayed into deep waters and had no idea how to get out.

"Your father uses you well," Duarte said eventually, his tone level. "A man allows himself to be diverted by your wit. He starts to enjoy the lash of your sharp tongue and quite forgets you are a merchant's daughter. Since the piece is broken, your question is no longer relevant, Mistress Paula."

I was so offended I found myself without a reply. Maybe I had offered to obtain information from Duarte and others by exercising my limited charms on them, but the question I had just asked had been framed out of genuine curiosity, nothing more devious. And did I really have a sharp tongue? I heard Irene draw a deep, indignant breath, ready to speak.

"Kyria." A deep voice from behind me: Stoyan's. I breathed a sigh of relief. "Your father is ready to go."

"Then I will bid you good night, Mistress Paula." Duarte was all smooth courtesy, but he was looking over my head, and his eyes were full of challenge.

"Good night, Senhor Duarte," I said. "It's been . . . interesting . . . talking to you."

"Good night, Mistress Irene."

Irene gave the Portuguese a frosty nod, then Stoyan steered us away like an efficient sheepdog gathering up strays from a flock. I could think of no reason why we would ever see Duarte da Costa Aguiar again. I should have been relieved. He had flattered me and insulted me, made me feel warm with pleasure, intrigued, confused, and angered me all in the space of an evening. Talking to him was like treading a path across stepping-stones set a little too far apart. But what I felt most strongly was disappointment.

* * *

I was in the storeroom of Irene's library, poring over another leaf from the Persian manuscript. It was quiet. I was alone, standing by a high desk on which the piece had been laid out with care, its corners weighted down by squat creatures with bulbous toes. The light was fitful, and I could not see the tiny illustration clearly. Inside the lamp, fireflies swarmed, their bodies glowing behind the glass shade. I winced as they blundered against it. I had never been fond of insects.

The miniature. I must concentrate. I must study it, for time was running out. I narrowed my eyes, trying to focus. Was that a figure standing on another's shoulders? A girl? She was wearing trousers—most indecorous—and was reaching up to grasp something above her head. Picking apples? The man supporting her was balancing on something himself. It all looked quite precarious. And there was something else there. . . . I must carry this out into better light. But carefully. Nobody must see.

The hanging was down over the door to the main chamber, and when I brushed against the cloth, a swarm of little flies arose from within its fibers to hover around my head. I held my breath and squeezed my eyes shut, ducking around into the library proper.

I opened my eyes. There was a scholar at every table: a hooded soothsayer, a wizard in a hat with stars on it, a tiny gnome hunched over a map, an old man dipping a peacock-feather quill into an inkwell of faceted crystal. Light poured down from above, an otherworldly light as pale as dawn and pure as springwater, but not from the holes pierced in the plasterwork or from a torch or a lamp. A sphere floated there, two arms' lengths above the scholars, held by nothing but sheer magic. I walked forward, but nobody so much as gave me a cursory glance. I opened my mouth to greet them, for they were all dear and familiar, my friends from the Other Kingdom with whom I had argued and debated on every night of full moon through the years of my childhood. A moment later, everything shifted and changed, and I was no longer in the library but in Dancing Glade, scene of the fairy revels I knew so well. Ileana, queen of the forest, sat on her willow wood throne, and before her knelt my sister Tati, clad in a white gown with her dark hair flowing down her back and her big violet-blue eyes desperate with feeling. Around them were gathered the same folk I had just seen in the library. Many others, from dwarf to giant, from salamander to owl, watched on in silence. I was part of that crowd, and yet I knew I was there only in dream form, unable to speak or move.

"I need to see them!" Tati was pleading. "You know I have accepted this way of life. I have done my best to become part of your realm. Love brought me to the Other Kingdom, and it will hold me here forever. I mean no disloyalty to you and yours. But my love for Sorrow did not cancel out my love for my family, Your Majesty. It seems cruel that I can never go back. I just want to hug my sisters and talk to them a little. I need to know they're safe and well and to show my father that I am all right."

Ileana was wearing her feathered headdress. She towered above my sister, her robe swirling around her with a life of its own. In its folds, clouds of small bright butterflies danced. Her eyes were cool. "Do you not speak with those of our own folk who are permitted to go across?" she asked. "Grigori or the dwarves? They can report to you on your sisters' progress. I expect they're all doing very well, Jena in particular, since we took such a hand in her learning. I can't imagine why you would concern yourself about them."

"They're my sisters," Tati said simply. "I love them. I miss them. I want to see them so much it hurts. Such things are important to human folk, Your Majesty. Isn't there some way I can earn the right? Or if I can't go across, couldn't I win them the privilege of coming back here, just for a little?"

Ileana gave a slow smile. On the trees around her throne, the leaves shivered. "You do not know what you ask, Tatiana," she said softly.

"With respect, Your Majesty, I do know," Tati said. "I've talked to Sorrow about it, and he agrees. I am prepared to undertake a quest."

"I see. And if you had to choose just one of your sisters to see, which would it be? Jena, to whom you owe so much? Little Stela, who lost the most by being forbidden the Other Kingdom, since she was only a child when the portal was closed? Clever Paula, whom our scholars miss so badly, or Iulia, who danced like moonlight?"

Tati's eyes had widened. "Only one of them?" she whispered. "How could I possibly choose?"

"How indeed?" Ileana looked amused. My heart was pounding fast as I wondered what Tati would do, what cruel choice she would make. "As it is," the forest queen went on, "you need not decide that part of it until your quest is complete. It will link very neatly with a mission we have for your sister Paula, who happens to be right where we need her. Drăguţa has been asked for assistance—an old, old friend in another part of the world requires human intervention to set matters right. This can become a threefold mission: We can assist Drăguţa's friend, give you your chance, and, at the same time, help no fewer than three human folk to learn and grow. Tell me, how brave is your sister?"

Then, before I could hear more, the scene dissolved around me, Tati, Ileana, the scholars of the Other Kingdom fading away as if they had never been, and I was lying in my bed at the han, with darkness outside and only my tears for company.

Poor Tati! In all those years of missing her, I had not imagined she, too, might be unhappy. She had been so sure of her love for Sorrow, so certain in her choice to leave us. If only I had been able to hold the dream a little longer. I had so wanted to walk forward, to put my arms around her and tell her we loved her and missed her, as she did us. As for being brave, I hoped very much that I could be as brave as I needed to be.

Now I had to go to the privy. Stoyan was asleep, lying across the outer doorway, through which I must pass to make my way along the gallery. I fumbled for my cloak, then tiptoed out of my closet and across the larger chamber in my bare feet. Stoyan was lying on his back with one arm flung over his eyes and the other relaxed by his side, the blanket loose around him. His pose was that of a small boy exhausted by a day's activity. For all my confusion, it made me smile. I put one hand against the door frame and stepped across him.

A powerful hand seized my ankle. I teetered, then sprawled at full length onto the hard floor of the gallery. "Ahh!" I exclaimed as a spear of pain stabbed through my ankle.

The hand released its viselike grip. "Paula!" He was on

his knees, lifting me with an arm around my shoulders, his voice rough with comprehension come a moment too late. "I hurt you! Why were you out of bed? What is wrong—"

"Nothing," I said, grimacing as I gingerly felt my ankle. "I got up to go to the privy, that's all. I didn't want to wake you. I'm fine, really." But my ankle still hurt, and as soon as I tried to rise to my feet, it was obvious. I hobbled to one of the chairs by the little gallery table and lowered myself carefully onto it. "I've just wrenched it," I said.

Stoyan looked devastated at what he had done. "You are crying." He crouched by me, reaching a hand to brush my cheek. "You are badly hurt. I should wake Master Teodor—"

"Don't. I will be all right soon, Stoyan. They're not tears of pain. I had another dream. I really didn't want to disturb you again. I'm sorry. And now I'm going to have to hobble to the privy. You might need to help me. So much for lessons in self-defense."

Leaning on him, I got there and back well enough. Then I was wide awake, the image of Tati clear in my mind and the mission teasing at my thoughts. "I won't be able to sleep for a while," I said. "You don't need to stay up with me. I'll just sit here and think."

"I will put a strapping on your ankle." He was already looking in his bundle of belongings, stowed on a shelf just inside the main doorway of our quarters. "If you permit. It will swell before morning; this will make it more comfortable."

The ankle hurt too much for me to worry about propriety. "Thank you," I said. "Stoyan, I need to go back to the library in the morning. I dreamed about Tati again; she's here because she's earning the right to visit us—her sisters, I mean.

That's the reward for her quest. And it's tied up with mine. Stoyan, if we go to Irene's, I might see Tati again and be given my last clues so I can work out what it is we have to do. Will you have time to take me there before you escort Father to the blue house?"

The end to this evening had been interesting. Father hadn't said a single word about Cybele's Gift until we had parted ways with Irene and Murat and returned to the han. Then he had calmly reminded me that our own buyer was a scholarly collector of advanced years with a passionate devotion to religious antiquities. This man, unwed and something of a recluse, would care little about the supposed capacity of Cybele's Gift to bestow a future of good fortune and prosperity on its owner. Chances were he would not be troubled by the availability of only half the piece; he would still want it for its historical interest. Indeed, Father had said, our buyer should be delighted to obtain the item at a reduced price. Slightly reduced. Father had no intention of letting anyone else outbid him now that success was within his grasp. Before we had left the blue house, he had told Barsam he would be back in the morning with a revised bid, one that was likely to be acceptable. He had asked the Armenian to hold Cybele's Gift until the midday call to prayer.

"There is only one possible problem," Father had added. "Perhaps one or two of the others might consider coming back to Barsam with revised bids, but I don't believe anyone was keen enough to act immediately. Except for Duarte Aguiar. He was still there when we left Barsam's house; I imagine he remains in the race. And they say he's ruthless. I expect he, too, will be there in the morning, ready with an offer. I'll go early, but not so early that I disturb Barsam's household and risk offending him. I can outbid Duarte. The man's purse cannot be bottomless."

"He must be quite wealthy," I'd said. "He couldn't maintain the *Esperança* without a good source of funds, surely."

"Perhaps he has a rich family," Father had said. "Stoyan, I will need you in the morning. Not straight after breakfast, but a little later."

Now, in the semidarkness of our quarters, Stoyan had found what he was looking for: a strip of linen and a small pot of something pungent. "A salve," he explained. "It should bring down the swelling. Will you . . . ?"

I hitched the skirt of my nightrobe up toward my knee and put my foot on the other chair. I made myself breathe slowly as I felt Stoyan's hands on my ankle, gently massaging in the ointment. A confusion of sensations filled me: pain, certainly, but something else as well, something I liked more than was appropriate. I valued our friendship; I knew he did, too. I liked the way he was there when I needed him, strong, quiet, and capable. Anything further between us—the sort of relationship Irene had hinted at—would be all wrong. There were so many arguments against such a development that I would not even entertain the idea of it.

When he was done, Stoyan wrapped my ankle in a neat bandage. "This Aguiar," he murmured as he bent to fasten the ends of the linen securely, "you like him?"

A startling question. "What do you mean by 'like him'?" I asked.

"You spoke much to him tonight. As if he were not an acquaintance but a friend. There was a smile in your eyes as you did so. I wonder if you have not heeded my warning. He seeks to exploit you, Paula. I see this in his face."

Cautiously, I returned my foot to the ground. "It does feel much better with the strapping," I acknowledged. "Thank you, Stoyan. And don't worry about Duarte. He loves to flirt. If it hadn't been with me, it would have been with some other woman. It means nothing."

"You did not answer my question." He was rolling up the extra bandage, stowing things away.

I tried to summon an honest answer. "It seems wrong to say I like him if there's any possibility he was the one who threatened Antonio. But he appeared quite shocked when I suggested that, so maybe I was wrong. Duarte is interesting to talk to, full of surprises. He seems to enjoy the same kinds of things I do, books and ideas in particular. I'm flattered that he wants to talk to me. But I don't trust him. And maybe you can't actually like someone unless you have trust in them." The topic was uncomfortable, especially in the middle of the night. "You should go back to sleep," I said.

"Why were you crying? What did you see in your dream?"

"I dreamed about Tati." My voice sounded small and forlorn; I couldn't help it. "She was in the Other Kingdom, and she was saying how much she missed her family and that she would undertake a quest just to be allowed to see us. . . ."

A sudden wave of homesickness came over me. I covered my face with my hands, unable to stop the tears. Stoyan moved to kneel by my chair and put his arm around my shoulders, muttering something indistinct. I gave myself up to weeping. It was only when the flood began to abate that I realized I was holding on tightly with my face pressed against his shoulder and that he was whispering words of comfort against my hair and doing his own share of holding. So much for heeding my own good advice.

"Oh, I'm sorry," I muttered, pulling back. "How embarrassing for you. I can't believe I did that. It may be hard for you to believe, but I'm actually not the crying sort of girl. In your company, I seem to have been doing it regularly. Please don't tell Father I was so upset. He'd be worried."

"As you wish." Stoyan had withdrawn to a safe distance. His face was in the shadows, and I had no idea what he thought of my inappropriate behavior or my attempt at an apology. "Master Teodor is not the only one who worries," he went on. "With your ankle injured, you are still more vulnerable. I cannot teach you what I planned to; not yet. But I can show you a trick that you may use even when not at your full strength. Let me demonstrate. . . ."

So it was that, in the middle of the night, I learned a way of getting out of someone's grasp by cunning rather than by physical strength. We even practiced it, in a modified form that would not strain my ankle. It kept me so occupied that there was no chance to brood on anything else. When the combat session was over, I felt obliged to deliver a lesson in return. By the light of a candle, I made Stoyan practice the letters of the Greek alphabet. He had a remarkably steady hand; I had observed that with our tree exercise. All the same, his fingers holding the twig trembled as he wrote in the sand tray, as if this task were something of which he was deeply fearful. It seemed to me he expected to fail, and the prospect terrified him. I realized I would have to take it more slowly than I had planned. Would a month be long enough to convince him that he could do this? Could he find the will to continue after I was gone?

"We must try to sleep," I said when we were done and the implements of the lesson were neatly packed away. "Tomorrow is a big day."

"Today," said Stoyan. "Thank you, Paula. I hurt you. You responded with kindness. What can I say?"

I smiled. Didn't he realize he was a very model of kindness? "You can just say good night and sweet dreams," I told him. "Or no dreams, that might be better. We're friends, Stoyan. Friends do this sort of thing for each other; it comes with the job."

"Good night, Paula." His voice was almost inaudible. "I am honored to be your friend."

I was in the library, the real one this time, with a second box of manuscripts beside me and my mind darting from one thing to another. I was on my own. Perhaps my pale face and shadowed eyes had alerted Irene to my need for time alone this morning.

If it hadn't been for the dream, I might have preferred a quiet day at the han waiting for Father to do his deal with Barsam the Elusive and bring Cybele's Gift safely back. Once we had obtained it, we planned to lock it away and not to take it out again until we were due to board the *Stea de Mare* in a few weeks' time. But if there was any chance I might see Tati again, if there was even the slightest possibility I could tell her that I missed her just as much as she missed me and that I would do everything I could to help her win the right to visit us, then I was bound to be in the library waiting for her today.

I began sorting through the contents of the box, hoping the unseen hands that were guiding my mission might provide me with the document I'd been studying in my dream, with its apple-picking girl. I was willing Tati to appear again today with clues for me. I certainly didn't have enough information yet to perform any sort of quest. Besides, Cybele's Gift was to be sold today, almost certainly to my father. Once he had acquired it, all that lay ahead was the voyage home. What was it the folk of the Other Kingdom needed me to do? *Make me whole*, said a voice in my mind, and a chill went through me. They couldn't want me to seek out the missing half of the statue myself, surely. The other part could be anywhere. It would take immense resources and unlimited time to mount such a search, with no guarantee of success. If that was what needed doing, they had chosen the wrong person.

It was hard to concentrate. My eyes were on the papers, but my thoughts kept returning to last night and the sensations that had passed through me as Stoyan's big hands worked so gently on my ankle. I remembered embracing him as I wept and how good it had felt to have his arms around me, tender and comforting. I must not let such a thing happen again. He and I were a world apart. To imagine any future for us beyond the *Stea de Mare*'s next sailing was pointless.

"Forget it, Paula," I muttered to myself. "Where men are concerned, you're not exactly an expert."

That was certainly true in Duarte's case. I had no idea how to deal with the man. Everything he did broke the rules. I was obliged to admit that this was one of many things I liked about the Portuguese. He could be guaranteed to surprise me every time I set eyes on him. Not that I was likely to do so again now that the competition for Cybele's Gift was almost over. I caught myself imagining going home to Piscul Dracului accompanied by the dashing pirate and the dramatic impression this would make on my sisters. I firmly ordered myself to stop acting like a silly girl of thirteen. I must start concentrating on these papers or Irene would think I was simply using her library as a bolt-hole where I could hide and feel sorry for myself.

I went right through the second box, but there were no pages there to match the two I had from the Persian manuscript. The exercise had been a waste of time. Worst of all, Tati had not come. I kept glancing up, hoping to see her black-robed figure seated opposite me, with the embroidered figure of Stela on her handiwork, but there was nothing. Women came in and out of the library, their voices muted, though I thought I caught an undercurrent of excitement in their tone today. Some new item of gossip, no doubt. I probably wouldn't hear what it was, since I did not intend to visit the hamam with Stoyan away.

Irene came to fetch me for coffee late in the morning. I had been sitting awkwardly and my neck hurt. So did my ankle. It was a relief to accompany her out to the colonnade, where a dainty repast had been laid out for us.

"Did you find what you were looking for, Paula?" Irene asked as she poured the coffee into tiny cups patterned with rich swirls of color and handed one to me.

I shook my head. "I don't seem to be very efficient today; I'm tired. Maybe another time."

"Of course." She sounded calm, but I sensed the same kind of restlessness in her that had been present in the other women, as if she were anticipating some diversion of great interest. But all she said was, "You seem upset, Paula. Is something wrong? You can talk to me. I am the soul of discretion."

"It's nothing." I would not tell her the story of Tati. What if, after all this, my sister never reappeared? What if the puzzles and clues came to nothing? "I twisted my ankle; it is painful after the walk and then keeping still for so long."

"You poor girl," said Irene. "You know, the hamam is the perfect thing for relaxing an injured limb and helping with other kinds of hurt as well." Her eyes were shrewd as she scrutinized my face. "Why not give up on work for the morning and allow Olena to tend to you? Not her usual vigorous massage, of course. She is expert in a gentler form of treatment, which will ease the pain and relax you at the same time. You seem very much on edge this morning."

"I'm fine." I took another sip of coffee. The cup shook in my hand.

"You're not fine at all." Irene leaned forward, her tone solicitous. "You are stretched as tight as a bowstring. Let me guess. Perhaps your father has gone out on another visit, and you are anxious as to whether it will be successful? Worried that Duarte Aguiar may get there first or bid higher?"

I stared at her.

Irene laughed. "I'm only guessing, Paula. Wasn't it extraordinary that, here in my library, you found that image exactly matching the artifact? I could hardly believe my eyes when we saw the piece. Your father spoke to Barsam after the viewing—after you had announced Cybele's Gift was not as it should be. I deduce that Master Teodor did not plan to back out of the deal altogether but had perhaps asked for more time. Maybe he thought himself the only bidder left, in which case he might obtain the item for a much lower price. I could not fail to notice that one guest remained at the blue house after we left: Duarte Aguiar."

"You probably know him better than I do. Do you think he'll still bid?" There didn't seem much point in pretending ignorance.

Her eyes went cold. "Oh, yes," she said. "Duarte will bid. Tell me, why is your father still interested in Cybele's Gift? Won't his buyer be disappointed? Or do the two of you plan to search for the missing half before returning home?"

"Hardly. We haven't the resources to mount a search across the whole region from here to Tabriz. That's supposing the fellow who sold it to Barsam ever had the other half."

"I have a theory, Paula."

"Oh?"

"You heard Duarte say he planned to return the piece to its place of origin, wherever that may be? I believe that once he has obtained the half statue we saw last night, he will go straight after its other half if he knows where it is. If he doesn't know, he will search for it. That man has the instinct of a migrating bird; he wings direct for his destination."

"He could only do that if he was the successful bidder," I said. "Father has years of experience in the merchant business. And he was going early. I'm certain he will bring the piece back." I had not intended to state quite so baldly what Father was doing this morning, but it was too late to make any difference now. In all probability, the transaction was already concluded and he and Stoyan on their way home.

"Duarte will stop at nothing, Paula. I did warn you. You

saw how he behaved last night—rude, presumptuous, in complete disregard of social niceties. You should have left me to deal with him."

"Maybe I should go back to the han," I said, not wanting to pursue this topic. In fact, I thought I had handled Duarte quite well. "I don't know when Stoyan is coming for me; it depends on how things go this morning. Could Murat escort me back?"

"Unfortunately, Murat is away from home this morning, Paula. Why not take a bath and let Olena tend to your ankle?" Irene rose to her feet. "I cannot allow you to keep working when you are in pain and upset. Come, you'll feel so much better for a massage."

I gave in. My ankle was not up to spending the rest of the day in the library, and I could not go home before Stoyan came, so it made sense. There were several women in the hot room, sitting on the benches, lying on the slab, or washing at the basins. As we entered, they were talking animatedly, a fast chatter in Turkish, but at a word from Irene, they fell silent. Perhaps she had told them that I was tired and that the noise might disturb me. It was a little disconcerting. I had not understood any of what they were saying.

Irene and I sat in the steam for quite some time, long enough for me to start feeling extremely sleepy. Then Olena worked on my ankle. By the time she was finished, all the others had gone. I woke myself up by taking a plunge in the deep pool. We settled in the camekan, where Ariadne brought us fresh coffee. I judged it was about time for the midday call to prayer.

"If you wish to lie down," Irene said, "you may do so here on one of the divans. I can wake you when it's time to go—"

There was a sound of running footsteps on the path outside, and a moment later the door from the camekan out to the garden crashed open and there was Stoyan, fully dressed, fully armed, and wearing an expression that made me spring to my feet in alarm, completely forgetting that I was clad in only a skimpy length of fine silk. He was as white as linen, and there were dark blotches like bruises under his eyes. His scar stood out vividly against the pallor of his face.

"What?" I took a step, grasping at the silk as it slid precariously downward. "What's happened?"

"You must come now, Paula. Right away. Get dressed and come quickly."

Irene was on her feet, her expression furious. "Out!" she commanded. "Turn your eyes away and walk back through that door before I call my men to throw you out!"

"Father, is Father all right?" I babbled, reaching around for my clothes.

"He is safe. Come now, please." Stoyan was leaving as he spoke. I dropped the silk wrapping and began to scramble into the things Ariadne had set out for me.

"Outrageous," muttered Irene. "What was my gate guard thinking, to allow this? Paula, that young man is not welcome here in the future. You should dismiss the fellow from your service immediately. . . ."

I was hardly listening, scarcely aware of the garments I was flinging on, another set of this household's spare clothing. My own things had been bundled up for me; I threw a veil over my hair and seized the package. "I'm sorry," I said. "Something's happened to Father; I can tell. I must go."

Outside, Stoyan was pacing just beyond the door. Farther down the garden, I caught a glimpse of the women from the hamam, fully dressed now, laughing together as they carried bundles and boxes along a pathway.

"Young man," my hostess said severely, "account for yourself! What is so vital that it warrants a violent intrusion into a private realm of women?"

Stoyan did not so much as glance at her. His eyes were on me. A flush of red now softened the unhealthy pallor of his cheeks. "We must go now," he said. "Do you have all your things?"

I nodded. "Tell me," I said. "What's happened?"

He shook his head and reached to take my arm. "Come," he said. "Now."

"I'm sorry, Irene," I said over my shoulder as he hustled me along the colonnade to the main gate. "I will explain later. Thank you for your hospitality."

We made our way down the street toward the square with the flowering tree.

"Stoyan, say something!" I hissed.

He was walking very fast. My ankle, which had felt almost normal not long ago, began to throb with pain.

"I can't keep up," I gasped. "My ankle hurts. Stoyan, please tell me." Tears of pain and frustration welled in my eyes.

"I will tell you. We must be where nobody can hear us. The corner of the square, there, by the public fountain." It was quiet; the call to prayer must have sounded while I was in the hamam. We paused in a spot where the trickling water of the fountain masked our words. "Sit down," Stoyan said. "I am sorry. I did not know you were in pain. Paula—"

"Just say it, whatever it is, Stoyan. What my mind can

invent will be far worse than the truth. What's happened to him?"

"While we were walking to the Greek lady's establishment this morning, a guard was sent to the han, from Barsam the Elusive, offering to escort your father to the blue house. Master Teodor should have waited for me."

I went cold all over. Salem bin Afazi had died in the street. "You said he was safe," I whispered.

"He is safe. Master Teodor is back at the han but injured, Paula."

"Injured? How?" I half rose from my perch on the rim of the fountain, and my ankle reacted with a stab of pain.

"I do not know yet how bad it is. I have arranged a doctor, a learned Jew, to tend to him. Master Giacomo and his wife are also with him. He was beaten."

I shivered. Father was not exactly young, and his health was less than robust. "What did he tell you?" I asked.

"He was deeply unconscious when I found him and not on a straight path to the blue house but in an alley at some distance. I wasted valuable time searching for him. There was no sign of the guard who had collected your father from the han. I have been worried about you, Paula; I wanted to come straight to fetch you, but I could not. Once I brought your father home, I had to find the doctor, make a formal report to the authorities, send a messenger to Barsam the Elusive. It took some time for Master Teodor to regain consciousness, and even then his mind was not fully itself. There was one thing he stated plainly: that he wanted to ask Barsam for more time. I sent the tea merchant's boy with that request."

"Oh, God. So he was set upon before he even got to Barsam's house." And there was only one bidder left in the race. My heart plummeted. I did not want Duarte Aguiar to have done this, but there could be only one conclusion.

"So it seems. If Barsam denies sending an escort for him, which I believe he will, then it appears this guard was a means of luring Master Teodor out unprotected. He should have waited for me."

I looked up at him, seeing the desolation in his eyes. "Let's go on now," I said. "I'll walk as fast as I can. You've done all the right things, Stoyan. Without you, we might not have found him in time."

"When he needed me, I was not there," he said, as if there were no possible excuse for this.

"You weren't there because I made you take me to Irene's. That makes it my fault. If not for me, he would have had you to protect him."

"This is not your fault, Paula."

"No," I agreed. "And it's not yours either. I very much suspect the fault lies with Duarte Aguiar. And if he's hurt my father, I'm going to make sure he's held accountable."

Chapter Nine

Father had been moved to a different apartment, next to Giacomo's. He lay against his pillows, his face pale beneath bruises, a bandage swathing his head. The doctor, a youngish man wearing spectacles similar to the ones I used for reading, was seated by the bed, a hand on his patient's wrist. I took heart from his calm demeanor.

"Paula!" Father said weakly. "You're safe, thank God."

I put this together with Stoyan's dramatic arrival at the hamam and realized they had genuinely believed that whoever had attacked Father might decide to assault me as well.

"Of course I'm safe," I told him. "I was at Irene's. And, unlike you, I waited for Stoyan to come and fetch me. Father, what possessed you to go out without him? You must have known—" At the look in his eyes, I stopped myself. "Are you seriously hurt?" I asked him, then glanced across at the doctor.

"Master Teodor has received severe bruising to his back and legs," the doctor said quietly, speaking in Greek as we were. "No bones are broken. It could be said he was lucky."

"What about his head? Why is it bandaged?"

"All I can remember is a thump on the back of the skull," Father said. "The next thing I knew, I was waking up here with Stoyan hovering over me, looking like death. He'd carried me all the way back. I didn't see my attacker at all. Paula, is there a message from Barsam yet? It's well past the deadline. I must know if I have an extension of time."

"I will see if the boy has returned," Stoyan said. "If not, I will go to the blue house. Write a message if you wish; I will take it there."

But the boy had returned, and he had brought a note. We asked the doctor if he would mind stepping out of the chamber for a little, and then I read it aloud, my voice faltering before I got halfway down the page.

"'It is now well past the hour to which we agreed. As I had another party interested, I must regretfully advise you that the item in question has been sold. I wish you every good fortune in your future business. . . .'"

Below the bandage, Father's face was desolate. I struggled to find words through a rising tide of anger. What sort of way was this to conduct a transaction, using physical violence against a man of fifty to ensure he could not outbid you in what should have been a fair and proper contest? Father could have died.

"Duarte Aguiar shouldn't be allowed to get away with this," I muttered, trying to mask my distress.

"As I told you, I have reported the attack," said Stoyan. "I was asked what party I suspected might have been responsible. I told the authorities that Master Teodor was involved in a sensitive trading matter. Without your permission, I could go no further."

"Father," I said in a tone that sounded falsely cheerful even to me, "you're alive and you're not seriously hurt. Nothing's more important than that. Later, perhaps we can give the authorities more information and bring the perpetrator to justice. Right now you need to rest and do what the doctor tells you. Stoyan, will you please let him back in?"

Father put his head on the pillows and closed his eyes. His face was a study in white and gray. Seeing him like that filled me with fury. Underneath it, my resolve strengthened. I wasn't going to let this pass. I was going to see justice done. And it wouldn't be through the authorities, whoever they were. That would be too slow. This needed attention now.

I asked the doctor how long he was able to stay, and he said until sunset. Maria was recovered from yesterday's illness, and she and Giacomo had been coming in and out, tending to Father. They offered to take turns sitting up with him overnight so I could sleep. I was certain Stoyan would remain on duty here, guarding the door against intruders, at least until it was time for me to go to bed.

As I sat sipping the tea Maria had brought in and watching Father fall into a restless slumber, my mind was working quickly. I'd wager a silver piece against a wooden spoon that the *Esperança* was on the point of sailing, her master and his prize safely aboard already. If Irene had been right, he would be heading off in search of the other half of Cybele's Gift.

Tabriz, that was the town Barsam had mentioned. I delved into my memory of geography. By water, it would be northward up the Bosphorus, then eastward along the Black Sea before starting a difficult overland journey. Even if Irene's theory was off the mark, Duarte would want to be gone from Istanbul straightaway. Perhaps he'd purchased Cybele's Gift by legitimate sale, but the means he'd used to gain the advantage were criminal. He knew we had friends in the merchant community of the city. He must realize that influential people like Giacomo, Alonso di Parma, and Irene of Volos would rally around Father and demand justice. If I waited too long, the *Esperança* would be gone and Duarte da Costa Aguiar with it.

I finished my tea. Father was asleep. I leaned over and kissed his cheek, feeling like a traitor.

"Stoyan," I said quietly, "my ankle's hurting. I'm going back to our apartment to lie down for a while."

Stoyan nodded. "Of course," he said. "I will watch over Master Teodor. Rest well."

In our own quarters, with the door hanging concealing the interior from curious eyes, I hunted in my storage chest until I found what I needed. The full-length garment, all in black, went on easily over the Greek-style clothing I had donned in such haste at Irene's hamam. I had practiced arranging the two parts of the veil until I could do it quickly and neatly. One went around my brow, tying at the back. The other went over the top of my head, coming down to fasten under my chin. Together, they hid every last curl. There was an additional piece that wrapped from side to side, hiding my nose and mouth and leaving only the smallest window through which I could peer out. In this outfit I might be anyone.

I left the han with a group of folk who had come in to talk to traders on the lower level. As I had suspected, in the swathing dark garments I had become more or less invisible.

My anger drove me quickly. I knew the general direction, and once out of the han, I followed my instincts, scurrying along as fast as I could, trying not to look too obviously lost. Directions would have helped, but to ask for them was to reveal that I was both young and a foreigner, on the streets all by myself. Ideally, I would fulfill my mission and get back to the han before anyone noticed I was gone.

I made errors and lost time, backtracking and moving in circles. It might have been better to tell Stoyan where I was going and why. No; he would have stopped me. If he'd been consulted, I'd never have got the chance to go within five miles of Duarte Aguiar again. I'd just have to be quick and hope Stoyan did not decide to tap on my bedroom door and ask if I was feeling better.

I found myself in a narrow alleyway I was sure I had walked down before: cats in the corners, shuttered windows, shadows creeping out to remind me that the afternoon was passing all too quickly. I closed my eyes and tried to get a sense of direction. When I opened them again, it was to find I was not the only black-clad woman in the deserted alley. Up ahead of me was someone who might or might not be Tati. She was looking at me and beckoning. As I started forward, she whisked around a corner and out of sight.

I hurried after her, ignoring the ache in my ankle. She was quick; I found it hard to keep up. She led me through streets crowded with market stalls, across the courtyard of a mosque whose walls gleamed with blue tiles, down a precipitous flight of stone steps. I turned a corner, panting, and the glittering expanse of the Golden Horn opened up before me, its bank lined with moorings and jetties. Not far away, amidst a confusion of masts and sails, I spotted the *Esperança*, still at anchor. Her deck was alive with activity; she was almost ready to sail. The path ahead of me was teeming with life, porters bearing bundles, men urging on oxen or donkeys pulling carts of goods, overseers cracking whips, small boys darting in and out of the throng. My guide had disappeared.

I took a deep breath and dived into the crowd, making for the *Esperança*. My heart was racing, and I felt a cold sweat on my body that had nothing to do with my chase through the city to get here. I had not really thought out what I would say to Duarte when I reached his ship. It was naive and stupid to imagine he would hand over Cybele's Gift if I asked him for it. I had no money on me beyond a few coppers. Why would he bother to listen to me?

Ahead, I could see men climbing the masts of the pirate ship, readying her sails. There was still a plank down to the dock and people going up and down carrying goods. I would slip on board and find Duarte. I could at least confront him with what he had done. I could give him something to think about while he sailed away with the piece that should have been ours. I could remind him that Father was a middle-aged man with children and grandchildren who loved him and that he could have died from that blow to the head. I could point out what a difference the acquisition of Cybele's Gift might have made to our whole family. Not that a man like him would care about such things. His family had probably disowned him long ago.

Calm down, Paula, I ordered myself as I approached the ship. How far could I go before someone challenged me? I hesitated, not wanting to step out from the crowd until I had a clear run up to the three-master's deck. No sign of Duarte himself, though there were many crewmen busy on the ship. The stocky fellow I had seen before with Duarte was issuing orders at a shout.

Here were three men carrying something awkward between them, a crate of some kind. Chickens? The noise from inside the container suggested so. Halfway up the plank, they came close to dropping the whole thing into the water. A chorus of squawking protest ensued, and the crewmen on deck fell about laughing. I was on my toes, ready to move in an instant. They maneuvered their crate up and in, then stood around it with their backs to me as the first mate addressed them in scathing tones. For a moment, all eyes were on him. Quick as a flash, I was up the plank, around a corner, and down a ladder to the area I thought most likely to house sleeping or living quarters.

I found myself in a short passageway with doors on the right side. One of them was open, and people were moving about in the compartment within. I shrank against the wall, trying to blend with the shadows. Under the black robe, I was shaking with nerves.

A voice came from within the cabin, a voice I recognized, though the tone was sharp and crisp, not the lazy drawl I was used to. The words were foreign to me, probably Portuguese.

A man came out into the passageway. Not Duarte; a crewman. I held myself very still, and he went right past me and up the ladder as if I were not there. No sound from the cabin now. Was Duarte alone? Creaks and shouts from the deck suggested I could not wait to find out. Wherever the *Esperança* was headed, I certainly didn't plan to go with her. Still, I reasoned, they would not sail until the captain was on deck. I stepped over to the doorway and tapped on it. "Excuse me." It sounded stupid, as if I was making a polite social call. I cleared my throat as Duarte Aguiar looked up from the chart he was studying and gazed at me in astonishment. "I must talk to you."

He rose very slowly to his feet. "Who—" he began; then as I removed the veil from my face, his eyes widened. "We're about to sail," he said, his tone incredulous. "What are you doing on board my ship, Paula? Where is your father?"

It was like a red rag to a bull. "How dare you!" I burst out, striding into the tiny cabin. "When you know quite well what was done to him today, how dare you stand there so cool and calm, acting as if nothing was wrong? I can see the ship's about to sail, and I know you've got Cybele's Gift on board! You've robbed us!"

Duarte gave a slow smile, and I clenched my fists in rage. Not only was he pretending ignorance but he was mocking me as well. "Perhaps you should take a deep breath and count to ten," he said lightly. "Then begin at the beginning. But be quick. I have a voyage to make, and there are reasons why I cannot delay it."

"I bet!" I retorted. "Like being charged with organizing an attack on someone who was just going about his legitimate business. My father could have been killed!"

He pushed the chart to the back of the table and perched himself on the edge. "Paula," he said with infuriating calm, "if something has happened to your father, I'm sorry. But this has nothing to do with me. You shouldn't be here on my ship, and you shouldn't be out on the streets of Istanbul alone. Where's your guard? And how on earth did you get in here without anyone seeing you?"

"Tell me the truth," I demanded, hands on hips. "You've got it, haven't you? Cybele's Gift?" Casting my eyes around the cabin, I spotted a very familiar box at the foot of the narrow bunk that ran along one wall. The iron lock and reinforcing bands were unmistakable.

"As you see."

"Father would have outbid you," I said. "You knew he was going back there this morning; you knew he would make a better offer than anything you could scrape together. Instead of going through with the process properly, as any self-respecting trader would, you sent in your band of thugs to beat him in the street before he could even get to Barsam's house. I have only one word for a man who does that sort of thing: heartless. Your behavior sickens me. You were planning this, weren't you, even as you practiced your charms on me last night over supper? You're disgusting!" I drew a deep breath. My whole body was vibrating with rage.

Duarte rose to his feet. He was a tall man; the cabin seemed too small to accommodate him. "Paula—" he began; then I heard a commotion from the dock outside: shouts, crashing, the sounds of a street brawl of momentous proportions. Duarte took a quick look through the porthole and an instant later was gone, slamming the door behind him. I flung myself across the cabin, wrenching at the handle, but the wretched thing wouldn't open. He'd locked me in.

I hammered and shouted, but nothing happened. The din from outside was loud enough to drown my pathetic efforts completely. I kept trying anyway, until my hands hurt and my throat ached. I cursed my own stupidity. It had been pointless to come here. Duarte was never going to listen to me. Why should he? He was the sort of man who went straight for what he wanted, not caring at all who fell by the wayside.

The sounds from outside were getting louder—mostly

grunts, screams, and oaths in several languages. There was one word I picked out clearly above the rest of it. "Paula!" The voice was familiar.

I clambered onto a stool and looked out the porthole. At the foot of the gangway, a full-scale brawl was in progress. Kicks and blows were meeting flesh, men were flying through the air to land with sickening thuds on the boards of the landing or, in one instance, with a splash in the waters of the Golden Horn. People were bleeding—this was no spur-of-the-moment scrap but brutal and serious combat. At quite some distance stood an official-looking figure, a big, tur-baned man with a staff in one hand. He was watching with every appearance of being mightily entertained and made no move to intervene.

It was wrong. It was all wrong. It was the most one-sided contest anyone could imagine. What I could see below me, through the narrow view the porthole offered, was quite clearly a mob attack on one solitary individual. It was amaz-ing that the white-faced, black-haired, rather busy person in the center of it all had managed to keep his feet for so long. His eyes were blazing with determination, his mouth was fixed in a snarl, his clothing was soaked with sweat, and he was using every bit of skill and strength he had to keep the mob at bay. While they maintained their assault, there was no way he could get a foot onto the plank laid from the dock up to the *Esperança's* deck. There could be only one reason why he had come here. If they killed him, it would be my fault.

"Stoyan!" I shrieked. "Behind you, there!" For I had seen what he could not: the flash of a knife in a man's hand.

He couldn't hear me. He couldn't hear the scream that built up in me as I waited to see him struck down and trampled beneath the booted feet of the mob. As the weapon rose, ready to stab, something flew through the air to crash onto the heads of two of the attackers and splinter with explosive effect into the general fray. A rain of similar missiles followed. From the deck of the *Esperança*, people were shouting: *"Vinde, por aqui, saltai! Soltai-o, seus filhos de cães!"* Then again, in the tone of a command, *"Saltai! Saltai!"*

I was screaming with the best of them by now and pounding my fists on the wall beside the porthole—"Watch out! Duck! Look left!"—as Stoyan whirled and dodged and staggered right on the edge of the dock, his assailants moving like a dragging garment all around him. A hurled stone struck him on the forehead, and a crimson stream began to pour down into his eye, half blinding him. He put up a hand to dash the blood away, and in a sudden flashing movement, someone struck at his arm. He stumbled. "No!" I screamed. "Stoyan, no!" For I could see what might be next, and it froze my heart.

The gangplank was being pulled up; Duarte did not want this unruly crowd on his well-kept ship. A gap of two arms' lengths opened up between the plank and the dock. Someone on the ship, recognizing belatedly that Stoyan could not understand the crew's shouts, yelled out in Greek, "Jump! Come on, jump!"

With the hands of several attackers grabbing at his dolman and sash, Stoyan jumped. I saw the leap. The landing was beyond my line of vision. I didn't hear a splash; but then I probably wouldn't. The mob was howling for Stoyan's blood, and the crew of the *Esperança* were shouting imprecations in return. I needed no Portuguese to interpret those; I could guess. Then, from the deck, a command rang out in a voice I recognized. A moment later the ship shuddered and creaked and, to a chorus of angry shouts from the shore, began to edge away from her mooring. Duarte da Costa Aguiar was sailing his ship out of Istanbul with me on board.

"What do you think you're doing?" I demanded. The *Esperança* was heading north up the Bosphorus under full sail. The crew had settled to their various tasks with the ease of well-oiled pieces of machinery, and having finally been liberated by a tongue-tied sailor, I stood on the deck facing Duarte, the wind whipping the folds of the long black garment around my body and tossing my hair into my eyes. "Why didn't you wait until I was safely ashore before you sailed? And where's Stoyan?"

"To answer the last question first," Duarte said, his expression somewhere between amusement and irritation, "your friend is on board and being tended to by one of my crew. He'll live; his injuries are more spectacular than serious. Why didn't I wait? It's bad enough having a hotheaded young woman on my ship, not to speak of her pugnacious bodyguard, without throwing in a brawling mob for good measure. What do I think I'm doing? Taking my ship on the voyage I always intended to make, for perfectly legitimate reasons."

"Legitimate. I doubt it. Why the rush? Couldn't you have pulled away from the docks and waited until the crowd dispersed? Then you could have put the two of us back onshore. In case you missed it when I mentioned this before, my father was set upon by thugs this morning and severely beaten. I need to get back before—" I faltered, realizing how this sounded.

"Before he learns that you left him on his sickbed to race out and get yourself in trouble? Before Master Teodor discovers he is not only without his daughter, but has lost his bodyguard as well, thanks to the fellow's need to chase after that same daughter and bring her to her senses? You are too ready with your accusations, Paula. If you did not want your father worried, you should have stayed at home."

I swallowed a retort. It was clear to me that, in the matter of the assault on my father, the most likely perpetrator was Duarte or his agent—I did not think he would perform deeds of that kind in person. Hadn't someone said he always took care to avoid being caught? He wasn't going to admit it to me, and I'd made a big mistake in ever thinking he might. Now I'd almost got Stoyan killed, though who those men had been and why they had attacked him I could not imagine. I could not blame that on Duarte; his crew had saved Stoyan's life. I should cut my losses and concentrate on getting us both off the boat and back to Father as quickly as possible. He might still be asleep. He might not need to be told.

"You didn't answer my question," I said as Duarte shifted restlessly, his eyes on the activities of his crew. "Listen to me! They look as if they can sail the boat pretty well without you. Now tell me, if you're not fleeing from punishment for what you did, why are you in such a hurry?"

He leaned on the rail, and behind him the shores of the Bosphorus passed, a soft, leafy parade of green banks dotted with the white walls of dwellings. Now a fortress tower . . . Dear God, we were already passing Rumeli Hisari.

"Duarte," I said, trying to suppress a hysterical note in my voice, "you must put in to shore and let Stoyan and me get off the ship. We need to go back to Istanbul."

A wary look had appeared in his dark eyes. "I can't," he said.

"You have to!" Now I sounded shrill, but I couldn't help it. With every moment that passed, we were less likely to be back in the city by nightfall. Father might think I had been beaten and left for dead, as he had been. He might think Stoyan and I had run off together. No, probably not that; he knew both of us too well. But I suspected that would be what everyone else would believe. The news of our disappearance would spread like wildfire through the trading community of the Galata quarter. Father would certainly be distressed and anxious. What if the shock proved fatal to him in his weakened state?

"You have to," I repeated. "Why would you want to abduct us? We have absolutely nothing to offer you."

He smiled. It was not the mischievous smile he used when flirting, nor the rapacious one he had turned on the traders of the çarşi, but a smile that seemed genuinely apologetic. He shrugged, gesturing helplessness. "I can't do it, Paula," he said. "There are reasons, very good ones, which I will explain to you in due course; that's if you are prepared to stop shouting at me long enough to hear them. In brief, I believe it's possible we may be pursued. We must make what speed we can to avoid being overtaken. I hope to stay far enough ahead so we can lose them once we reach the Black Sea."

"Pursued?" This was not what I had expected. "By whom? And why?" I wondered who else he had injured, what other property he had obtained by devious means, what other innocent folk he had kidnapped.

"Later," Duarte said. "You were right, my crew can do

the job without my interference. But when I put them under exceptional pressure, it seems only right to take my share of the responsibility. It's not simply a matter of tricky sailing. It's the need to tolerate passengers on board. I hope you are a quick learner."

I stared at him, unable to interpret this.

"If all you can offer are insults and false accusations," Duarte said coolly, "you should keep your mouth shut. My men are loyal. They won't take kindly to a barrage of invective."

"I'll make sure I don't do it in Portuguese," I said. "Anything else?"

"My cabin is at your disposal. I'll move my things elsewhere. Be careful with the door; it has a tendency to stick. Don't go anywhere else. You can't use the crew's facilities for washing and . . . er . . ."

"If you stop and set me ashore, you'll have no need to bother with such embarrassing details, senhor." My heart shrank at the prospect of spending a night on board while the *Esperança* plowed on northward.

"What are you wearing under that?"

I felt my face grow hot. The question seemed grossly inappropriate.

"Never mind." Duarte was showing signs of exasperation. "Without the robe, you'll get cold. And if you keep it on, you won't be safe on the ladders. Pero, my first mate, will find you some clothing. When he does, don't argue, put it on. Now you're to go to the cabin and keep quiet until further notice. Don't slow me down, Paula, or I'll throw you over the side as a treat for the fish."

After a moment I said, "I want to see Stoyan."

"You will find him in the adjacent cabin, which is Pero's. Cozy for you. Go on, and I don't want to see either of you on deck again until you're called for."

Stoyan had a dressing on his forehead and another on his left arm, which was in a sling. A sailor with a tattooed chin was tying this neatly at the shoulder when I came in. The man grinned at me and said something in Portuguese. As soon as the knot was fastened, Stoyan stood up, hitting his head on the ceiling, and conveyed by gestures that he and I were to be left alone.

"How could you do that?" he said as soon as the man was out the door. His voice was shaking with fury. "What on earth possessed you?" A moment later he added, "Kyria."

I had expected him to be angry. I had not expected to be so upset by it. Perhaps it was knowing I was in the wrong that hurt so much. "Are you all right?" I asked him. "Who were those men?"

"That is unimportant. What were you doing, Paula? How could you leave the han on your own?"

I took a deep breath. "I'm sorry," I said. "Truly sorry. If I'd known you were going to come running after me and get yourself half killed, I would have . . ." I paused. Even that would probably not have stopped me. It had seemed so important to make Duarte see the error of his ways before he traveled out of reach, taking Cybele's Gift with him. "I had to talk to him, to Senhor Aguiar," I said. "And it's nothing to do with falling for his charms. He must be responsible for the attack on my father. He's got Cybele's Gift on board, in that cabin through there. He made no attempt to deny it. Father was beaten to stop him from getting to the blue house in time. He was attacked because Duarte knew Father would outbid him if he was allowed to compete fairly."

He stood there looking at me, lips tight.

"Stoyan, I couldn't just let this go. I couldn't let Duarte sail away without accounting for himself. I had to tell him what this meant to us, to me and Father. I was hoping he might see sense."

"And did he?" Stoyan's tone was deeply skeptical.

"No. He denied having anything to do with the beating."

"And here we are on the ship."

"There's worse," I said, reluctant to give him any further reason to be angry with me.

"Tell me. What is worse than doing this to Master Teodor when he is already weak and despondent?"

"Stop it! I feel guilty enough already. I asked Duarte to put in at one of the anchorages on the Bosphorus and let us get off so we could make our way back to the city by road. He said he can't. Something about pursuers and needing to reach the Black Sea before they catch up. I have no idea who would be interested in following him."

Stoyan sat down abruptly on the edge of Pero's narrow bunk and put his good hand up to touch the bandage around his brow. "A slight headache only," he said, perhaps seeing some change in my expression. "Paula, I already know about that part of it. That fellow who was here knew enough Turkish to tell me. You know of the raids on various trading centers by representatives of the Sheikh-ul-Islam. It is this party Aguiar suspects of following him. That makes sense—who else would have the resources to mount a chase by sea?"

"The Mufti? But why? Isn't he only interested in tracking down the cult in Istanbul, if it exists?"

"That, you must ask Aguiar. I do know his crew anticipates an attempt to seize Cybele's Gift, either at sea or in the place to which we sail, wherever that may be. They think they can outrun the other vessel if it does not leave the city too soon after the *Esperança*. But they have no time for unscheduled stops. It seems we are with them all the way."

I gaped at him, astonished that he had learned so much when I had failed to get any of this out of Duarte. After a moment, Stoyan managed a smile.

"The man was keen to ask me about some tricks I used on the docks," he said. "Techniques that may be employed to good effect when a fight is uneven. We exchanged information. I think the crewmen are friendly enough. They did get me out of trouble. But I do not like your being on the ship. One woman and a lengthy voyage . . . You must stay down here and let me guard you, Paula. No more risky ventures on your own."

His words had turned me cold. "How do you know it's going to be a lengthy voyage?" I asked him. "How long is 'lengthy' anyway?" More than the one night I had been dreading, I was certain.

"It depends on the wind. Unless the conditions are unusually good, the fellow said it will be six days or more." And, as my jaw dropped, he added, "For the return trip, twice that."

Father with no news for nearly two weeks. Father desperately searching. Father ill and distressed, perhaps thinking me dead. I wrapped my arms around myself and turned away, temporarily speechless.

"Paula." The anger was gone from Stoyan's voice. "We will come through this safely. Don't cry, please."

"I'm not!" I said fiercely. "Curse Duarte Aguiar! This is all his fault!"

But it wasn't. Maybe Duarte had done something bad, two things at least, and set the whole chain of events in motion. But I was forced to acknowledge that a large part of the responsibility was mine.

Chapter Ten

I wanted explanations, but the ones I got did not satisfy me. With the sky fading to dusk and the *Esperança* still plowing a choppy way northward, Duarte came down to his cabin, where Stoyan was sitting on the floor just inside the doorway and I was cross-legged on the bunk with my spectacles on, reading aloud. In the captain's quarters I had found a small collection of books, some in Portuguese, others in Greek. Whether Stoyan really wanted to listen to classical poetry under the present circumstances was debatable. I had thought it would help to divert us from our predicament.

"Very fetching," Duarte commented as he ducked under the lintel and came in. He was eyeing the outfit I was now wearing. The trousers, shirt, and boots had belonged to a young crewman of diminutive size, Pero had told me in careful Greek, a lad who very sadly had suffered a mishap on an earlier voyage and was no longer with the *Esperança*. This boy might have been small, but the garments hung loose on me, and the shirt fabric was on the flimsy side, almost transparent. After trying everything on while Stoyan waited outside, I had searched through Duarte's storage chest and made the adjustment my outfit required to be acceptably modest, if still unconventional. I had no intention of spending a two-week voyage shut up in this box of a chamber for want of appropriate clothing.

"Isn't that one of mine?" Duarte queried, his gaze traveling up and down the belted tunic I wore over the things Pero had provided. This garment was made of very fine wool in a blue-gray shade and covered me from neck to knees. The sash I was using as a belt went around my waist twice.

"As you said, it's cold up on deck. I needed it," I said. "If you don't want to share, you shouldn't shut strangers in your cabin."

"It looks much better on you than it ever did on me." Duarte glanced toward the locked box at the foot of the bunk. "You've been through my meager wardrobe and raided my library, but you haven't bothered with Cybele's Gift," he said. "The key's right on the table there."

"There wouldn't be any point." I made my tone coolly polite. "What do you imagine I would do, smash her and drop her over the side just to spite you? I'm not vindictive, senhor. I wanted to see justice done, that was all. But I imagine you don't have much concept of that."

"Your imagination is sadly limited, then," he retorted. "I had been planning to offer you some clarification, since you were so keen for me to account for myself. But I'm beginning to realize it would be pointless. You've already judged me, and your opinion cannot be swayed by any words of logic."

Stoyan had risen to his feet, awkward with the sling, and fixed the pirate with a stare that would have made another man shrink. "Neither of us wishes to be here, senhor, and it is clear that you, too, wish we had remained behind in Istanbul. I am grateful to your crew for getting me out of a predicament. But I cannot tolerate your manner toward Paula. She acted in good faith in an attempt to help her father. Do you not value family loyalty?"

Duarte sighed. "Perhaps we should start again. I have made some arrangements that I hope will relieve some of your anxiety. Paula, the crew have agreed to give you access to our ablution area three times daily. They will not disturb you while you make use of it. Stoyan here can stand guard if you're worried; it's not exactly private. You won't be used to life aboard a ship. We don't wash much and we don't cook. There's dried meat, olives, hard bread. You'll be pleased to hear we took on fresh water in Istanbul." He glanced at Stoyan. "Once that arm's back to normal, you can make yourself useful. A man of your strength will be an asset to the crew."

"I guard Paula."

"Paula doesn't need a guard all day and all night. I run a tight ship. She'll be quite safe."

"So I don't have to stay in here?" I ventured, not meeting Stoyan's eye. I was struck by the fact that both of them were calling me Paula, even when speaking to each other. I suspected it was the first of many changes to come.

"I'll tell you when you can come on deck and where you can sit to keep out of folk's way," Duarte said. "You'll need a cloak; Pero will find you one. Remember that we're in a hurry. Don't expect fascinating conversation and nonstop entertainment."

I gave him a scathing look. "We'll amuse ourselves," I

said. "Provided we can have access to your books. And some writing materials, if you have them."

"You plan to pen missives home complaining that you are captive on a pirate ship? Place them in a corked jar, perhaps, and throw them overboard with a hopeful prayer?"

I did not dignify this suggestion with an answer.

"Do we sail through the night?" Stoyan asked.

Duarte shook his head. "We'll drop anchor in a bay somewhere tonight and be off again at first light. Night sailing is too risky, and I imagine the pursuers will adopt the same caution. In the Black Sea, I plan to lose them. At the end of the voyage, I must take Cybele's Gift overland. If I can, I want to make that landfall unobserved. A chase across a mountain pass is not a prospect I relish."

Stoyan and I both looked at him. Duarte seemed to be waiting for us to speak.

"All right," I said, laying the poetry book down on the bed. "Tell us exactly what it is you're doing. Where are you taking Cybele and why? And while you're about it, tell me who those men were who attacked Stoyan on the docks. Not yours, I presume, since your crew rescued him."

Duarte sat down on the bunk beside me. I edged away, knowing there was no chance of following normal rules of propriety in such a place but wary all the same. Stoyan remained standing, his eyes narrow.

"I find that I am not quite prepared to trust you," Duarte said, glancing at me and away. For the first time, his tone sounded less than fully confident, and that surprised me. "Much rides on this. A personal stake that cannot be measured in gold or silver. I became aware some time ago that, alongside the merchants who were bidding for Cybele's Gift, another party wished to track down the artifact for his own reasons. The interest of the religious authorities in Istanbul was at first a tightly guarded secret but became common knowledge as the raids began."

"Go on," I said.

"You will know that I speak of the Sheikh-ul-Islam," Duarte said gravely. "He is a ruthless man, and he has a long reach. In hindsight, I suspect his hand in the murder of your father's Turkish colleague. Salem bin Afazi was a devout Muslim. He made the error of putting personal friendship before the strict observance of his faith when he gave Master Teodor advance notice of this artifact's arrival in the city. That alone, I believe, would have been enough to attract the Mufti's attention. The religious authorities being what they are, it may have been interpreted as a personal interest in pagan idolatry. I cannot say how the Sheikh-ul-Islam came by the information, but the punishment was quick and deadly."

This was shocking and, I was forced to admit, entirely believable. It was the same idea Stoyan had hinted at when we first discussed Cybele's Gift. And if Duarte was telling the truth about this, perhaps he had also been honest when he'd said the attack on my father was not his doing. If that was the case, I had behaved appallingly toward him.

"Is there other evidence to back up your theory?" asked Stoyan.

"Indeed. Men have been tailing the bidders around Istanbul." Duarte gave Stoyan an appraising glance. "Until you came rushing on board to accuse me of attacking Master Teodor, Paula, I believed your father was the one bidder, apart from myself, who had managed to move about the city untracked. Pero and I discussed this and put it down to his cool head, his experience, and the presence of Stoyan. I was taken aback to hear that Master Teodor had been assaulted this morning. The timing was odd, since it was clear the Mufti's attention was on me today—he has finally learned of my interest in Cybele's Gift. Pero recognized several of those who set upon Stoyan. Our friend here happened to be in the wrong place at a crucial time. The Mufti's men were trying to board the *Esperança* and carry out a search before we sailed. Stoyan got in their way. In the ensuing confusion, he was lucky to escape with his life. Pero holds the theory that once a brawl commences in such a public spot, passersby have a tendency to join in for no better reason than entertainment. Hence we had folk pushing in all directions, when a little co-operation might have enabled the Mufti's party to board quite easily. You did us a favor, Stoyan."

"Which your crew returned," Stoyan said. "I did not know who had dispatched that mob to the dock. I did know that if there was any chance Paula had reached your ship, I did not want them on board."

"A search?" I was puzzled by Duarte's theory. "But wouldn't the Mufti send uniformed Janissaries? Or officials? That just looked like a band of thugs."

Duarte smiled thinly. "Officials carry out inspections, in-terviews, visits. In this case, I suspect what was intended was brazen theft, backed up by violence as required. In broad daylight, on a crowded dock, with a crew such as mine to confront, it could not be done covertly. Hence the thugs: unidentifiable by passersby, with nothing to connect them with the Sheikh-ul-Islam. But we know who sent them. Pero is extremely well informed about who hires whom at a certain level of activity."

"How can you call it theft," I challenged, "when the artifact is stolen already?"

Duarte sighed in exasperation. "Paula, my silver is as good as your father's. I paid a fair price; Barsam was happy. Cybele's Gift is legitimately mine. For a short time."

"For a short time," I said flatly. "Until when, exactly? Where is it we're going?" I remembered the trip from Constanţa and the few moments when the prospect of being boarded and attacked had seemed all too real.

Duarte hesitated.

"Senhor," Stoyan said, frowning, "you have made it clear you do not intend to set us ashore along the way. That means Paula and I must accompany you to this destination. There seems to me no reason to withhold its name from us."

"Paula is a merchant's daughter," Duarte said. "She came on board my ship clad in a disguise. Maybe she's on the *Esperança* for the reason she gave me, incoherent as it was. Maybe it's pique at being outbid combined with concern for her father's predicament. Maybe it's more. Until I know that, I don't plan to confide any secrets. Not in the lady, and not in you, since it is blindingly clear to me that you would jump through fire for her."

A muscle twitched at Stoyan's temple. I heard him draw a deliberate breath, as if to stop himself from answering in anger.

"So you don't trust me, Senhor Duarte," I said quickly. "The feeling is mutual. I'll make this easier for you. I noticed a certain lack of surprise on your face when you saw the artifact for the first time. You remained cool and calm when I announced that half of it was missing. Answer me one question: Did you already know it was broken? Do you know where the other half is?"

"That's two questions." Duarte was smiling. He had the ability to look entirely charming even when he was in his most adversarial mood. "If I answer yes and yes, will you believe me?"

So Irene had guessed right about him. "How did you find out? Documentation about Cybele's Gift is as scarce as hen's teeth." There were, of course, the papers I had found, but I suspected an uncanny hand had set those before me.

"You are not the only scholar in the world, Paula," Duarte said smoothly. I could tell he was holding something back.

"You said something about returning the artifact to its original owners. Who are they? Have they paid you to acquire it for them?"

Duarte laughed, though I could not see anything funny about it. "They are hardly in a position to do so. Let us simply say that I owe a debt and that I am repaying that debt. I'm on a mission. I don't plan to give you the details; at least, not yet. You'll have to earn my trust first."

A mission. Mine, Stoyan's, Tati's. The forest queen had said nothing about Duarte. All the same, it rang true for me. I remembered that Tati had helped me reach the ship. In fact, Tati had been on the ship the first time I had seen her black-robed form.

Duarte addressed Stoyan rather pointedly. "Why don't you go up and stretch your legs awhile? It's cramped here, especially for a man of your build. You could find your mistress something to eat. Ask for Cristiano. He's in charge of rations."

Stoyan looked at me. Beneath the bandage, his face was paler than usual.

"I will stay with Paula until you return," Duarte added. "I have no intention of harming her in any way, though I must confess to a strong urge to shake some of her prejudices out of her. No, no, don't look like that. I won't touch her, I swear. With you to answer to, not one of the *Esperança*'s crew would dare look at her in the wrong way, and that includes the captain."

"Go on, Stoyan," I said. "We're going to have to sample this dried meat sometime. Don't ask them what kind it is. I'd rather not know."

I could see Stoyan thinking, weighing up the relative dangers of leaving me alone here with Duarte and taking me up on deck, where I would be visible to the *Esperança*'s crew. He left, looking anything but willing.

"Well, now," Duarte said, sitting down again by the small table that held his charts, "are we going to continue fighting, or shall we attempt some kind of truce?"

"You still have questions to answer—" I began, but Duarte waved a hand, hushing me.

"Not now. We will only argue, and I am weary of that. Once we drop anchor for the night, we must quench all lights on board, the better to remain invisible to certain eyes. Until then, perhaps you and I might engage in some other activity, one that will not have us at each other's throats."

A prickle of unease crept across my flesh. "What activity?" I asked, trying for the sort of tone Irene might have employed in a similar situation.

"I could teach you a game," he suggested with an expression that could only be described as wicked, all dimples and snapping dark eyes.

Out of my depth already, I struggled not to make my misgivings too obvious. "I'm not sure I'd care for your sort of games, senhor."

"Call me Duarte; you did before. Forget the teaching, then. Tell me what games you already know, and we will try one of those."

"Chess?" I had already observed a board and pieces amongst his things when I went through them in the hunt for clothing.

Duarte grinned. It was the fierce, combative smile he had used in the çarşi. "Done," he said, crouching to retrieve the set from the small chest where it was stored. "I warn you, I'm good. I've been playing since you were a babe in swaddling."

"Then I imagine you will defeat me before Stoyan returns with our supper," I said demurely. "How convenient. I'm sorry I won't be able to offer you a challenging bout."

"Ah, well, perhaps that is best. Otherwise we may fight again."

"Oh, I don't fight when I play," I said. "Getting the emotions involved is not at all appropriate. A cool head is the thing."

I saw the flash of his teeth. "Then I will certainly beat you, Paula. You're incapable of keeping your temper for more than the space of a few breaths."

I refused to be baited. "Black or white?" I asked him calmly.

"For a villain such as Duarte da Costa Aguiar, it must be black, of course. For an innocent maiden held captive on a pirate ship, pure white."

We were just getting into the game when Stoyan returned, bearing a platter of food. I was playing carefully, wanting to show enough skill to keep Duarte interested but avoiding any displays of expertise. I planned to trap him at a far later stage and thereby secure a victory. He was good, certainly: an experienced player, as he had said. But he was far beneath the folk who had shared the scholars' table with me in the Other Kingdom. They had taught me a rare assortment of strategies and tricks; they had trained me to see far ahead and to read my opponent's subtlest gesture, his faintest sigh.

"You play well," Duarte said grudgingly. "We should pause awhile and eat. Is there sufficient here for three?"

Stoyan set the platter down without comment. I exercised my teeth on the chewy strips of meat and managed a few bites of hard-baked bread. The olives were the only thing worth eating. I finished my share in unseemly haste, for it had been a long time since Irene's sweetmeats. What would Irene think of my current predicament? She'd be shocked, certainly. She'd also tell me I had only myself to blame for disregarding her warnings about the charming Senhor Aguiar.

Duarte ate steadily, no doubt long accustomed to sailors' fare.

"You're not eating, Stoyan," I said, noticing how pale he still was. "Are you sure you're all right?"

"I am sure, kyria. This man Cristiano tells me we will soon be at our anchorage for the night. You will wish privacy to prepare for sleep."

"Not quite yet," Duarte said. "I need to win the game first."

"I don't suppose that will take you long," I said with a

sweet smile that brought a suspicious frown to his face. "Stoyan, you may as well go to the cabin next door and lie down. Chess is boring to watch if you don't know how to play."

Stoyan's features tightened. "I will stay," he said, and settled on the floor again. The size of the cabin meant he could not quite stretch out his legs. He looked uncomfortable in more ways than one, but I decided not to press the point.

As the game advanced, I became more and more absorbed. So, it seemed, did my opponent. Knights, rooks, bishops, and pawns fell and were removed from the board. Strategies were put into play and countered. Once or twice I was aware of Stoyan asking if we were nearly finished and Duarte murmuring something in return. At a point when I was beginning to set up my endgame, Stoyan observed that the ship had stopped moving and that we should surely be quenching the lantern, since he had been told all lights on board were to be extinguished once we reached our mooring. "Not yet," I muttered, moving a critical piece into play. A little later, Pero came to the door, said something in Portuguese, and at a murmur from Duarte left us.

And somewhat after that, I won the game. It was only then, looking up with a triumphant grin and surprising an unguarded smile of pure delight on Duarte's aquiline features, that I realized how quiet it was. Stoyan had his head tipped back against the wall; he was half asleep. The *Esperança* was at anchor, and beyond our door, all I could hear was the gentle creak of the timbers and the faint wash of the sea. The last time I had been so caught up in the thrill of a true intellectual challenge had been six whole years ago—the night I made my final farewell to the Other Kingdom.

With each day that passed on board the *Esperança*, I felt guiltier. Looking back, I could hardly believe I had acted so rashly. Father would be distraught. I imagined him using up all our profits in mounting a fruitless search for me. I thought of him sinking into a decline. At the same time, I found myself glancing into odd corners of the ship, wondering when Tati was going to make another appearance and give me some clear instructions as to what exactly I was supposed to be doing. For, despite my guilt and anxiety, I felt in my bones the certainty that Stoyan and I were exactly where the powers of the Other Kingdom wanted us to be. We had begun our quest.

Duarte relaxed his rules. I was allowed up on deck, except at times when the crewmen were under particular pressure and needed to be without distractions. He showed me where I could sit or stand and not be in the way. I obeyed his instructions, understanding that on a ship the captain's word is law and it is foolhardy to disregard it. I knew next to nothing about sailing. I tried to learn by observation how things worked: the sails in particular, with their complex arrangement of ropes and the different deployment of them in varying conditions.

Many of the crewmen spoke some Greek, Turkish, or French, and they put these together to answer my questions or invite me to learn a certain knot or help haul on a particular rope. They were indulging me in the latter. My strength was puny by comparison with that of the slightest of them, but they congratulated me heartily and, after a day or two, took to singing a certain ditty as they worked:

Paula, de brancura singela
Faz corar uma rosa
Gaivota graciosa, do navio
Marinheira mais bela!

I heard Stoyan and Duarte arguing about it later. Duarte was assuring my guard that there was nothing at all ribald in it and that it was the kind of song a man might make up about his little sister. He would never, Duarte declared, allow crude comments about a lady like Mistress Paula on board the *Esperança*. The crew knew he would have their guts for garters if they tried anything of the sort.

I could not help noticing that Duarte was regularly seeking me out. That surprised me. It seemed we had managed to outrun the pursuing vessel as our captain had intended, for she had not been sighted. But we were in a race of sorts, with Duarte keen to reach landfall and move on before there was any chance of the Mufti's crew spotting where he was headed.

A mountain pass, he'd said. That sounded difficult. I knew from my studies of geography that there were high mountains quite close to the shore at the eastern end of the Black Sea. I judged we were still a long way short of that region. In view of the urgency, it was odd that Duarte so often found time to stand beside me on deck, explaining how far we had traveled and telling me the names of landmarks as we passed them. I asked him about something that was puzzling me.

"Isn't it supposed to be unlucky to have a woman on board? On the *Stea de Mare,* I kept getting funny looks. But your men have made me welcome."

Duarte smiled. "For a few memorable years, we had a woman amongst our crew. Carlota captains her own ship now; her name is much feared across the Mediterranean. My men have never forgotten the lessons she taught them. Besides, they understand that you are my guest."

After dark he made a habit of coming down to the cabin for a game of chess or a conversation about politics or philosophy or literature. He had a strong grasp of the classics, and his knowledge of matters scientific was wider than mine. He was not so strong on mythology and folklore, which surprised me, since the object of his personal mission was a statue of Cybele. As I grew to know him better, I realized he was not quite the evildoer I had once believed him. He spoke of my father with such genuine respect that I became convinced that he was not responsible for that attack. It had been luck rather than violence that had enabled him to acquire Cybele's Gift that morning. I stumbled through an apology for so misjudging him, and he told me to put it behind me. I toyed with the notion of telling him about Tati and the mysterious messages I had been receiving since the day I first arrived in Istanbul, but I held back. Maybe there was some genuine feeling for me hidden in his smooth flattery, but he didn't trust me. He still hadn't told me where we were going. He still hadn't said why after paying good money for Cybele's Gift, he seemed to be planning to give it away.

Of course, there were times when the *Esperança*'s crew, expert as they were, needed their captain's guidance, and to keep those times from passing too slowly, I prevailed upon Stoyan to let me continue his reading lessons. As my ankle and his arm were both now completely recovered, Stoyan in his turn worked on my skills in unarmed combat. This was made easier by my new outfit of practical trousers and tunic. I was certain Stoyan would not have allowed either reading or combat lessons had he not disapproved so strongly of the interest Duarte was showing in me. It was harmless, of course—something Duarte did without even thinking. It meant absolutely nothing. I tried to explain this to Stoyan but got tangled up in words.

"He likes books," I said. "He likes talking about ideas. I don't suppose there are many men in the crew who enjoy doing that; they're probably all so tired at the end of a shift that they want nothing more than a platter of that miserable dried meat and a few hours' sleep. Duarte likes games, and I'm good at them."

"His motives cannot be so simple." Stoyan's tone was grimly judgmental. "He wants something from you, Paula."

"I just happen to be here and able to entertain him, that's all. He means nothing by it. As soon as this voyage is over, he will forget all about me, Stoyan."

"You cannot read the look in his eyes."

"And you can?" I challenged, exasperated with his edginess. I wished he would go off and help sail the ship.

Stoyan did not answer, and when I looked at him, there was such a closed expression on his strong features that I glanced quickly away. I remembered Duarte saying: *You would jump through fire for her.* At the time, I had thought this a flowery Portuguese overstatement. Now I was not so sure.

By afternoon on the third day, Stoyan had memorized the Greek alphabet and could inscribe all the letters. We improvised a sand tray, since there was a supply on board as a first precaution against fire. We wrote and erased and wrote again. We usually performed the task in the cabin, since the deck was too windy for such a delicate activity.

At first, there were frequent interruptions. When Duarte saw what we were doing, he raised his brows in apparent astonishment, making spots of color appear on Stoyan's cheeks. Pero was fascinated and wanted a turn. Others followed; had time permitted, I could have provided the Portuguese pirate ship with the most literate crew to be found anywhere between Istanbul and Lisbon. The cabin was small, and I could tell Stoyan was acutely uncomfortable performing his tasks under any scrutiny other than mine. I shooed the others away with assurances that I would teach them another time.

Then there were the lessons in which I was the pupil. I perfected the technique for escaping an assailant who grabbed me from behind. I learned an unpleasant move involving a kick to a certain part of a man's anatomy, but I refused to practice this on Stoyan. I began to understand that the relative strengths of a pair of opponents were not the determinants of who would prevail. He taught me to use my adversary's superior size against him.

"This is much more complicated than I thought," I panted, every part of me aching with effort after an attempt to bring Stoyan down by edging him just slightly off balance so he would fall at a subtle push to the back of the knee combined with a particular grip on the wrist. "I thought it was a simple matter of brute force. I didn't expect to have to calculate exactly the right way to stand or the perfect spot to push."

"You learn quickly," Stoyan said, bending to pick up my

sash, which had come undone during our contest. "Our audience does not disturb your concentration?"

I followed his glance and spotted five or six seamen clustered at a vantage point above us. Our activities must have made an entertaining diversion from their daily work. Embarrassed, I looked away, wrapping the sash around my waist over Duarte's tunic, which was getting rather grubby. "At least they're not singing now," I said.

"I have heard this Paula song, but I do not know its meaning. I hope the words are not offensive."

I felt very awkward. *"Paula, of a natural pallor, makes a rose blush,"* I muttered, not meeting his eye. *"Graceful seagull, the prettiest sailor on our ship.* Duarte translated it for me."

"I see," Stoyan said. "Well, it is accurate. But these sailors see only the outer beauty; their verse says nothing of your courage, Paula, nor of your honesty and strength. This is a beauty far deeper than the blush of a rose." Without another word, he turned and headed off toward the cabin, leaving me speechless.

Before dusk, a crewman spotted the sails of a three-master behind us, rusty red against the slate gray of the sky. He called to Pero, who swore and fetched Duarte. It didn't matter that Stoyan and I could not understand what they were saying. It was clear the pursuer was on our tail.

Commands rang out, and men moved efficiently to obey, climbing masts, putting on extra sail, doing what could be done to make speed before night fell. I was ordered below, and obeyed. Stoyan remained on deck, a useful extra hand. Alone in the cabin, I sat on the bunk as the ship gained speed, rolling as she went. What would happen if we were boarded?

Would Stoyan come down to protect me or fall in some bloody encounter above my head, leaving me as prey for an attacker? I eyed the bound strongbox that housed Cybele's Gift. Suddenly, this seemed an awful lot of fuss for one little statue.

"What if they're all killed?" I whispered, half to the bee goddess, half to myself. I thought of the crewmen and their song; I thought of Pero asking eagerly if he could be taught to read. I considered Duarte with his delightful dimples and his sharp wit; I pictured Stoyan at the han by night, his fingers gentle against my face as he whispered away my terror. "This is wrong," I murmured. "This can't be what you want."

The sky was covered with heavy cloud. With the waxing moon obscured, there could be no sailing after nightfall. Fortunately, if we could not go on, neither could the red-sailed vessel, unless she was crewed by bats and owls. Stoyan came down to tell me the crewmen were running the *Esperança* into a narrow inlet for the night. Duarte had ordered all lights to be extinguished as soon as possible; there would be no games this evening. We would move on as soon as the sky began to lighten. Everyone was praying for a favorable wind. Duarte, Stoyan said, was consulting over a chart with Pero and two other crewmen.

After passing on his information, Stoyan went silent. As for me, I was still pondering the remark he'd made earlier about inner beauty. His words had made my cheeks grow hot. What did this mean? Duarte and Irene had both on occasion tried to imply that Stoyan harbored feelings for me beyond those appropriate between a merchant's daughter and her bodyguard. I recognized there was a bond between us now that went far beyond my friendship with, say, my two brothers-in-law. Those nights at the han had been like something that belonged in a different part of my life from everything else: a place that was secret, private, special.

I reminded myself that we were on a pirate ship, headed for an unknown destination with someone dangerous on our tail. Under the circumstances, I could not afford to spend time mulling over what Stoyan might or might not think of me and whether or not it was inappropriate. I'd got us into enough of a mess already without creating further complications.

Stoyan sat on the floor in his usual spot, in the dark, and I sat on the bed.

"What if they catch up?" I mused. "Will they board us? I'm sure these men would fight hard. They may not care about Cybele's Gift, but they worship Duarte. They'd die for him, every last one of them, I'm certain. I'd much rather not die yet, Stoyan. I've got so many more things I want to do. I wonder if they can sail the *Esperança* out of trouble?"

No response.

"I thought Tati might come back," I said. "There's been one more sister on her embroidery each time she manifested, and she hasn't shown me Stela yet, the youngest. If we saw her on the ship, it would confirm that this is part of the mission we're supposed to accomplish."

"We?" murmured Stoyan.

"You and I. And Duarte, I suppose. I wish he'd tell us exactly where we're going."

"I will do so." Duarte's voice came from the doorway, and a moment later he stepped over Stoyan's legs and entered the cabin, a tall shadow coming to perch on the edge of the bunk. This time I did not move away. "We have made a decision about tomorrow, and it is time for me to explain that to you, as well as some other matters. Then you must rest."

"What about tomorrow?" I asked nervously. "Can we outsail them, Duarte?"

"We must do so." His voice held a darkness of its own; its intensity scared me. "Their vessel seems of similar size and capability to the *Esperança*. However, there is one element they lack: a crew to equal mine. If the pursuer remains within sight after a morning's sailing, there is a particular option we can take. It is dangerous; I will not lie to you. By midday we will be close to a place where the land juts out in a large promontory on which steep cliffs rise from the water's edge. A mountain range lies not far inland. I believe certain conditions will be in place when we reach that area allowing us to utilize a wind that comes down over the mountains, then creates a powerful, funneling effect around the promontory. A columnate wind, the phenomenon is called. The closer to the cliffs we sail, the more speed we can make. That way we can open sufficient distance so the Mufti's crew loses sight of us until after nightfall. From that point on, I believe I can evade them."

"Dangerous, you say," said Stoyan when it became apparent I was not going to comment. "How dangerous? What are our chances of surviving such a maneuver with the ship intact and no lives lost?"

I imagined Duarte's fierce grin in the dark.

"Better than those of the other ship," the pirate said. "And I prefer them greatly to the prospect of a hand-to-hand battle should the pursuer overtake us and attempt to board. My men are sailors, not warriors. They can account for themselves with sword or club, but I would rather they did not have to."

"This may seem like a silly question," I said, trying not to sound shaky, "but I imagine falling overboard in that area you mentioned, near the cliffs, would mean one could not swim to land. Yes?"

"I will keep you safe, Paula." Stoyan's tone was steady as a rock, and I felt marginally better for it, even though I doubted his capacity to save me from deep waters, strong winds, and precipitous cliffs all at the same time.

"It's not decided yet." Duarte remained calm. "I wanted to warn you, since tomorrow will be a busy day, and if we must attempt that maneuver, nobody will have time for explanations."

"You said that in due course you would tell us about our destination," Stoyan said. "Is now the time for that?"

Duarte cleared his throat. "Very well. Let us assume tomorrow's sailing is successful, we outrun the pursuer and lose him, we continue on a certain distance to the east. Two more days of sailing, by Pero's estimation. Our landfall will be in a settlement so small it is not recorded on maps. There I will be put ashore with the artifact while the ship is taken to a place of concealment not far away to await my return. There is a track from that settlement up into the mountains— it is a region of high peaks and thick vegetation, a place of much rain. To take Cybele's Gift home requires the crossing of a mountain pass. A steep and arduous climb. I will take only a small party with me. On the other side of the pass is a village, remote and . . . unusual. It is to that place that the artifact must be returned."

Stoyan and I both spoke at once.

"Is that where—"

"A party, what—"

"You would ask, is that where one might find the other part of Cybele's Gift?" Duarte's voice was very soft. "So I have been told, Paula. Maybe the rumors that attracted the Mufti's attention are accurate. Maybe someone has revived the cult of Cybele in the heart of Istanbul. But its true observance belongs not in that great trading city but in the most obscure of mountain villages, where a community that has loved and guarded the statue for generations is awaiting its return. The goddess Cybele is said to have retreated from this world long ago, when humankind had become deaf to the old messages of the earth that are so central to her lore. This mountain was her most holy of places, and the people who dwelt high on its flank were entrusted with her last words of wisdom, inscribed on a little statue formed in her likeness. Many years ago, an unscrupulous man found the secret village and attempted to steal the artifact. In that raid, the statue was broken. Half was taken away. Half remained with the mountain folk, held safe until the other should be returned and Cybele mended again."

I tried to take all this in. "If that's true," I said, thinking hard, "why are you the only person who seems to know about it? What are your sources?"

"This mission was laid on me by a man born and bred in that place, a man who saved my life at the price of his own. He told me everything I know about Cybele's Gift, including details of its appearance. I believe I was the only bidder un-surprised when the statue was revealed at the house of Barsam the Elusive."

There was a silence while we contemplated this. Then Stoyan said, "This mission is a debt of honor for you?"

"Acquired when I was young and still testing myself against the world," said Duarte. "I come from a merchant family, respectable, prosperous, but I had turned my back on them in a foolish desire to prove myself unaided. Mustafa and I were crew together on a spice ship. He spoke much of the remote place of his birth. He hoped in time to earn suffi-cient silver to set out on a very particular quest. Mustafa hoped he might find the missing piece of this statue that was so central to the faith of his home community and return it there. Each night he muttered a prayer to Cybele that she would help him find what he sought and deliver him safely home to his loved ones.

"There was a shipwreck. My friend and I found ourselves washed up on an unknown shore together. We were set upon by tribesmen and imprisoned in a little hut, injured and weak. I think they believed us to be devils. Peering out through the cracks in this meager dwelling, I could see preparations for a ritual killing, perhaps to be carried out at dawn. We discovered a chink through which escape might be possible, if we were prepared to risk the jungle and its wild creatures. But Mustafa's leg was broken; he could not walk. At first, I refused to leave without him. 'I will carry you,' I said, knowing we would not get far. 'No,' he said. 'Go. Live.' I told him, 'I will not go without you. What about your mis-sion? What about Cybele's Gift?' Mustafa smiled through his pain. 'You will find it for me,' he said. 'Fair trade. I give you a life. You give my people a future. Go, Duarte. I will talk through the night to cover your escape. Go now!'

"I hope I never again have to make such a choice. I do not know, still, if I did right or wrong. I squeezed out of the hut and fled into the jungle. I left Mustafa to his fate. The rest of the story is unimportant. All I brought home from that unfortunate voyage were the rags on my back and my debt of honor. Mustafa's mission had become mine. I have searched for Cybele's Gift a long time. I will not let anyone stop me from taking it back. Not even the Sheikh-ul-Islam."

We rewarded this narrative with a few moments' respectful silence. There was no doubt Duarte was telling the truth. His voice was trembling with emotion. As for the future of Cybele's Gift, I realized I would have to rethink my attitude toward it. If there was indeed a place where folk still believed in the bee goddess and pinned their hopes on the return of this symbol, it was hard to argue that the artifact belonged anywhere else. Even a scholarly and respectful collector such as the one for whom Father had been working could not better such a claim. With a certain sadness, I felt my belief in the mission that had brought Father and me all the way to Istanbul slipping away.

"How many men do you plan to take ashore?" Stoyan asked Duarte. "A climb through a mountain pass, you said. How long will that take, and what if the ship is attacked while you are gone?"

"I will take as few as possible. A small party will be quicker, but there must be enough so we can defend ourselves if necessary. Pero has volunteered. The ship will be concealed; you should be quite safe. If the *Esperança* can set my party down, then sail to its waiting point unobserved, I do not think the pursuer will track us. The village is difficult to reach, isolated and small. Those who seek to take Cybele's Gift from me will only find the place by walking in my footsteps. I wish to ensure they cannot do so."

All through this speech, I was becoming increasingly edgy. Duarte had no way of knowing that the powers of the Other Kingdom had decided Stoyan and I had a quest, too. If there was some old friend of Drǎguţa, the wood witch, in this part of the world, someone who needed a favor, Mustafa's mountain village sounded just the kind of place where we might find her. It would be remiss of me not to warn Duarte. It seemed to me that he might not fulfill his mission unless both of us helped him. I hesitated.

"You have little to say, Paula." Duarte's voice came through a darkness in which I was aware that the movement of the ship had lessened and the sounds of voices from above had quieted. The *Esperança* had reached tonight's safe mooring. "Can it be that you do not believe me?"

"I do believe you, Duarte," I said, realizing I was clutching my hands together nervously and making myself relax them. "Stoyan and I have something to tell you. We have listened to your tale. Now you should listen to ours, because I believe it may be tied up with what you plan to do."

"Very well."

I told him everything. That my sister, who lived in a world beyond the human one, had come to us and told us about a quest. I spoke of her appearance on this very ship the day we reached Istanbul. I outlined the strange happenings in Irene's library, the manuscript pages I suspected had been set out for me to find, the tree puzzle, the miniatures that seemed like clues to a task we were bid to undertake. I repeated the cryptic words: *Find the heart, for there lies wisdom. The crown is the destination* and *Make me whole*. When I was finished, there were a few moments of utter silence. Then Duarte chuckled.

"Well, Paula, you are an imaginative storyteller. I place no credence in the supernatural. I acknowledge that such beliefs remain strong in isolated places and amongst those who have good reason to adhere to them—the simpler kind of seafaring men, for instance. Folk cling to their gods and spirits in hope of finding comfort and meaning in difficult lives, and the return of items like Cybele's Gift provides such people with heart and purpose. But I would not expect an educated young woman to have a head full of visions, dreams, and wild imaginings. Perhaps your true calling is not as a scholar but as a writer of diverting romances for the entertainment of noble ladies."

A tumult of emotions churned inside me: anger, hurt, bitter disappointment that this man I'd been beginning to trust and to like very much had dismissed the precious secret I had confided in him as if it were nonsense. I sat there, mute, as furious tears welled in my eyes. I held them back and found words.

"You're a fool," I told Duarte bluntly. "I have firsthand experience of such phenomena—not dreams and visions but reality. During the years of my childhood, I regularly visited a place beyond the human world. That was a magical time, the best time of my whole life, and that realm was just as real as my everyday world. The two exist side by side. One is not fact and the other imagination. They are equal but different. If you cannot accept that, then I believe your mission is doomed to failure, because what Stoyan and I have been shown tells me you cannot succeed without us. Dismiss that at your peril."

"Paula is right." Stoyan's voice was deep and certain. "I did not wish to say this, for the last thing I want is to see her put in still more danger. But I believe, Senhor Duarte, that unless she accompanies you up this mountain of yours, your quest cannot be achieved. And where she goes, I go. You have no choice but to take both of us with you."

Chapter Eleven

The next day, after sailing eastward from first light until the sun was roughly overhead, we still had not shaken off the red sails of our pursuer. I went up on deck to use the rudimentary privy and washing facilities and caught sight of our captain with Pero by the rail, the two of them shading their eyes as they gazed intently forward. I followed their gaze and my heart skipped a beat.

"Those are the cliffs he spoke of, no doubt," said Stoyan, coming to stand beside me. A massive rock face rose above the sea a few miles ahead of us. It was formidable, a bastion. Behind it were the purple-green forms of mountains, the highest of them capped with snow. I considered my single set of borrowed clothing, in which I often got quite cold up on deck. If that was where Duarte intended to walk, I was not sure I wanted to go with him.

"I thought he was crazy before," I said. "Now I'm sure of it."

"And he believes we are out of our wits, the two of us—

you because of a young girl's overactive imagination, and I because . . ."

"Because of what? An excess of duty?"

Stoyan shrugged. "I can imagine what he thinks."

I didn't press the issue, for Duarte was striding over to us now, looking grim. "We'll be there soon," he told us. "You'd best go below, Paula. Once we come close to the cliffs, get into a small space and try to keep hold of something solid. If we need to tack to take advantage of the wind, things will get uncomfortable for you. Make sure everything is in the boxes or trunks, safely stowed."

I nodded, my words deserting me, and headed for the ladder down to the cabins. Stoyan came behind me.

"Not you," Duarte said. "We'll need every able-bodied man on deck. Don't look like that; Paula's capable of fending for herself. We need those muscles of yours."

In the cabin, I stowed everything in perfect order, then wedged myself into a corner, knowing that beyond the porthole the wall of cliffs must be looming closer and closer. I had lashed the strongbox that held Cybele's Gift to the foot of the bunk with a length of rope. I might break if we had an accident, but with luck she wouldn't. And since this whole sorry affair was because of her, that seemed the right order of priorities.

"I'm your best chance," I told her. "You keep me safe and I'll do the same for you. I just wish I knew what it is Stoyan and I have to do. Help Duarte get you over the mountains safely? Or something more?" The quests set by the Other Kingdom were always designed to make human folk grow and learn and lead better lives by achieving whatever task it was. They'd done it to Jena and Costi and they'd done it to Tati and Sorrow. They'd tried to do it to my cousin Cezar, but it had been too late for him to mend his ways; he had not been able to learn. "Why can't I work it out?" I whispered.

I did not expect an answer, spectral or otherwise, and I got none. Before I could draw another breath, the *Esperança* leaned heavily to starboard, and I was pressed back against the wall, my stomach dropping in terror. After a little, the ship righted herself, and I got up, staggering over to the port-hole and dragging out the stool to balance on it and look out. A wall of stone confronted me for an instant; then a wave of white water buffeted the glazed window as the ship heeled over the other way.

I crept back to the bunk and hugged the blanket around my shoulders. I wondered if God would be angry if I prayed to him now, since I had not been particularly good about seeking out an Orthodox church in Istanbul. Some had been converted to mosques when the Turks took over the city, but the Sultan had allowed several to remain open for Istanbul's Christian residents. It was a long time since Father or I had attended a service.

I muttered a prayer, the kind that comes out of abject fear, in which I said I was sorry for a lot of things, such as losing my temper too quickly and not taking time to think before I spoke, and in particular for deserting my father and causing him grief. I asked God to keep Father safe and well, and to protect all of us on this voyage, and to look after my sisters, the three who were back home in Transylvania and the one in the Other Kingdom. "And look after Stoyan," I said. "He's the grandson of a . . . a znaharka, I think it was. That's some-thing like a white witch, the human kind. Some folk frown on people like that. Some folk believe all manifestations of the Other Kingdom are evil, that they're the same as the devil. But I don't think that can be true. I think all things exist together and their destinies are tied up together, like a great book of stories that weave and pass and thread through one another, making the most astonishing tale anyone could dream up. Keep us all safe, Heavenly Father, and please, please help me work out what my mission is. I need to know what I'm supposed to learn from this."

I did feel slightly better after that. But only slightly; the *Esperança* was creaking and groaning like a huge, dying creature, and beyond the porthole it was almost dark. How close to the cliffs would Duarte sail? Was he so reckless, or in such haste, that he would risk battering his beloved ship to smithereens?

It was probably a good thing that I could not see out properly without staggering to the porthole and climbing up. Glancing over, I thought perhaps it was underwater for a bit. My teeth were chattering. I clenched them together until my jaw ached, then buried my face in the blanket, pressing my back into the corner. I felt how fast the ship was moving, hurled forward by the fearsome funneling of the wind. I saw it in my mind, the vessel skirting so close to the cliff face that scraps of sail caught on rocky protuberances and tore off, the gale so strong the men on deck struggled not to be blown bodily overboard, the masts bending and flexing under the strain of yards and yards of wind-stretched canvas. It was insanity. I was too scared even to cry.

The *Esperança* changed tack again, everything tipping the other way, and a groan of protest shuddered through her timbers. I fell off the bunk and landed in a heap on the boards of the cabin floor, jarring my elbow and bruising my knee. There was shouting from the deck, a series of commands and responses, and we barreled forward like a piece of debris washing down a chute, as if even the crazy pace of that last run had not been quite quick enough for our captain. I lay where I had fallen, one hand gripping on to the bunk to stop me from sliding helplessly around the floor. My arm hurt, and my leg. Tears came to my eyes, stupid tears, for if a person was going to drown anyway, what did a few scrapes and bruises matter?

"Paula!"

A pair of large boots appeared at eye level; then a pair of strong arms reached down and lifted me up, depositing me gently on the bunk in a sitting position. I held on to Stoyan as if he were a lifeline, burying my head against his chest.

"You are hurt? You fell?"

"It's nothing," I muttered against the none-too-clean wool of his tunic. "I'm fine. How much longer?"

"Not long. I will stay with you."

"Don't they need you up there?" I sniffed, the tears really flowing now that I felt almost all right again. It was amazing what a difference it made, not being alone.

"I do not care what they need. I will stay with you." His words sent an odd feeling through me, like the ringing of a low, soft bell or the sudden sensation of falling into deep water. Then his arms came around me, more tentative than his voice. He had held me like this once before, for comfort, and I had accepted it gratefully without thinking beyond that. But something had shifted between us on this voyage, and I knew this time was different. With my cheek pressed against Stoyan's heart and his body warming mine, I had a clear image of my sister Iulia, the one who was knowledgeable about men, lifting her brows and saying to me, *This is only natural, Paula. You're a healthy young woman; he's a fine-looking man. What else do you expect? Just don't make it into something it can't be, that's all. He's a farmer, uneducated and penniless. He's a foreigner. Imagine what Aunt Bogdana would say!* As the wind carried us on through churning waves and blinding spray, past murderous cliffs and jagged rocks, I sheltered in Stoyan's arms and pondered this. At last, the *Esperança* sailed into the smoother waters of a wide bay. We had survived the suicide run, and when we disengaged ourselves a little awkwardly and ventured on deck, it was to find that the red sails of the pursuing vessel were nowhere to be seen.

We sailed out of the bay on an easterly course. The necessary things happened on the run: an inspection of the ship to ascertain whether she had sustained any damage—it seemed not—and hasty individual trips to pick up rations from Cristiano. I smiled at him and he gave me a double scoop of olives.

"You survived, then," observed Duarte laconically as Stoyan and I walked past him on our way to a sheltered corner where we could eat our meal.

"What did you imagine?" I raised my brows at the captain. "That I would expire from a fit of the vapors? I'm made of stronger stuff than that, Duarte. They tell me we've made good distance and lost the pursuer. Your gamble paid off."

"I don't gamble. Not where human lives are concerned. I was certain we could do it. Almost certain. Now we are ahead, and we must stay ahead. I hope to reach the place the day after tomorrow, by midday if we are lucky. The moon is waxing; we may attempt to make some progress by night. If there is any chance the pursuer can sail by moonlight, we must do the same."

"Your crew will be tired."

"I am not as heartless as you imagine. They sleep in shifts, a few hours at a time. Once we make landfall, there will be no rest for those who continue on foot until Cybele's Gift is safely delivered." There seemed to be a question in his eyes.

"Then it's fortunate you are taking us," I said. "We, of everyone, have the best opportunity for sleep, thanks to your generosity in allowing us the use of your cabins."

Duarte regarded me through slitted eyes. "I have made no decision on that matter," he said. "It's a hard climb, and I'm not convinced you can keep up."

"I see you have decided not to take me seriously," I said in withering tones. "I thought you had better judgment. Come, Stoyan, I'm getting the impression Senhor Aguiar doesn't want us here."

"Not at all," came Duarte's mocking voice from behind us. "Baiting you is great entertainment."

"Let it go, Stoyan," I warned as my companion's cheeks flushed angry red. "He means nothing by it. And if he does end up taking us with him, we're all going to have to cooperate whether we like it or not."

"With one breath he praises you, with the next he insults you. What is his game?"

"Sheer mischief," I said, sitting beside him on a wooden shelf out of everyone's way and wondering whether to eat the olives first, while I was hungry, or save them until last.

"Or maybe nobody ever taught him good manners. Would you like some of these olives? I have extra."

We reached our destination at the time Duarte had predicted. It was at that point I realized there were some possibilities even our well-organized captain had not allowed for in his planning. For the last few miles, we had sailed close to the southern coastline, and Stoyan and I had stayed on deck, well wrapped in borrowed cloaks, watching with awe as the mountains marched closer and closer to the water, their dark forms towering over us, their upper reaches thick with vegetation until the blanket of trees gave way to stark, rocky peaks patched with snow. Pero came up to me, pointed ahead, and said, "Village there. High path. We come soon." We had almost reached our landfall. Not that it mattered so much now. Duarte had told us we could not come with him.

The village had a scattering of low buildings and a little wooden mosque with a single minaret. The *Esperança* sailed into the bay, ready to drop anchor while a rowing boat ferried Duarte's party ashore. Stoyan and I were to remain with the ship, in hiding, until he and Pero, with three other men, returned from their mission. There had been no point in pleading with him. On the surface, his decision made good sense. I willed Tati to appear and explain to Duarte that he was making a terrible mistake, but she did not. The cruelest thing about this was that if I failed to complete my own mission, that would mean Tati failed hers as well.

The rowing boat was about to be lowered into the water when Duarte gave a sharp, one-word order. The men who were untying the ropes paused.

A flag was being raised in the settlement: a black flag. Pero crossed himself, muttering in Portuguese. I heard him say *peste*, and the men close at hand echoed the same word as the color drained from their faces. As we watched, a boat headed out from the shore with two men rowing. They came within shouting distance, shipped their oars, and called in Turkish across the water between us. Duarte shouted a response in the same tongue, asking a question. When the reply came, he gave a series of quick orders to the crew. We put on canvas. The *Esperança* shuddered and creaked and turned, and we sailed out of the bay. *Peste.* I did not know any Portuguese, but I did know Latin. The word meant "plague."

The charts came back out. Duarte and Pero pored over them as the ship headed along the coast to the east and the mountains lowered on our starboard flank.

"I can't see anywhere at all where there could be a track over," I said to Stoyan. "What do you think he'll do?"

Stoyan frowned. "He will not return home," he said. "Such a man never abandons his mission. Besides, he must continue to evade this pursuer. He will search for another way."

We gazed up at the impossible slopes, where mountain goats, if they were especially nimble, might perhaps find a path.

"I don't suppose it's our problem anymore," I was saying when I caught sight of it out of the corner of my eye: a tattered scrap of black against the white of the *Esperança*'s bellying sails. I hardly dared turn lest she vanish the moment I did so. "Stoyan," I hissed.

"What?" He had heard the change in my voice and answered in hushed tones.

"She's there. Tati. I can see her up amongst the sails. Over there, near the mainmast."

After a moment, while we both pretended not to be looking, Stoyan said, "I see her, Paula. What now?"

"She's pointing," I said. "That way, back toward the shore but beyond that rocky headland to the east of us." Still I did not turn directly toward her, but I could see her figure perched improbably halfway up, her feet on a spar, one hand clutching the mast, the other gesturing with confidence in the direction I had mentioned, as if to command the course of the ship. I could not see what lay beyond the headland; the mountains seemed as impassable as they were here, but maybe there was a path. On the deck and on watch atop the mast, crewmen went about their business as if there were no robed woman clinging to the timbers of their ship. It seemed she was invisible to them.

"She's fading," said Stoyan, and before our eyes the dark figure wavered and broke up and vanished. "Do we tell him?"

"Maybe we don't need to," I said, seeing Duarte coming across the deck toward us. I addressed the captain with what confidence I could muster. "There could be plague all the way along this shore. You realize that, I suppose?" I said. "Landing anywhere nearby might risk the lives of your entire crew. May we see your maps?"

Duarte was looking haggard. "Why not?" he said flatly, as if it hardly mattered.

Pero showed us our current position on the map and the site of the stricken village. I shivered to think of that. Plague had spread across our region more than once and had swept whole towns and districts bare of living souls. It was indiscriminate, taking men, women, and children alike, the poor, the wealthy, the wicked, and the saintly. That settlement had looked so small. I imagined the inhabitants perhaps gathered at their little mosque to pray, fewer by the day. I imagined mothers watching their children die or children left alone, confused and helpless. The worst thing was, there was nothing to be done about it. To land and offer assistance was to invite a death sentence. Still, it had felt bad to sail on by.

I found what I thought was the big headland, and beyond it a pair of narrow, slitlike bays. The map was lacking in detail. I could not tell if any paths led up the mountains from one or the other of these.

"You could put in here," I said, stabbing the spot with my finger. "There may well be a way up into the mountains, perhaps a path that meets the one you intended to walk. And the ship could anchor in the second bay, out of sight. Of course, you may find plague in the settlement over the pass; it might be everywhere in the region. That's your risk, which I suppose you must take on behalf of your whole party. You could always sail back to Istanbul, taking care to evade the Mufti's vessel. You've got a fine crew. They could do it."

Duarte looked at me, his dark eyes inscrutable. "Put yourself in my place," he said, for once not mocking but entirely serious. "What would your decision be?"

I blinked, surprised. "I could not make it so quickly," I said. "I know which choice is right but . . . I understand what it means to be dedicated to a mission, too. My head and my heart would do battle over it. I would need time to decide."

"I have no time. We are here, and sooner or later the other ship will find us. If we go ahead, it must be quickly."

I looked at Duarte closely. There were lines on his face that I had not noticed before, grooves between his nose and the corners of his mouth that made him look older. His dark brows were drawn into a frown. "You have a little time," I said. "Until we sail around the headland and into the bay, and then until we see if there's a path. You could talk to your crew."

He gave a curt nod, then turned his back and went to the rail, where he stood looking ahead as the *Esperança* sailed on a steady course toward the promontory. I remembered how I had said before that I believed his crew would die for him. That was what he had to decide now: whether to put them in the path of death.

Without further talk, Stoyan and I went down to the cabin. It was cold. Out on the water, at times it was hard to believe the season was late spring. I held my cloak around me, watching Stoyan as he stood by the porthole staring out. He was tall enough to do so without standing on anything; indeed, he had to stoop a little.

"This is hard for Duarte," I said. "It's one thing asking his men to defend him against attackers; I expect they do that quite often. It's quite another expecting them to enter what may be a plague village. What if he got there with Cybele's Gift and found everyone dead?" A shiver ran through me; I could see the scene, what should have been a triumph turned to ashes. "He can't attempt the climb alone. That would be foolhardy. If he sails back to Istanbul, he'll be sacrificing the mission. And putting himself in the way of the Sheikh-ul-Islam."

"So what would your answer be?"

"I don't know. Imagine watching a friend die of plague, knowing you could have prevented it. Can a mission really be worth that?"

"I ask myself," Stoyan said solemnly, "what would my choice be if I had to risk the lives of companions, of friends, in order to find my brother. Not so long ago, I would have told you yes, I would do so without hesitation."

I waited for more, but it was not forthcoming. "And now?" I asked him.

"I believe that, like you, I could not do it. That I could not bear what might ensue. And that wounds me; it is as if I have set Taidjut aside." His voice was full of pain now.

"Then we must both be glad the decision is not ours to make," I said quietly. "Do you think of him all the time? Taidjut?"

"I count the grief I have caused, the losses, in my quest to find him. Salem bin Afazi, slain through my neglect of my duties, because I asked for leave to follow a thread of information. Your father, alone and unprotected in Istanbul because I did not keep a proper watch on you. Others before. I have acquitted myself miserably, Paula."

I stood and laid a comforting hand on his back. "You'll find him, Stoyan," I said. "You're strong of heart. And you've acquitted yourself bravely. When things went wrong, it was not your doing. It's my fault entirely that you and I are in our current predicament."

I pondered the future. If Duarte decided not to risk the climb, we could be back in Istanbul sooner than we had expected, and I would be able to end Father's anxiety. He and I would sail back home, and Stoyan could pick up his search for his lost brother again. That was good. But I was filled with sadness: for those who were suffering in that little village, for Stoyan and Taidjut, for Duarte, torn between the duty laid on him by his friend's sacrifice and his responsibility to his crew. And what about Cybele's Gift? How could I set aside my own mission? How could I ignore my sister?

"Maybe the decision will be made for us," I said. A cold feeling came over me, a certainty that what I had just said was true. "Maybe . . ." No, I refused to believe the plague had somehow been sent so that we would land in another bay, take another path, do the will of the Other Kingdom. That was too dark a possibility to be contemplated.

"What is wrong, Paula?" Stoyan turned, putting a hand on my shoulder.

"Nothing, I . . . no, nothing." I shivered, drawing the cloak tighter. "I just . . ." I realized that I was afraid. "Stoyan . . ."

"What? You frighten me, Paula, when you look like that. Come, sit down." He sat me on the bunk, squatting in front of me, unclamping my hands from the cloak and putting his around them. "Now tell me."

I shook my head. "It's nothing. A fit of the vapors. But stay there, please." His grasp was warm; it pushed the fear away a little. Soon, very soon, I suspected, nothing would have the power to do that.

After a while, Duarte came down to the cabin. We had sailed around the promontory and were heading into the first of the narrow bays. Stoyan had got up from time to time to look out and report to me. I was trying to read aloud—*Aesop's Fables*—and he was seated on the floor with his back against the bunk, next to my legs. It was extremely hard to concentrate.

"I have a question to ask you." Our captain was standing in the doorway, hands up on the frame, expression neutral.

"Both of us?" I asked, closing the book and feeling my heart pick up its pace.

"Stoyan only. If I find a track from this bay or the next, will you come up the mountain with me?"

We stared at him in stunned silence.

"I cannot," Stoyan said after a little. "My place is with Paula. You cannot expect her to put herself in the path of plague. And if she stays on the boat, I do not go."

"And if she comes, too?" Duarte's dark gaze moved to me.

Now I was really cold. I knew why I had been afraid. At no point in the journey thus far had I really believed that I might die. Perhaps that was not quite true; the whirlwind sail around the cliffs had had its moments. But this . . . "Before, you said you wouldn't take us," I said, trying to sound calm. "What has changed your mind?"

Duarte gave a bitter smile. "If I could go alone, I would," he said. "But I must have two men with me at least, one as a guard, a second to come back for help if one of us is injured. Pero has volunteered. Stoyan is the strongest man on board, an unparalleled fighter."

"And the others?" I asked, knowing the answer before he spoke.

"Pero is a friend; we understand each other. I will not ask the others to risk their lives out of personal loyalty. Accidents, mishaps, bandits, yes. Plague, no."

"You didn't ever consider not going yourself?" I queried, clutching my hands together to conceal the way they were shaking. Because, of course, I did want to go. Despite the plague, despite the danger, I still believed I was meant to go.

"No. Paula, will you release Stoyan from his obligation to you? My crew will keep you safe. They will treat you with respect. You have my word—"

"I said no." Stoyan's voice was heavy with finality. "I will not go, and neither will Paula. She stays, and I am her guard. Take your little statue and make your climb, pirate, and if your loyal mate loses his life to those ills you list—bandits, accidents, plague—live with the knowledge of that. You will not take Paula with you."

Duarte's brows shot up. For a moment, he looked like his old self. "Ah, but Paula is very much her own woman," he said. "I thought you'd have learned that by now. Besides, she's your employer, unless I've got things wrong. Why don't we let her answer?"

God help me. I had to say yes; everything that had happened up till now made that clear. A force beyond the worldly wanted Cybele's Gift returned. My instincts and the messages of the Other Kingdom told me all three of us were required to make that happen. I was prepared to go. Terrified, but willing. I was not so sure I was ready to put Stoyan in the path of plague.

"We need to talk about this alone," I told Duarte. "Stoyan and I."

"There's no time." The captain's features had a set look.

"It won't take long. Please."

He went out without a word, and I got to my feet. Stoyan stood, too, his face ashen in the bright light from the porthole. His scar made a sharp line across his cheek; his lips were pressed together.

"I don't want to argue with you," I said. "I believe I must do this. But I don't want you to come because of duty, because it's your job to look after me and protect me. I couldn't bear to put you in such peril because of that, Stoyan."

"That was the reason you hired me. As a bodyguard."

"Then I'll unhire you, if that makes this any easier. Consider yourself no longer in my employment. You are your own man, and you can make your decision based only on your own wishes. You can make it not as a bodyguard but as a . . . friend." My voice had started to shake. I so much wanted him to come with me, but I shrank from the prospect of watching him perish from plague, or in combat, or from cold or injury. I realized, with a jolt of the heart, that I would not be able to bear it. I reached out and took his hand, and his fingers closed around mine. I had never seen him like this; he looked stricken.

"I will ask you one question, Paula," he said.

"Ask, then."

"You will go, I see that, despite anything I may say or do. I know you. I know how determined you are. Do you want me to come with you?"

I nodded, tears of relief and sadness brimming in my eyes.

"Then I will come," Stoyan said on a sigh.

"Duarte!" I called, and he was there in the doorway again; probably he'd heard the whole thing. Side by side, Stoyan and I faced him, our hands still clasped. "We'll come," I said. "Both of us. It's what we're meant to do. But no more mockery. No more dismissive remarks. We'll do our best to help you, and you'll treat us with respect, as equal members of your party. Now ask Pero to find us some really warm clothing. It looks as if we're going to be up there overnight."

Four crewmen rowed us ashore and waited while we searched for a path. The shore was rocky here with only a tiny flat patch for landing, and the tree cover came down almost to the water. The pitch of the hillside was steep. There was no obvious track up from the shore. We were about to give up and sail around to investigate the second cove when Stoyan, who had scrambled higher up the rocks, called out, "Here!"

There was a tree there, a juniper that crawled over the stony ground and up the rock wall with a tenacity like that of a strong old woman. Its gnarled branches were festooned with offerings, scraps of cloth, lengths of colored wool, snippets of braid, human hair twisted and tied, beads, fraying threads, and tarnished buckles. Behind it, the slightest of gaps in the close-growing foliage could be observed. Nearby, a tiny stream of freshwater trickled through a natural channel in the rock to fill a bowllike indentation before spilling over and down into the sea. Stoyan's eyes met mine, questioning, and I gave a nod. Everything about this place suggested the Other Kingdom. When Duarte and Pero climbed up to us, I said, "This is the way."

Duarte peered up between the trees, looking doubtful. He began to say something, then closed his mouth, perhaps remembering he had promised not to make dismissive remarks. "All right," he said, "for want of anything better, we'll try it."

A little later we headed off up the mountain, the vista of

open sea behind us rapidly disappearing as we entered a realm of damp, dark forest. The small boat would be taken back out to the *Esperança,* which would sail into the neighboring bay and wait for our return. They would row around to look for us the day after tomorrow, and then every day until we reappeared.

The men carried packs. I had offered to bear my own supplies, but Stoyan would have none of it. My blanket, water bottle, and share of the rations were stowed away with his. We all had weapons. Stoyan had given me one of his to put in my belt: a small, very sharp knife in a leather sheath. I could not imagine using it and was not at all sure it made me feel safer. Duarte carried an extra burden. In his pack, liberated from its box and tied up instead in many layers of soft cloth, traveled Cybele's Gift.

It was already late in the day. I knew the most important thing was to get as far as we could while it was still light, then find a place of shelter. We wasted no breath in talking. We climbed, keeping the pace as steady as we could, and for a long time the track went straight up and the terrain remained the same: a dense forest of conifers mixed with broad-leaved oaks and beeches, floored with mud, leaf litter, and, here and there, stony outcrops that were a test for my short legs. Many small streams gushed down the hillside, evidence of heavy spring rains. Each time we stopped to check our progress and catch our breath, Duarte stared at me in apparent amazement.

"Don't look so surprised," I said eventually. "I was born and bred on slopes like these, just as Stoyan was."

"I'm grateful you're not slowing us down," said Duarte. He spoke to Pero in rapid Portuguese, then turned back to us. "If we can reach that big outcrop before the light fades too much further, we may be able to see whether this track meets the one we wanted. No point in going up if we can't get over the—"

He had gone suddenly still, staring up to the rocks he had mentioned, an odd formation that looked a little like a cat's head.

"What?" I asked. "Did you see something?"

Duarte frowned. "I thought—no, it's not there now. Something fluttering, like a flag, up above the rocks. I must have been mistaken."

"What color?" I asked. "Black?"

He gave me a searching look. "Why?"

"Nothing." I had not forgotten the way he dismissed my visions as those of an impressionable young girl. He would learn, I thought. Tati was probably up there even now, beckoning us onward. I hoped very much that she did not expect us to traverse this hillside at night. Very soon the only light would be the moon, and it would be deathly cold.

"You're shivering." Stoyan was by my side, taking my hands between his and massaging them to warm them up. We both wore sheepskin gloves. Mine were several sizes too big, and I could not wear them on the steepest pitches, where I needed to slip my fingers between the rocks to haul myself up.

"I'm all right." Our breath was making clouds before our lips. A thin mist was rising up the slopes, insinuating itself between the trees to wrap around our ankles. "We should move on."

By the time we reached the outcrop, it was clear we would have to camp there for the night. The light was going and with it the last traces of warmth from the air. We halted at the foot of the massive rock formation. Pero and Duarte went off to climb up and assess the wider terrain while they still could. Stoyan and I looked for a place of shelter and found a shallow cave with a patch of open ground in front. He gathered fallen wood for a fire, finding some dryish branches under the natural cover of protruding rocks. I undid the pack and got out our blankets and rations. I found a flint and dry tinder, neatly wrapped in oiled cloth.

"Stoyan, I suppose it is all right for us to make a fire? What about that other ship?"

"Without it, we freeze." Stoyan dragged a larger log across toward the stack he had made. "Your Portuguese friend may be obsessed with his quest, but I do not think he is a fool."

"It may not matter anyway," I said, thinking aloud. "We're well ahead of the Mufti's men, and perhaps it's not so very far to this place." I wouldn't even think about plague. "Maybe the two tracks meet at the top, and we can still go over the pass as Duarte originally intended."

We had the fire crackling by the time the others returned. I saw Duarte's face and spoke before he could. "I know someone might see it. We weighed that against the possibility of dying of cold or being too cramped to go on in the morning. This is our decision." He raised his eyebrows but said nothing. "Duarte, what could you see from up there?"

"Nothing conclusive. We should go on up at first light. This track must lead somewhere, and it seems the only possible option for reaching this village, if we cannot use the path from the plague settlement. It's just that . . ."

My heart sank still further. "What?" I asked.

"The map is incomplete, so I must rely on the long-ago account of my shipmate for clues to the way. I have not visited this place before. There seemed no point in that unless I had found Cybele's Gift. I did not think to learn the terrain here, to anticipate difficulties. I should have planned more carefully."

"You couldn't have foreseen plague," I pointed out. "Nor that you would have us with you. What did your shipmate tell you?"

"He did not mention a second path. Indeed, I could swear he said the village was so isolated there was only one track in and out."

"Then why are you suggesting we go on in the morning?" asked Stoyan, frowning. "What is the point of that if you believe this track will not take us to our destination?"

"Wait a bit." I was thinking hard as I held my hands up to the fire, trying to get some feeling back into my fingers. "Perhaps Mustafa wouldn't have told you. Perhaps this path is secret, a way that would only reveal itself to the person who brought back Cybele's Gift." As soon as I said this, I felt instinctively that it was true. "You saw that tree down at the bottom," I added. "Gifts for a deity of some kind, a nature god or goddess—that's the kind of place where folk leave them, an old tree by a spring. A spot where earth meets water. Cybele's path."

"That is more leap of imagination than logical deduction," Duarte said, but he was gazing into the fire as if giving the idea serious consideration.

"No, Duarte," I said. "It's a mixture of scholarship and

intuition. And experience, but I am not going to discuss that part of it with you, since you more or less called me a liar last time I mentioned it. I know about this kind of thing. This is the right path. We just have to keep going up and following the signs."

"Signs?"

"Trust me," I said with more confidence than I felt. "Now, are we going to try cooking, or is supper to be strips of dried meat eaten cold?"

I'd been worrying about our sleeping arrangements. It was one thing to have Stoyan lying on guard across the outer doorway at the han, or in the next-door cabin on the *Esperança* listening for intruders. It was quite another for me, at seventeen, to have to share a small cave with three adult men and to be obliged to lie close to at least one of them to keep even tolerably warm. Now that it was time to bed down for the night, I found myself suddenly bereft of all social confidence. I stood shivering by the fire, wishing I was back home again.

"Here." Pero spoke in halting Greek from within the cave, where he had been quietly laying out bedding. "*Senhora* Paula, Stoyan, Pero, Duarte. Senhora near fire. Good for sleep. Yes?"

"Thank you, Pero," I said. "That arrangement sounds extremely sensible."

Pero grinned at me, showing several gaps in his teeth. "I am father of seven children, senhora. Seven children, two beds. Is the same, yes?"

"Not quite," observed Duarte. "Still, it would take a man

with more fortitude than mine to consider getting up to any tricks when it's as cold as this. Sweet dreams, my friends."

Before he rolled himself into his blanket next to Pero, he set Cybele's Gift in the cave, safely to one side where nobody could harm it with a sudden movement. Within its shroud of wrappings, it cast an odd shadow on the cave wall, round and bulging. *Make me whole.* Tomorrow, perhaps we would do just that.

Even with the fire in front of me and the solid form of Stoyan at my back, I was almost too cold to sleep. I kept dropping off, then waking with a start to the deep silence of the nighttime forest, punctuated by the cries of birds and by vague squeakings and rustlings. The first time I did this, Stoyan adjusted his blanket so it was over the two of us. The second time he murmured something that sounded like poetry as I gradually fell asleep again. The tone was soothing, though I could not understand the language. The third time I woke, trembling with cold, his arm came around me, moving me closer against him, and the chill began to retreat from my body. "Thank you," I whispered. I felt his breath warm against my hair, but now he said nothing at all.

I awoke in the morning groggy with tiredness and sore from lying on the ground, but certainly not cold. As I sat up and rubbed my eyes, I realized that I had four blankets and someone's cloak over me, with a folded jacket under my head. The cave was empty; all the others were up. The fire had been quenched, and Duarte was busy covering the ashes with soil. Pero was stuffing items into a pack.

"I was about to wake you," Stoyan said. He was sitting on the rocks near me with a cup in his hands. "Please drink this. You need something in your stomach before we move on."

I drank. It was a hideous brew of dried meat and stale bread soaked in water; I hoped I would never have to sample it again. Still, it was food and it was warm. They must have only just put out the fire. The sun wasn't even up yet.

"We're heading on straightaway," said Duarte as Pero gathered the blankets, folding and stowing them each in turn. "With luck we'll reach the mountain village while the sun is high and have shelter tonight. I don't want you sleeping out in the open again if it can be avoided."

"I'm an equal member of the expedition, remember?" I said, trying for a smile. "No special privileges, no concessions. Not that I'll refuse a warmer bed if it's offered. Excuse me, I need to go off into the forest for a little."

I was squatting under a tree, making sure none of the men could see me, when a black-robed woman manifested in the shadows nearby: not Tati this time but an old crone, peering at me with her sunken dark eyes, her face as pale and crumpled as worn parchment. She could have been a sister of the ancient juniper down at the water's edge, a thing of old earth, a survivor of many lifetimes of men. I had never felt more exposed or more vulnerable.

"It's time," she said, and once again I did not know what language she spoke, only that I understood it from instinct. "Sharpen your wits. You will have sore need of them before this day is out. Tighten your courage. And watch your balance."

I nodded, wondering if I could ask questions or whether she might vanish if I spoke.

"Remember," she said. "Remember what once seemed

the most important thing of all. And learn. Learn wisdom. Go safely, Paula." And she was gone, not fading away, not stumping off into the forest, not disappearing in a flash and a bang, just . . . gone.

I didn't say anything when I got back to the outcrop, though Duarte observed that I was looking paler than usual and whistled the first line of *Paula, de brancura singela* in a thoughtful sort of way. The men already had their packs on their backs, and we set off up the mountain as the sun appeared above the horizon, veiled by clouds. The first part was steep. We scaled the side of the outcrop to pause on a level patch and gaze out at the view Stoyan and I had missed yesterday: a broad vista over the Black Sea, with headlands to both sides. The mist was rapidly clearing from the tree-clad slopes below us. We could see the *Esperança* at anchor in the next inlet, her sails furled, and several little islands not far from shore. There was a coastal settlement in the distance, a long way farther to the east. And moored in the cove from which we had begun our assault on the mountain, small as a toy on the sheltered water, there floated a stately three-master with sails of an unmistakable russet red.

Chapter Twelve

The pursuers must have sailed by night to catch us. It was possible they'd reached the cove in darkness and begun to climb while we were still asleep. The ascent became a race, and I gritted my teeth and got on with it, determined not to hold the men back. Mountain-bred I might be, but my legs were shorter than everyone else's, and my hands were soon bleeding with the effort of clinging on and hauling myself up.

The men weren't saying much, and nor was I. I tried not to think too hard about what would happen if the pursuers caught up with us. I remembered the Janissary guards at the han, big, well-armed men with purposeful faces. We were only four; who knew how many of them might be climbing after us?

To distract myself, I thought about what the crone had said to me. It seemed I had a job to do and that it was possible for me to succeed at it, provided I followed her instructions. Wits: Yes, I was not short of those. Courage: If I failed there, Stoyan had enough for two. Balance: It depended, I thought as I clambered up a rock face, stretching for an impossible grip, on what kind of balance was meant. Pero reached down from above, seized my wrists, and pulled me bodily up. I gasped a thank-you before tackling the next climb. ·

Remember what once seemed the most important thing of all. What could that be? My family? My home? The Other Kingdom? I hoped I would understand what the old woman had meant before it was too late. As for *Learn wisdom,* I was a scholar, wasn't I? I'd been trying to make myself wiser for years. I pictured the crone stopping the people who were on our trail and giving them the same advice she had offered me. Under the sweat that now coated my body, I felt cold. Perhaps it was a game for her, like chess, black against white, and the four of us a team of king, queen, knight, rook, playing it out on the mountain as if on an inlaid board. Maybe the old woman didn't care who won. Maybe we were just entertainment.

We paused high on the flank of the mountain, beside a field of loose scree. One false step would mean a rapid, sliding descent back to the tree line.

"I can't see a path from this point," Duarte said. "We'll have to find some sort of goat track around those cliffs. But I don't see how that could lead to the place we want; there would have to be a—" He stopped short.

"A what?" I asked, wishing we had not stopped to confer, for the moment I ceased walking, my body began to remind me that it hurt all over and needed a good rest.

"A bridge," Duarte muttered, his eyes distant. "Mustafa mentioned a bridge. Something about taxes and trade."

"It seems unlikely," Stoyan said. "How could trade affect

such an out-of-the-way place? There must be nothing up here but the most isolated villages. Imagine it in winter."

"Maybe there is a back way in," I said. "There is a bigger settlement along the coast to the east; we saw it. If that has an anchorage for trading vessels and tax is payable there before the goods are sent off with caravans inland, this could be a way to sneak things by."

"Whether your theory is correct or not," said Duarte, "we must try the cliffs or retreat and meet the pursuer on his way up. No choice, in my view. I hope you have a good head for heights." He glanced at me, not altogether joking.

"Come," said Stoyan. "If we must negotiate a cliff path, let us do so while the Mufti's men are well behind."

"Of course," I felt obliged to say, "if there is a bridge, it would be more logical for it to connect with a path down to that eastern settlement, not to a village on the other side of the mountains."

"So," Duarte said, hands on hips, "what is your advice?"

"Logic tells me this path doesn't go where we need it to. Instinct tells me it's the right path. Make of that what you will." A bird had alighted on the rocks just ahead of us as I spoke, a large black crow. Its wings had a tattered look, its eyes a bright wildness, intent, unsettling. "In fact, I'm absolutely sure this is the way," I added. *Follow the crow,* I nearly said, but stopped myself. I didn't want Duarte to think me completely mad.

There was a path around the cliffs. It was so narrow I did not dare look down. The rock surface was pitted and crumbling. My limbs shook. My mind went numb with terror. I could not imagine any goat in its right mind choosing to go this way.

Duarte went first, with me next. I kept forgetting to breathe. Stoyan came after me, once or twice reaching out an arm to steady me or offering calm, quiet instructions. Pero was at the end, dogged and silent. I did have the advantage of being smaller and lighter than any of them, but the boots I'd been lent on the *Esperança* were not a good fit, and I was never more relieved than the moment I stepped off the tiny ledge onto more solid ground, to be enveloped in an embrace by Duarte before seeing the others in turn reach the safety of the broad, treed hollow where we stood.

"You're a brave girl, Paula," the pirate said. He still had me folded to his chest and seemed in no hurry to let go. My heart was beating fast, whether through terror, relief, or something quite different I was not sure. "I'm proud of you," Duarte added in a murmur.

"It's the thought of doing it all again on the way back that really bothers me," I said with a shaky smile, and stepped away from his embrace.

"If we can find another way, we will," he said. "Trust me on that. Now—"

There was a whir and a thump, and Pero gave a strangled gasp before collapsing to his knees by our side. My eyes went wide with horror. Something was sticking out of his calf, and he moaned as he clutched at it. Blood ran down his trouser leg and onto his boot. I had just time to identify the thing as a crossbow bolt; then Stoyan grabbed me and shoved me back under the cover of some straggly bushes. The crow, with a derisive caw, settled on a branch above me.

I stayed where I'd been put, watching Duarte and Stoyan as they moved like a team, keeping their voices low. Neither looked back along the cliff path. To lean out was to put oneself in the path of a second missile. I did not hear any sounds of pursuit, falling stones, or voices, but I knew we did not have long. Stoyan picked Pero up without apparent effort and shifted him to a more sheltered position. Duarte hunted items out of his pack. The two of them crouched beside the stricken man, busying themselves. I could see blood on Pero's face; he had sunk his teeth into his lip to stop himself from crying out. I wasn't prepared to stay crouching in cover while they worked, so I came out and held things for them as Stoyan set his hands to the bolt and drew it out with an unpleasant sucking noise. Duarte applied pressure to the wound. Pero endured the operation without a sound. Stoyan ripped lengths off his own shirt to improvise a dressing.

"Where are they?" I whispered as the last knot was tied. Fresh blood was already seeping through the linen. "How far behind us?"

"Too close," muttered Duarte. "They must have been climbing in the dark, or they'd never have caught up. They must be right at the other end of the cliff path, probably waiting for us to move on. They'll be vulnerable once they start to come along that ledge. We must go now. Pero . . ." He addressed his friend in Portuguese, his tone confident and warm. Pero's face was an unlikely shade of gray. He was trying to smile. I looked at Stoyan and he looked at me. He was transferring items from Pero's pack to his own.

"I can carry it," I said. "You've got too much already."

"I'll take it, Paula. Pero's going to need help. I want you to go ahead and find the path."

Duarte indicated agreement with a jerk of his head. Perhaps the grim, weary look on his face was reflected on mine; I could not tell. I knew that forcing Pero to go on went against all rules for the care of the seriously injured. But now that our pursuers had shown their true colors, we had no choice.

"And, Paula," said Stoyan as the two of them helped Pero to rise, supporting him between them, "if you need to use that knife I gave you, don't hesitate. Promise me."

The cliff path had taken us below the level of the scree, and we now entered another area of trees, where a broader, easier way opened out. We kept up a reasonable pace thanks to the combined strength of Stoyan and Duarte, who helped Pero as we went, but before long the path began to climb again, winding uphill between rocks overhung with creeping thorn bushes. The crow was still with us, flying ahead to land and wait, gazing at us with its impenetrable eyes.

I paused on top of a rise, turning to look back, and caught a flash of something between the trees lower down: a color that did not belong in the grays and browns and greens of the forested hillside, a movement I thought was human. "I can see them," I muttered as Stoyan came up beside me. "I don't think we can keep ahead much longer."

"Where's the bird?"

"You noticed? Still following this path. So I suppose all we can do is go on and hope." Now I could see more of them, five, six men, moving purposefully up the hill a few hundred yards behind us. My heart felt like a cold stone in my chest.

"Keep going, Paula," Stoyan said. "If the ground levels out up there, run."

Duarte was helping Pero up the rise; Stoyan reached out a strong hand and hauled the injured man up beside us. Pero said something in Portuguese and made a gesture indicating that he could walk and that we should go on and stop worrying about him. The bandage on his leg was stained red.

"Quickly," Duarte said. "Go."

The ground leveled, and I ran. The path, such as it was, went around a bluff, then cut between high rock walls where mountain plants grew in crevices, their tiny flower faces turned up toward the cloud-veiled sun. The crow flew ahead, not crying out now but winging with intent along the narrow way. My legs ached; my head was dizzy; my breath rasped in my chest. I knew, deep inside me, that even with Stoyan on our side, we could not hope to prevail against so many attackers. Crossbows were probably only the first step. It was very possible we were all about to die. Wits, courage, balance. How could I employ any of them when I was so frightened I couldn't think straight?

The rock walls opened out. I halted so abruptly that Duarte, who was next in line, almost crashed into me. We were standing on the very lip of a deep, narrow rift in the mountainside. I made myself look down and saw a thread of pale blue: a waterway far below us. Birds were wheeling in space above the river, mere dots against the gray of rock, the dark green of forest. It was a fearsome drop. A short distance along the path that skirted this ravine was a little hut and beside it a fire with smoke rising in a lazy plume up the side of the gorge. And there was a bridge: a ramshackle suspended construction of ropes and wooden slats, with a single knotted line as a handhold. It spanned the gap, a tenuous link to the other side, where the path began again, winding across a bare expanse of hillside to a great wall of rock. Dark foliage in a band screened the foot of that cliff. An odd formation of low cloud, like a localized mist, clung to its top, blotting out the view of the mountain behind. In and out of this haze flew waves of dark birds. I heard their screaming cries, like warnings to come no closer. It seemed to me a place of magic, strange and mysterious. Gazing at it, I felt an odd sense of recognition. The crow took wing and headed across the divide; it needed no bridge.

"Over there," I said as Pero came up beside us. Stoyan had not yet appeared. "Where those cliffs are, that's the place we must go." After that first glance, I tried not to look at the bridge.

Duarte muttered something in Portuguese, and we headed along the path. We had taken only a few steps when a commanding voice shouted in Turkish, "Halt!" From inside the little hut appeared a man with a sword in one hand and a dagger in the other. He wore a soldier's gear, protective leather over garments of padded cotton. "What is your business here? No passing!" At least that was how I interpreted his words.

Duarte began an explanation in fluent Turkish, accompanied by much eloquent waving of hands. The guard shook his head, pointing back the way we had come. A moment later a second man, then a third, emerged from the small hut. All were heavily armed; each wore the same implacable expression. Duarte began again, and this time the first guard cut him off with a single, snapped word.

"What is he saying? Tell them we must get over!" I said, wondering why there was no sign of Stoyan. Could he be back there fighting off the pursuers all by himself? "Tell them we're being followed by men with crossbows!"

"They say nobody can pass without the authority of the

local administrator," Duarte said. "Something about taxes and contraband. They suggested a thorough search of our packs and our persons might be in order."

"There's no time!" I thought I could hear noises back along the path, the sound of many booted feet. I tried my basic Turkish. "Please let us pass!"

The first guard glared at me. "The bridge is closed!" he barked.

An impasse. We would stand here arguing until the enemy came up and killed us. It would be all too easy on the edge of a precipice. These guards would probably stand by their little fire drinking tea and watching it happen.

"Go back," the first guard said. "Leave this place."

"We could fight them, I suppose," said Duarte quietly, in Greek. "But—"

Then, before our eyes, the adversarial scowls on the faces of the guards were abruptly transformed into expressions of combined shock, embarrassment, and servile apology. They were looking over my shoulder, down the path.

"Your Excellency!" exclaimed the first guard. "A thousand apologies! We are most honored . . ."

I turned my head, wondering if the pursuers were here already and had a dignitary amongst them. But the only person standing there was Stoyan, looking as bemused as I felt. He opened his mouth to speak, but Duarte, quick as a whip, got in first.

"His Excellency is traveling incognito," was what I thought he said. "You are not to speak of this, you understand? Now let us pass, and be quick about it."

And they did, ushering the four of us up to the bridge with many bows and polite apologies.

"Your Excellency, I did not realize . . ."

"We regret greatly . . . We wished only to carry out our orders. . . ."

"Yes, yes," Duarte told them airily. "His Excellency understands." And he added something about others, speaking too fast for me to follow.

Stoyan said nothing at all. That was wise. If, as it seemed, he had been mistaken for someone else, the moment he opened his mouth and spoke with a Bulgarian accent, our permission to cross the bridge would be snatched away.

"Paula," Duarte said, "you should go first. You are light-footed; we will be slower."

I swallowed nervously, knowing I had to do it, wondering if I was going to be sick with sheer fright.

"One hand on the rope," Duarte went on, his voice calm. "Don't look down, don't look back, keep moving whatever happens. Fix your gaze on a point opposite and walk toward that. Go now, Paula."

Stoyan reached out, wordless; his fingers brushed my hair. Then I was on the shaky structure, stepping from one narrow, weathered plank to the next, my teeth clenched with terror, my whole body drenched in nervous sweat as the bridge began to bounce and sway under my weight.

Sometimes there is nothing to do but keep going. I didn't like heights; the cliff path had tested me severely. If I'd been traveling alone, I'd never have dreamed of trying this. But somehow I did it. With one hand holding the rope and the other out to the side for balance, I walked across in my ill-fitting boots, keeping my eyes on the wall of rock ahead with its odd cap of mist, knowing instinctively that up there lay the key to the mystery. *Find the heart, for there lies wisdom. The crown is the destination.* Could that have something to do with this? Hearts. Crowns. Kings and queens had both, and maybe Cybele was a kind of queen. I imagined her bulbous form crowned with leaves and berries. She was also like a tree, I reminded myself as I stepped over a gap where one board had fallen from the bridge. I teetered, catching a glimpse of the ribbon of water far below me. *Concentrate, Paula. Use your balance.* Heart of wood; crownlike canopy. That was what Stoyan had suggested. And the tile pattern was a tree. What was the connection?

The men were on the bridge. I felt it shudder and sway with the extra weight and the movement. This would be hard for Pero. I was almost over. There were about four strides in it. . . .

Someone shouted. *Don't look back,* I ordered myself. I stepped forward, one slat, two, three, and I was on the far side of the rift, where the path continued up across the rocky slope. I breathed, relief spreading all through my body. I was here, I had done it.

Another shout. I turned and my heart froze. Halfway across the bridge, Pero had fallen. He was clutching on to the slats with both arms, his legs dangling down into the void. Beside him, Duarte was lowering himself into a crouch on the violently swaying structure, trying to establish his balance so he could use both hands to help his crewman. Stoyan was between these two and the far end of the bridge. As I stared in horror, more yelling broke out from over the gap— our pursuers had reached the sentry post. There was a small crowd of men there now, in spirited argument with the guards. Someone drew a curved sword.

On the bridge, Duarte had let go of the handhold and

was lying at full length on the slats, grasping Pero's shoulders, trying to haul him up to safety. Stoyan stood immobile; if he moved toward them, he would set the flimsy structure bouncing and swinging and perhaps topple the two of them into the depths. On the other side, the shouts rose in a crescendo. Weapons flashed. A moment later there was a scream, and someone fell from the path near the hut, disappearing down the cliff like a discarded garment. Stoyan looked back. As he did so, Duarte managed to pull Pero up a little, and the stricken sailor got one knee onto the boards of the bridge.

I was cold with terror. I prayed with every fiber of my being—*Keep them safe, don't let them fall, please, please*—but on the other side was someone with different priorities. A calm figure stood there, turban neat, green dolman sashed in clean white, crossbow aimed squarely at the spot where Duarte and Pero balanced between life and death.

"No!" I shrieked. "Don't shoot!" But this archer cared nothing for my protests. The bolt was ready—he fired. Not at Duarte, leader of this expedition; not at foolish Paula, who had thought her presence might make some difference in this pattern of darkness and death. Not even at Stoyan, the strongest and most dangerous of our party. No, this weapon was aimed at the weakest, the man whose life depended on the strength and skill of another. The bolt struck Pero through the chest. He grunted and went limp, half on, half off the bridge. Duarte lay there, holding on. I could not see his face.

"Stop it!" I screamed again. "Leave us alone!"

"Let him go, Duarte." It was Stoyan, speaking calmly as he walked across the bridge toward the place where the

Portuguese was lying, supporting the body of his first mate and friend. "You must let him go."

I saw Pero fall, down, down, a last flight to oblivion. The seven children would wait forever for their father's homecoming. He'd never again tuck them into bed, solving their small territorial disputes with benign efficiency.

Stoyan bent to help Duarte up, to guide his hand back to the supporting rope. The crossbow leveled once more, aiming toward them. This time I got a better view, and I saw the archer's face. My heart stopped. It was the court-trained eunuch Murat: Irene's jewel. And behind him, clad in an outfit that was a perfectly cut blend of Greek fashion and Anatolian mountain dress, full gathered trousers tucked into boots, long woolen tunic and embroidered waistcoat, was Irene herself, her expression cold as winter. Now that the shouting had died down, I could hear her voice with perfect clarity through the thin mountain air.

"Leave the girl, Murat," she said. "Her head's a mine of information; she may be useful to us. Don't harm the Portuguese. He'll have the artifact in his pack, and he knows the way. Kill the guard dog."

Stoyan was getting Duarte up, ensuring the other man did not fall as he regained his balance on the swaying bridge. He was a clear and easy target. Murat sighted.

I had no time to think, no time to consider the monstrous betrayal that had taken place. I ran back out onto the bridge, heedless of falling. I saw the shock on Stoyan's face, saw him open his mouth to shout at me, but all that mattered was to save him—somehow to save all of us. I reached Duarte, who was half up. Murat was holding fire. With me on the bridge as well, the thing was moving erratically, and he had been ordered to kill only one of three.

I reached up to Duarte's pack, undid the strap, and lifted out a rolled bundle of cloth. Something beyond my own body seemed to be moving me—I do not know how I managed to work so quickly. I took a step back and yelled toward Irene: "You see what I'm holding? Harm Stoyan, harm any of us, and I'll drop it. It'll smash into a thousand pieces, and this will all be for nothing! You think I value a piece of broken pottery above the lives of my friends?"

She was staring at me, and I thought perhaps there was a little smile on her lips. "What, sacrifice Cybele's Gift?" she called across the divide. "You couldn't do it, Paula. Kill him, Murat."

"You think I'm bluffing? Just watch me!" I shouted, and dangled the bundle out over the drop. It was only when I saw the horrified faces of the two men on the bridge next to me that I realized I had let go of the hand rope. I wobbled, arms outstretched, and my burden swung wildly, almost falling.

"Slowly over," muttered Stoyan. "One step at a time. Stay close together."

I did as he said, inching back with the two men following. I waited for a cry, the sound of another terrible descent, but there was nothing. It seemed Irene had at last believed me. In the balance, Cybele's Gift meant more to her than the chance to pick off another of Duarte's protectors.

When we set foot on solid ground, there was no time to speak of what had happened. Duarte was gray-faced, his hands visibly trembling. My legs felt like jelly and my head was whirling. The pursuer was not the Sheikh-ul-Islam but Irene of Volos, Irene, who had been so kind to me with her library and her hamam and her interest in seeing me reach my potential as an independent woman. . . . How could she do this? And why? Could Murat's past connections with the Sultan's household include some kind of link with the Sheikh-ul-Islam? Could Irene and her steward be here on the Mufti's behalf? Not possible; an Islamic cleric would not use an infidel woman as his agent. The pursuit probably had nothing to do with the Mufti. Irene was wealthy. She could have paid for a ship and crew. Had she been using me all the time, cultivating my friendship so she could find out my father's plans? I had been the one to invite her to Barsam's supper, but she had offered her services as chaperone before I did so. . . . How could she have known Maria would be ill on the day? Surely she hadn't had a hand in that? It didn't bear thinking about. I felt cold with shock.

Stoyan took charge with quiet competence. "They will be over quickly," he said. "They have killed the guards. No time to cut the bridge. You think the way is up there, Paula?"

I nodded.

"You must go first. Run ahead and find cover. We will hold them back. You have the artifact; get it to safety."

I looked at Duarte. He eased off his pack, reached in, took out a wrapped bundle. I stuffed the rolled-up shirt I had been holding back in and took Cybele's Gift from him.

"You mean—" Stoyan's brows rose.

"It's what people believe that matters, not what actually is," I said. "They're coming; there are three men on the bridge. Can't we all run? What if—"

"Go, Paula," Duarte said. "Forget about us. Run as fast as you can. Go with God, little *marinheira*."

So, clutching Cybele's Gift in both hands, I ran. I told myself that I would not look back, that I would carry the precious artifact safely all the way to the shelter of the bushes and not even think about who might have fallen and how many friends I might lose today. Behind me men shouted, arrows hissed, and swords clashed. The mist was freakish. It lay now in strands across the open ground, and when at last I looked behind me, I caught only glimpses of what was unfolding. I saw Stoyan with his sword drawn and three assailants around him. I saw Duarte with a knife in each hand, his eyes ferocious above a savage grin. In a fog of terror, I tried to count the opposition and failed, for the shreds of mist now concealed and now revealed five warriors, seven, ten, a whole small army. There were many. We were grossly outnumbered. Now Duarte and Stoyan were standing back to back, snarling and brandishing their weapons, a fearsome two-man fighting force. The crow shrieked in my ear. Unable to dash away my tears because my hands held the priceless burden Duarte had entrusted to me, I turned my back and headed for the cliffs.

The bird led me. Under cover of the bushes, in semidarkness, I paused to wipe my eyes. The crow's harsh cawing hurried me on along the base of the cliff, following a snaking path between the myriad plants that grew thickly beside this rearing edifice of stone. I could no longer hear the sounds of battle on the hillside below. My mind refused to take in the possibility that it was all over, that my friends were lying in their blood out there while the enemy came on after me.

Irene. I still couldn't believe it. She had described Duarte to me as obsessive, a man who would do anything to get what he wanted. But she was the obsessive one. Not only had she exploited me and lied to me, but it seemed she was prepared to see innocent men die so she could get her hands on Cybele's Gift. It made no sense at all. If she had the resources to mount this chase, why hadn't she simply outbid Duarte? Why make such a secret of the fact that she wanted the artifact?

The crow had settled on a branch of a young pine, not far from the cliff face. I halted, my chest heaving.

"Is this the place?" I whispered, looking about me. The wind sighed in the trees; I could hear the trickling of a stream nearby. The breeze parted the bushes, and on the rock wall in front of me was revealed a brilliant display of color, gleaming white, blue, green, and a very particular red in the dim sunlight filtering through the leaves. Tiles. I blinked, stepping closer. Here in this unlikely spot, far from the mosques and palaces of the great cities, away from the well-traveled trade routes, someone had created a small masterpiece. The pattern seldom repeated itself but flowed along the rocks with its own life—vines, fruit, foliage, here and there the taller form of a tree. I tucked Cybele under one arm and reached out to touch the smooth surface, drawing my fingers across it and marveling that in such a wild corner of the country it seemed unscathed, not a crack or mark on it, only a glowing patina, as if its perfection had increased with the passing of time. What was it, a temple wall? The ruins of an ancient home of kings?

The bird croaked again, and I came back to myself. What to do? The tiles, the pattern, the tree . . . I was meant to make something of this. To find a way. I hurried along the wall, following the pattern to its end, where gleaming color gave way once more to bare stone. I went back; perhaps there had been an opening of some kind and I had missed it. But I found nothing, only that smooth unbroken fresco, the tiles stretching up twice a man's height and running a good fifty paces along the cliff.

Shouting came from beyond the trees. I heard Stoyan's voice—thank God, he was still alive—and those of other men. They were much closer and heading my way. *Think, Paula.* I had been right along the tiled area; the only other course was to go all the way across the foot of the cliff, hoping somewhere there might be a cave or signs of a clearer way out. No time for that; they were coming now. *Think.*

There was a crashing in the bushes nearby. I hugged Cybele to my chest and backed against the tiles. A moment later Stoyan came bursting through, his garments stained with blood and sweat, his breathing labored. His hair had come untied and was over his shoulders and in his eyes, a wild dark cloud. Behind him was Duarte, still gripping his two knives. They halted in front of me, staring at the tiles.

"Where's the path?" Duarte gasped. "Quick, Paula!"

Sounds of pursuit close at hand. My heart hammered. My mind edged into blank terror. *Remember, remember, Paula. You are a scholar. Find what you need.* I gazed wildly up at the pattern on the cliff, and something the crone had said to me, the part I had not understood, sprang into my mind. *Remember what once seemed the most important thing of all.*

"Paula," Stoyan said suddenly, his gaze on the tiles. "That's the tree. Cybele's tree."

I had been too distraught, too dazzled to distinguish one

tree from the others on the tiled wall, but he was right. Every branch, every leaf and little bird was the same as the image we had made in our sand tray, the one we had done our best to memorize. The tiny patterns hidden in the decorative border of the Persian manuscript were here in complete order, and Cybele's tree flowered on the wall before us.

"They're here," Duarte muttered, and through the bushes came five or six of Irene's men, not running to attack, simply moving toward us in a tightening semicircle, weapons in hand. My companions turned to face them.

"Paula," came Irene's voice, not in the least out of breath. She sounded as if she were welcoming me to a day of study, bathing, and good coffee. "How very clever of you. This must indeed be the place. I'm so glad you and the artifact have both come this far unharmed. You have such potential; I'd hate to see that snuffed out. Now might be the right moment to dispense with Paula's guard at last, Murat. I feel he's going to get in our way. Not the pirate. He'll know the path. And make sure you spare Paula; she's a real scholar, and that may come in useful to us. Besides, she'll change sides quickly enough once she realizes how serious we are. Separate the Bulgar from the others, and let her watch him die."

I was a hairbreadth from asking Duarte to hand over Cybele's Gift to her. But that had to be wrong. The quest couldn't end so bitterly. I must do the job I'd been given and trust Duarte and Stoyan to do theirs. As the two of them moved closer together, forming a protective shield between me and the attackers, I forced myself to look away, to concentrate on the tiled tree. Metal clashed, and Stoyan gave a muffled cry. It took all my will not to turn and launch myself into the conflict in a futile effort to help him.

A moment later I had it. *Remember what once seemed the most important thing of all.* The Other Kingdom. The key to a new portal. When my sisters and I had lost our doorway to the fairy realm, I had been given a bundle of papers and manuscripts. I had always believed that if Stela and I worked out the clues in them, we would be able to find another portal and go back. But we never had, and after six years of trying, I had given up hope of ever doing so. For all that time, there had been nothing in the world more important to me than that. And that was where I had seen the pattern before. In those papers, somewhere in the complex tangle of clues and maps and puzzles the scholars of the Other Kingdom had given me as a parting gift, this tree image had been present. No wonder it had teased at me so in Irene's library.

"It's a doorway," I breathed as Stoyan was forced backward to the rocks by three fighters. Duarte, trying desperately to get close to him, was being held off by a blank-eyed Murat. "A secret portal . . ." *Find the heart, for there lies wisdom.* I reached out my hand toward the tiled tree, imagining its rotund form was that of Cybele. I placed my palm exactly where I thought her heart would be, closed my eyes, and prayed harder than I had ever prayed before.

Under my touch, a door opened. The whole panel where the tree was depicted swung inward, creating an entry just big enough for a person to step through. I glanced behind me. Stoyan had lost his sword and was on his knees, fending off his three assailants with sweeps of a knife. Murat and Duarte were wrestling for control of a dagger.

"Now!" I yelled. "Now, quickly!" But there was no way my companions could follow me. "Help us!" I added for good measure, not at all sure whom I was addressing, just knowing I could not do this alone.

The crow rose from its tree with a strong beat of the wings. As it flew by me, it became an old woman in flowing black, eyes fierce, seamed face deathly pale, arms extended toward the struggling men, long fingers tipped with pointed nails like the claws of a predatory bird. She shrieked; it was a sound to freeze the blood in the bravest man's veins. For a moment, shock held everyone immobile. The combatants stared at the crone, their faces drained of color. One man crossed himself.

"Now!" I said again, pointing toward the dark opening that had been revealed in the rock wall. Stoyan was up with one quick slash of the knife and across to my side. Duarte slipped out of Murat's grip and followed. Without another word, the three of us darted through the portal and into a shadowy subterranean passageway. A moment later the crow flew by us, heading deeper into the mountain.

Somewhere ahead of us there was a flickering light, perhaps from a candle. Behind us, on the other side of the portal, Irene was issuing sharp orders.

"Can you shut it after us?" hissed Duarte. "No, forget that, just run."

We ran, not looking back. I heard Irene's voice again behind us, and Murat's, and shortly after they spoke, a creaking sound as if the doorway was being closed, or perhaps closing of itself. The passage had an earthen floor that muffled the sound of our feet and of theirs. It was not pitch-dark; the unsteady light was always there in front of us, though we saw no candle, lantern, or fire. The path curved around, went up sharply, then descended and became precipitous steps. At the foot of these, it branched three ways.

I halted abruptly. Each path was lit by the same uneven glow. There was no saying which our guide, if that name could be used for a crow, had taken. *Sharpen your wits.* My mind refused to cooperate. I had no idea.

"Paula." Stoyan spoke hesitantly.

"Yes?"

"The tree. I think the tree is the path."

"What?"

"A map. You put your hand on a certain point; that's where we started, the heart. The shape of the tree we made, the one on those tiles, is the map of this underground tunnel. We are exactly at a place where the main trunk branched three ways."

I remembered him on the night we had made the image in the sand poring over the tray and telling me he would memorize the pattern rather than sleep. "The crown is the destination," I murmured. "We have to go to the top of the tree, the highest point. How well can you remember the image?"

"Well enough, I hope. Shall I go first?"

"Hurry up," muttered Duarte. "I'm the one in position for a knife in the back. Can we run?"

So we ran, and the passageways grew narrower, and my nightmare engulfed me once more. Stoyan was leading, his strong hand clasping mine. Duarte came after me. The walls were close and the light dim. When we paused to check a turning or assess the safety of a crumbling stairway or shadowy tunnel, the pad of footsteps or the murmur of voices behind us was a reminder that death was only a heart-beat away.

Now our pursuers seemed to be keeping pace, letting us lead them, perhaps by footprints, perhaps by sound. I could not tell how many had followed us into the cave system, but I was sure they could have caught up with us if they'd so chosen. It came to me suddenly that it was Irene who had told me Duarte would head off in search of the second piece of Cybele's Gift once he had acquired the first. That must be what she wanted—to put the whole together, just as he did. To follow him to his destination so she could have both. Perhaps she had gone to Barsam's supper intending to bid. But once she knew the piece was incomplete, she had let Duarte do the job for her instead. A chill ran through me. She had wanted him to buy Cybele's Gift so he could lead her to the missing piece. She had made sure the other serious bidder was out of the way before Duarte went to the blue house that morning. While I sat oblivious under her very nose, her henchmen had been attacking my father in the street. Irene had done that; Irene, whom I had trusted. In the nightmare, I had imagined the enemy a monster, a thing from the dark-ness. Remembering the look in the Greek woman's eyes, cold and implacable, as she'd ordered Pero's death, I recognized that the human monster was infinitely more frightening.

Chapter Thirteen

We emerged, panting, into a cavern. It was markedly colder and darker than the passageways we had come through. I took a step forward and Stoyan, with a sudden shout, grabbed me roughly by the arm, dragging me back.

"Wha—" I protested, then saw that across the center of the chamber was a deep crack in the stone floor, a chasm three yards wide and so deep that when I crept closer to peer into it, I could see nothing but fathomless dark. A rough rope hung down from the roof of the cavern above the gap and was hooked up against the rock wall on our side. No, not a rope, a tree root, perhaps the dangling remnant of an age when Cybele herself walked the earth, for only a forest giant of ancient lineage could have sent its feet so deep in search of nourishment. This was an old place, old and powerful.

"Dear God," muttered Duarte. "The way across is to grab hold of that and swing."

My eyes were growing more accustomed to the darkness. I saw that on the other side of the gap were five passages branching off from the cavern. Beside me, Stoyan stood gazing at them and moving his lips in silence, as if repeating a pattern. If his theory was correct, we needed to remember every bough and limb of that tree design, every leaf and flower and twig, to guide us through this maze of caves and tunnels. I hoped very much that if we chose the right way, we would reach the mountain village where Cybele's Gift belonged. That seemed the only reason the crow, or the old woman, would have guided us in here.

I tried not to think too much about where we actually were. I had discovered that I did not especially enjoy being underground. My bones sensed the weight of earth above me. I found it hard to breathe.

We stood in silence as Stoyan did his best to remember the way. I thought it was the second from the right, but I did not say so, not until he had made his own choice. It seemed to me that he had more talent than I for tasks involving shapes and patterns and that in this matter he was more likely to be correct.

Stoyan cleared his throat, but it was someone else who spoke, the voice coming from a particularly dark corner. "You cannot simply make a choice here," it said, and its tone reminded me of warm afternoons and rich cream and the smell of freshly mown grass. "In my chamber, the key to the door is using your wits. Which of you will attempt it? Choose one and one only."

A figure emerged from the shadows, not the dark-robed crone as I had expected but a smaller personage, wrapped in a cloak of pale fur. The garment had a deep hood, and under this, all I could see was a pair of shining eyes. They were elongated and mysterious, the irises gleaming, one of brilliant blue, the other golden yellow. "Be quick," the creature warned. "Others come after you. If you would pass swiftly, choose your cleverest and take the test."

Both men looked straight at me. "Paula," said Duarte. "The obvious choice. She'll do it, whatever it is." Considering his avowed disbelief in all things supernatural, he was coping well, but I could hear the nervous edge in his voice. His calm self-possession was not so much in evidence now.

I remembered the miniatures: someone talking to a cat. Great heavens, must we complete a whole set of challenges before we could get to wherever it was we were going? My mind shied away from memories of a figure dangling from a rope; another fighting; the girl who was possibly not picking apples, not if she was underground, but doing something a great deal more difficult. . . . I made myself fix on the fact that my companions had selected me as their champion this time around, that they respected my intelligence, that they trusted me. That the others were coming, so I'd better get on with this.

"I'm ready," I told the catlike figure, passing Cybele's Gift to Duarte, just in case. He stowed it in his pack.

"Good," the creature purred. "Three riddles, Paula, one for each traveler, though you will answer all. With each correct answer, you win passage forward for one of your party. Here is the first:

Stronger than iron
Crueler than death
Sweeter than springtime
It lives beyond breath."

"Love," I said straightaway, hoping the other riddles were as easy.

The creature motioned toward the dangling root rope with a hand whose human fingers were clad in soft fur. "One may pass," it said solemnly.

We waited, and after a moment the catlike being gestured again. "One must go now," it said.

Stoyan looked over his shoulder and made a little sound under his breath. Following his gaze, I saw two figures emerging from the shadows of the tunnel from which we had come. A turbaned man in green and a stylish figure in a tunic and trousers, with her black hair piled atop her head. Only the two of them. All they had to do was listen to my answers and they'd be over the chasm in a flash.

"Too easy," Irene said as if reading my thoughts. She walked forward, and Murat came a step behind, a tall shadow.

"Wait!" The cat creature's voice was commanding, and the two of them halted. Irene lifted her brows. "Each in his turn," the creature said, and now its tone was closer to a growl.

"That's all very well." Irene sounded cool and controlled. "But—" She fell suddenly silent, looking at the rift in the ground and the rope. "Astonishing," she breathed. "Just the same as those miniatures in the library, the ones our little scholar here mysteriously found for us . . . What are you up to, Paula? What is this?"

Nobody answered. The cat creature looked at Duarte. "Go now," it repeated.

Duarte unhooked the vinelike tree root, testing it for strength. His glance moved from time to time toward our unusual puzzle master but did not settle for long. I reminded myself that, of the three of us, only I was familiar with the

Other Kingdom. I was frightened and nervous, but the creature itself did not trouble me. I had seen far odder in my time.

"You go first," Duarte said to Stoyan. "I'll bring Paula."

"I will bring her." Stoyan wore his most dogged look even as he, like Duarte, cast furtive glances at the robed figure. "She cannot do this alone. It requires too much strength in the arms and shoulders. I can support her and swing us both over."

"Go now or lose your chance," said the catlike creature. "One at a time. That is the rule."

"I'm a sailor," Duarte said, setting the dangling root firmly in Stoyan's hand. "I know ropes. Besides, what about your shoulder? And I need you to catch her on the other side. Now go."

"Shoulder?" I asked in alarm. "Are you hurt, Stoyan?" His clothing was so bloodstained, as was Duarte's, that it was impossible to tell whether either had been wounded in the fight. Because both were able to talk, to run, to make decisions, I had assumed most of the blood was that of their enemies.

"Only a scratch," Stoyan muttered. "It's nothing." Tight-jawed, he gripped the root, took a few steps back to gain momentum, then ran to the edge and swung. My heart did not beat again until he was safely over and had sent the rope back into Duarte's hand.

"*Gift of a raven*
Sharp as a blade
Black is its burden
Wisdom its trade."

The catlike being regarded me with its luminous, odd

eyes, and I stared back, thinking hard. Raven, crow, what sort of gift might they offer . . . a feather . . . *black is its burden* . . . a black feather . . . no, something carried by the feather, something used to create wisdom . . .

"A pen," I said. Crow feathers were the most commonly used for quills, being strong and relatively easy to obtain. Black ink, words of wisdom . . . The riddle was a good choice for a scholar. Perhaps these folk wanted me to get them right.

"Good," said the questioner, and fixed its eyes on Duarte. "Go now. Do not delay. Time passes."

"Paula, you must go next," Duarte said, doing something to the rope. "We're not leaving you to come last." He glanced toward Irene and Murat.

"You will go now." The creature sounded displeased. Its voice no longer held the melting softness of its first greeting but was all sharp edges. "She answers the riddles," it hissed. "You chose her. She swings last. Go!"

"I'm not leaving her here on her own!" Duarte protested. "These people mean us harm!"

"Go, or forfeit your right to proceed." The voice was implacable.

"Go on," I muttered.

Duarte's expression was stricken. "I'm sorry," he said. "Look, I've made a loop. When it's time, put your foot in that; it will be easier to stay on. Watch me, and when it's your turn, try to do the same. Don't be afraid; we'll catch you." He sounded more confident than he looked.

"Just go, Duarte. Let's get this over with," I said, not daring to glance across at Stoyan.

The pirate was, as he had said, familiar with ropes. I recalled my first glimpse of him on the deck of the *Esperança*, a nonchalant figure leaning far over the turbulent water of the Black Sea, one hand carelessly holding on, the other extended to whisk my scarf out of midair. As if the two of us shared the same thoughts, Duarte reached now to touch a corner of red fabric that protruded above his belt and turned his dimpled smile on me. He set his hands to the tree root and backed up, then ran almost to the brink, slipped his foot neatly into the loop, and swung across the divide as if it were nothing, jumping down nimbly by Stoyan's side. They sent the rope back to me; I caught it and looped it ready. Paula, the scholar. Paula, who was not particularly good at tasks requiring agility or strength. Well, I had gone across that bridge. I could do this, too.

"Give me your last riddle, please," I said, trying not to dwell on what was to come. Too much imagination can be a drawback in such situations. I did not want to consider what might lie in that pit, beneath the shadows.

"It sees the sailor and his crew
Through winter's fiercest storm
It draws the traveler home at last
To the place where he was born;
It keeps the scholar working long
Though wisdom's hard to find,
It soothes the weary, eases pain
And calms the troubled mind."

Irene was coming toward me, eyes dark with purpose. Behind her, Murat walked with knife in hand. Now the cat being was making no attempt to hold them back. What they intended, I did not know. Not to kill me, surely. Hadn't Irene said my head was a mine of useful information? But maybe once I'd answered the third riddle, they would already have all the information they needed. After this, maybe I would become superfluous.

"Lay a hand on her and your life will be measured not in days but in minutes!" yelled Duarte from the opposite side of the chasm.

Stoyan said nothing. His amber eyes were fixed on Murat, his expression truly frightening. He raised one hand above his shoulder. In it was a little knife, poised for flight. It was a warrior's pose, full of a graceful, deadly purpose.

"Wait, Murat." Irene did not raise her voice. She and her steward halted, three paces from me. "Aren't you going to answer the riddle for us, Paula?" the Greek scholar went on. "You must know the solution. You know everything. Don't you?"

I hesitated, my heart thudding with tension. How to respond? It was a riddle that could have several answers, any one of them appropriate. A trick? I had not asked what would happen if I got any of the riddles wrong. Would the others be allowed to go on, leaving me behind? What if I could not guess it and Irene could? I cleared my throat nervously.

"Have you an answer for me?" the catlike creature asked. "Time runs short. You have other challenges to face."

"Don't disappoint me, Paula." Irene's voice was almost friendly. When I glanced at her, I saw the sly smile with which she usually accompanied her little comments about my naiveté where men were concerned or my inadequate understanding of fashions in dress. "You're such a clever girl. I hate to see you squander your talents and your fresh-ness on a misguided fool like Duarte da Costa Aguiar. Now would be a very suitable moment to change your allegiance.

Answer your riddle, then come with Murat and me. You must know why we're here. With your talent for working things out, you must have seen it quickly. I was on the verge of making you part of the secret, you know. The first time you visited the hamam, I was so tempted to offer you an invitation to join our sisterhood, but it was too soon. . . . You'd love it, Paula. I need an assistant, a clever younger woman whom I can train in the rituals . . . someone who can share with me the rare and dangerous thrill that comes from outwitting the most powerful of men . . . someone who will, in time, learn to love being a leader as deeply as I do. Your father would let you stay. An opportunity to remain in Istanbul, housed with a respectable matron, studying Anatolian culture. . . . Do it, Paula. Let go of your misguided pirate and your Bulgar brute."

I tried to take in what she was telling me while some part of my mind still wrestled feverishly with the riddle. "Tell me," I said, "was it you who had my father beaten so Duarte would be the one to acquire Cybele's Gift and lead you to this place? Did you befriend me just so you could get to Barsam's supper without revealing you were a buyer? Why did you need to be so secret about it? Why not just bid like everyone else?"

She gave a slow smile. "Oh, you are quick, Paula," she said. "And observant. I saw the miniature, but it did not occur to me that the artifact was broken until you pointed it out. I would give much to know how it was those manuscripts came to your attention when I did not know they were in my own collection." Her voice changed abruptly; her lovely eyes gleamed with a new emotion, something intense and dangerous. "The statue is rightfully mine," she said. "I am Cybele's priestess in Istanbul. I revived her worship; I drew women from all cultures and levels of society to the temple I established, a secret temple within the safe walls of my home. You do not imagine those women visit me solely to study, gossip, and enjoy my hamam, surely? That is what visitors such as yourself are shown—those whose worthiness to join us is still being assessed and those like your acquaintance Maria who come quite innocently, without knowing the true purpose of my establishment. In fact, you almost stumbled on the secret the very first time you were in the hamam, when the women were talking about the Mufti's interest in our cult—it is most fortunate that your Turkish is not as good as your Greek, or you might have understood better. Once we knew you were awake, we altered the conversation somewhat. I did intend you to hear us mention Cybele. I wanted you to be intrigued, excited, eager to return."

"I can't believe this," I breathed. "You, a devotee of a pagan earth goddess? I know you have always valued freedom for women, but . . ." It was hard to accept. Irene's elegance, her sophistication, her smooth manner, none of these seemed right for wild, earthy Cybele with her bloody rituals and her affinity with creatures. There was neither love nor reverence in Irene's voice when she spoke the goddess's name. "A temple. Where?"

"Behind the library is another part of my house, an inner sanctum where we enact our rites. What better place for Cybele's Gift to be displayed? Why should the pirate be entrusted with such a powerful symbol? Why should he be allowed to carry it over the mountains to some complete backwater? Folk in such places don't know how to cherish precious things. The statue will be broken and chipped and forgotten within one generation. Or Duarte will bear it away from the mountain and sell it for his own profit. We cannot allow that to happen, Paula. Cybele's Gift belongs to me. Join me, and in time it could belong to you: the statue, the cult, the power. And the unparalleled excitement of the game—a true battle of wits. On one side, the Sheikh-ul-Islam and the other leaders of established religion in the city; on the other, myself, a mere woman and an infidel, presiding over such rites as would turn their hair white in a day if they could be present. I am always a step ahead, always just out of their reach. What clever girl could resist that?"

Irene glanced at Murat as she ended this extraordinary speech, and I saw him smile for the first time since I had met him. It was a little, tender, intimate smile, and for a moment, as he gazed back at her, his icy blue eyes warmed. Only a moment. The smile faded, the eyes were once more remote. As for me, I was having difficulty taking it all in. The whole thing a sham, a facade—the library and the hamam and the gracious lady with a reputation for good works—and behind it a covert temple in which the worship of the bee goddess was carried out right under the noses of Istanbul's religious establishment, perhaps for the sole purpose of Irene's personal entertainment.

"You'd better answer the riddle," Irene said pleasantly, "or we'll be here all day. Your men are growing agitated. I'd hate one of them to start throwing things."

I turned to the robed creature. "What happens if I get the answer wrong?" I asked. "Couldn't I just swing across anyway?"

There was a gleam of pointed teeth under the hood. "You

would fall," the creature said in a tone of absolute certainty. "Answer now." It glanced toward Irene. "For those who follow," it added, "there are new riddles."

As a scholar, I had learned to focus my mind, though that skill had deserted me once or twice on the journey here. I blocked out Irene's startling revelations. I blocked out Murat, who had killed a good man today. I set aside Stoyan and Duarte; I did not even think of Cybele's Gift. I narrowed my thoughts to the riddle itself and the three possible answers I had: trust, faith, hope. Some parts of it were better suited by one, some by another. But, in fact, there was only one answer that worked for the whole verse. It had to be right. If it wasn't, I was going to the bottom of the chasm.

"Hope," I said.

There was a moment's charged silence; then the creature said quietly, "Go now."

I let out my breath in a rush. Then, without allowing myself to think too hard, I grasped the rope, backed up, and ran toward the chasm. Duarte was shouting instructions. But I was not looking at him. Stoyan had put the knife back in his sash; he stood like a rock on the other side, arms outstretched to catch me, his anguish and terror in full view on his broad features. If I fell, he would fail again, as he had done with Salem bin Afazi; as he had done with my father. I could not fall. I would break his heart.

On the brink, I slipped my foot into the loop and launched myself into space. It was over in a heartbeat, and I was on safe ground again, Stoyan's strong grip steadying me, Duarte grabbing the rope and disentangling my foot. The pirate stood there with the tree root in his hand, gazing back across the chasm. The cat creature was speaking quietly to Murat and Irene.

"Of course," mused Duarte as Stoyan brushed my hair from my eyes with gentle fingers, "I could hook the thing up on this side, out of reach, or only send it as far as the middle."

"I think that would be considered cheating," I said shakily. "I'm certain that to get to the end of this, we must follow the rules, even if they sometimes seem unfair."

He swung the rope back across the divide. Not a flicker of expression crossed Murat's face as he caught it. Irene was saying something to the robed creature; I imagined she was already answering her riddles.

"Second from the right," Stoyan said, taking my hand. "Now run!"

We ran. The passages grew narrower, their corners sharper, the light dimmer. I held on to Stoyan as if he were my lifeline. The ground under our feet changed. There was a scuttling, a rustling, as if many tiny creatures were moving along the passage beside us, above us, under our feet. I slipped and skidded, knocking my elbow on the rock wall. Something crunched under my boot. Behind me, Duarte cursed. Still Stoyan's confident hand drew me forward. I was out of breath, damp with sweat, feeling the vast weight of rock above me, wondering where the air came from down here and whether it would last. Then, suddenly, everything went dark.

There is the darkness of a moonless night out of doors, and there is the darkness of a house with its shutters closed and the lamps quenched. There is the darkness of sleep, relieved by the bright images of dreams. But no darkness is as complete, as blanketing, as terrifying as the utter darkness of underground.

Stoyan's hand tightened on mine. He slowed his pace but kept going, and there was no choice but to follow. The scuttling, whirring sounds seemed louder now that the light was gone. Something buzzed by my ear. Something blundered across my face, brushing my eye. Spindly legs were crawling up my neck, over my hands, inside my tunic. Panic swept through me—I couldn't breathe. *Make it stop. Make it stop. I have to get out.* There was no holding on to common sense. My heart was knocking in my chest. I made some kind of sound, not speech, more of a whimper that, in normal times, I would have been ashamed of.

"I'm here, Paula." Stoyan's voice was firm, his grip the same. "Keep hold, I'll guide you."

"I can't," I squeaked, despising my weakness. "I hate this, I hate the dark—"

Stoyan swore, staggered, and let go of my hand. I froze. If this was the next challenge, to be all alone in a darkness so deep it was like a smothering blanket around me, I couldn't do it. I couldn't be here, I couldn't bear it a moment longer. . . .

"Paula?" Stoyan's voice was coming from somewhere ahead of and below us. It was a lot less steady now. "Duarte? Are you there?"

A hand closed on my shoulder; I started violently.

"It's me, Paula," said Duarte. "Stoyan, where are you? What's happened?"

"There's a sharp drop. Be careful. Hold on to Paula and edge forward slowly." Then, after a little, "I think it's a dead end."

Dear God; all that way back, and Murat behind us with his expressionless eyes and his crossbow. "It can't be," I said in a thread of a voice as the darkness crowded in. "Not unless we chose the wrong way."

"Wait a bit."

I breathed again as Stoyan spoke. I could hear him moving about on some lower level of the cave system. I did not go forward. I had felt the edge of the drop but did not know how deep it was. Duarte and I stood waiting, his arm around my shoulders. That human warmth barely held hysteria at bay. *Too dark, too dark . . .*

"Duarte? Paula?" Stoyan's voice was coming from a new direction, over to our right and much lower down. "I think there's a way through. But it's tight. I can see a place beyond where it's lighter. Duarte, you'll need to help Paula down. Don't let go of each other. Follow my voice."

Duarte scrambled down, then lifted me after him. Hand in hand, we made our way across a more open cavern, with Stoyan's steady instructions our only guide. The darkness remained absolute. I strained to hear footsteps behind us but there were none. There was only the susurration of many small wings, the scurrying of tiny claws, the occasional sound of something smashing underfoot. Cobwebs tangled in my hair and draped themselves in clinging intimacy across my nose and mouth, and I dashed them away.

"I'm here," Stoyan said. His hand brushed against me and I grasped it. "The place is down at the foot of the cave wall, here beside me. If I lie on the ground, I can see faint light coming through. The way is narrow, not much more than a crawl space. You'll get through easily, Paula. Duarte should be all right as well. I'll come last."

I crouched, and he guided my hand to the outline of what felt like a very tiny opening in the rock wall. I lay down, peering into the black, and wondered if the impression of a faint lightening was created purely by our longing to be out of this place, able to see, able to breathe. "What about the packs?" I asked, getting up again. "It's really tight. What about Cybele's Gift?"

"Time to leave a few things behind," Duarte said. "When you get through, Paula, reach back and I'll pass the statue to you. Then if . . ."

"Then if what?"

I could hear the two of them removing their burdens, throwing items out. So much for rations, blankets, the means to make fire.

"Did you hear what Irene was saying?" I muttered into the darkness. "The cult—she said she was the leader of Cybele's cult—"

"I heard," said Duarte as he emptied his pack. "I curse myself for not seeing it sooner. If it's true, she's been expert at concealment—her reputation as a pillar of the community has no doubt helped. No wonder the Mufti couldn't work out who it was. He'd never have dreamed of looking in her house. Her husband is a personal friend of his."

"I wonder what her followers would think if they knew she was prepared to kill for a symbol of Cybele," I said, remembering the women at the hamam, who had seemed quite normal and friendly. Just now, Irene had suggested that the peril of flouting the authorities was the most exciting part of the whole thing. How could she possibly run a secret religion in her own house without her husband knowing? She must be in love with danger.

"I've no plans to hand it to her, Paula," Duarte said. "Are we ready?"

"Keep your knife," Stoyan said to me. "Watch you don't lose it crawling through."

"And pray that this is the right way," added Duarte.

I lay down again and wriggled forward into the narrow opening. If I survived today, if I got through all of this, the snow-pale skin Irene had admired would be patched all over with livid bruises. What if Stoyan had been wrong and this went nowhere? What if I got stuck? The tunnel bent around. I struggled to fit my body to the curve. A protruding spear of rock dug sharply into my hip, making me gasp with pain. How would I reach back around that corner to take Cybele's Gift? How far was it until I could get out of this hole? I ordered myself sternly not to dwell on the possibility that I might crawl on and on until I was so exhausted I could go neither forward nor back. I would not consider how Stoyan, a muscular giant of a man, could pass safely through this tiny space.

And then light. Oh, God, I had never been so grateful for light. A dim glow first, then, as I wriggled forward, a gradual brightening, a flicker, a golden gleam as of a lantern, and at last the tunnel opened up to a cave, and I made my clawing, sobbing, undignified exit, rising to stand unsteadily and run shaking fingers over the tattered remnants of Duarte's blue tunic. I was in a far larger space than those we had passed through before. There were lamps on the walls, and a strange, rippling brightness played across the high vault of the roof. Not important now. I crouched down again.

"Duarte? I'm through. Come now!"

With the light had come fresh courage. I knew I could not

stand here long, savoring release. I must go back in. Duarte with his broad shoulders could not get himself around that curve in the tunnel while holding Cybele's Gift safely. I made quicker progress this time, reaching the place before he did, calling instructions to him for the trickiest part so that when our hands touched, he was ready to manipulate the artifact, still safely bundled in its cloth wrapping, around the corner to me. I backed out, grazing my elbows as I held Cybele's Gift away from the rough stones. Not long after, Duarte emerged into the cavern, his clothing in the same state of disrepair as mine. We exchanged a look. In it was a shared relief that we were safe and a shared fear for our larger companion. Duarte fished the red scarf out of his belt and tied it around his neck.

"Talk to him," he said. "Talk him through. His misplaced heroism is all to do with you. Tell him you can't do without him. That should do the trick, even if he has to break a few bones to manage it."

"Misplaced heroism?" I echoed, outraged on Stoyan's behalf, but Duarte's words made a kind of sense. I crouched by the tunnel exit, my voice eerie in the echoing space of this larger cave. "Come now, Stoyan! It's not far. There's only one part that isn't straight; you might need to wriggle a bit to get through. We've got Cybele's Gift safely out. You'll be all right. I'm just on the other side here. . . ." I kept my tone as reassuring as I could, even as my heart quailed at the thought of my friend stuck halfway and the terrible range of choices that would lie before us if that happened. I could hear him coming, his progress slow, his breathing labored. It was taking a long time. It was taking too long.

"You're crying," Duarte observed.

"Shut up," I muttered. Then I bent down again and called out, "Stoyan! Come on, you can do this! I need you!" My voice cracked. "I can't go on without you!" Glancing up, I caught the fleeting smile that flickered across Duarte's features. "Please, please," I whispered, holding Cybele's Gift to my chest. "Let him get through. Let him be safe. He doesn't deserve this."

"None of us does," Duarte observed. "But it could be said each of us has brought it on himself, for whatever reason. And see, here our friend comes at last. Your prayers have been answered."

We helped Stoyan out; he would have bruises far worse than mine. I fought the urge to throw my arms around him and burst into full-scale tears. He was struggling to catch his breath.

"I apologize," he gasped. "I was too slow. What now?"

As he straightened, a voice came from higher up, a smoky, insubstantial voice that brought to mind polished brass and fine silks and the smell of pungent spices.

"Travelers, you draw close to your destination. A new challenge awaits you."

This cave floor was on an incline, rising from the place where we stood to a high shelf shielded by a fringe of old roots, fronded brown and gray. The lamps were odd, glowing without visible wicks, their brightness doing nothing to relieve the deep chill of the cavern. I could hear a trickling nearby, and when we reached the topmost point, I saw that the canopied shelf led through into a higher chamber whose floor was gleaming blue-green water. Here, the roof was lower, perhaps twice the height of a tall man above the rippling surface. The place was filled with a curious droning sound.

On the rocks that bordered this subterranean lake stood the source of the instructions: not a man or woman, not a creature such as the catlike being we had encountered before, but something that seemed made up of smoke and mist and illusions. It swirled and changed and twisted itself in and out of various shapes, but if I narrowed my eyes, I could make out, vaguely, the form of a portly man of Turkish appearance, his full trousers, billowing shirt, and bejeweled caftan winking in and out of view as if he did not really want us to see him at all.

"A djinn," whispered Stoyan.

He was probably right. I had read stories in which such magical beings appeared, usually as a result of a human accidentally summoning them by polishing a mysterious old lamp or uncorking a forbidden bottle. I could not remember whether they were of a helpful disposition or not.

"Who are you?" I asked, aware that I had shown my worst side during the last ordeal and determined to start as strongly as I could this time. "What challenge?"

"We need to move on," Duarte muttered, half to me, half to the djinn, which he was rather pointedly not looking at. "We mean no harm here; I do not understand why there are so many barriers to our progress. What must we do to pass forward?"

I was recalling the miniatures. The cat and the riddles, the rope swing. What came next?

"This task is for two," said the djinn in its vaporous voice, waving its evanescent arms toward the lake. "Choose the two with the greatest bond of trust, those who will work best as a team. The third need not endure this trial."

No choice, I thought. Duarte and Stoyan had, at best, a wary truce. The fledgling trust between Duarte and myself was too new to be put to such a test. "It has to be Stoyan and me," I said, glancing at the others.

A crimson flush spread slowly across Stoyan's pale skin. He uttered not a word.

"But . . . ," Duarte began, looking from me to Stoyan and back again. Then, to the djinn, he added, "This is unreasonable. We need to know what this task is first. If it's a feat of strength, we'd want Paula to be the one who is spared from having to attempt it."

"In this place, the rules are not yours to make," the djinn said solemnly. "Your quest brought your companions here. Either they will help you or they will hinder you. The choice is made."

"So you do know why I've come here. Then I don't understand these obstacles that have been set in our way. What purpose—"

"It is required," said the djinn, gesturing with its incorporeal hand. "It is foretold."

"It's the way of things in the Other Kingdom," I said under my breath. "Tests and trials. They love them."

There was a little flat boat on the lake, tied up by the rock shelf. It looked unstable. I could not remember anything in the miniatures that matched this.

"Balance," said the djinn. "The boat must be guided through the cave. There is a pole to propel the craft forward. That will require strength."

It sounded suspiciously easy, something Stoyan could do without even thinking. "And?" I asked.

Somewhere within the vaporous form of its rotund

countenance, the djinn seemed to be smiling. "Balance," it said again. "You bring the goddess home. She cannot come without an entourage, a celebratory throng to accompany her. You will find them here, in the cavern of the lake. While your companion guides the boat, you must gather them."

"Gather?" My voice had shrunk to a wisp of sound. The bee goddess. A celebratory throng. I recalled the miniature, the image of Cybele with her hair flowing wild, garlanded with flying insects. High above us, the strange humming sound echoed around the cavern. "You mean gather . . . bees? How?" The nightmare again, the sensation of crawling creatures on my face, in my ears, swarming down my throat . . . My gorge rose.

"How could she reach them?" Duarte was staring up at the cave roof. "It's too high even for the tallest of men. Besides, she'd be stung. You can't ask Paula to do this!"

"Shh," I said, forcing down both physical sickness and fresh panic. "We have to do it; that's the way these things work. If I'm supposed to get through without being stung to death, then I will. Stoyan, that day you came bursting into Irene's hamam, I thought I might find another picture. I dreamed it the night before; I thought the girl was picking fruit. I know what we have to do." I bent down and took off my boots.

As if this were not already hard enough, the djinn insisted I carry Cybele's Gift. Perhaps it was to prevent Duarte from abandoning his crazy friends and somehow bolting ahead with the artifact, leaving us to what did indeed seem an impossible endeavor. I tied a loop of the cloth around my belt so the artifact hung by my side. Stoyan stepped into the boat. It rocked wildly under his weight until he balanced it, standing with legs apart.

"You realize what we're going to have to do," I said, meeting his eyes. As I spoke, I heard sounds from the lower cavern—voices, footsteps. I had believed the run through the darkness and the hideous, squeezing passage through the rocks might have defeated our pursuers. It seemed I was wrong. Irene was every bit as determined as we were. And she was taller than me.

"I know what must be done, and I do not like it at all," said Stoyan through gritted teeth. I could feel his unease in my own belly.

"Here," I said, picking up the pole by which the boat was guided and leaning it against him with one end wedged in the boat and the other by his shoulder. "Once you're supporting me, you won't be able to bend and pick it up. I'm not quite sure how to do this next part. . . ."

"Paula," said Duarte, his tone incredulous, "you can't be going to—" Then, seeing that I was, he fell silent.

I stepped into the boat. Stoyan gripped my hands; I climbed via his knees to his shoulders. It was not a particularly graceful performance, but his strength and my light weight made it easier than it might have been. In addition, we had practiced maneuvers of a similar kind when rehearsing our combat sequences. It all helped.

The next part was the most difficult. I was no acrobat, and I did not like the look of that rather odd-colored water or the long dark shadows I could see moving in its depths. Sitting on the shoulders of a tall man who was standing in a rocking boat was quite challenging enough. But the cave ceiling was still too high for me to reach. I let go of Stoyan's hands and set mine on his head. Shakily I brought one leg up, then the other, until I was in a crouching position. Then, as Stoyan held my ankles, I took my hands away and straightened to stand. The boat tilted, and Stoyan adjusted his balance. I stretched my arms out to the sides, trying to ignore the awful churning feeling in my stomach. All this and bees, too.

"I'm ready," I murmured.

"Great God Almighty," Duarte said from the shore, and crossed himself.

I wobbled as Stoyan took away his right hand; I almost fell as he removed his left. There would be no steering the boat if he could not grip the pole. He must use all his skill to maintain a controlled course and to keep the craft as stable as possible. It was up to me to stand straight and not fall.

We moved off slowly across the lake, leaving Duarte and his strange companion behind us on the shore. I thought I heard the djinn say behind me, "You must complete your own task, mariner."

The watery light rippled all around us, casting uncanny shadows on the rock walls. *Don't look down,* I ordered myself. *Keep your back straight. Don't lock your knees.*

"Breathe slowly, Paula," Stoyan said. "I can see a place where something is moving about up above. I will steer for that corner." I could hear how he was pacing his breathing, trying to keep calm. His body was strung tight; I felt it through the soles of my feet. "If you are stung, if you are in pain, tell me. We need not go on with this."

"Mmm," I managed. Of course we had to go on. If we failed to do so, what had this all been for? We were almost there. If Cybele required a triumphal procession complete with attendant insects, then we must provide one.

The buzzing above us became louder. I made myself tilt my head back and look up as Stoyan dug the pole in, bringing the little craft to a halt. A mistake—I teetered, a hairbreadth from falling as a wave of dizziness swept over me.

"Reach up slowly," Stoyan said. "Be careful. There are odd currents in this water. I may not be able to hold us here for long."

Without looking, I reached a hand above my head. My face screwed itself up, waiting for stings. There was a slight soft motion against my fingers, and when I brought the hand back down, a single bee was crawling there. The soft light of the cavern touched every hair on its body to a small miracle of brown and gold. Its legs were delicate threads, its eyes bright and strange. I put my hand to my shoulder, and the bee crawled onto my tunic and settled there with every appearance of purpose.

"Listen," Stoyan said. "The buzzing has stopped. But I can hear something else."

I was holding both hands up again, trying to get a glimpse of what was above me without moving my head. My reach was well short of the cave ceiling, and no more bees came. "I can't get high enough, and I've only got one," I said. "If I had a net or something . . ."

"I cannot hold the boat here any longer, Paula. The current is too strong." And, indeed, we were moving off quite quickly now, Stoyan's efforts with the pole futile against the pull of the water. If he dug in too hard, I would fall. I was already struggling to stay upright. The boat was making its own course for the far end of the lake, traveling faster and faster. Stoyan's hands came around my ankles once more. His touch gave me heart. I hoped the pole was somewhere he could still reach it.

The boat took us to a place where the sound overhead was higher and softer. This time the creatures flew down to investigate the intrusion. Not bees, but bee-sized birds, brightly hued, fantailed, each no larger than a thimble. They whirred around my head and around Stoyan's, causing him to curse and sway. I had to bend down and clutch his hair again to keep from falling.

"Sorry," I muttered. "I've got one." A scrap of vivid red had joined the bee on my shoulder. As soon as the miniature avian settled, the others flew up in a flock to vanish into the shadows above. The boat moved off again before I could so much as stretch a hand up. Tears of frustration welled in my eyes.

"Paula," Stoyan said quietly.

"What? Stoyan, this is no good, I can't reach properly—"

"Paula, I think this is right. The current moves us despite my efforts, as if on a predetermined course. Perhaps we need collect only one of each kind: one bee, one bird, one of whatever else we find here. We should not struggle against the pull of the water but let it carry us where it will."

I drew a deep, shaky breath. Perhaps he was right. The more I thought about his suggestion, the wiser it seemed.

"All right," I said. "Let's see what happens."

We stopped in another place, and whatever was scuttling about overhead dropped down a spiky creature like a small gargoyle. I caught it, wincing, and set it on the other shoulder in case it had a taste for poultry.

"Stoyan?"

"Mmm?"

"Can you see back to the shore where we started? Is there any sign of Irene and Murat? I thought I heard the djinn telling Duarte he had his own task to complete."

"I cannot see, Paula. I hear the sound of some larger creature. Perhaps—"

The boat moved off toward a rock shelf near the end of the lake. I fought for my balance; Stoyan could do no more than try to hold steady. The closer we came, the louder the cacophony from ahead, a wild howling and barking that sent echoes all around the cavern. Here, a tunnel led from the rocks on into the system of caves. Guarding the passage was an enormous creature, perhaps some kind of mountain wolf, perhaps an outsize dog, though I had never seen such an intimidating animal before. Its barking mouth revealed a ferocious display of sharp teeth and slavering tongue. Its body was all harnessed power, muscles bunched, legs planted, every part of it gathered for a leap. I looked into its eyes, an odd light green unusual in a dog, and thought I read there a blind greed for human blood. There had been many bees, many birds, a number of gargoyles. There was only one dog. This was the one we had to take with us. As the boat drew closer to the shelf where it stood, the animal drew back its lips and growled low in its throat.

"Stoyan," I whispered. "It doesn't look very . . . What if . . . ?"

"Come down slowly; let me help you," Stoyan said. "This is the way out. It fits with our tree map. Stay behind me. No sudden movements."

"Yes, but . . ." I crouched, then slid down to stand behind Stoyan in the boat, my legs threatening to collapse under me.

"It's not just a matter of getting past; we have to . . ." I fell silent as the wolf, or dog, sidled toward the boat, its growl acquiring a menacing edge. On my shoulders, the three little creatures maintained their silence.

Stoyan stepped out onto the rocks, one hand holding the boat against the shore. "Stay there for now," he warned me. He remained crouching, his gaze not on the dog but directed away, though I could see he had the animal in the edge of his sight. His free hand was relaxed by his side, in a position where the dog could smell it but not actually reaching out. He was keeping up a continuous flow of quiet talk. It was Bulgarian, and I could not understand the words, but the meaning was clear in the tone. *I am a friend. I can be trusted. I know you are afraid. Smell my scent. I mean you no harm. You are safe with me.*

Slowly the creature settled and the fearsome challenge died down. The dog crept closer. It sniffed at Stoyan's hand. He waited awhile longer, murmuring all the time, before he tried a deliberate touch, a caress at the base of the ear, then a stroke down the neck. Gradually, with remarkable control, Stoyan got me out of the boat and squatting beside him while all the time petting the dog, talking to it, making sure my movements did not startle it into another defensive frenzy.

"Now extend your hand slowly; that's it." He put his large hand around mine, and we stretched out together to let the dog assess this new scent. Then Stoyan rose carefully to his feet, drawing me up after him, keeping close enough to grab me if he needed to. The dog was still nervous. I imagined few human creatures made their way to this subterranean realm and fewer still penetrated to the depths we had reached. Behind us, the boat had floated away.

"We can go on now," Stoyan said quietly. "He will come with us." He spoke a few words to the dog, and it moved to stand by his side, turning its eyes up to him expectantly.

"How did you do that?" I asked in wonderment. "How did you know?"

"I saw it was a good dog, but wary and afraid. One must take time to earn the trust of such a creature. With a more damaged animal it would be far longer—days, weeks of patience. This one is strong of heart. Paula, we can go on."

For a moment we paused, looking at each other.

"You chose the right team," murmured Stoyan.

A sudden thought came to me. "What about Duarte? We can't go back to fetch him. The boat's gone."

"You have the artifact," Stoyan said, and now his tone set a distance between us. "Whatever has happened, he would want you to take it on."

There were possibilities behind this that I could barely bring myself to think of: Duarte at the mercy of Murat and his crossbow; Duarte carrying out a task of equal difficulty to ours, somewhere in the caves alone; Duarte trapped on the other side of the lake, unable to leave. I said nothing. If our mission was to take Cybele's Gift on the last part of its journey and leave the pirate to his fate, the powers of the Other Kingdom were cruel indeed.

As we passed through another tunnel, leaving the lake behind us, the little creatures I had gathered from the cavern grew more and more excited, two flying up from my shoulder to dance around my head like a strange garland, the third creeping to and fro and making anticipatory wheezing sounds. The dog was silent, padding beside Stoyan as we emerged to the grandest chamber of all.

The sight that lay before us stopped us in our tracks. The walls were pillared, the ceiling vaulted, and in the central space . . . My eyes widened with amazement. Here lay every sort of treasure one could imagine: jewelry, gold coins, silver ewers and basins and platters encrusted with decoration, statues and vases and coffers of precious stones. Scattered amongst this wealth were books with covers of the finest tooled calf leather and manuscripts whose delicate calligraphy and dazzling decoration caught and enthralled my scholar's eye. All was jumbled together, a brilliant chaos of merchandise, a veritable dragon's hoard. If only my father could see this!

"Welcome," someone said, and there before us was the old woman in black. "You have passed through Cybele's Heart. I am the keeper of Cybele's mysteries. We have waited a long time for your coming. Many years. Many long years."

My hand slipped into Stoyan's. "We greet you respectfully," I said, wondering if we should have brought gifts. "Perhaps you are a friend of Drăguţa, the witch of the wood. If so, she would want me to give you her best regards. I understand that each of us has a quest to fulfill. Stoyan and I have traveled here as helpers to Duarte Aguiar. He is bringing the last words of the goddess home and should be close behind us." How far across the lake would Murat and Irene have traveled by now? Was there another bee, another bird, another gargoyle and dog waiting for them? By my side, Cybele's Gift in its soft wrapping hung against my thigh. "There are others following," I told her, "people who think they have a claim to the statue." I was not sure whether to warn her, to tell her Irene wanted to snatch Cybele's Gift and keep it for herself to enhance her prestige with the cult in Istanbul—if what Irene had told us was true. I thought it must be; what else could have brought her all this way? Should I say it? The folk of the Other Kingdom tended to take offense when human folk tried to tell them how to conduct their own affairs. It was possible this crone already knew all about Irene and considered her a more suitable custodian for the artifact than the inhabitants of Mustafa's mountain village.

"Ah," said the old woman, "but Cybele's Gift is in your possession, Paula. Why do you not go forward with it yourself?"

I shivered. It was like what Stoyan had said before, a choice that implied Duarte might be left behind. "It's not right for me to do it," I said. "Duarte made a promise to a friend, someone who saved his life. Duarte should be the one to finish this."

"Let me make this plain to you," the crone said. "There are two ways to Cybele's treasure trove, which you must pass to complete your mission. One is before your eyes—simply walk forward across this chamber, and you will reach it. You have Cybele's Gift. You are safe and so is your companion. That is the first way: the easy way."

"And the second?" Stoyan asked.

"The second lies there." The old woman pointed a long-nailed finger toward what had seemed a plain rock wall, and an archway appeared, through which a smaller cavern could be glimpsed. A reddish light flickered there.

"Which will you choose?" the crone asked quietly. "How brave are you, Paula?"

It was an echo of the dream, the one in which Ileana had interrogated my sister about my part of the mission. This was not the simple choice it seemed to be. Take the wrong path and it might not be just Duarte I abandoned to whatever fate awaited him but Tati as well. "The second one," I said, glancing at Stoyan, who gave a nod. "We'll go that way. I hope I'm brave enough for whatever it is." *Let this be right,* I prayed. *Let all of us be safe.* Almost as much as that, I wanted Cybele to go to Mustafa's people. It couldn't be right for Irene and her cult to have the statue. The goddess was an old thing of earth, simple, wild, and good. She did not belong in the hands of a devious person like Irene, a woman who was prepared to lie and dissemble and kill to get the statue for herself.

"Be quick," the old woman warned. "Those whom you have brought after you are almost here. Each in turn will have a chance to make a claim. If you would have Duarte be first, show us what you have learned."

Hand in hand, Stoyan and I went through the arch into the smaller cave. The crone did not follow us, for there was another guide here, an ethereal woman whose hair was a shimmering cloud like spun silk, its color pure white. Tiny twinkling stars dotted her locks, and her gown seemed made of sea, or summer sky, or the wings of delicate blue-green butterflies. A peri, I thought, an Anatolian fairy woman. Her eyes were lustrous, her face creamy pale, but not as pale as Tati's. I gasped in a shocked breath, then fell silent.

My sister was standing very still halfway across the chamber, which was rimmed by a ledge onto which we had emerged. Tati was on the lower level. She was blindfolded and her wrists were bound together. The floor of the cavern was a metal grille of elaborate design. Most of the holes in it were quite large, big enough for a slender woman like Tati to fall through. A red light came from beneath, as of fire not so far down, and the chamber was hot. Tati stood right at the center on a little platform. If she tried to move blind, she would quickly fall to those flames beneath the treacherous floor. There was a strange smell here, like bone, or iron, or something old beyond counting.

Across the narrow bars of the grille moved a number of creatures similar to the one I bore on my left shoulder, things like gargoyles, though these were much bigger and their mouths were open wide to show knifelike teeth. Their little avid eyes, shining red in the flickering light, were uniformly fixed on Tati, as if they were only waiting for her to stumble and fall. They scuttled from one crossing point to another, apparently heedless of the danger. When they met face to face, which was often, they snarled and scratched at each other. As they ran past my sister, this way, that way, each took a snap at her legs. I heard her suppress a cry as, through the cloth of her robe, a set of teeth found its mark. The gargoyle on my shoulder made an anxious chittering noise and hid its face under a wing. The shelf where we stood seemed too high for the creatures to attempt a leap up. If Tati could make her way over to us, we could haul her up beside us, out of danger. All she needed was a set of clear instructions. Or, better still, someone who was prepared to cross over and lead her back.

Footsteps behind us. I spun around, fearing Murat and Irene had reached us already, but it was Duarte, his face parchment white. He had an oozing slash on one cheek, as if from a whip. Around one arm was coiled a bright green snake, clinging but apparently quiescent, its pale eyes narrowed to slits.

"Don't ask," he said with a crooked smile. "Let me just say that this amiable little fellow had a lot of far less friendly and much bigger brothers and that I've changed my mind about my skill with ropes. If anyone ever asks me to climb one again, I'll tie the thing around his neck." What he saw on my face and on Stoyan's stopped the flow of words. His eyes went to my sister, all alone amidst the circling creatures. "What in heaven's name is this? Don't tell me we're not finished yet."

"None may speak!" the peri ordered, raising her hand. "None may approach her!"

Tati had heard this interchange, despite the cacophony of the creatures' shrill cries. She turned her head toward us. The blindfold concealed all but her mouth, the lips pressed tightly together. Perhaps she, too, was forbidden to speak. Fury and frustration welled up in me. To subject Tati to this kind of trial was barbaric. This was just too much. I was a hairbreadth from screaming childishly that it wasn't fair, that they couldn't treat my sister like this, that I'd never asked for a quest, and that I wasn't doing it anymore.

I looked at the peri, wondering if I was allowed to speak to her, if not to Tati, but she made a sharp negative gesture.

"You must all remain silent," she murmured. "You must remain here at the side, the three of you. There is a solution. Find it."

It was horribly unfair. My mind ran in circles as my sister stood frozen on her little platform amidst the circling, slavering creatures. Cruel. Ridiculous. This seemed so arbitrary, so violent, when all Tati wanted was a chance to visit her loved ones, so simple and modest a reward. Why had the crone asked me how brave I was? What difference did that make if all I could do was stand by and watch?

"Curse it," muttered Duarte. "What is the purpose of these tests? I'm here in good faith to return Cybele's Gift to its people. Who is that woman anyway?"

"Shh!" hissed the peri, frowning at him.

Learning. The purpose is learning. I did not say it aloud. Duarte might be prepared to risk speech, but my knowledge of the Other Kingdom held me mute. With Tati's life in the balance, we could not afford a single error.

Tati took an unsteady step forward, the direction apparently random, and one of the gargoyles fastened its teeth into her ankle and hung on, jaws firm. She could not suppress a cry of pain.

Think, Paula. You're the scholar, work this puzzle out. Stay calm and concentrate. Words: we were forbidden to speak. Signs: useless with Tati blindfolded. Clapping, stamping, clicking: only helpful if everyone agreed in advance what they meant. Something to throw, a knife or rock, to deter those hideous creatures: it might get rid of one, if the aim was good, but there were so many of them, enough to use up within moments every missile we could lay hands on.

Struggling to dislodge the creature from her ankle, Tati lost her balance and fell to one knee. Immediately, four or five of the gargoyles leaped to cling to her, growling and shrieking. Stay calm? My heart was pounding and my breath was coming in panicky gasps. My blood was boiling with outrage on my sister's behalf. A pox on the Other Kingdom! I gathered myself to break every rule I knew about quests.

No peri was going to make me stand by and watch my sister being bitten to death.

Stoyan's hand fastened around my arm, holding me back. He gestured, pointing to himself, then to Tati. He looked from me to Duarte and back again, his expression clearly saying, *Let me do it.*

I could not see any way he could manage it other than by disobeying the peri's order and rushing across to try to pluck Tati to safety. Let that happen, and no doubt a terrible fate would befall the two of them, likely a plunge through the grating to the flames below. In a place like this, rules were rules—even Duarte, a man who in the outside world was a law unto himself, was not supposed to break the codes of the Other Kingdom. If I trusted Stoyan with this, two people I loved would suffer a horrible death right before my eyes. I looked desperately at Duarte, thinking he, of all of us, might have some surprising solution, some brilliant, quirky answer to this apparently impossible challenge. But he only shrugged and shook his head.

My sister was crouched down, her head bowed toward her knees. The gargoyles were all over her, eight or ten of them, snapping. Her body jerked and flinched as the teeth made their mark. I could see blood on her bound hands. Stoyan touched my shoulder, making sure he had my attention. There was a smile on his lips and in his amber eyes a shining confidence, and suddenly I understood the crone's words to me. *How brave are you, Paula? Are you brave enough to admit your weakness? Brave enough to trust?* Swallowing my tears, I laid my hand against Stoyan's ragged tunic, over his heart, and nodded. Then I stepped back.

Stoyan clicked his fingers. The dog moved up beside

him, alert, quiet. I'd been so shocked by Tati's predicament that I had forgotten it was there. Stoyan made a simple gesture, hand slightly cupped down by the dog's face, motioning it forward.

The dog moved steadily, advancing with confidence across the narrow spans, ignoring the menacing light, the rushes of heat from the gaps between. It padded toward the quivering form of my sister. It did not hesitate, even when three of the creatures came scuttling straight toward it, hissing and shrieking defiance. The hound opened its massive jaws and uttered a single, monstrous bark of warning that echoed around the cavern as if it had summoned a whole pack of great dogs in its support. The creatures hesitated, then retreated.

The hound reached Tati and barked again, right next to her head. Unsurprisingly, Tati cowered lower. One gargoyle, particularly bold, was creeping toward the dog now, ready to seize a leg in its jaws. A piercing shriek sounded in my ear, momentarily deafening me: The creature on my shoulder, the one that looked like a miniature cousin of those attackers out there, had sounded a shrill warning. The dog made a snatch, a snap, a jerk of the head, and the would-be attacker was flung across the grille to fall neatly into one of the gaping holes. There was a little fizzing sound, a puff of dark smoke, then silence. Beside my left ear, my own gargoyle gave a muted hum of satisfaction.

Stoyan clapped his hands twice, sharply. The dog looked across at him. Tati was huddled down as if trying to press her face into the ground. How could he do it? How could he let her know she was under a friend's guidance now and would be safe if she could only bring herself to trust?

Stoyan motioned to the hound, keeping the gesture clear. *Come. Lead her.*

The dog nosed at Tati's cheek, gentle as a loved household pet. It gave a little whine, licking her face. Tati stirred.

Duarte began to whistle. The tune he chose was a jig, innocent and jaunty, a melody full of the joy of life. It was entirely alien in this place of darkness, fire, and pain. He could not have known the power such a sound would have to lift my sister's spirits, for he had dismissed as fantasy my tale of full moon revels in a mysterious fairy kingdom. But we knew jigs, Tati and I. We'd pranced our way through hundreds of them over the years with our uncanny companions. In this cavern speech was forbidden. But nobody had said anything about music.

Tati sat up, turning her head toward the sound. A foolish gargoyle was creeping closer, eyes glinting with greed. The dog, intent on washing my sister's face, had not seen it. The gargoyle sprang, landing on the hound's neck and sinking in its fangs. The dog yelped and twisted, struggling to dislodge its unwelcome passenger. It was perilously close to the platform's edge.

The bee left my shoulder, winging across the divide. I could not see exactly what it did, but suddenly the clinging gargoyle was thrashing on the platform, and a moment later it was gone, fallen into the fire. The dog shook itself and returned its attention to Tati. The bee alighted on my shoulder once more. Perhaps all it had needed to do was provide a diversion. Or maybe the bees of the Other Kingdom sting and sting again and do not die.

Tati was on her feet, her bound hands against the dog's neck and her blindfolded face turned toward us. Duarte whistled on, the tune more muted now, for Stoyan had begun to coax the animal back. Without benefit of his voice, he used his body with eloquence, crouching, gesturing, mouthing words of encouragement, clapping his hands when he wanted the creature to pay attention, for here and there it was necessary to turn sharply, to circle, to backtrack in order to reach us. Tati held on, her face chalk-white below the dark cloth of the blindfold, her feet wobbling on the narrow tracks of the grille. On my right shoulder, the little bird twittered a counterpoint to Duarte's melody.

Tati was almost here. She was moving across the treacherous path, leaving the gargoyles behind. They were clustered on the edge of the platform, watching us with crestfallen expressions on their odd little faces. I breathed again, a great gasp for air, my relief like a spasm all through my body. He had saved her. Against the odds, Stoyan had found a remarkable, ingenious way to solve the seemingly impossible puzzle.

Tati had reached us. The two men stretched down to help her up to safety, and the dog jumped up after her.

"Oh, Stoyan, thank you," I breathed; then, at a nod from our guide, I untied my sister's blindfold and threw my arms around her.

Chapter Fourteen

"It is good," said the peri coolly as Duarte undid the bonds around Tati's wrists, and my sister hugged me back. Stoyan spoke quietly to the dog, praising it for its courage and obedience. Then Tati, looking over my shoulder, suddenly shrieked, "Emerald!" and released her hold on me. She reached out a hand toward Duarte, and the green snake uncoiled itself from his arm and flowed onto hers, making its way up to her shoulders.

"Where was she? Where did you find her?" Tati was addressing a bemused Duarte, using the language of the Other Kingdom. "Oh, thank you so much for bringing her back!"

"Delighted to oblige," Duarte said smoothly. He had no doubt noticed that, even when she was pale with shock, my sister was a woman of exceptional beauty. "Your Emerald had discovered some far bigger companions; they made it somewhat difficult for me to reach her, but my instructions were to retrieve one particular creature, and that was what I did. And put myself off climbing for the rest of my life." He examined his palms, which now bore rope burns in addition to the damage inflicted by our passage through the mountain. "A little friend of yours, I take it?"

"My dear companion," Tati said. "Given to me by Drăguţa, the witch of the wood. I thought I'd lost her forever. She insisted on coming, and then she slithered off on her own. Oh, Paula, I have so much to tell you—"

The peri interrupted, using the same language Tati had, that nameless tongue we could all understand but not identify. "If you would be first to reach Cybele's treasure trove and make your claim, you must move on now. Say your goodbyes."

"What?" I gasped. It was the first proper chance I'd had to talk to my sister since she left us for the Other Kingdom six years ago. "Already? But Tati's hurt; she's bleeding. It's so soon—"

"I'm all right, Paula." Tati's voice was shaky, but as she showed me her hands, I could see no trace of injury—her skin was ghostly white but unmarked. "The fear was real enough, the pain as well," she said, "but the rest was mostly illusion, I think. We must do as they tell us. Maybe I'll see you again soon, if I've got this right. Oh, Paula, I did so want to be able to explain what I was doing, but there were rules. . . ."

I was wordless. I felt as if I had been thumped in the chest and all the air pushed out of me. "You can't go," I whispered. But I was not so foolish as to believe I could change the laws of the Other Kingdom. If her quest depended on obedience, then she must obey, and so must I.

"Sorrow's waiting for me," Tati said, and as we walked back under the archway to the larger cavern, I saw to my surprise that it was so. The crone still waited there, not far from the pile of treasure, and at a slight distance stood the pale-faced, black-clad form of my sister's sweetheart, his grave gaze leaping instantly to her as we appeared. She had not come all this way alone, then. I was glad of that. Still, I could feel that pain in my chest, the bittersweet hurt of holding her so briefly, then losing her again. I had not told her anything, our family news—marriages and babies and merchant voyages—our small triumphs and disasters over the years since she had left us. I had not even said how much we loved her and missed her. But perhaps she knew that. *How brave are you, Paula? Brave enough to say goodbye?*

"It's time, Tatiana," the crone said solemnly. "Your part in this is over. It is for your sister and her companions to take the quest forward now. Make your thanks and depart. Pay my respects to Drăguţa. An old friend."

Tati smiled at Stoyan and reached to touch his arm, a gesture of gratitude. She acknowledged Duarte with a little bow of the head. Then she put her hands on either side of my face and kissed me on the brow. "Be safe, Paula. It looks as if you have good companions for your quest. I hope you'll be happy." The snake on her shoulders gave a faint hiss. Whether this was an objection or a farewell there was no telling.

"Goodbye, Tati," I said, choking on my tears, and watched her walk over to Sorrow. He put his arm around her shoulders; she slipped hers around his waist. The snake moved to drape itself across the two of them. I saw in Sorrow's face that he loved my sister every bit as much as he had when we let him take her away to the Other Kingdom—more, perhaps. His care for her was in the curve of his somber lips, the tenderness of his touch, the dark intensity of his eyes. With her free hand, Tati gave us a little wave, and the two of them walked away into the shadows. I did not think they would travel home by merchant ship or cart, on the paths of men, but by a different way.

There was a little cough behind us. Irene and Murat had emerged into the treasure cavern. They were looking less immaculate now. Their skin bore bruises and scratches, and their clothing was as torn and filthy as ours. By Murat's side a cat stalked, palest gray, sleek and aloof. I thought it bore an uncanny resemblance to the eunuch, and this made me look again at the dog that had been so quick to obey Stoyan's unspoken commands. On Irene's shoulders perched creatures similar to mine: a bee and a bird—hers were green. Instead of the gargoyle, she had a rat. Her eyes met mine, the look in them supremely confident. She gave me a little crooked smile.

"You are all assembled. You have triumphed in the tests we set for you." The old woman's tone was solemn. "Few pass through this mountain, and still fewer emerge with wiser hearts. Perhaps you thought the tests unreasonable." She looked at Duarte. "But this is a secret way. If you cannot learn, you will not pass through. To reach this point has required much of you. In recognition of that, the goddess offers each of you a reward." Her gaze passed over us in turn, Stoyan and I close together, Duarte a little apart, looking exhausted, with Cybele's Gift in his hands. Irene was holding her head high. Murat stood, impassive, by her side.

"Each of you may take one item from our treasure trove before you pass on," the keeper of Cybele's mysteries continued. "I am certain each can find something to please. Weapons for warriors. Books for scholars. Jewels and gold for those who lack resource. Collector's items such as are seen but once in a lifetime. Choose with care, and only when I call your name."

"Wait!" I could not stop myself from speaking out, though Stoyan squeezed my hand in warning. "You shouldn't let those two pass through the cavern; they mean us only harm! They only got here because they followed us to find the way. That isn't fair—"

The old woman fixed me with her obsidian-dark eyes. "You will choose first," she said. "If there are rules in this place of the goddess, it is not for you to make them, Paula. Come, let us see what you have learned on your journey. Which do you value most highly now, wisdom or scholarship?"

I might have known the trials and tests were not yet over. As I considered her question, I pictured Stoyan quieting the dog, taking time, staying calm, knowing from both instinct and experience what to do. He had quickly worked out how to help Tati, though neither Duarte nor I could see a solution. I recalled, with shame, that I had at first expected my friend to use muscle, not mind, to solve that problem. I remembered him poring over the little drawings I had found so hard to make sense of, then saying, *Perhaps it is less complex than you imagine.*

"I have overestimated the role scholarship plays in finding answers and in understanding the world," I told her. "I have learned that there are deeper kinds of wisdom." I thought of Duarte supporting his friend as he dangled over the void and his stricken expression when he lost him. I heard him telling me to run ahead with Cybele's Gift—to save it and myself. I thought of Irene's cool voice as she ordered Murat to kill. "And I've learned it's a mistake to judge people too quickly," I added.

"Well spoken, Paula," Irene said approvingly, as if the original question had been hers. "I do hope you will reconsider your decision now. Move on with Murat and me, and a brilliant future awaits you. You are young; perhaps the attention of these men of yours flatters you. Believe me, neither has anything of worth to offer you."

"Choose your reward," said the crone, waving toward the mound of treasure.

It seemed I had answered the question to her satisfaction, and now I was supposed to take some kind of prize. I had only to reach an arm's length to pick up any one of five items, each worth a king's ransom. My eyes fell on a lovely manuscript not far from my foot, its borders embellished in gold leaf, with little images of minarets against a night sky painted in rich deep blue. Beside it was a tiny bound book, open to show delicate calligraphy on creamy vellum. Either would make a miraculous start for my business, for each was an item nobody from here to Transylvania would be able to match.

"Oh, Paula," said Irene. "Such riches. Such a beginning for your collection. How can you possibly choose?"

I stood gazing at the lovely things, the precious and glittering assortment of treasures, and I knew I didn't want any of them. I just wanted to see Duarte achieve his mission and the three of us get safely out and home again. I wanted to hug Father and tell him how sorry I was. Most of all, I wanted my sisters.

"Choose, Paula," the old woman said.

The little red bird flew from my shoulder to the heap,

alighting with precision on an item tucked behind a grand silver jug. A hint of bright color told me what it was even as I reached across to retrieve it. Tati's embroidery was finished now. The crumpled rag unfolded, its creases disappearing before my eyes, and there were five girls dancing proudly across the linen hand in hand, their faces wreathed in smiles. Tati, Jena, Iulia, Paula, Stela. We were all there, together, strong and alive. *No more tears, Paula*, I ordered myself. "May I have this?" I asked.

Irene sucked in her breath. It seemed an odd choice, I suppose, with such riches on offer.

"It is yours," said the crone, and a rare smile curved her withered lips. "And I will give you another. As you are a scholar of some note, I am certain you would appreciate an additional riddle."

I refrained from telling her that right now I was incapable of dealing with a riddle for three-year-olds, let alone anything more taxing.

"It is not to solve now," the old woman said, apparently reading my mind. "Take it away with you, consider its meaning, find the solution in good time. But don't wait too long. It goes thus:
Water and stone
Flesh and bone
Night and morn
Rose and thorn
Tree and wind
Heart and mind."

There was a silence. Nobody offered me a solution, and nothing immediately suggested itself to me. But then, she had told me to take time. "Thank you," I said with mixed feelings. The trouble with being a scholar is that once someone sets you a puzzle, your mind starts working away at it even if you are too tired to get anywhere.

"You, young man"—the crone motioned to Stoyan—"choose next. Three rewards you have earned, one for the courage that saw you take an arrow for a man who was not yet your friend; one for the steadfastness that held Paula safe and strong as she endured her trials; and one for the openness of your mind to this world beyond the human, a world in which trust and cooperation take many forms. Make your choice: One item from the pile is yours."

He was far quicker than I. "If you permit," he said to the old woman, and reached out to take a diadem of gold. It was an opulent piece, thickly crusted with precious stones: an adornment fit for the Sultan himself. I was surprised by his choice and a little disappointed. After all this, after what we had been through together, my friend would measure his reward in riches? A moment later, I realized an item like this would allow him to stop earning his keep as a guard and get on with the search for Taidjut.

"I understand your choice, Stoyan," the old woman told him. "This is the first of your rewards and the only one fully in my power to give you. Although you have earned all three, the long-sought second and the deeply desired third do not depend on the decisions of the Other Kingdom but on those of your own kind. You are a good man. I hope both will come in time."

I met Stoyan's eye as he slipped the priceless ornament into his sash, then looked away, full of shame that I had doubted his motives even for a moment. And what had the crone meant about an arrow? He'd said his wound was only a scratch.

The crone did not ask Stoyan what he had learned but turned her attention to our companion. "Duarte da Costa Aguiar," she said. "You have come farthest of all to make your choice. Step forward now and do so, bold adventurer." Her tone was warm.

Duarte stood there a long time with the cloth-wrapped artifact in his hands. He was scanning the hoard, searching for something, not necessarily the most valuable item, or the most unusual, or the rarest. It became clear to me that he was looking for one particular object amidst a hundred, a thousand individual treasures. We stood waiting, and Duarte walked around the pile of precious things, hunting high and low. Irene tapped her foot. Beside her, Murat waited quietly.

I think both Stoyan and I realized at the same time what it was Duarte was looking for, and we joined him in the hunt. It wasn't easy. Gold and silver dazzled the eyes; parchment and vellum, unrolled and tumbling down, screened what lay behind. Vessels spilled forth small rivers of rubies and amethysts. Necklaces, bracelets, and decorated swords vied for attention. But then, perhaps we were meant to find it.

"Duarte," I said, suddenly still. "There." I pointed to a low corner where something protruded slightly from beneath an ornate sword hilt.

Duarte smiled. He knelt and the crone moved closer. I held my breath. He cleared away the sword and a bronze platter the size of a small table, and there it was, a modest piece of broken pottery, like the lower half of a bulbous gourd in shape, its upper edge snapped off cleanly. Amongst the thousand rare and expensive items in the hoard, this was a thing of unpretentious clay fashioned with modest craft, unadorned save for a scrawl of cryptic writing curling across it.

Duarte placed the small bundle he was carrying beside the broken fragment. He untied the cloth and drew out Cybele's Gift. In the cavern, there was utter silence. On my shoulders, the three attendant creatures had become preternaturally still.

"I have come not to take, but to give," the pirate said, glancing up at the old woman. He lifted Cybele's Gift in hands that were remarkably steady and placed the top part of the little statue on the base.

Something changed. I could not say what it was, for there was no sound, no dazzling light, no sudden cold or warmth. Nobody spoke a word. But I sensed a profound difference in the cavern, as if a drought had broken or a pestilence had been cured. Before our eyes, the two parts of Cybele knitted together, joining up as smoothly as if the artifact had never been broken.

Duarte rose to his feet, leaving the statue where it was. As he moved, the creatures moved as well, bee and bird soaring upward, small gargoyle jumping down from my shoulder to scamper away. The hound padded off more slowly, pausing once or twice to look back at Stoyan, its heart in its eyes. The creatures that had accompanied Irene and Murat made their own departure, the cat stalking off without a backward glance.

"Cybele thanks you," the crone said softly. "You have been dogged in your task, Duarte. You have never taken your eyes from the horizon. What have you learned?"

He grinned disarmingly. Solemn as the moment was, he was still himself. "I don't know where to begin," he said, glancing at me. "Trust would be the first lesson. I've learned the hard way not to discount tales of the remarkable and uncanny. And I've been forced to acknowledge that I am not, in fact, entirely devoid of human weakness. Not that I plan to make that widely known. It might get in the way of business."

"Good," said the old woman. "The three of you have acquitted yourselves as we hoped you would: bravely, wisely, with love and balance. It was ever decreed thus, but the fulfillment of the quest has been long in coming."

"Have we permission to pass on through the mountain?" Duarte asked her. "My intention was to take the statue to the village on the other side, a place where, I was told, Cybele is still revered and loved. That quest was laid on me by a friend long ago. Is it right to carry it out of this cavern?"

"Perhaps," the crone said, turning her gaze on the others, the ones who had not earned the right to be here. "We are not yet finished. Murat, come forward."

She was actually going to do it. She was going to grant them the same privileges as we'd been given.

"But—" I began, and wilted at the look in her eye. Whatever was to unfold, I could see it would happen whether we liked it or not. I clutched Stoyan's hand and prayed that this would come out right, that justice and goodness would prevail.

Murat stepped up beside us. He bowed his head respectfully to the crone and said, "I serve the lady of Volos. Her reward is my reward."

The old woman fixed him with her eyes. The eunuch met

them with perfect calm, and I watched him, thinking of what he had done at the swinging bridge and before. Today he had rendered seven children fatherless; he had forced Duarte to drop his friend into the void. If not for my desperate bluff, he would have killed Stoyan. What mad loyalty could inspire a man to act thus, with no regard for what was fair and right?

"Very well," the old woman said. "Irene of Volos. You like lovely things. What will you choose?"

The chamber grew darker. On either side of me Duarte and Stoyan moved in closer. We had become vulnerable, all of us. There would be no bluffing our way to safety now.

The lovely line of Irene's throat was exposed as she tilted back her head and laughed. The sound rang around the cavern. "You mean it," she said to the old woman. "Anything. I may take away anything from this remarkable treasure trove." Her brows lifted in mock astonishment.

"The rule is the same for all," the crone said. "One item as reward. Then all will pass onward."

"This is—" Duarte began, and this time it was I who hushed him.

"Let it go," I muttered. "We can't control this; we have to let it happen." I had seen enough of the workings of the Other Kingdom to understand that human intervention could go only a certain distance. There were patterns here far larger and older than our minds could encompass. Wisdom, a deeper form of wisdom than any scholarship could unlock.

"Very astute of you, Paula," said Irene in her most charming tone. "I knew I was right about you; I saw your potential from the first." And, bending gracefully, she picked up Cybele's Gift. She rose with it cradled in her arms. Her lips shaped a benevolent smile. Her eyes were alight with the triumph of her win. "You disappoint me, pirate," she said to Duarte. "You have led me here, and now you have passed over your treasure as if, all the time, you did not really want it."

"Want it?" Duarte's face was a ghost's, a hollow-eyed study in black and white. "I never sought to possess Cybele's Gift. I wish only to repay a debt of honor." His gaze went to Murat. "But, of course, this is a concept your mind cannot encompass. I have seen today that you do not know the value of a human life."

It seemed Irene was not listening. She had one hand under the little statue, and the other was caressing the wild hair of the miniature goddess, whose hollow eyes gazed out at us from her broad earthenware face. "The artifact is mine," the Greek woman said. "As head of the cult, I have the only legitimate claim to it. The statue will be safe with me, hidden within my home in our gathering place. Through possession of such a fabled item, my position as leader of Cybele's rites will be absolute. It would be ludicrous to leave the artifact up in the mountains. That would result not only in the statue crumbling away because folk are too ignorant to preserve it properly but also in bitter disappointment when it's proven to have no more mystical power than any other lump of clay. I imagine these villagers actually believe in Cybele. They'll be pinning all their hopes on the conviction that this scrap of pottery can magically bestow instant peace and plenty. It's a forlorn hope of extricating themselves from their destined lot on the earth, which, unfortunately, must be one of grinding poverty. Senhor Aguiar, your quest to take the statue there is sheer folly. Cybele's Gift belongs to me and to my followers. Paula, now might be a good time to make your choice. Come back with Murat and me. Whatever impulsive reason you may have had for accompanying Senhor Aguiar on his journey, you can rely on me to provide an acceptable explanation for your father. When Master Teodor has come to terms with that, we'll ask him if he will let you stay in Istanbul awhile and extend your knowledge of Turkish culture. I will initiate you personally."

A shudder of sheer horror ran through me. "Never," I said, meeting Irene's eyes and seeing on her face an expression that truly scared me. "I'll never betray my friends. You told me you value freedom for women, and of course I believe in that; it's central to the way I live my life. But you are a poor example, Irene. You're selfish to the core—all you want is to be admired, to be the center of your so-called cult, with your devotees clustering about you like bees around a flower. You call yourself a priestess, and yet you tell us quite openly that you don't believe in the goddess you claim to represent. That's immoral. It's despicable. People have died because of this, good people. You may thrive on the foolish risks you take, but what about those other women? Your hunger for power could draw them and their families into terrible consequences. Look at what happened to Salem bin Afazi, and he wasn't even part of the cult."

"Salem made an error; he attracted the Mufti's notice. I do not make errors." Her voice was chill. "Have you more to say, Paula?"

"In one breath you tell us Cybele's statue belongs to you, and in the next you express scorn for what she represents: the ancient wisdom of earth. You dismiss people's faith just because they are poor and isolated. But these old gods are powerful. Perhaps they are sleeping now, waiting out a long time of change in the world, but that doesn't mean they are only the imaginings of simple folk. You sicken me, Irene. I can't believe I ever trusted you."

"Well, well," she said, eyes slitted, "there is indeed some passion in that scholarly breast. I'm disappointed, Paula. I had believed we might make something of you. You realize, of course, what an enormous difference your decision will make to your future?" She turned to Duarte. "Senhor, now that you have seen me here, it will unfortunately be necessary for me to ensure that you and your companions do not return to Istanbul to tell the tale. The Sheikh-ul-Islam and his cronies don't care for the revival of pagan practices in their Muslim city. As for the possibility that such a group might be headed by a woman, I imagine that terrifies them. For the sake of my husband's career, if not for myself, I must continue to keep this particular interest secret. . . ."

Around us the light was rapidly fading. Murat was drawing a knife from his belt. Beside me, Stoyan reached for the hilt of his dagger. The old woman had stood quietly in the shadows during this interchange; it did not seem she was planning to intervene.

In my mind, I saw how it might be, how, in seeking to do the right thing, the three of us would be slaughtered here beneath the ground, our corpses slowly turning to bone and dust in Cybele's treasure chamber while the Greek scholar and her protector made their way to the surface and home to Istanbul with the prize. The guardian of Cybele's cave was going to let this false priestess walk away with the statue, and Mustafa's people, who had kept the faith all these years, would never see it again. How could this be? Back in Transylvania, I had seen the folk who ruled the Other

Kingdom make some strange choices—choices that, on occasion, had seemed quite cruel. But everything they had done had been for the greater good.

"Take it, then," the crone said to Irene, and smiled. Irene was looking at the statue and did not see the old woman's expression, but I did. It was inimical, so full of danger it made my stomach clench tight. "Take it and go on your way. Move swiftly; Cybele's doors will not remain open much longer. Not even for a priestess."

With that, the old woman vanished into nothing. Before our eyes the pile of treasure disappeared, leaving the five of us in the dimly lit cavern. I felt under my sash; the folded embroidery was still there where I had tucked it. As my fingers touched its soft form, a solution presented itself to me, a possible solution at least. For although Irene had the artifact, there was one bargaining piece still in our possession.

"Irene," I said as calmly as I could, my eyes on the knife in Murat's capable hand. "Did you wonder how we knew the way to this chamber through the underground passages? It's a kind of code, a map—I found it in your library. Each of us knows part of it; it was too complex for one person to remember. If you kill any one of us, you won't be able to get out."

Murat had taken a step forward. She halted him with a hand. "Each of you?" she queried. "When had the pirate an opportunity to learn this secret map? I don't recall seeing him in my library. And your big dog there?" Her eyes were contemptuous as they raked over Stoyan. "A man like that couldn't memorize his own mother's name."

Stoyan hissed, surging forward.

"No!" I shouted, and a moment later I found myself

seized in a powerful grip and spun around as Murat took advantage of the moment. Duarte had grabbed Stoyan, halting his charge. And now I was pinned in front of the eunuch, with the sharp blade of his knife laid cold as ice across my throat.

My companions were suddenly still.

"Drop your weapons, both of you." Murat's tone was cool. "All of them." He waited while knives and daggers clattered to the ground.

"Very well," Irene said when it was done. "We go forward. Let us test whether Paula's faith in the two of you is justified. I see three ways from this cavern. Who will choose for us?"

Stoyan moved, heading for the left-hand opening. We followed, Murat dragging me with him, the others behind us. I thought I could feel the knife breaking the skin, blood trickling down my neck. Wrong, all wrong. This could not be intended to finish so miserably. Why had we been rewarded if we were to fail in the quest?

I was crying. I sniffed back the tears, unable to wipe my eyes with that powerful arm holding me, that cold metal kissing my throat. Where had I gone wrong? What had I failed to learn? What pieces of the puzzle had I forgotten?

"This way," said Stoyan, making another choice of paths. The ground was rising; we were getting closer to the surface. I fought down terror and made myself focus. *Think, Paula. What have you learned?*

Murat jerked me around a corner. The knife dug in. *Concentrate.* I had learned the difference between knowledge and wisdom. I had experienced a lesson in trust. At least, I'd started to understand these things. A whole lifetime was probably not enough to learn them completely. Especially if that life was cut short before one reached one's eighteenth birthday. *Think.* And I'd learned other things that I hadn't mentioned. How to escape from the grip of someone much stronger, who grabbed me from behind . . . Of course, the lesson had not included dealing with the complication of a knife. But Stoyan had taught me to look for the right moment, the kind of moment Murat had just used to his advantage. And if Stoyan, walking in front of us, also knew the right moment . . .

All along, I had tried to keep my own image of the tree map clear in my mind. I had not retained it as well as Stoyan had; without him, we would indeed have been lost. Now I made myself concentrate on this section. There could have been several possible ways from the treasure chamber up to the top. Stoyan was taking the most central route, past a place where the tree image had been thick with fruit of many shapes. We moved forward along a winding way—a particularly wayward branch—passing small caverns to either side, each with its own peculiar form. I saw them as they had appeared on the tiles—pear, apple, plum, bunch of cherries.

We came to a fork: two ways, left and right. Stoyan paused, glancing back.

"Move, Bulgar!" Murat said. "Which is it? Make up your mind!"

For a brief moment, Stoyan's eyes met mine. I tried to convey something to him, intent, purpose, and I thought he gave the smallest of nods. "We go right," he said.

I knew it should be left. I moved forward, still clasped in Murat's menacing embrace. Behind, I heard the soft footsteps of the others.

Something creaked above us, jolting my heart. The rocks were shifting. Murat tensed; his knife fell momentarily away from my neck. I sagged in his arms, making my body abruptly limp. Stoyan leaped toward us, eyes blazing, ready to tackle the well-armed eunuch with his bare hands. Murat dropped me, bracing to defend himself. Suddenly he had a knife in each hand. I rolled to the side and came up on one knee as I'd been taught during those practice sessions on the *Esperança*. Stoyan stuck out a hand in my direction; I drew the little knife he had given me out of my sash and tossed it to him. Nobody had thought to ask *me* to throw down my weapons.

The struggle was brief but intense. Duarte could do no more than crouch by me, shielding me, for the combatants moved so fast there was no getting between them. Murat fought like a dancer, with elegant economy of movement and a sequence of practiced swings and turns and kicks. Someone had trained him to perfection. Stoyan's style was brutal and efficient. They grappled and wrestled and fell, rose and came together once more, muscles bulging, eyes glaring, feet slipping on the rock floor. Above them, the earth trembled and groaned; showers of little stones fell from the tunnel's roof. Irene stood watching, mute, with Cybele's Gift clutched to her breast. Huddled by the wall, I felt the rocks shuddering under my hand.

Murat had Stoyan pinned against the opposite wall, his right forearm pressed across his adversary's chest. It wasn't looking good. With his left hand, he held Stoyan's wrist in a painful grip clearly designed to make him drop the little knife that was his only weapon. As soon as the knife fell, the eunuch would use his own head to smash Stoyan's skull back against the rock wall or employ a dagger to stab my friend in the heart.

Stoyan drew a deep, shuddering breath.

Then, with an odd sort of twist that suggested getting himself pinned against the wall had been a planned combat move, he hooked a leg around Murat's and toppled him. There was a hideous crunching sound as the eunuch's head went down on the rocks. Stoyan knelt and, with deliberation, drew the little knife across Murat's throat.

"Quick, Paula!" Duarte was helping me up, pulling me back along the passageway. The place was alive with the sounds of warning, rock grumbling, creaking, moaning as it shifted. More stones fell, bigger ones this time. *Cybele's doors will not remain open much longer.*

"Stoyan," I whispered, and he was there beside me, wiping his knife on his tunic and sticking it in his sash.

"Run," he said.

Irene was blocking our way. She stood stock-still in the middle of the passage, staring at the prone form of her steward. She had set the artifact down on the stone floor.

"The place is coming down," Duarte said to her. "If you value your life, follow us out." As we pushed past Irene and ran, he scooped up Cybele's Gift.

Over the sound of the shifting rocks, I could not hear if Irene was coming or not. When we reached the place where Stoyan had deliberately led us down the wrong branch, I snatched one backward glance. Irene was kneeling on the ground. She had gathered Murat's body close, his head resting on her knees; her hands, cradling him, were dyed crimson. On her features was a look of such grief and pain it hit me like a blow. She turned her face upward and wailed, a wordless, primal sound of sorrow that rang all through the subterranean passageway, making the hairs stand up on the back of my neck.

A moment later, her cry was drowned by a roaring like the voice of a huge wild creature, a monstrous rumbling above, beneath, on either side of us.

"Paula!" shouted Stoyan. "Come on!" Not waiting for me to obey, he picked me up and slung me over his shoulder as he sprinted down the left-hand passageway. A jerking, bobbing vista of rock and earth and shadow passed before my eyes. We ran around corners, dashed through caverns, ducked into openings not much bigger than the portholes on the *Esperança*.

"Lights," panted Duarte. "Ahead, see there. . . ."

Stoyan halted. He put me down, and when I sagged against his chest, too dizzy to hold myself upright, he gripped my arms to steady me. His touch left smears of blood on my shirt. The rhythm of my heart was like the galloping of a warhorse.

"We're out," Duarte gasped. "Look, stars, the moon. . . ."

"And lanterns," I said, gazing along the tunnel to the place where a view of the outside world could be seen.

We walked forward. As we did, the mountain sent a last warning rumble after us, and I thought I could feel the ground shaking. We ran and did not stop until we came out into an open place, a bowllike depression high on the flank of the mountain, where an old, gnarled tree whose shape was familiar to me stood alone amongst rocks. A bonfire blazed in the open space before it. There were lanterns and torches and musicians playing long horns and drums and little cymbals.

There was a crowd of people, young and old, clad in embroidered felt and sheepskin and fur and fringed leather: a whole village of folk dressed in their best, ready for a celebration. I saw masks and painted faces. Over on one side, people were beating on drums of many sizes and styles. A great shout greeted our appearance. But behind us, the mountain had fallen quiet. Cybele's doors were closed. I could not forget the look on the crone's face as she bade us farewell. I suspected the old woman had known, in that moment, that it would end this way—that Irene, Cybele's so-called priestess, would never walk out of the mountain to see the goddess come home.

As we approached the assembled folk, beaming smiles broke out all around and the music rose to an exuberant climax. It looked as if they had been expecting us. *It is foretold,* the djinn had said.

Duarte stepped forward, a lean, handsome figure in his tattered clothing. Two old women in bright woolens came up to greet him with formal kisses on both cheeks. These two were not veiled. Indeed, none of these women were—some wore hats or little decorative kerchiefs, but most of them had their hair luxuriantly loose, flying about them in wild banners as they danced. Their dress was loose trousers under shift and caftan. The men's outfits were similar, though more sober in color. The dancers formed long lines, hands held at shoulder level, bodies snaking and weaving as feet followed an intricate pattern. The drums made a shifting heartbeat in the spark-brightened air.

The old women were slipping a garland of leaves over Duarte's head; others came forward to decorate Stoyan and me in the same way. Duarte had begun an explanation in Turkish. I picked up *Mustafa,* and *Cybele,* and *bringing it home.* At a certain point, he said, *Paula and Stoyan,* glancing toward us with a slight frown. I was leaning on Stoyan; he had his arm around my shoulders. I felt the uneven rise and fall of his chest, heard the wheezing catch in his breath.

"Stoyan, what did the old woman mean about an arrow? You're badly hurt, aren't you?"

Duarte was handing Cybele's Gift to one of the elders, bowing, stepping back. A high ululation arose from the villagers, and out on the mountain, there was an echo that sounded like the voices of wolves.

"It's nothing," Stoyan murmured. "You're shivering, Paula. Here." Our packs had been left behind in the caves. Now he loosened his sash and set the priceless diadem on the ground. He took off the garland and slipped his tunic over his head. I saw him wince as he raised his arms. "Put this on," he said, draping the garment around my shoulders. The touch of his hands filled me with warmth; I wanted him to leave them there. Then I saw a fresh bloodstain on his shirt, near the shoulder.

"You're bleeding!"

"I told you, it's nothing."

"I don't believe you. Show me—"

"It's not important, Paula. It looks worse than it is. Sit down, here. You're exhausted. Look, this woman is bringing you a blanket."

I sat, and by signs I conveyed to the woman that Stoyan needed attention. With some reluctance, he let himself be persuaded to sit down on the rocks while she removed his shirt and tended to what appeared to be quite a nasty flesh wound. There was no shortage of volunteers to help her. Much to their patient's embarrassment, as they performed the job, they kept up an animated commentary complete with gestures. It was evident that they thought him a magnificent example of manhood. They kept glancing at me.

"When did that happen?" I asked, trying not to meet Stoyan's eye.

"It was before we entered the caves. The fight on the mountainside. An arrow at an inconvenient moment."

"You said that was only a scratch. I believed you. How did you carry me on your shoulders with an injury like that?"

Stoyan stared into the distance as the women dabbed at the injury. "Your weight is light, Paula, and you balance like a bird."

I said nothing. Despite my exhaustion, I was full of the need to touch Stoyan, to be close to him, to put into words the realization that had become stronger every moment as we made our perilous journey through the mountain. Every step of the way, he had been my rock, my guide, my protector, and my indispensable friend. *Don't lie to yourself, Paula. Not just a friend.* His waiting arms had given me the courage to swing across that chasm. His had been the hand that was my grip on sanity, my guard against mindless terror, my lifeline. I had known, when he was squeezing himself through that impossibly narrow tunnel, that I could not bear it if I lost him. Stoyan was far more than a friend, and if I'd been brave enough to get through Cybele's mountain, I could surely find the courage to tell him how I felt. So why was my heart thumping with trepidation?

I looked across the open space and saw Duarte now

enveloped in a small, enthusiastic crowd, both men and women. He was listening hard as the elders who had welcomed him offered a lengthy explanation of something. I was too tired to make any sense of what little I could hear.

The women who were tending to Stoyan found him a clean shirt and a dolman of dark red wool. Folk brought us more blankets, cups of a steaming beverage, sheepskin hats. So high on the mountain, it was bitterly cold. And nighttime. The moon was high. Our progress through that underground place had taken many hours.

"What are they saying, Stoyan? Can you hear?"

"They say the statue has returned to the place of its origin," he said. "That it was foretold. Everything—three travelers, a mariner, a warrior, and a scholar. That the mountain would roar when Cybele came home. That the secret path would be opened and then closed again. And . . ." He hesitated.

"What?" I asked, hugging the blanket around me and thinking I had never understood how wonderful it was to be warm until now.

"The tree," Stoyan said. "Something about the tree . . ."

The moon was shining between the branches now, a perfect disk of silver. The crowd was suddenly hushed; the music died down. Every eye was turned toward the tree. It looked immensely old and so shriveled it must surely no longer hold any life within it. The little statue had been placed amongst the roots; the hollow eyes of Cybele gazed out at us, inscrutable and strange.

"It has borne neither leaves nor buds nor fruit in living memory," said Stoyan. "But the old women said to Duarte that tonight it will be different. On the night of Cybele's return, everything will change. The words will be spoken—the last wisdom of the goddess."

Into the stillness, the two old women cried out together, chanting in a tongue unfamiliar to me. The firelight touched their faces as they raised both arms toward the rotund trunk and gnarled branches of Cybele's tree. A swarm of insects arose, circling and dancing amongst the boughs. And on the tips of the twigs, where before had been only hard, dry wood, now sprouted the greenest of new growth, tiny leaves that uncurled under the darkness of night, hesitant and fresh. Amongst the tender shoots, a multitude of little bright birds hopped and fluttered and sang. There was no doubt about it: The goddess had come home.

"Don't cry, Paula," murmured Stoyan, and folded his arms around me.

But I put my hands up to my face and wept against his shoulder. The beauty of the moment was too much to take in. I heard the wild music start up again, felt the thud of many feet around me as the folk of the village danced around the fire, celebrating the return of their community's heart. It was good. It was a rightful ending to Duarte's quest. But this outpouring of happiness, not to mention the sheer delight of being in Stoyan's arms, did not outweigh the death of Pero, the terrible fates of Murat and Irene. Some of the responsibility for those deaths lay with me. If I had not wanted so badly to prove to Duarte that my father had a better claim to Cybele's Gift, I would not be here now, and nor would Stoyan. If we had not been here, Irene and Murat could not have found their way into the mountain.

"Paula." It was Duarte's voice. I wiped my cheeks and moved away from Stoyan. Duarte was squatting in front of us, with several smiling villagers behind him. "No tears. This is a party. Mustafa's people have expressed profound thanks to all of us for returning the statue here. It is their belief that in this time when other religious faiths are gaining strength in the world outside, Cybele should be sheltered here, where she will be safe from the destructive hands of those who do not understand her message."

"We almost brought a pair of those destructive hands right to them," I said. "What message?"

"They are singing the words now, this time in Turkish."

"Words?" I asked stupidly.

"The words of the goddess, those written on her belly. First they were spoken by the elders in the old tongue, and now they are echoed by all. *Eat of my deep earth, drink of my living streams, for I am your Mother. Your heart is my wild drum, your breath my eternal song. If you would live, dance with me!* Somewhat obscure in meaning, but I'm told that's an accurate translation. These people expected us tonight. Our arrival was foretold down to the exact hour."

I nodded. After all the strange things that had happened today, a prophecy was not so difficult to accept. I was not sure I understood exactly what Cybele's fabled last message meant. Perhaps I was simply too tired to understand.

"They honor the earth," Stoyan said quietly, as if he could read my mind. "The earth that nurtures crops and gives them clay for their houses, the water that sustains life. In these words, Cybele bids us live in harmony with that which gave us birth. From that arises a mode of living that is simple and wise, one in which man and woman understand their part in the wholeness of things."

I was without words. How was it he could understand so

quickly, as if he had the answers stored somewhere deep inside him? That grandmother of his must have been an exceptional woman.

"These folk expect us to join them for dancing and feasting," Duarte said. "They've asked me to bring my sweetheart—their word, not mine—out into the circle where they can see you properly. I know you're tired and upset, Paula. But we owe it to them to try, at least."

When he put it like that, there really was no choice. I got up and took off my blanket. One of the women brought me a shawl instead, dark blue with little mirrors sewn all over it, so that when I moved, I carried the moonlight with me. I put my hand in Duarte's and we joined the dancing. Now that I had let it rest for a little, my body was protesting about the bruises and scratches it had sustained during our journey through the mountain, and I was surprised I could even walk, let alone perform any sort of capering. But the moment the music began again and the circle started to move— clapping, swaying, stamping—memories of the Other Kingdom and Ileana's revels came flooding back to me, and the rhythm crept into my bones and my blood and made my feet light. So I danced, and with each dance I floated further away from my worldly cares, seeing an answering spark of joy on Duarte's drawn features as we turned and stepped and moved as a pair. And after a while, this was the only place I wanted to be, my body's surrender to the music the only thing that was keeping me from breaking apart. Even in the center of such celebration, I knew sadness was only a breath away.

The night wore on, dance following dance. Various men came up and asked shyly if they could partner me, but

Duarte kept a firm grip on my hand, and one by one they withdrew. Later, a line of men in animal masks performed what looked like a stylized version of the trials and tests of Cybele's mountain. Within the sequence of dancelike moves was a part where a man in a woman's gown balanced on another's shoulders and then a part where a blindfolded man made a dangerous progress between two rows of women using sharp-toothed puppets on sticks. There was mock combat, tumbling, and juggling. All the while, the drummers beat out their throbbing rhythm. Flasks of drink went around; whatever it was, it kindled fire in the belly, banishing the deep chill of the mountain night. I drank very little. The dancing had kept me warm, but I became too tired to take another step. Besides, I had not spoken to Stoyan yet, not properly, and I knew that, nervous as I felt, tonight was the time to do it. I had become more and more aware of his somber expression, his narrowed eyes fixed on me and Duarte as we navigated the steps of one dance after another. I had not expected Stoyan to join in, injured as he was, though I had been thinking how much nicer this would be if he were the one out here holding my hand. But the look on his face worried me. Caught up in the thrill of the revels, I had allowed myself to forget for a little that I had something important to say to him, something that was going to take all the courage I could find.

I gave my excuses to Duarte, pleading weariness, and walked out of the dancing throng.

"You like to dance," Stoyan observed flatly as I went over to sit by him.

For a little I did not answer. Now that I had stopped moving, the bitter cold was creeping into my bones.

"Stoyan?" I ventured.

"Mmm?"

"I have so much to thank you for I don't know where to begin. Without you, we wouldn't be here, the three of us. And you saved my sister." I still could hardly believe how cleverly he had done that. "How did you think of that, using the dog to help you?"

"I simply knew what to do, Paula. It was not such a great thing."

"My sisters are very dear to me. You probably know that already. But I didn't realize how much I loved Tati until I saw her in trouble and couldn't work out how to help her. Now maybe I will be able to see her again. There's no way I can thank you for such a gift."

He said what I expected him to say: "It is nothing, Paula."

"I have something to ask you, Stoyan."

"Ask, then."

I drew a breath, ready to say the all-important words. But I couldn't get them out. He looked so serious, almost disapproving. So I asked a different question. "You remember what happened at the swinging bridge, when those guards called you Your Excellency and let us across. Do you think . . . I mean, clearly they mistook you for somebody else. Did it occur to you—"

Stoyan stared down at his hands. "That perhaps I was mistaken for my brother?" he said quietly. "Yes, I thought of it. There have been many false hopes, Paula, many threads of information that frayed to nothing. I have taught myself to expect little."

"But it could be," I said. "If a devshirme boy proved

clever and apt, it is possible, isn't it, that even at the young age of eighteen he could be in a position of some power or authority in a region such as this? There cannot be many men who look like you, Stoyan."

He turned his gaze on me. If I felt sick with tension, he looked worse. His jaw was tight, his eyes miserable. "It could be so," he said. "I do not know if my brother grew up to resemble me. When they took him, he was only a child."

"You must find out," I said. "He could be somewhere really close, perhaps in that town farther along the coast. Some of these folk might know of him. You should look for him now, Stoyan."

There was a little silence. Not far off, Duarte was dancing in a circle of admiring women, young girls, elderly matrons, and everything in between. On the tree above him, the leaf canopy was burgeoning into a shady mantle touched by the moonlight to uncanny silver-blue. A high chorus of birdsong rang forth from it.

"No," Stoyan said.

"No? You can't mean that, Stoyan. It's your mission, your quest! It would be crazy not to pursue it when you may be so close."

"I will take you back to Istanbul. Your father will be worried. You need to go home."

"Duarte can take me. I'll be fine."

"You will travel on the *Esperança*, of course. But not without your guard. I must see you safely back to your father."

A silence followed. This was the moment when I should speak, when I should be honest and tell him I could not face the prospect of being back in Istanbul and having to say goodbye to him. Maybe once we had been mistress and servant, but that had changed long ago, well before I had flippantly dismissed him from his position as bodyguard. He must know how his smile warmed me, how his touch awakened me. It had seemed to me, in the caves and before, that he felt the same. I was an adult woman, wasn't I? So why was I trembling with nerves at the very thought of putting such feelings into words?

"Stoyan . . . I . . ."

He said nothing.

"I have something to say to you. Please hear me out." My heart was pounding. "Stoyan . . . I know we are worlds apart, the two of us. When Father and I came to Istanbul, when we hired you, all we needed was someone who would be strong and reliable and keep trouble away. We never . . . I never . . ." This was going badly already. I cleared my throat and tried again. "We've become friends, you and I. Good friends. What just happened in the caves, that seemed to show . . . I mean, I do know there are enormous differences between us, education and background, language, profession, the fact that your home is in Bulgaria and mine far away in Transylvania. People—society, the world—would view anything between us as ridiculous, impossible. And there's your quest for your brother. That means you'll have to stay in the region well after Father and I have to leave. Any sensible person would tell us we should just say goodbye when we get back to Istanbul and enjoy the memory of what we've shared here, a remarkable, exceptional adventure. . . ." Now I was going to cry. I ordered myself to get the most important words out, the ones I was leading up to, but my stupid tongue would not obey.

Stoyan's features were transformed by the firelight into a

mask of orange-gold, his scar a sharp slash across his cheek, his mouth particularly tight. That look was less than encouraging. It seemed to me that the more I blundered on, the further inside himself my friend was retreating. While I struggled to find the right words, the ones that would tell him what was in my heart, his grimness set a chill on me, making such honesty almost impossible. What had happened to the closeness we had felt in the mountain, the desperate clinging of our hands on our wild chase through the dark, the unspoken trust we had shared in the cave of the creatures? He had touched me with tenderness after I crossed that bridge. His eyes had spoken sweet words after we came across the lake. Now he was as silent as stone.

"What I'm trying to say is that despite all those things, despite the many reasons people would think it's unsuitable, I . . . I don't want to say goodbye when we get back to Istanbul. And I did wonder if . . ." I could hardly launch into a marriage proposal. Maybe I was not the most conventional of young women, but it seemed wrong to take the initiative in this most traditionally male of duties. "If there might be some way we could . . . we could be together." That sounded even worse, as if I were proposing something quite improper. "I don't mean . . ." I added hastily, then faltered to a halt. His face remained guarded and wary, even after that. It was quite obvious he was not going to come out with an expression of love. From an arm's length away, I could tell that his whole body was strung up with tension.

"Are you finished, Paula?" he asked.

"Don't worry," I said, wrapping my arms around myself and looking at the ground. "It's obvious you think it's a silly idea, so just forget I ever suggested it." There was hurt all through me, a pain I could never have believed possible. He didn't need to say a single thing more for me to know I had messed this up completely. Yet I had been sure, almost sure, that he felt the same way I did.

"One cannot argue with this logic." Stoyan's voice cracked, and although my heart had gone cold, I reached out, intending to take his hand. He drew it away. "You say, let us be together despite this, despite that. If a man truly loves, Paula, such a word as this does not enter his mind. He does not consider the obstacles, the restrictions, the reasons why his choice may be flawed or impractical. He gives no heed to what others may think. His heart has no room for that, for it is filled to the brim with the unutterable truth of his feelings."

"But—" I blurted out, desperate to make him understand that I did love him and that if I hadn't been so tired and nervous, I would have said it much better.

"Hear me out, Paula, please. I cannot say this twice over. As you have reminded me in such a timely fashion, your future is one of wealth and opportunity, of scholarship and achievement. You will move in circles far beyond the reach of a man like me. If we imagine things might be otherwise, we entertain a delusion born of the strange adventures we have undertaken together. Were we to seek something further, and I cannot pretend the idea has never entered my mind, we would soon find ourselves at war. You would seek from me an erudition and cleverness I have no capacity to offer, and you would become bitter that you had tied yourself to a man of such limitations. I would . . . Never mind that. By the time we return to Istanbul, you will look back with gratitude that I answered you thus, Paula. You inhabit one world, the same world as Duarte, with its privileges and its possibilities. I exist in another entirely."

It felt as if he'd hit me. With that well-phrased speech, he had effectively severed the bond between us, and it was like cutting off my supply of fresh air. I sat there, miserable and silent, with Stoyan close enough to touch but separated from me as completely as if there were a wall between us.

Duarte strode forth from the dancing, a hand extended toward me, a smile softening his features. He was flushed from the activity and from the fire, which crackled high, lighting up the night. "One more dance, come on! You too, Stoyan. We must show these folk we appreciate their welcome. After this, we're invited to go back to their village for some sleep. Tomorrow they'll take us down to another anchorage. A fishing boat can ferry us around to the *Esperança*. Home's in sight, my friends!"

I got to my feet. One thing was certain—I could not remain here with Stoyan after that speech, or I would break apart.

"Come on, Stoyan," Duarte said, grabbing his hand and hauling him to his feet. "Unless that arrow you stopped for me has winged you too badly." He turned to me. "I imagine our friend here didn't give you the full story; he's never keen to draw attention to his own exploits. If he hadn't pushed me out of its path, that barb would have taken me right in the chest. So just when I've finally repaid my debt to Mustafa, I've acquired another."

"There is no obligation," Stoyan said in a voice that

sounded gray and drained. "It was a battle; in a battle one protects one's comrades. Must I dance?"

"We all must," I said grimly, since the alternative was to sit about feeling utterly wretched until it was time to go. We owed it to Cybele, I thought, to honor her with celebration. Our personal feelings played no part in that.

So we danced, the three of us, I in the middle, my friends on either side, part of a big circle of folk all with hands on each other's shoulders, working through a complicated sequence of repeated steps as the music got gradually faster and faster. The pipe shrilled, the drums pounded, the horns bellowed in turn and then together, blasting a wild fanfare into the night. Duarte managed an exhausted smile. To these folk, he was a hero, his debt of honor paid at last. But he had lost a good friend on the way. Stoyan was pale, his expression forbidding, his hands still stained with Murat's blood. He, in his borrowed clothes, looked tidier than Duarte or I did. But all of us showed the signs of our ordeal, our eyes shadowed with weariness and shock, our hair tangled, our bodies battered and sore. Still we danced, heads held high, in tribute to the mountain people who had held on to faith and hope for so long.

The moon crossed the sky; the tree rustled in a light breeze. Sparks from the great fire rose into the night air. And while my feet trod the intricate patterns of the dance and my mouth formed a smile, inside I was aching with sadness. Stoyan's words had been like nails driven into my heart. I had thought what we had was strong enough to defy custom and expectation, to leap barriers of distance and difference. He had thrown my stumbling arguments back in my face. Tonight, this dance, was the last time I would be able to touch his strong shoulder, to feel his warm presence by my side, to glance up and know he would be there. Until the music ended, I could pretend we did not have to say goodbye.

Chapter Fifteen

We left the next morning. The villagers gave us warm clothing and an escort down a precipitous track, and a fisherman
ferried us back to the *Esperança*. Plague had not yet touched
the mountain village, but the people knew it was not far
away, and they did not linger.

The mood on the ship was somber, the loss of Pero
weighing heavily on Duarte and on his crewmen. Arrangements were changed. Stoyan asked to be a full member of the
crew on the way back, and Duarte accepted his offer. That
meant Stoyan slept with the other men and Duarte reoccu-
pied his cabin, putting me in Pero's. I was sure Stoyan had
done this less from a wish to be useful than from a need to
avoid talking to me. On the rare occasions when we crossed
paths, he greeted me with courteous formality, just as any
other crewman might, though the others generally gave me a
smile. My blundering attempt to tell him what I felt for him
appeared to have destroyed not only the future we might
have shared but also the close friendship we already had.
And yet the more I thought about it, the more I recognized

the depth of my feelings for him, feelings that had been creeping up on me long before our passage through the mountain had awoken me to their true nature. I was so wounded by his attitude that I spent most of the time in my cabin, brooding. I tried to make sense of everything that had happened.

I thought a lot about Irene and what she had done at the end. I went back over what I had observed of her relationship with Murat, the wordless understanding that had shown itself in everything from the pouring of a perfect cup of coffee to the instant deployment of a murderous weapon. I had seen, in that moment of terrible grief as she cradled her dying steward in her arms, that she loved him. It had been clear that she had never considered he might fall in her service and that, for a little at least, the loss of him had far outweighed the value of Cybele's Gift. Had she realized, in that moment, that she did not want to go on without him? Perhaps; she could have escaped with us, and she had chosen to stay behind. As for the nature of their love, that I would never know, and maybe it did not matter. Maybe it was enough to be aware that Irene had possessed the capacity for such feelings.

Stoyan's behavior, to which he adhered with stern resolve throughout the voyage, meant I was thrown into Duarte's company. He, at least, seemed happy to spend time with me. I heard about his family. They were wealthy; the *Esperança* was not the only vessel they owned. He told me about his early rebellion against his father's expectations, his travels as a lowly crewman on various ships, how he had risen to be captain of his own vessel—not the *Esperança*, which had been a later acquisition, but a more modest one-master. He had indeed supplemented his income with acts of piracy in those early years and had garnered a reputation as ruthless and successful. The long debt of honor to Mustafa had gradually changed him. He said that he no longer employed the kind of tactics he once had, and I believed him, for our journey had convinced me he was a good man at heart. Indeed, he was now a wealthy man in his own right, with no need to engage in underhand practices. He was, in fact, the respectable trader his father had always wanted him to be—he had just taken a little longer to get there than his father would have liked.

I asked him what he would do now that his mission was over, and he said he would go home for a while. The crew was overdue for time off. And Pero's wife must be told that she was a widow. She would be provided for, as would the fatherless children. There was a code amongst seafarers that required this.

It seemed to me that this account was not quite complete, that there was something on Duarte's mind he was not telling me. I saw it in the quality of his smile and in the guarded eyes. I did not press it. We were all tired. But it seemed to me Duarte was somewhat adrift now, as a man might well be when his energies have gone for so long toward a single purpose and that purpose suddenly ceases to exist. He needed time to come to terms with the change, to work out what it meant. We read poetry together, drank wine, sometimes sat in companionable silence. It was pleasant, but it could not soothe the ache in my chest that never went away.

We did not encounter the red-sailed ship. Perhaps it was still moored in that little bay, waiting for Irene and Murat to return. Without her orders, I did not suppose the crew would bother pursuing us. I wondered if I would have to report her death and Murat's to the authorities in Istanbul. I was much relieved when Duarte told me he would take care of this. He would, he said, give a version of our story that could not lead the authorities to Mustafa's village or expose Irene's secret to the world. If there was evidence of the cult in her house, something that would reveal the truth to her husband, there was very little we could do about it.

And so fifteen days after our departure, we sailed back into the Golden Horn. The moment the *Esperança* was tied up at the dock, Duarte got a boy to run up to the Genoese han to advise my father that I was back safe and well and would be there shortly. Stoyan took my little bundle, which contained Tati's embroidery and the clothing I had been wearing, an Anatolian countrywoman's outfit given to me in the mountain village to replace my shredded sailor's clothes. I wore the Greek-style dress that Irene had given me the last time I was in her hamam, the day when Stoyan burst in on us. I could not believe that was less than three weeks ago.

Duarte gave me a book—the *Odyssey*—and kissed me on the lips at the top of the gangway to a chorus of whistles and amiable catcalls from the crew. As Stoyan and I walked down, their voices rang out behind us: *Paula, de brancura singela* . . . I was close to tears and annoyed with myself for being so upset. We had all known it could not last forever.

Father did not utter a single word of reproach but simply gathered me in his arms and thanked God that I was safe. I told him the bare bones of the story but omitted quite a bit of detail, knowing how upset he would be to hear of the physical hardships and danger Tati and I had faced. He listened quietly, as he had six years ago when we had been obliged to explain to him that his eldest daughter had gone to the Other Kingdom and that he would never see her again. When I was finished, Father asked a couple of questions: Was Tati looking well? Had I been injured at all? And lastly, was I happy with the final fate of Cybele's Gift? If so, Father said, he would draw a line under that matter and we would simply move on. I assured him that what we had done was for the best, even though it meant his voyage had been a commercial failure. It was not an easy conversation.

Stoyan was silent and tense, though when Father embraced him and thanked him for bringing me back safely, he thawed a little. We would be leaving on the *Stea de Mare* in a few days' time, and there was much still to be done. If we had not returned when we had, Father would have stayed in Istanbul and kept on searching for us. Because of that uncertainty, he had not finalized the accounts or completed packing the goods we had purchased to take back to Transylvania. He would need me to help with the former and Stoyan for the latter.

I was so tired I could hardly stay on my feet. I greeted Giacomo and Maria and thanked them for their help. They had not only nursed my father back to health but had also put a great deal of effort into assisting him with the search. Father scrutinized me as I swayed and yawned, then told me the accounts could wait until tomorrow. I went to bed and slept for fourteen hours. I got up, washed, and ate breakfast, then went back to bed, promising Father I would do the work in the afternoon. He and Stoyan were busy in the downstairs chamber we were using for our goods, packing up silks.

I did not wake until the midday call to prayer rang out

over the Genoese mahalle. I found Father out on the gallery drinking tea. He had sent Stoyan to the docks with a cartload of items to be stowed on the ship.

"I've had a visitor," Father said. "Sit down, Paula. You still look exhausted." He stood and gestured to the tea vendor down in the courtyard.

"A visitor?" I queried, subsiding onto a chair. "Who?"

"Your friend Duarte Aguiar. He paid me a formal call."

"I'm sorry I missed him." It was unsurprising. Duarte would have felt obliged to give some explanation, I imagined, for what must appear to the outside world as a kind of abduction. "When is Stoyan coming back, Father?"

"In time for supper, I imagine." Father was looking at me quizzically. "Why do you ask?"

"No special reason." I couldn't bear that we should leave with things the way they were between Stoyan and me. But he had made it clear that he didn't want to entertain my suggestion. On all sorts of levels, this was perfectly logical. We were completely different. Our homes were many miles apart. I was a scholarly girl of prosperous merchant stock, he an uneducated farmer from a remote village. He had sworn to find his brother and take the news to his mother, and I was on my way back home. It could be years before I traveled this way again. I might never come. What chance of success could a partnership between us possibly have?

"Mmm-hmm," murmured Father. "Have you two argued? I've noticed quite a frosty atmosphere between you. And Stoyan seems . . ." He hesitated, searching for the right word. "He seems disturbed."

"We had a disagreement. Don't trouble yourself with it." Oh, how I wished one of my sisters were here, Jena in particular, so I could unburden my sadness and confusion to her and seek some practical advice. This wasn't something I could tell Father.

After I'd been scowling into the middle distance for a while, Father said, "Aren't you going to ask me what Aguiar wanted?"

"Wanted? Wasn't he here to apologize to you?"

The tea vendor's boy had come up with a laden tray. I helped myself to a glass and sipped gratefully.

"He asked for your hand in marriage." Father sounded mildly amused as he delivered this thunderbolt.

"He . . . what?"

"Made a formal proposal of marriage, accompanied by all the information a father expects at such a time. It sounds as if the fellow is quite wealthy, Paula. And the family is well thought of by the rulers of that country, if Aguiar is to be believed. All this, of course, weighed against his dubious personal reputation. He spoke highly of you. You've clearly made an impression."

I was almost speechless. "Why didn't he say anything to me?" Never in my wildest flight of imagination had I foreseen this. I struggled to make sense of how I felt. Confused and unsettled, certainly. But pleased as well. After Stoyan's rebuff, this made me feel just a little better about myself. Duarte did have a lot to offer, far more than my father could learn from a quick interview. "What did you tell him?" I asked.

"I said no, of course." Father was calm, his gaze fixed on me.

"You said no? Just like that? Without even asking me?" I was outraged. Perhaps this was what run-of-the-mill fathers did, fathers of the kind who did not view their daughters as intelligent, independent human beings with opinions of their own. But not my father.

"You needed your sleep. Don't be upset, Paula. A man who gives up after a single refusal is not worth considering as a son-in-law, in my view. I expect he'll be back. Are you saying you actually want to marry the fellow?"

I felt a blush rising to my cheeks. "I'm not saying that at all, Father. Only that I would like to be consulted before such a decision is made. It is the rest of my life, after all."

"Portugal is a long way off." He looked suddenly desolate. I got up and went to put my arms around him.

"He might not come back anyway," I said. "Don't worry, Father. Now where are these accounts?"

Stoyan returned briefly, procured supper for the three of us, then asked my father if he might absent himself until tomorrow morning. He was still trying to avoid me, I knew it. There were questions in my eyes, perhaps—questions whose answers would be too painful to speak aloud.

As we ate in awkward silence, it came to me that I did not need to look at Stoyan to make an inventory of all the things that pleased me about him: his imposing height and broad shoulders, his muscular arms, the cascade of thick dark hair, the amber eyes that could be as gentle as a dove's or as fierce as a wolf's. The pale intensity of his complexion, marked by the jagged scar whose trajectory I would like to trace with my fingers. The strong bones of cheeks and jaw. Most of all, his rare wisdom, an inner stillness and understanding that went far beyond such surface cleverness as a capacity to read and write or a facility with numbers. There was so little time left. His silence troubled me, and so did the forbidding look on his face. I knew how strong-minded he was. The shield he had set up around himself was almost perfect. But tonight, for the first time since the voyage home, I thought I could see through that barrier to the pain it concealed. In Stoyan's guarded eyes, I glimpsed a perfect reflection of what was in my own heart, and a tiny flame of hope flared inside me. Perhaps, after all, it was not too late. I must talk to him again, and this time I must get it right. When he came back tomorrow morning, I would do it.

Father gave Stoyan leave of absence, and we spent the evening quietly packing our personal items. There was only one load of goods to go to the ship now. We would be sailing the day after tomorrow. We talked a little more about Cybele's Gift and what its true importance was. So many folk had wanted to track it down for so many different reasons. Irene and Murat had been prepared to kill for it. So had the Sheikh-ul-Islam, if it was true that the Mufti had ordered Salem's death for, as he saw it, encouraging pagan practices within the city.

"The leaders of the Other Kingdom back home always intend good for human folk provided we can learn our lessons," I told Father. "I'm sure their counterparts here, like the crone we met in the caves, are exactly the same, though their methods are more brutal. They wanted Cybele's Gift to go back to Mustafa's village. It's more than just another primitive artifact; it's a recognition of old, good ways. It's the same lesson they tried to teach Cezar when he intended to chop down our forest rather than harbor Ileana's people. Respect for . . . for Mother Earth, I suppose you could say."

"I had heard," Father said as he tightened a cord around

a box and knotted it, "that Cybele's rites were somewhat violent and bloody. That does not seem entirely apt for this message you set out."

"Maybe they once were. What we saw was stylized: people in masks, men in women's clothing, and so on. No bloodletting, just dancing, games, and music. Irene set herself up as a priestess of Cybele. But I think she got things wrong when she restricted her rites to women only, with Murat, as a eunuch, the only exception. Up in that mountain village, men and women mingled freely and seemed equal, though it was the old women who led the ritual."

"And what of the inscription?" Father asked. "Did you discover its meaning?"

"It's not a key to instant good fortune. That legend must have grown up around Cybele's Gift over the years it couldn't be found. The inscription is just simple advice on how to live our lives well. Cybele tells her followers that if they live in harmony with the earth, respecting what she provides, she will continue to nurture them. And she tells them to celebrate the lives they have. That's a message for everyone, men and women both. The villagers seemed to think the world was going through a time when that wisdom might not be understood. They said Cybele's Gift, and her words, needed to be hidden away for a while, kept safe."

"With folk like Irene of Volos in the world, as well as the Sheikh-ul-Islam, no doubt that is wise," Father said. "Christian leaders in Istanbul would be equally determined to stamp out any evidence of idolatry, as they would see it. As for me, I am somewhat stunned by the whole sequence of events. I do not believe I will be trading in religious artifacts for some time. I'm certain you are not giving me the whole story, Paula. You think to spare a frail old man, perhaps." There was a twinkle in his eye.

"You, frail?" I said. "You're an exceptional parent, Father. I've always known that." It was true. How many fathers would be so ready to accept what I had told him? How many would have allowed a daughter to come on the voyage in the first place, let alone forgiven so quickly the impetuous and crazy act that had seen her spirited away on a pirate ship?

Morning came, and with it not Stoyan but Duarte da Costa Aguiar, striding into the courtyard at an hour perhaps a little too early for a social visit but not too early for my father and me. We had been up since the morning call to prayer, getting the last of the goods ready for Stoyan to take down to the docks when he arrived. I was wearing my plainest gown and had my hair pinned tightly back under a scarf.

Father saw Duarte coming and said to me, "Choose wisely, Paula. You're a fine girl, full of spirit and intelligence. I may not like this man very much, but I can see that in many ways he's ideal for you. You and he have a great deal in common. I suggest you take him up to the gallery and leave me to get on with this."

I wiped clammy hands on my skirt, suddenly overcome with nerves. I would have liked a chance to wash, to brush my hair, to put on a better outfit, perhaps the plum-colored silk and the lovely veil Duarte had given me.

"You look fine, Paula," Father said, setting his hands on my shoulders and kissing me gently on the cheek. "Go on now."

Well, Duarte had seen me grimy and sweaty with my clothing in rags, so perhaps it didn't matter. Now he greeted me with a smile, exchanged courteous words with my father, then followed me up the steps to the gallery, where we seated ourselves at the little table. I wished I had brought something to occupy my hands. I clutched them together in my lap and cleared my throat.

"Father told me about yesterday," I said awkwardly. "I was . . . surprised. Very surprised."

Duarte had dressed for the occasion. His shirt was of pristine linen, his tunic and trousers of finest wool in the light blue-gray he seemed to favor. His boots were buffed to a shine. Around his neck he wore my red scarf. I considered the aristocratic features, the mischievous dark eyes, the glossy black hair caught neatly back with a ribbon. The upright, athletic body. I tried to imagine being his wife. "To be honest," I added, "you've never struck me as the marrying kind of man."

"Up until recently, I was not," he said, and I heard the slight tremor in his voice. He was nervous, too. "Our recent journey, the pleasure we took in each other's company, the way the whole ship came to life while we had you on board . . . these things have changed my mind on the issue. The fulfillment of my debt of honor has caused me to reassess the future. Master Teodor will have told you, no doubt, that I gave him an inventory of my personal resources and those of my family. I want you to know that I did so not because I believe the final decision will be made on the basis of my wealth but so that your father will be reassured that I can offer you a secure future."

"I see," I said, wondering if I should tell him there was no need to set such details out for me.

"Paula, you know what kind of man I am. My past conduct has not always been entirely ethical. My life is one of constant movement and change. The success of this mission will not alter that. I love the sea. I love the adventure of it, the opportunities it offers, the surprises and challenges." He had risen to his feet now and was standing by the railing with his back to me, tapping his fingers against his leg.

"Duarte," I said, "why don't you sit down? We are friends, aren't we?"

He seated himself on the very edge of a chair.

"Good," I said. "I've got a question for you. That life you just described, the life of a seafarer—it doesn't sound like a life that has much room in it for wives. I could never be the sort of woman who tended the hearth and kept everything in place for a husband who dropped in once or twice a year when he felt like it. That seems to me quite pointless; one might as well stay single and live one's own life."

Duarte smiled. I liked that smile; it reminded me of our conversations on the *Esperança*, the way we sparked each other off with lively banter, each seeking to outwit the other in our debates on every topic under the sun. I had enjoyed those times. Father was right; Duarte was my intellectual equal, a partner such as I might have great difficulty in finding within my limited circle back home in Transylvania. He was clever, witty, possessed of a quirky sense of humor. He was also courageous, strong, and resourceful, not to speak of his physical charms and his considerable wealth. Not so long ago, I would have considered him completely unsuitable to be my husband or indeed anyone else's. But he had proven himself to be a different man from the unscrupulous pirate I had once believed him.

"That wasn't what I had in mind," Duarte said quietly.

"Nobody could imagine that a woman like you would be satisfied with that role, the stay-at-home wife waiting patiently while her husband goes off on adventures at a whim. It was for that reason I decided, long ago, that I would not marry. Such a partnership would be too uneven, and the kind of woman who wanted it would not be the kind of woman to interest me."

I could not work out where he was heading. Down in the courtyard, near the area where Father was working, I glimpsed a tall, dark-haired figure in a dolman, with knives stuck in his sash. Suddenly every nerve in my body was on edge.

"Of course, when I made that decision, I had not met you, Paula," Duarte said. "And I confess, during our earlier encounters, I had very mixed feelings about you. But I have entirely reassessed those feelings. I found it difficult to say farewell to you down at the docks. Then it came to me—I thought, perhaps I need not do this. Why should we not go forward together, side by side, companions in an even greater adventure? I believe we would continue to surprise and delight each other and add spice and sweetness to each other's life."

Down in the courtyard, Stoyan was moving in and out of the storage room, talking to Father. He looked as if he hadn't slept a wink. My heart did a strange kind of flip-flop, as if to remind me to be honest with myself.

"You know I admire you, Duarte," I managed. "I have greatly enjoyed your company. The voyage, your determination to fulfill your debt of honor, the way you conducted yourself . . . I can't fail to hold you in high regard after that." I drew a deep breath, struggling to keep calm. It wouldn't be fair to cut him off short; he was a friend, and I owed him respect. "You still haven't really answered my question. If I accepted you, where would I fit into the future you have said you want, the future of voyages and adventures and discoveries?"

"I was hoping," he said, coming closer and dropping to one knee beside me, "that you would share it with me, Paula. Be my partner on the *Esperança*, travel with me, share my adventures. We would make an invincible team. Together, we could achieve anything. And think what enjoyment we would have doing so. Paula, I don't think I am wrong in interpreting your willingness to spend time in my company as perhaps indicating you feel more than friendship toward me. I know your father intends to sail for home tomorrow. We don't have much time. Can you give me an answer?"

The han seemed suddenly hushed. My answer trembled on my lips, reluctant to become sound, for I valued Duarte's friendship and I respected the honesty with which he had presented his proposal—while it had scarcely been romantic in nature, he had said it in plain words, not masked by empty compliments. I rose to my feet, moving to stand at the railing. "Please don't kneel like that," I said, feeling tears somewhere close. "You're making me feel awkward. Come over here, take my hand."

He knew, then, that I was going to say no. I saw it on his face as he moved closer and put his hands around mine.

"I can't," I said bluntly. "I have a high regard for you, Duarte, and if the circumstances were different, I would accept your offer gladly. But I can't."

"Just like that you refuse me? Will you not at least take a little time to consider this? We could . . ." His words trailed off as he met my gaze. "You mean it," he said simply. "You won't change your mind."

"I'm sorry, Duarte." Cheeks flaming, I tried not to glance down to the courtyard. "You're a fine man, and it hurts me to cause you pain. But I know I could never love you the way I should."

He shrugged, lifting his brows and giving me that sardonic little smile. It made me want to cry.

"Ah, well," he said, "I can see it's back to a life of piracy for me. So much for redemption through the love of a good woman. It's time I was off. But first . . ." And before I could so much as draw breath, he swept me into his arms and kissed me full on the lips, not the cheeky, joking kind of kiss he had given me as I left the *Esperança* but a proper kiss of a sort I had never before experienced. It was lovely: passionate, tender, a little frightening. It was a kiss that said, *This is what you're giving up. This is what we might have had.* He did not release me for a while. When at last he did so, it was to turn abruptly on his heel and head off down the steps without another word.

I watched him cross the courtyard and vanish out the arched entry. As I turned back, I found myself looking directly at Stoyan, who was standing motionless in the open doorway of the storage room where he and Father had been working, gazing up at me. If he had appeared tired and dispirited before, now he looked like a man betrayed. There was no guard on his expression: The amber eyes were blazing with hurt, the lips twisted in furious outrage. If I had thought his feelings less strong than mine, I'd been wrong. I opened my mouth to call out, to offer some explanation, but he turned and disappeared inside. He must have seen us, Duarte and me. He had probably seen everything.

I was in no state to run down and explain myself, especially not in Father's presence. I retreated to my closet, where I sat on the pallet and stared at the wall. Tati's embroidery was spread across my pillow. I ran my fingers over the dancing figures, longing for my sisters to be here. Stela would give me a comforting hug; Jena would provide wise advice. Iulia would make a joke about men and how impossible they were. But my sisters were far away, and I felt utterly alone. The thrilling peril of the journey, the tragedy and triumph and the bond of friendship I had shared with these two men, each so lovely, each so different, seemed further away than ever. I had managed to wound both of them and to make myself utterly miserable.

A little later, after washing away the tearstains, I went down to the storage area. If I had to, I would ask Father if I could speak to Stoyan alone. I would tell Stoyan that I wanted to spend my life with him, no matter what. If there were obstacles, surely the two of us together had the strength to deal with them. We'd proved that on our journey through the mountain, hadn't we? It sounded logical, but I was trembling with nerves as I went down the steps. *How brave are you, Paula?* I asked myself. *Brave enough to put your heart on a chopping block and invite your dearest friend to cut it up?*

The storage room was empty. Father and Stoyan had taken the last of our goods to the waterfront. I borrowed a millet broom and gave the chamber a vigorous sweeping. Under the rhythmic swishing sound, words came to me, a verse I had come close to forgetting in the turmoil that my life had become since our passage through the mountain. *Water and stone, flesh and bone. Night and morn, rose and thorn. . . .* I had not taken one gift out of Cybele's treasure cave but two. How could I forget something as important as a riddle? At the time, it had seemed no more than nonsense pairs of contrasting words. *Tree and wind, heart and mind.*

Now, abruptly, I knew exactly why the crone had given it to me. I imagined strong stone supporting and aiding the passage of fluid water; a delicate flower protected by its sharp thorn, the two interdependent, contrasting parts of the same whole. I pictured a gale shivering through the trees, seeds spiraling downward to start a new forest. I considered how day followed night in inevitable sequence, each giving meaning to the other. The perfect team could be two people who were as unlike as rock and stream, high peak and west wind, bare earth and green shoot. They could complement and enhance each other's strengths and make up for each other's weaknesses. They could be so close it was as if they shared flesh and bone, heart and mind. That was how it had felt with Stoyan and me as we traversed the cave of the lake. We had worked together as if we were two parts of the same self. And that was how it felt now. I knew that if I lost him, something inside me would break beyond mending. There was no need to present him with logical arguments to support my case. There was no need for *despite.* All I needed to say was *I love you.*

The sweeping finished, I paced up and down the courtyard until Maria called me up to her quarters, saying she couldn't bear to watch me any longer, and plied me with coffee and little honeyed pastries. I could tell she had seen me talking to Duarte, but I offered no explanations, and she was not quite prepared to ask what had occurred between us. I did wonder what damage my reputation had suffered after the journey and how much impact that might have on Father's continuing success in these parts as a trader. Once we sailed back home, the stories would all die down, I thought. People would forget as soon as some new scandal took their interest.

"I think your father's back, Paula," Maria said, looking down toward the courtyard. We had been standing by the railing, finishing a second glass of tea and enjoying the warmth of the day while the activity of the han went on below us. She was smiling; it was clear she knew my mind was far away.

Father had come in through the arched entrance and was heading for the steps to the gallery. There was no sign of Stoyan.

"Thank you for the tea," I said. "I'm sorry if I seem a little out of sorts. I'm still tired and there's so much to do before we leave. . . ."

"No trouble, Paula. Let me know if there's anything more Giacomo and I can do to help."

When I reached our apartment, Father was taking off his hat and cloak. He looked unusually somber.

"Father, is something wrong? You were gone a long time. Was there a problem with the goods?"

He shook his head. "No, Paula, everything is loaded and the *Stea de Mare*'s captain is confident of leaving on time tomorrow morning. I can hardly believe we're headed home at last. It's felt like a lifetime."

"I'm sorry—"

He hushed me with an uncharacteristically sharp gesture. "No, no. Let's not have that. What's happened has happened, and you acted with the best intentions. You are safe, and I have come through my experience undamaged, if somewhat prematurely aged, so no more need be said on that score. I suppose I should ask what answer you gave Senhor Aguiar."

"I refused him, Father. I like Duarte very much, but we are not suited as life companions. He accepted my answer, though I could see he was upset. Father, where is Stoyan?"

He did not answer immediately but looked at me with a little frown, as if he had some news he was unwilling to tell me.

"What, Father? You're worrying me. What is it?" I put my hand on his sleeve.

"You won't like this at all."

I waited, heart suddenly racing.

"Stoyan's gone," Father told me flatly. "Once we'd seen the goods safely loaded onto the *Stea de Mare,* he announced that as we were to sail tomorrow, his duties for us were effectively at an end. He requested to be released forthwith. I had already paid him what he was owed and a little more for service beyond the call of duty. I did protest. I told him you'd be most upset if you couldn't say goodbye, but he wouldn't change his mind. On the face of it, his request was entirely reasonable. I had no choice but to let him go."

I felt as if my insides had plummeted to the ground. Stoyan couldn't do this! He couldn't! I clutched Father's arm. "Father, I have to see him! I have to go down to the docks. He might still be there! We must go right now—"

"Shh, shh, Paula, take a deep breath. It's much too late for that, I'm afraid. The goods are already loaded; Stoyan could be anywhere. You know what that crowd is like—"

"I can't let him go like this, Father, I just can't. I never told him . . . And then he saw us, me and Duarte, and . . . I can go by myself. I'll run all the way—" I heard what I was saying and came to a shuddering, tearful halt. "Please, Father," I said, struggling to sound calm. "Can we try?"

"Oh, dear," Father observed mildly, getting back to his feet. "I suppose Giacomo might be prevailed on to lend us a cart. Come, then. Please don't get your hopes up, Paula. I have no idea where he was headed, and this city is a very easy place to get lost in."

We made good progress, Father driving the horse himself, I seated beside him with my veil up over my nose, trying to scan the crowd in all directions for a very tall man with dark hair, a pale, scarred face, and a wounded look in his eyes. Deep inside, I was muttering a silent prayer to whomever would listen, to bring him back to me just long enough for me to tell him I loved him, even if he heard it and chose to walk away again. Why hadn't I got those words out the night of Cybele's return? Why had I left it so long that he had seen me in Duarte's arms and probably leaped to all sorts of conclusions? Why, oh, why had I forgotten the riddle? He had chosen to step back, on the voyage home, and give me and Duarte time alone together. He'd probably made a decision that the pirate, with his wealth, status, education, and ready wit, was better suited to me than he was. In the eyes of the world, perhaps this was so. But not in mine. And if I told him how I felt, if I was brave enough to come right out with it, maybe not in Stoyan's either. *If a man truly loves . . . he gives no heed to what others may think. His heart has no room for that,*

for it is filled to the brim with the unutterable truth of his feelings.
That hadn't been a speech about me and my pathetic attempt
to express myself or he would have said, *If a woman truly
loves.* Those had been the words of his own heart. And I'd
missed it; I'd missed it. I'd been so stupid, and now, if we
didn't hurry up, I was going to lose him forever. . . .

Halfway down the last road to the docks, a cart had lost a
wheel and was blocking the way completely. A group of men
stood around it arguing while a boy worked to unharness the
two horses.

"Oh, please, oh, please," I breathed as Father used skills I
had not realized he possessed to turn our vehicle and head
off down a side way. We went through a maze of smaller
streets. A dog that had been sleeping outside a doorway fled
at our approach. I found myself wishing Tati were still here
to guide us safely to the waterfront, but there were no eerie
presences about today, only obstacles in the form of crates
and barrels, fruit vendors' little stalls, porters bearing bundles, stray cats streaking across our path.

"Breathe, Paula," my father advised as he turned the cart
onto the dockside and we were enveloped in a press of folk.
"You're wound as tight as a spring. Stay on the cart or you'll
be trampled. I'll drive along to the *Stea de Mare,* but if you
can't see him anywhere on the docks, there's nothing more I
can do."

I bit my nails to the quick as we made a painfully gradual
progress along the busy waterfront to the place where our
vessel was moored, her decks shipshape, the last of her cargo
being neatly stowed as we watched. Farther along, the
Esperança was at anchor. I looked ahead, behind, into the
mass of dockworkers and trading folk, visiting dignitaries

and port officials, anonymous robed travelers and sweating slaves. I looked until my vision blurred, until my neck was stiff, until an aching flood of unshed tears had built behind my eyes. At the *Stea de Mare*, despite Father's warning, I got down from the cart—he followed quickly, motioning a crewman to come and hold the reins for him—and went on board to question the crew about Stoyan. Nobody had seen anything of him since he and Father had brought the last load down. I came back down the plank and stood very still by the cart a moment. Then I climbed up to the seat and put my head in my hands.

"I'm sorry, Paula," Father said as he got up beside me. "Truly sorry. But the fact is, if he doesn't want to be found, there will be no finding him. This will fade in time, my dear. Once we're at sea and on our way home, things may not seem so desperate."

I said nothing as he flicked the reins and the horse headed back toward the han.

Are you brave enough, Paula? I asked myself as the tears began to fall. *Are you brave enough to live with a broken heart?* And I could not dismiss his words because, after my mother had died, that was exactly what my father had done.

Chapter Sixteen

"Tell us about going across the swinging bridge! No, tell us about balancing on that man's shoulders and collecting the animals!"

It was spring, almost a year since Father and I had left Istanbul, and Stela was still thirsty for the story, no matter how many times I told it. My younger sister found the tale of desperate pursuit at sea, deeds of courage and magical trials, a devious Greek scholar and a charming pirate captain utterly thrilling. The pirate, especially. As for the news of Tati, all my sisters had greeted that with mixed feelings when I told them. They were happy that she was well, impressed by her bravery, and sad that she was missing us so badly. Iulia and Stela were also, I suspected, a little jealous that I had been the one chosen for an Other Kingdom quest. For the first few months, we had expected Tati to turn up one day, out of the blue, ready for the visit she had earned. But so far there had been no sign.

"Tell us about the time Duarte gave you the shell scarf," Stela urged now, glancing at our other sisters, who were seated with us on a rug. It was a beautiful day, the warm air heady with the scent of hawthorn and wood smoke. The charcoal burners were busy farther down the valley.

It was unusual for the whole family to be here at Piscul Dracului. Iulia and her husband, Răzvan, were visiting Jena and Costi, who lived on the estate next door to ours, and to-day all of them, with the children, had come down through the woods to see Father, Stela, and me. The narrow stairways and crooked passages of the old castle where we lived had been full of shouts and laughter and running feet. Now the sun had drawn us outside with a basket of provisions. We were in a field not far from the house, just below the spot where grazing land met wildwood. On a stretch of level ground a little farther down the hill, Răzvan and Costi were energetically teaching four-year-old Nicolae the best way to kick a ball into an improvised goal. Father was on the side-lines offering expert advice and keeping an eye on Iulia's son, Gavril, who had a tendency to wander out into the middle of it all with no warning. His self-confidence was admirable but, at two, a little perilous.

"Father seems happy," observed Jena. "I haven't seen him looking so well since you came home, Paula."

"Of course," put in Iulia, who was busy spooning a gluti-nous substance into the gaping mouth of her daughter, Mirela, "it must have helped that you and Costi scored such a coup in Vienna. That's set the business on its feet for an-other five years at least. It's entirely made up for Father's dis-appointment over the failure of his deal in Istanbul."

She was partly right. A lucrative long-term agreement had been struck by Costi and Jena with a trading house in the great northern city, and the profits from that would remove our financial worries for the foreseeable future. Thank heavens for that. Despite his avowal to put the whole episode of Cybele's Gift behind him, his perceived failure had left Father feeling low, and he still wasn't back to his old self. He did remind me quite frequently that he, too, had learned a vital lesson during that time: He knew now that no trading deal, however advantageous, meant anything at all beside the life and safety of a loved one. All the same, the events of last spring had saddened him, and I was glad to see him today with a smile on his face and a sparkle in his eyes.

"Come on, Paula, tell the story." Stela wasn't going to give up. She reached into the basket, helped herself to a bread roll, and began to munch, fixing expectant blue eyes on me. At twelve, she still had the enthusiasms and energies of a child, but she was hovering on the edge of womanhood. Her figure was rounding out, her features gaining a bloom that hinted at future beauty. She would be like Tati: the kind of woman men's eyes were drawn to despite themselves. "Please, Paula."

"Not today," I said, leaning back on my elbows and narrowing my eyes against the sun. "Everyone's heard it a hundred times before. And it's over; all I want to do now is forget."

In the silence that ensued, I felt Jena's eyes on me. I knew that she, of all the family, understood how much the season of Cybele's Gift had changed me.

"Stela," said Iulia, "will you go down to the kitchen and ask Florica for another bottle of her elderberry wine? And maybe some more cheese . . . Răzvan's sure to be starving when they finish running around."

Stela's expression told me she knew this was a ploy to get

her out of the way, but she went without question, dark hair streaming behind her as she ran across the hillside to the stile. The grass under her feet was dotted with wildflowers, blue, purple, yellow, pink. Down the hill, I could see a cart coming up the track to the castle. The red tassels on the horse's bridle swung as it moved. On the driver's seat was Dorin, our man of all work. He and Petru had a big job on hand, something to do with drains. The cart would be loaded with building supplies.

"Paula," said Jena in a big-sisterly voice, "we're worried about you."

"You're not yourself," added Iulia. "Florica says you're only picking at your food these days, and you can't afford to lose weight. You're skin and bone already." She herself was a shapely woman, the delight of her husband's eye, and had been telling me for years I was too thin.

"Worse than that," put in Jena, "Father says you haven't even been reading much lately. Or at least not the way you used to, as if you could never get enough of books and learning. If I didn't know you better, I would say you're exhibiting all the signs of having been unlucky in love."

"You should come and stay with Răzvan and me," Iulia suggested, reaching out to grab Mirela's smock before the child could grasp a bee that had caught her interest. "It would take your mind off things."

"What things?" I could hear the growl in my voice. I did not want to talk about it, not even to my sisters. I'd been doing my best to forget, to pick up the threads of my old life, helping Father, teaching Stela, making myself useful around house and farm. It was just unfortunate that I wasn't better at hiding how unhappy I was.

"Come on, Paula," Jena said. "We're your sisters. We're here to help. There's a part of this story you've held back, Iulia and I are certain of it. You need to talk about it sometime, get it off your chest."

"I'm fine," I muttered. "Anyway, it's much too late now."

Down the hill, Dorin had driven into the courtyard, and Petru's farm dogs were going crazy. The frenzy of barking went far beyond the greeting they usually provided when someone came home.

"Paula." Jena's tone was stern. "You can't fool us. Before you went to Istanbul, you were bubbling with plans for the future. You were so confident and hopeful. You convinced all of us that you'd achieve your dream one day. That's all changed since you came back. You seem . . . adrift. Not simply unhappy, but unsure of yourself. And yet you had such adventures during that trip. You were tested to the limit. That was terrifying, I know, but wonderful, too. To go back to the Other Kingdom, to see Tati again . . ." I could hear the longing in my sister's voice. "And to be given such an important task, a quest of your own . . . You've told the story pretty modestly, I suspect. It sounds as if you had to call upon all your reserves of courage and intelligence to get through it. I can't understand how you've lost faith in yourself."

"Unrequited love," said Iulia. "It's written all over you. Come and spend the summer at our place, and we'll introduce you to any number of suitable men. In a pinch, I may even find one or two who like books."

The noise from below had not abated. I was trying to think of a reply when Stela came sprinting back across the field, babbling something that did not become clear until she arrived in our midst. "Paula! There's something for you! Dorin brought it, a . . . a delivery. Come now! You have to see this!"

"A delivery?" I tried to remember if I had ordered anything, books maybe or some household supplies that might have been packaged under my name rather than Father's. "Can't Dorin deal with it? I'll come down later."

"No!" Stela was beside herself with excitement. "You have to come!" She grabbed my arm and hauled me up, tugging me after her in the general direction of the house. With a grimace at my elder sisters, I followed.

In the courtyard, Dorin was unloading the supplies. The farm dogs were clustered around the front door, barking hysterically.

"What's wrong?" I shouted.

"In there," Dorin yelled, pointing to the doorway.

The dogs did not follow me inside; they were well trained. Their raucous challenge died down behind me as I walked along the red-tiled passageway to the kitchen. I went in to find a crate in the middle of the floor and our farmer, Petru, crouched down beside it, peering through a narrow opening in the top. His wife, our housekeeper, Florica, stood by the stove, lips pursed, eyes thoughtful.

"Apparently it's for you," she said dryly, glancing at me.

"Look, Paula!" Stela was already by Petru's side, poking her fingers between the slats of the crate. "Petru, can we take the top off? He's probably been in there all day, the poor thing. . . ."

The flood of words abated as I moved closer, and Petru edged aside to make room for me. I peered into the crate. Through the opening, a pair of soft, expressive eyes gazed up at me. There was a low growling, a sound I interpreted as a token challenge. My heart was doing a dance. I had never really believed in tears of joy, but those were what seemed to be welling in my eyes right now.

"Open that and the creature'll take your finger off," said Florica. "It's huge. That's the last thing I'd be expecting you to want, Paula. A crate of books, now, or a box of paper and pens, but not a dog."

"It's a gift," Stela said importantly. "Not something Paula ordered for herself, something someone's sent her. Open it up, Paula. Maybe it's from that pirate. He sounded as if he liked you. Perhaps he's right here in the valley!"

Her words flowed over me as I borrowed Petru's knife and prized off the side slats of the crate. The dog emerged, at first not entirely steady on his legs. He sniffed at my skirt, looked around, then ambled over to relieve himself against the wall. "I'll clean up," I said hastily.

I could see the message on Florica's face: No dogs inside the house. Before she could say a word, Petru snapped his fingers to bring the animal close—I noticed how ready it was to obey—then ran his gnarled hands over its noble head, its straight, strong back, its extremely large feet.

"A handsome creature," he observed. "Only half grown; I'd say he's six months at the most. He's going to be a fine big dog." The animal was already larger than our adult herding dogs. "Unusual gift for a young lady." Petru glanced at me, eyes shrewd. "I've never seen this breed before. Foreign, is it?"

"It's called a Bugarski Goran," I said absently as I hunted inside the crate for a note or message. "A special kind of mountain dog known for its strength, heart, and loyalty. Generally they're treated as members of the family. That's

straint was remarkable; I could not have wished for a more understanding parent.

Around midday, Florica bundled me off outdoors, saying the dog needed exercise and so did I. As I went out, I heard her say, "Now, Stela, I've a mind to make those walnut pastries just in case we have guests. I'll need your help with chopping the nuts; it's too much for my old hands these days. . . ."

I hadn't intended to go far, but it was another lovely day and the dog's enthusiasm was hard to resist. I took a ball up to the top field and tried to teach him to fetch. He was good at the chasing and catching part, taking off like an arrow, seizing the ball and shaking it to and fro as if he planned to kill it on the spot. Then he would drop it at his own feet and stand watching me expectantly. Having never trained a dog before, I had trouble conveying to him exactly what he was supposed to do. We worked on it together. I became tired; the dog was keen to go on forever. I slipped and got grass stains on my skirt; the dog rolled in something interesting. At least the activity had distracted me from my anxieties for a little, I thought as I sat down for a breather and he took up a relaxed guard position next to me, tongue lolling. But Stoyan had never been far from my thoughts. What if he didn't come? What if he turned up and I found myself lost for words? What if all he had in mind was a polite visit? Just because I was feeling like this, as if I wanted to laugh and cry and sing and dance all at once, did not mean he would be feeling the same. A year might have cured him entirely of those feelings that had made him look so drained the day we parted. Best stay calm. Best think out carefully what I would say, word by word. . . .

The dog went from a lying pose to a hurtling run in an instant, barking wildly. I started, then rose slowly to my feet. A familiar figure was climbing over the stile at the bottom of the field, a big, pale-skinned figure with thick dark hair and a scar on his cheek. He was not in his Turkish-style dolman now but wore a linen shirt, a plain waistcoat, close-fitting trousers, and serviceable boots. The dog reached him and jumped up ecstatically. Stoyan made a firm gesture, and the creature dropped obediently to sit. He bent to scratch the dog behind the ears, then straightened, shading his eyes with a hand, gazing up toward me.

I realized the dog had the right idea. The best words for such a moment were no words at all. I ran down the hill through the grass and the bright spring flowers, not even thinking about the stains on my skirt or my untidy hair or anything but the fact that Stoyan was here at last and that in an instant we would be together again. At ten paces away, he opened his arms, and when I reached him, I threw myself into them and was picked up and whirled around as if I were a little child. When he stopped turning, he brought me slowly down, my body against his all the way, until my feet were on the bottom step of the stile. His arms folded around me like a barrier against all the ills of the world; his cheek was wet against mine. I was crying, too, crying and laughing and wondering how it was possible to have such tumultuous, thrilling sensations coursing through me and at the same time feel utterly safe.

"Paula," Stoyan murmured. "Oh, Paula. . . ."

"I thought I'd never see you again," I whispered, my arms around his neck, my lips against his cheek. "You didn't even say goodbye—"

Stoyan stopped my words with a kiss. And if Duarte's kiss had been nice, enjoyable, a little exciting, this one eclipsed it in every way. I drowned in it, my body melting with delight. For a precious few moments, there was more magic here than in all the realms of the Other Kingdom. When we broke apart, we were both breathless.

"Stoyan," I said, "any moment now my little sister's going to come running up here to tell me you've arrived; she's beside herself with curiosity. I have to say something before she gets here, just in case you . . ." It no longer seemed possible that he would turn me down. His kiss had told me eloquently that he felt the same as I did. "I love you, Stoyan," I said, feeling suddenly shy. "I was working up to telling you that night after we came out of the cave, but I got it all wrong, and then you were so grim and forbidding, and . . ."

"Shall we sit down on the grass here?" Stoyan said gently, drawing me down beside him. "If we are below the line of the wall, perhaps this sister may not see us until we have said what we must say." He settled himself against the stone wall, placing me between his knees, my back against his chest. In this position he could wrap his arms around me from behind, which I found I liked very much. The dog flopped down beside us. "I hope you like my gift," he went on. "I know our wager was canceled, but I was not quite brave enough to come here in person until I knew you would receive me. I made an error of judgment, Paula, a grievous one. I ran away. I could not bring myself to say goodbye to you. I have caused you pain; myself as well."

"Did you actually think I would marry Duarte? Couldn't you see how I felt about you?"

There was a lengthy pause, and then Stoyan said, "Your

father had told me of Duarte's visit and offer of marriage. Not knowing the depth of my feelings for you, he saw no harm in sharing that news. And when Duarte returned, you kissed him. He held you as a lover does. You gave him your lips as if you . . . as if you felt more than friendship for him. It seemed plain to me that you had accepted his offer. I knew Duarte could give you what you wanted, what you needed. Our journey had shown me that he was a good man beneath the surface and that he cared for you. I could protect you. I could be brave. I could be a friend of sorts. But I could never be your equal in learning, in conversation, in skills of the mind. He was your equal. He could offer a life rich with possibilities. I had my brother to find, my mother waiting at home for news. I had a path to follow that must take me far from you."

"So you stepped back. After all the trials we had been through together, after we had become so close, you believed I would accept Duarte?" I brought his palm to my lips and heard his indrawn breath.

"It had seemed to me thus ever since I watched the two of you dancing on the night of the celebration," Stoyan said. "Your list of reasons why we were ill matched wounded me even as I recognized its truth. I took it to mean your feelings were less strong than my own. I believed that to say yes to you would end in heartbreak for both of us, Paula. I am ashamed that I misjudged you so. At the time, to step away seemed the honorable choice. Indeed, I was angry with myself for being such a fool as to dream that you might love me as I did you, deeply, truly, with an intensity that crowded out all arguments to the contrary. So I went my own way, hoping the memory would fade in time."

"What brought you back? Stoyan, what about Taidjut? Did you find him?"

His tone became somber. "He lives. Your theory was correct; he carries a position of some authority, the second in charge to a provincial governor. After making some further inquiries, I went back to the region of our adventure. The plague had passed. Many were lost, but they are strong folk in those parts, and my brother and his superior had taken steps to limit the spread of the disease. He agreed to see me, not in public but in a carefully controlled setting where his privacy was strictly guarded. He seemed content. He spoke like a Turkish nobleman. He asked me to convey his respects to our mother but made it clear he wishes no further contact with his family. For him, that life is over, forgotten. Taidjut has a new religion, a new culture, a new responsibility. He wishes to obliterate from his mind what he was before the devshirme. To do otherwise would be to negate the years of learning, to reduce to nothing the sacrifices he has made. So he believes. There was no choice for me but to accept that."

"I'm so sorry," I said, deciding I would not ask if Taidjut was a eunuch or had been left a whole man. "I'm very sad for you and your mother. But at least he is well and has a good life."

"I came back through Istanbul, intending to bear the news home to my mother. To my surprise, I saw the *Esperança* in port. I had expected you and Duarte to sail back to Portugal when your father departed. Not long after my arrival, I met Duarte at a coffeehouse. It was then that I learned you had refused him, Paula, and from that moment my heart began to mend. I questioned him closely. Duarte assured me that your feelings for him were those of a dear friend only. This, he said, you had made very plain when you refused his offer. He added that it was quite apparent to him that your reasons for turning him down related to me. He urged me to seek you out and speak boldly of my love for you."

"Go on," I said, hoping very much that I would hear all of this before Stela made an appearance.

"I could not come to you straightaway. I had to travel home to see my mother. The news of Taidjut was difficult for her. I felt obliged to stay awhile and help her on the farm. At the same time, I undertook some studies with the priest and gave consideration to the future. Eventually, my mother told me quite firmly that it was time to sort things out with you. I was somewhat fearful. I did not know yet that you truly returned my feelings. When you came running toward me with your hair flying, when you threw your arms around me, that was the best moment of my life. And now, I have something for you." He fished in a leather bag he had slung over his shoulder.

"Another gift? The dog is plenty."

"The dog is part of the future," he said solemnly, drawing a kidskin pouch out of the bag and setting it in my hand. It was heavy. "This is another part. Open it, Paula."

I loosened the strings and looked inside, and my breath stopped in my throat. The pouch was stuffed with gold coins. By the weight, I knew it was a small fortune, more money than I had ever seen at one time before.

"Proceeds from the sale of my reward, the one the old woman said I might take from Cybele's treasure trove," he told me quietly. "I purchased this dog and another, a female, so we will have a breeding pair. I gave my mother enough to have some improvements made to the farm. But the remainder, the bulk of the funds, was always intended for you. I chose what to take away from the cave with a particular purpose in mind. The money is to help you start your bookselling business. When I thought you would marry Duarte, I could not bring myself to speak to you of this plan, for it made me seem foolish, deluded."

"I'm sorry," I murmured, imagining how awful that had been for him and wishing he had told me straightaway. "It makes sense now—what the old woman said about three rewards. The diadem and the gold it brought was the first. Finding Taidjut was the long-sought second. And . . ."

"And you are the deeply desired third," Stoyan said. He was blushing. "I know how proud you are, Paula. I know you will not ask your father for funds to realize your own dream. I hope you will take this from me, for we earned it together, you and I, and together we can make that dream reality. Paula, will you marry me? I cannot read very well yet, but I am learning, and you can teach me more. Booksellers need guards; they need folk who can load and unload carts, carry heavy boxes, protect expensive cargoes. . . ."

"Yes," I said.

"I studied as well as I could," Stoyan went on. "It was not easy; there were few books in the village—"

"Stoyan, I said yes, I will marry you. I'd marry you if you couldn't read a word. I would if you hadn't a single copper coin to your name." I wrapped my arms around his neck, spilling the coins into the grass. We let go of each other and gathered them as, at last, Stela could be seen coming up from the castle, face flushed from her cooking activities and from excitement. "I'm sure we can find a place for our business close to a town, but with enough room for dogs. And near Piscul Dracului, of course. I want to be able to visit Father and Stela and Jena and Costi. . . . But, Stoyan, what about your family? The farm, your mother . . . ?"

"Paula!" Stela had arrived. She clambered over the stile, then was unaccountably stricken by shyness as she examined the large and somewhat intimidating figure of Stoyan. It was clear to me that he was not at all what she had expected.

"This is Stoyan," I said in Greek. "Stoyan, this is my youngest sister, Stela. Stela, you'll need to use your Greek; that's the only language the two of you have in common. It will be good practice for you."

After a couple of false starts, Stela asked Stoyan, "Is it true you fought off twenty armed men single-handed? And walked into a Turkish bath when Paula was only wearing a sort of sheet?"

I felt my cheeks grow hot. I had forgotten the night I had told my sister this particular story.

"Entirely true," Stoyan said gravely. "Indeed, I was about to tell Paula that the occurrence at the hamam is one of the matters on which Senhor Duarte quizzed me when I met him not long ago. It had been mentioned in passing and had been exercising his imagination. I am happy to make your acquaintance, Kyria Stela."

Stela grinned, captivated by his courtesy as indeed I had been the very first time I met him. Then she remembered something. "Paula, there's a lady down at the castle. In the kitchen. She doesn't seem to speak any language we know, so I think you need to come."

"A lady?" I looked at Stoyan.

He seemed a little abashed. "My mother," he said. "I was

going to explain. It is true, she has no Greek. She sent me to find you. She insisted she did not need my help."

I began to feel quite worried. "We'd best go down right away," I said. "You're saying your mother has traveled all the way from Bulgaria with you?"

"That is correct, Paula." He helped me over the stile, then extended his hand to Stela. The dog went over the wall in a leap. "A cousin is looking after our farm. Depending on what is decided, my mother may remain in Transylvania with us. She wishes to . . ." The words trailed away awkwardly.

"She wants to inspect you," Stela said. "To see if you're suitable for her son. I'm right, aren't I?" she added, glancing at Stoyan in a way that if she had been slightly older, would have been flirtatious.

"She knows that Taidjut will never come home," Stoyan said. "It is natural that she wishes me to be happy. You should not worry about this, Paula. The decision is not hers, but ours, and is already made. Besides, she cannot do anything but love you on first sight, as I did."

Stela grinned with pure delight. I was glad she decided not to comment.

"On first sight?" I queried. "When I was trying to be a real merchant and putting on my sternest manner?"

"The moment I saw you, Paula," he said, putting his arm around my waist. "The first instant. Later, I will tell you all the reasons. For now, I think we must face the challenge of this family visit. There is nothing to fear. You have your dog, you have your sister, and you have me. Even the most alarming of mothers cannot prevail against such a show of strength."

* * *

It must have been a daunting journey for Stoyan's mother—all the way from Bulgaria by cart or on horseback, with not a word of our language or of any other that was common currency in this northern land. She was surely not equipped for such an adventure at her age. I made a picture of her in my mind as we walked down to the castle and indoors; I imagined her as frail, weary, and lost. It would be hard to make her feel at home when we had no common tongue. Holding Stoyan's hand tightly, I opened the kitchen door.

The kettle was steaming on the stove, and the room was full of a tempting smell of baking. Several pieces of Florica's best weaving were spread out across the well-scrubbed table. Our housekeeper was explaining that the flower border was based on a pattern her mother had taught her and that she had invented the dye for the gentian blue herself. As she spoke, her hands were busy illustrating her meaning.

Seated at the table admiring the weaving was an extremely imposing woman. She was younger than I had expected—a good ten years my father's junior, I thought. Her hair was as dark as Stoyan's, the braids pinned in a no-nonsense style atop her head. She was a big woman, tall and solidly built, and she sat bolt upright. I felt she was the kind of person who would tap me on the shoulder and correct me if I did not hold myself well. Her jacket was of black felt covered with multicolored embroidery, an intricate pattern of flower and leaf, vine and fruit. Under it she was clad in a linen blouse, a practical riding skirt with a slit up the side, and good though mud-spattered boots.

As we came in, she turned, then rose to her feet, looking me up and down. Her gaze was not unfriendly, but she was definitely assessing me. Perhaps she was deciding my hips were too narrow for childbearing. Perhaps she was thinking that if Stoyan was going to drag her all the way to Transylvania, he could at least have chosen a beauty. I swallowed nervously, then said in Greek, so that Stoyan, at least, could understand, "Welcome. I am very happy to meet you."

Stoyan said something with *Paula* in it, a translation, an introduction, and I stepped forward nervously to kiss my future mother-in-law on either cheek. She took my hands in hers, looked me in the eye, and said something to Stoyan in Bulgarian.

"For pity's sake, Paula, let the poor lady sit down," Florica said. "Stela, will you run and call your father again? And get that dog out of here. I'm not putting my pastries on the table while he's within range."

We sat. Stoyan's mother spoke again, nodding in my direction.

"My mother says she did not expect me to choose such a slight girl," Stoyan said apologetically. "She is a farmer, you understand; the women in our part of the world are of robust build. She says you remind her of the mountain flowers, small and pale but strong. She bids you welcome to our family." A flush rose to his cheeks. "She adds, she hopes you are aware of what a fine man you are getting. I think mothers are fond of making such remarks."

"Please tell your mother I know I'm getting the best man in the world," I said. "She must be very proud of you. Now perhaps I'd better make the tea, just to show reading and writing are not my only skills."

After that, the kitchen filled up with folk. First was my father, who threw his arms around Stoyan and was embraced in return. He engaged Stoyan's mother in conversation, with her son as interpreter, while I brewed tea and Florica set out the walnut pastries, cheese, little spiced sausages, and bread rolls, as well as a jug of fresh milk from our cow. Then Petru came in, taciturn as ever in company but clearly unable to curb his curiosity. The smell of Florica's baking drew in Dorin as well and then Father's secretary, Gabriel. Stoyan and his mother, whose name was Nadezhda, did not seem at all overwhelmed by this crowd, despite the constant need for everything to be rendered into Greek and then into Bulgarian and back again.

At a certain point, when fresh tea was being prepared and the pastries were almost finished, Stoyan spoke quietly to Father and the two of them went out together. They were gone awhile; long enough for me to begin to worry. Not that I believed it likely Father would refuse Stoyan permission to marry me, but I thought he might set conditions. He might want us to wait awhile so we would be sure we were making the right decision. Or perhaps he would think we should find our house and land first. My stomach churned. We'd waited a whole year already, a year in which both of us had been lonely and miserable. Now that Stoyan was here, I didn't want to let him out of my sight.

The door opened. Not Stoyan, not Father, but Jena and Costi with little Nicolae.

"We're on our way down to the village—" Jena began, then saw we had an unusual visitor. "Oh, I didn't realize— Paula, will you introduce us?"

I did my best without language. Stoyan's mother stood, bowed, kissed Jena and Costi on both cheeks. Then, her strong features softened by a smile, she crouched down to Nicolae's level and spoke to him quietly, asking him about

the toy he was carrying, a little wooden cart. Not much later, she had him sitting on her knee and was sharing her pastry with him. And I had a flash of foresight, or something similar. I saw her with a different child in her arms, a child who would be not my nephew as Nicolae was but my son, mine and Stoyan's. I could not see him clearly, only that he was big and strong with a fine head of dark hair and that his grandmother held him with a fierce pride. In my vision of the future, there had not been much room for children, but I saw in this moment that we owed her that. And I found, to my surprise, that I quite warmed to the idea myself. With this formidable lady as part of our family, Stoyan and I would juggle running a book business and breeding dogs and raising children quite capably. For we were a perfect team. I had known that in the caves of Cybele. I was even more sure of it now.

"He's a fine big man, your Stoyan," murmured Florica in my ear as I went to the stove for more hot water.

"I know," I said.

"You look after him, now," she added. "He'll need good feeding and plenty of love. Don't get so caught up in your books that you forget that."

"I love him, Florica," I said. "I won't forget."

At that moment, Stoyan and Father came into the kitchen, Stoyan looking as if he might laugh or cry at any moment, Father smiling broadly.

"A celebration is in order," Father said in Greek. "I'm gaining another son-in-law. It just goes to show my theory is correct, Paula. A man of true mettle is not deterred by a single refusal. I always believed Stoyan would come back eventually."

"He didn't get a refusal," I felt obliged to point out, as the rest of the household stood about listening with great interest. Stela was providing a running translation for Florica, Petru, and Dorin, none of whom understood Greek; I was proud of her. "Until today, he never asked."

"All the same, a refusal was what he sensed," Father said. "I am happy the two of you have sorted things out at last. It's been a little like having a brooding storm cloud in the house. Stoyan, we must explain all this to your mother."

Nadezhda appeared delighted with the news. When it was suggested she might come and stay at Piscul Dracului awhile, she was quick to accept. The hostelry where she and Stoyan were lodged was at some distance down the valley. Since he had talked of nothing but me since the day she prized the reason for his unhappiness out of him, she imagined that now he had found me, he would not wish to be too far away. She seemed quite taken by Father, who did indeed have a charming manner developed over years of dealing with fellow merchants and their wives.

Stoyan translated busily. I brought him tea, then sat beside him so I could lean against his shoulder and hold his hand, letting the talk flow around me.

The afternoon passed and faded into evening, and although Dorin, Gabriel, and Petru went back to their work, the rest of us sat on together talking. It had become easier for Stoyan with the arrival of Costi, who was fluent in Greek, and Jena, who knew enough to get by. As for Nadezhda, she did not say much, but her eyes were often on her son and on me, and I saw a quiet contentment in her face that warmed my heart.

Everyone would have to stay the night. Costi and Jena would not walk home in the dark with Nicolae, who was falling asleep on Jena's knee. Stoyan and his mother had come on horseback. Petru had settled the horses in the barn already, and it was too dark to ride down the valley safely anyway. We sisters offered to prepare bedchambers for our guests and went off upstairs while Florica made a start on supper. Nadezhda had rolled up her sleeves, donned a borrowed apron, and begun to chop vegetables with the casual assurance of a woman who is confident even in another's kitchen. I had a feeling I might not be called upon very often to prepare those large meals Florica thought Stoyan needed.

When we had made up beds for Costi and Jena, Nicolae, Stoyan, and his mother, we gathered for a moment in our own old bedchamber, the one where all five sisters had once slept and which would soon have only Stela left as its tenant.

"I wish Iulia had come down with us today," Jena said, flopping onto the bed that had been hers and Tati's. "I can't wait to tell her in the morning. She was so certain that if you ever married, you'd choose a weedy little scholar twice your age. You can expect her and Răzvan here sometime tomorrow. She won't be able to resist casting her eye over Stoyan at the first possible opportunity. He seems lovely, Paula."

"He is lovely," I said. As I had smoothed the sheet on the bed where Stoyan was to sleep tonight, I had not been able to avoid imagining what it would be like to share it with him.

Stela was over by the indentation in the wall, the place where, long ago, we had found our secret portal. She had set her candle on the table nearby and was making shadow patterns with her fingers across the stones. "I wonder if I'll ever get a turn?" she mused. "I mean, Tati told Paula her quest was to earn the right for her to visit us or for one of us to go across. It should be me next. You found your true love because of the Other Kingdom, Jena, and so did Tati. And now Paula's got Stoyan. And it can't be Iulia next, because she's already married Răzvan. So it's my turn. Not that I want a true love especially; I just want to go back. I want to so much sometimes I feel as if I could burst."

I had not yet told my sisters about last night's dream. Now did not seem the right time to break the news to Stela that it had sounded as if Tati would be visiting us, not the other way around.

"You can't apply logic to the workings of the Other Kingdom, Stela," Jena said. "We already know it has its own rules, and they're not like ours. Ileana and her kind do set tests for lovers; one of the lessons we've all learned is how difficult love is and how hard we have to keep on working at it. But there are other lessons built into these journeys. Hard ones. Ones that make us strong."

"It's not fair." Stela did not really seem to want a sensible answer. She was in a strange mood. After her excitement at Stoyan's arrival, she had become subdued and thoughtful. Perhaps it was the specter of impending change. Even with Jena living next door and the rest of us within a few days' journey, it would be lonely for her as the last sister left at home.

"There could be more in store for all of us," Jena said, her gaze traveling to the embroidery, where we five sisters danced hand in hand. "Just wait, that's my advice. And don't worry about it too much; worrying doesn't make things happen any faster. Paula, why don't you wear that lovely plum-colored outfit tonight and the veil with the little shells?"

"That wouldn't be suitable," I said. "I'll wear the green."

On the way downstairs, we met Stoyan coming up to tell us supper was almost ready. His eyes met mine.

Jena seized Stela by the arm. "We'll see you down in the kitchen," she announced, heading off without a backward glance and pulling Stela along with her.

The two of us were alone on a landing, outside the chamber where I had made the bed so carefully and set a handful of wildflowers in a little jug by the window.

"That's your room in there," I said as we stood with our arms around each other and the rest of the world fast receding. "I wish we were already married, Stoyan."

"I too, heart's dearest," whispered Stoyan against my hair. "Your father said we need not wait long. But I think it will seem long."

"Mmm," I murmured, then thought of something. "Stoyan, you know when we were in the cave and the old woman asked me what I'd learned? She never asked you that question. I wonder why?"

"I had not quite achieved my learning, Paula. It took a very long time. I almost lost sight of it. It is interesting that Duarte, whom I blamed for stealing it away, was the one to give it back to me. I should have listened more carefully to your riddles, the third especially."

"Hope," I breathed as it all fell into place. "You'd begun to lose hope—hope of finding your brother, hope of making a good future, and hope of . . ."

"And hope that my dearest might love me as I loved her; that is correct, Paula. There were times when it was almost within my grasp. Those nights we spent together at the han, each such a precious gift . . . I remember every word you spoke to me. I remember every touch. And when we came across the cavern of the lake, my hope was almost strong enough to let me speak the words of my heart to you. But then, at the dancing, it fled away again and I sank into despair. It was odd that Duarte was the one to lift it. This was a hard lesson, but a good one. I will never forget it. Do you think we should go down to supper?"

"Just one thing first—" I stood on tiptoe, slipped my arms up around his neck, and kissed him.

Time passed: a kind of lost time in which we were in another world, just the two of us alone with the thousand sensations drawn out by the touch of our lips and the beating of our hearts and the warmth of our bodies against each other. It was only Costi's voice from the foot of the steps that brought us back to Transylvania, and Piscul Dracului, and the landing where we stood folded in each other's arms.

"Suppertime!" called Costi. His mobile mouth was curved in a droll smile. "Even in this labyrinth of a house, nobody can escape the eagle eye of family. Florica expects everyone to taste Petru's best plum brandy."

I unwrapped my arms from around Stoyan's neck and clasped his hand instead. "Costi's right," I said. "There's no getting away from family. And now there's a wedding to plan. We'd best go downstairs and fortify ourselves. We're going to be busy."

Author's Note

Cybele's Secret is set mainly in the Istanbul of the early Ottoman period. While I undertook substantial research, it should be remembered that this is a work of historical fantasy. In some parts of the book, I have taken liberties with time and place in the interests of better storytelling. I received expert advice from several people whom I mention in the Acknowledgments. However, any errors of fact that may occur in the novel are entirely my own responsibility. In particular, if I have offended anyone with my depiction of Islamic culture or religious practice, I offer a sincere apology.

When I visited Turkey, I tried to see through Paula's eyes. Despite the many changes that have taken place since her time, it was easy for me to imagine the days when Istanbul was the hub of trade for the entire region. Everywhere in the city one can see its rich and complex history. Mosques and other public buildings are decorated with Iznik tiles like those Paula finds on the wall outside Cybele's cave, their colors rich and glowing. The covered markets provided me with a shopping experience not unlike Paula's frustrating attempt to haggle for silks. Farther afield, in Edirne I stayed in a converted han with the same layout as the Genoese trading center where Paula and her father are accommodated. I was able to view ancient manuscripts in various Turkish museums, and my description of the items Paula finds in Irene's library are based on these. At the Sadberk Hanim Museum in Büyükdere, I found an ancient earthenware jug in the shape of a rotund woman, and that was the inspiration for the form Cybele's Gift finally took in the story.

Readers may be interested to learn that the Turkish Van cat is known not only for its apparent enthusiasm for swimming but also for its unmatched eyes, one blue, one yellow. The Bugarski Goran, or Bulgarian shepherd, is a recognized breed of herding dog.

Dealing with languages in the book presented a challenge. The Istanbul of Paula's time was home to folk of many origins, and within the city there were several discrete communities in which particular languages were probably spoken almost exclusively. However, the city had been Greek before it was Turkish, and Greek remained a common tongue for traders after the Ottomans took control. I hope I have not stretched credibility too far by allowing most of the major characters fluency in this useful language. With few if any Romanian speakers in the city, Teodor would have needed to be fluent in Greek or Turkish, probably both, to conduct his trading business. Paula, a born scholar, would have learned Greek and Latin early so she could read the classics.

Glossary of non-English words

Bektaşi	beck-*tuh*-shee; dervish order in which women have equality in worship
Bugarski Goran	Bulgarian shepherd (breed of dog)
caïque	ka-*eek*; shallow-drafted vessel, powered by banks of oars
camekan	*ja*-muh-kahn; rest and refreshment area at the hamam
çarşi	*char*-shee; market comprising small streets lined with shops
dervish	an Islamic mystic
destur	make way
djinn	pronounced like the English word *gin*; genie, spirit
dolman	long robe opening in front, with narrow sleeves
hamam	ha-*mahm*; Turkish bathhouse

han	traders' building incorporating market area, storage for goods, and merchants' accommodation
haremlik	women's quarters
imam	ee-*mahm*; Islamic prayer leader
kyria	*kee*-ree-a; polite Greek form of address for a woman
mahalle	ma-*hahl*-luh; district or quarter
medrese	muh-*dra*-suh; Muslim religious school, usually associated with and situated near a mosque
muezzin	*mweh*-zin; person who gives the call to prayer
Mufti	*moof*-tee; authority on Islamic religious law. The Sheikh-ul-Islam was Mufti of Istanbul and the Sultan's principal authority on matters of religion and religious law

peri	Turkish fairy woman
peştamal	*pesh*-tuh-mahl; cloth used to cover the body while at the hamam
tulum	traditional musical instrument, similar to a bagpipe
Stea de Mare	*steh*-uh duh *mah*-reh; starfish (sea star)
Esperança	Eh-spuh-*rahn*-tsa; hope

Places

Aya Sofia	*eye*-uh so-*fee*-uh; Istanbul's most famous monument, a church built by the emperor Justinian and converted under Ottoman rulers to a mosque
Bosphorus	strait linking the Black Sea with the Sea of Marmara, separates Istanbul into

	western (European) and eastern (Asian) parts
Braşov	bra-*shove*; major trading town in Transylvania
Constanţa	kahn-*stahn*-tsa; trading port on the west coast of the Black Sea; loading point for overland travel through Transylvania
Galata	district of Istanbul, situated on the eastern side of the Golden Horn and populated mostly by foreign merchants
Golden Horn	broad horn-shaped inlet separating western Istanbul into two sections; main docks located here
Rumeli Hisari	*roo*-muh-luh hih-*sa*-ruh; fortress built by Mehmet the Conqueror at the narrowest point of the Bosphorus

Samarkand	city on the caravan route from Anatolia to the East
Tabriz	city on the caravan route from Anatolia to the East
Topkapi Palace	tahp-*ka*-puh; main residence of the Sultan's household in Istanbul